BEING PLUMVILLE

Savannah J. Frierson

SJF BOOKS

Being Plumville

Cover Art by Nuri Abdur-Rauf—nuriabdurrauf.com

This is a work of fiction. All of the characters, names, incidents, organizations, and dialogue in this novel are either the products of the author's imagination or are used fictitiously.

ISBN-13: 978-1500874094 (print)
ISBN-10: 1500874094 (print)

Printed in the United States of America

To all those who came before me.

ACKNOWLEDGMENTS

It's been almost six years since I've first released *Being Plumville*, and this book has opened up a world of opportunity and fulfilling relationships for me. Also fitting that this story is set forty-five years ago this year, and in that time we have been able to witness the election of the United States' first African-American president. I'd like to think Benjamin, Coralee, and all of their friends are beside themselves with joy and, yes, *hope*, for the future ahead.

Many thanks once again to my family and friends for being so supportive of me and for the readers who have helped me make my dreams of being a writer come true. Special thanks to Nuri Abdur-Rauf for her amazing cover art, and to BJ Thornton for her discerning eye and astute observations during the editing process.

Additionally, special acknowledgment to two people who truly loved this story but have passed away since the *Being Plumville's* initial release: Ruthy Charlot and Rhonda Scales. You are missed.

Lastly, these acknowledgments wouldn't be complete without mentioning my grandmother Lillie B. Glover, who passed away in 2010. I don't think anyone was as excited as she was when *Being Plumville* was first released. She is dearly loved and dearly missed.

PROLOGUE

1953

The screen door burst open and bounced against the wall a few times before creaking slowly back to its formerly closed position. Two children, the eldest being the one who first blundered through the door, talked hurriedly to the black woman in the small-print floral smock who was mixing batter for cornbread, and showed her the bleeding finger of the crying second child.

"Lawd, Ceelee, I told you you was too young to be playin' wit' them boys!" the woman replied on a sigh, setting the bowl down and taking the injured brown finger in her hand.

This child, Ceelee, sniffled, her bottom lip poking out far beyond its normal place. "They was mean, Mama!"

"They called her tar baby, Aunty Patty!" the first child said, lifting himself on the counter and dipping into the mix. Patty gave the boy a reproachful look, and he blushed, but put the offending finger in his mouth anyway.

"Mama, they pulled my hair, too," Ceelee croaked, following her mother as she led her to the sink. Patty turned on the faucet and lifted her daughter so her hands would reach the running water.

"Benny, what were y'all doin' so Ceelee hurt her finger? Y'all stayed in that backyard?"

He stood beside her, his attention focused on his friend's finger. "Yeah! We was swordfightin' with branches and stupid Tommy

Birch took a swipe at Ceelee's hand 'cause she wanted a turn holdin' the sword."

Patty rolled her eyes, rubbing a soap cake over Ceelee's hands. "Told you not to play wit' them boys, now!"

"But Mama, it's fun!" Ceelee declared, her pain gone and anxious to play again.

"Yeah, and I got ole Tommy—gave him a good lick in his jaw!"

"Excuse me, young man, you did *what*?!"

Ceelee and Benny looked at each other with wide eyes, scared at the new voice.

"Miss Florence..." Patty sighed, turning off the water and setting down Ceelee to the side. The other woman wore a smart, dark-blue cardigan over a crisp white blouse and a black skirt. Her blonde hair was short and curled around her head, making it appear as a soft halo, and her face was perfect with flawless makeup accentuating her thin lips, narrow nose, and aristocratic eyebrows. "I was just—"

Florence's hand cut off Patty's explanation, and she regarded her son with a stern look. "Benjamin Mark Drummond, tell me you did not hit Tommy Birch! Your father and I raised you better than that!"

Benny dropped his head and nodded, shuffling his feet and putting his hands in his pockets. "Sorry, Mama..."

Florence frowned at him once more before turning her attention to Patty. "Is dinner almost ready?"

Patty nodded, tying a napkin around Ceelee's finger in a make-shift bandage. "Ceelee got hurt playin' outside, so I had to take care of it. It'll be ready soon as the cornbread's done."

Florence clasped her hands at her stomach and tsked. "She shouldn't be playing with boys, Patty. She's a little girl; she should be doing girl things, like playing with dolls or learning how to cook. Why doesn't she stay in here and watch you? It'll be useful lessons for her, don't you think?"

Patty's smile was tight and she went back to the cornbread mix, her wrist action more vigorious than earlier. "Ceelee would be bored to death just sittin' in here lookin' at me, Miss Florence. Besides, she's used to playin' with boys; she plays with Luther Jr. and his friends while at home."

Florence scoffed, pulling off the lids of the pots on the stove to peek at what Patty was cooking. "But there aren't any appropriate children here for Coralee to play with—"

"She plays with me, Mama; I'm her friend! That's why I hit Tommy Birch! Because he called her a tar—"

"Ain't no use repeatin' it now, Benny," Patty said, knocking the mixing spoon against the side of the bowl for the excess batter to slide off it. "What's done is done."

"But Aunty Patty—"

"Why don't you go read Ceelee one o' yo' books, huh?" Patty suggested, giving her young charge a warm smile. "Ceelee loves to hear you read."

"Yeah!" the little girl squealed, "I wanna hear about Curious George again!"

The children left in excited chatter, and Patty grinned, secretly pleased little Benjamin treated her daughter as a true friend. Florence sighed and stood next to Patty as the housekeeper poured the mix in a buttered square tin pan. She felt Florence tense and Patty breathed out slowly. "Ma'am?"

"This is not good, Patty," Florence determined, the words surging out of her mouth. "Benjamin's becoming far too attached to Coralee."

Patty bit her lip, catching drops of the mix on her finger and wiping them on her apron. "They're just children, Miss Florence—"

"Benjamin is eight years old and in second grade! By the time I was his age I knew the way of the world!"

"I've nowhere to leave her, Miss Florence," Patty explained, placing the tin in the preheated oven. She turned the stove's eyes on simmer to keep the rest of the food warm. "Ceelee and Benny usually stay out of trouble; today was...special."

Florence's eyebrows quirked. "If they keep on going the way they are, they'll be in all sorts of *trouble* when they're older."

Patty, who had been wiping down the counter, slowed her movements and stared at the wet streaks on the marigold counter-top. "Miss Florence, they just children! Benny's at school most of the time, anyway, and Ceelee *does* help me here, but today was a holiday."

Florence leaned against the counter, speaking in low tones near Patty's cheek. "Don't tell me you can't see it, how protective *my* son is of *your* daughter! He feels too much affection for someone so obviously wrong for him! I mean, can you *really* imagine it? Benjamin in love with a *nigra*!"

"Miss Florence, now—"

The other woman placed her hand on top of Patty's. "I'm not saying Coralee's not a nice young girl, but she needs to be around *her* kind..."

Patty looked at Florence out of the corner of her eye, inhaling slowly before exhaling and starting her cleaning again. "You don't think you panickin' for nothin'? Ceelee's only five years old! Benny's eight! For all we know he probably still thinks girls have cooties!"

Florence said nothing, patting Patty's shoulder before going to the kitchen door and watching her son read to her housekeeper's daughter. Florence frowned when Benny wrapped an arm around Ceelee, bringing the girl closer to him.

She sniffed, leaving the door to stand in the middle of the kitchen, arms crossed at her chest. "My son certainly does *not* think Coralee has cooties!"

Patty shook her head and shrugged, going to the sink and wringing the excess water out the dishrag. "He probably thinks of Ceelee as a little sister."

Florence tilted her chin upward. "Nevertheless, I think you should stop bringing Coralee here. We wouldn't want this 'friendship' escalating to something indecent."

Patty laid the rag gently on the edge of the sink, clenching her jaw and counting to five before responding. "I won't bring her again."

A large smile bloomed on Florence's face, and she took a deep breath, tension seeping out of her posture. "I'm going to freshen up. Call me when dinner is ready? And don't forget to fix Paul a plate. He's having a long day at court today. I tell you, all this 'civil rights' legislation creates so much paperwork nowadays."

Florence arched a brow, glancing at the children, before making her retreat. Patty's rolled her eyes and she shook her head, pulling silverware out of its drawer to set the table. People like Florence Drummond kept progress from happening in Plumville, Georgia; yet as much as she didn't want to admit it, Miss Florence had a point. Benny and Ceelee's affection for one another could reach dangerous territory if it weren't stopped. Benny proved that today with his oblivious defense of Ceelee's feelings. In fact, Benny should be right beside that Birch boy calling her daughter names, but he wasn't. In fact, Benjamin had always treated both of her children no differently than any of the other kids.

But even when Patty had used to bring Luther, Jr. around, Benjamin and Coralee's friendship had always been unique. It was almost as if Coralee's brother had been a buffer to the *something* between the other two children. Whereas Benjamin and Luther had behaved like brothers, Benjamin and Coralee's relationship wasn't as familial. It was as if she were the most precious thing in the world to Benjamin, and she adored her playmate as well, talking about him constantly at home—to her father's consternation.

Patty hummed lowly as she completed the final place setting, lifting her eyes to the ceiling and asking for guidance. Patty was all for equality and togetherness, and saw Benjamin and Coralee as hope for the future...but not necessarily with the two being together *that way*.

The timer buzzed, jerking Patty out of her musings, and she slipped on mitts before pulling the golden-brown cornbread from the oven. She allowed it to cool on a trivet and checked the other pots and pans to make sure the food remained warm.

"Mama!" Patty fixed a plate for Mr. Drummond and smiled as her daughter held up a *Curious George* book. "Benny say I can keep it!"

Patty put the backs of her hands to her hips, arching an eyebrow when the boy in question entered the kitchen. "That's very nice of you to give that book to her, Benny."

Benny smiled sheepishly and shrugged. "I have loads of the books, and Ceelee likes it so..."

A slow smile crept on Patty's face. "You really like my daughter, don't you?"

He nodded excitedly. "Yes'm! When we get older we gonna get married!"

While Patty's mouth dropped open, Ceelee made a disgusted face. "*Married*? We gon' hafta do all that icky kissy stuff like my mama and daddy?"

Benny scrunched up his face and stuck out his tongue. "Oh, *no*! Just we can stay in the same house and play forever and ever and ever—"

"And read *Curious George*?" Ceelee interrupted excitedly.

Benny grinned and nodded, wrapping his arm around the smaller girl. "Yeah! I could read to you every night!"

"All right, Benny, before you begin makin' weddin' plans go get yo' Mama and tell her dinner's ready," Patty commanded, putting Mr. Drummond's plate in the oven and closing its door. Though the oven was off, the lingering heat inside would hold the food at a comfortable temperature.

"I'm gonna tell Mama!" Benny exclaimed as he did Patty's bidding, and Patty groaned.

"Mama?"

She set the prepared dinner plates on the table for the other two Drummonds, glancing over her shoulder at her daughter. "Yeah, Ceelee?"

"How old I gotta be befo' I get married?"

Patty smiled softly, crouching before her daughter and touching her cheek lightly. "Not fo' a long while, sweetheart. Right now you just concentrate on bein' the cutest five year old this side of Plumville!"

Ceelee smiled, pressing a kiss to her mother's cheek. "Yes'm, Mama."

Patty stood, taking her daughter's hand and they went to the backdoor. She helped the girl put on her coat, then slipped hers on, smiling as Ceelee buttoned the bottom while she handled the top. "Thank you, sweet pea."

"Welcome Mama!"

"Patty! A word."

Florence's face was pinched, her eyes following her son's progress to Coralee. Patty slid her purse on her arm, allowing Florence to guide her into the main dining room.

"Ma'am?"

"'They're just children,' eh?" Florence recalled, red creeping into her cheeks. "Coralee's a nice girl, but not for my Benjamin, you understand?"

Patty nodded slowly. "Yes'm."

Florence let out a slow breath, squeezing Patty's forearm. "I know it's hard for you, but Coralee needs another place to stay during the day; got to nip these fanciful notions in the bud."

"Yes'm."

Florence gave an assessing look. "I'll see you tomorrow, Patty."

Patty nodded curtly and walked briskly to the backdoor. "Say goodbye, Ceelee."

"Bye, Benny!" the little girl squealed and hugged her friend. "Thank you for the book!"

Benny blushed and gave stuttering pats to her back, mumbling, "You're welcome." It wasn't until Patty and Coralee had started down the steps did he grow confident in his voice again.

"See you later, Ceelee!" Benny called. Ceelee stopped and waved at him again, hugging her mother's leg as she did. An edge of the book dug into Patty's lower thigh.

Patty and Florence regarded each other, both holding onto their children as if they were lifelines. Florence nodded imperceptibly and ushered Benjamin inside, closing the door with a soft, creaking click.

Patty rubbed Ceelee's shoulders and exhaled. "C'mon, baby, let's go home."

She took her daughter's hand and they began the hour-long walk from the big, well-kept houses and businesses of downtown Plumville to the small, patched-together dwellings of its southern side. Patty listened to Ceelee chatter away about what she and Benjamin would do the next time they saw each other. Patty wondered how she would tell Coralee "next time" would never come.

ONE

1968

Benjamin Drummond huffed out a breath for the third time in as many minutes, his head lulling back so he could count the tiles in the ceiling.

It was a far more entertaining endeavor than listening to Professor Carmichael drone on about grade point averages and the importance of completing assignments.

But the Yankee professor didn't understand or appreciate Benjamin didn't have *time* to worry about stuff like that—he was too busy being the star quarterback of the Mighty Lions, after all. Sure, he had to keep a certain grade point average in order to be eligible, but that was why every other professor showed him some slack and made sure he passed just enough to play. Professor Carmichael refused to do the same, his woefully football-deficient Boston upbringing making him ignorant of the fact that in the South, football was king.

So now, Benjamin was flirting with academic probation during his senior year and final football season. Benjamin's grades hadn't risen above a C- on any assignment in Carmichael's English III class—a class he'd postponed during his junior year because he *hated* reading and everyone knew professors let seniors breeze during their last year. But Carmichael was *determined* to enlighten his students on the power, imagination, and beauty of the written word no matter how much they fought against it.

A kick to his ankle had Benjamin jumping and swallowing a yelp, turning affronted eyes to his glaring football coach. If Benjamin hadn't wanted to be there, Coach Norman had desired his own presence there even less.

"I have a compromise. I will allow you to finish playing provided you take on a tutor of my choosing—"

"*Tutor?*" Benjamin groaned, calming down after another sharp look from his coach.

Professor Carmichael raised his eyebrows, pushing his thick, black-framed glasses up the bridge of his nose. "You need a tutor, Mr. Drummond; your grades are getting worse and you've even stopped bothering to hand in your assignments. So, you can do this, or you cannot play. The choice is yours."

Coach Norman clenched his jaw and Benjamin gripped the arms of his chair, but both knew they really had no choice.

"Fine," Coach Norman said as if the word was wrenched out of his mouth. "We got a damn good chance at postseason play, and as much as it pains me, we'll get him a flippin' tutor."

Professor Carmichael smiled. "Great! I've secured a tutor for you, but she seems to be running late..."

"I can't have him missin' practice because of *your* desire to smart up my star player," Coach Norman grumbled, folding his arms at his chest. Professor Carmichael smirked slightly, shuffling papers on his desk. A knock sounded, and Professor Carmichael verbally granted entrance.

Benjamin had to work very hard not to call out her name in shock as Coralee entered with books in her arms, her hair in its typical chignon, and wearing a simple beige skirt and white-collared blouse with a light-pink cardigan over it. Her brown eyes locked with Benjamin's blue ones, and she stopped just short of the only empty seat in the room—next to him.

"You wanted to see me, Professor?"

Professor Carmichael smiled. "Yes, Miss Simmons, I have a tutoring assignment for you—"

"Are you crazy?!" Coach Norman exclaimed, his voice like sandpaper rubbing against eardrums. "You don't mean to tell me *she's* gonna tutor him—!"

Professor Carmichael took off his glasses and cleaned the lenses with a tissue. "Coralee Simmons is my best student, and the one with the best chance of helping Mr. Drummond improve his grades. Miss Simmons will tutor Mr. Drummond throughout the term; and if Mr. Drummond doesn't improve, all games in which he plays will be forfeited."

"I won't have it!" Coach Norman bellowed, spittle flying from his mouth.

Professor Carmichael scowled at the irate man. "Fine, but he doesn't play football."

Coralee remained silent and standing, and Benjamin noted the slight tension around her mouth and her arms practically strangling the books she held. Now that he thought about it, Benjamin shouldn't be so surprised she was his suggested tutor. She was among the smartest and most vocal people in English III, and quite obviously Professor Carmichael's favorite. And though many of his friends would heckle her for being a brownnoser (with particular licentious cackling at the intended pun) Benjamin had never been able to join them in it. In fact, sometimes he wanted to defend her, but that would raise suspicion and create rumors. White men just didn't defend a black woman's honor.

Just then, he remembered the last time he'd been this close to her, when he'd done just that with a wallop to Tommy Birch's head. The image of the branch exploding against Birch's noggin had him snickering.

"Somethin' funny?"

It was whispered, said out the corner of her mouth, but it made him start. "Huh?"

She smirked at him. "Smooth, Drummond."

Benjamin scowled back and slumped further in his seat, now more annoyed than ever. Who did she think she was, teasing him like that? They weren't friends anymore.

"I think it should be up to Mr. Drummond," Professor Carmichael suggested.

Benjamin rolled his eyes and shrugged. "I just wanna play. If I have to get tutored, then I'll get tutored."

"Imagine the field day the folks would have if—"

"No one will know." Coralee's firm voice arrested Benjamin's attention and he couldn't help but look at her. She stared at the nameplate on Carmichael's desk as she spoke, one of her hands picking at the spiral spine of her notebook, but her tone was clear. "No one would ever have to know Benjamin needs tutoring, let alone by someone like me."

Benjamin bristled at Coralee's insinuation while Coach Norman continued ranting. As Carmichael had said, Coralee was his best chance of bringing up his grades, so why *not* her? Coach should be happy instead of complaining. In fact, Benjamin himself was struck with a sense of irony that made him grin. When they'd been younger, it'd been he who'd helped Coralee understand books. Now it would be the other way around.

"I don't trust their kind, you know," the coach muttered, coming to the tail end of his tirade, and Benjamin's scowl returned.

"C'mon, Coach—"

"Dammit, I mean it!" Coach Norman insisted, jerking a thumb at a still-standing Coralee. "Nigra gals like that make upstandin' men turn their heads! I want another tutor!"

Professor Carmichael sighed and rubbed his temple. "I've said this already, Coach Norman. Coralee's the best student I have—"

"You can't make me believe this *darkie*—"

"We gotta do what he says, Coach. He has our entire season on the line," Benjamin reminded him.

No one spoke for a while, then Coach Norman shot out of his chair and stomped out the office, slamming the door soundly behind him. "I think that's a yes, Professor. He generally does that whenever he gives in to something."

"Duly noted, Mr. Drummond. I'll step out and give you time to set up a schedule."

Professor Carmichael's exit was far less energetic, yet the door's soft click sounded like an explosion to Benjamin. Coralee set her excess books on Carmichael's desk and took out her notebook and pencil.

She looked at him dead on. "What days are good for you?"

Benjamin blinked, suddenly confused. The question was simple enough, pertinent to the purpose of the meeting, but Benjamin's mind wasn't on scheduling tutoring sessions.

"You're much taller than I remember," he blurted.

And prettier, too, but he wouldn't say that out loud—partly because it wouldn't be on to flatter his tutor, but mostly because he shouldn't have even noticed in the first place. Yet he couldn't help taking in her smooth, flawless skin that was a shade or two darker than caramel. Her hair appeared softer, more relaxed, and would probably flow around her shoulders in thick curls had she not kept it tied back. She'd grown into her face as well, which featured wide, welcoming eyes and a slightly broad nose above a mouth with plump lips that made her appear the vixen she wasn't.

Her pencil's scratchy noise softened to a stop, and he watched her full bottom lip disappear between her teeth. "So are you," Coralee muttered. "Older too."

Benjamin smiled slightly and nodded, resting his forearms on his knees. "People tend to get older as time passes."

Coralee chuckled, the scratching beginning again. "Good thing I'm not wastin' my time teachin' you biology!"

He laughed and shook his head, bouncing his clasped hands between his knees. "No, you always took a shinin' to books."

She smiled genuinely at him then, and it was by far her best feature, opening up her face like a book and brightening it like a light "What about you? You used to read all the time."

The woodwork on Professor Carmichael's desk fascinated him now, and his eyes followed the swirling patterns on one of the panels. "Nobody to read to after you left, Ceelee."

Coralee sucked in an audible, her eyes widening. "Ceelee?"

He shrugged and furrowed his eyebrows. "I used to call you that, remember?"

Her eyes went from wide to narrow. "We used to be friends, re-member? Although, I'm not sure if that was even an accurate label." She suddenly became cold, and Benjamin almost shuddered at her changed demeanor. "But we're not friends, or otherwise, anymore, Mr. Drummond, and we haven't been for fifteen years."

Benjamin cursed silently at himself, wondering how their first, brief conversation in years deteriorated so spectacularly.

"Right, I forgot," he muttered sarcastically.

"Something you're clearly good at doing."

Blue eyes simmered with irritation as he looked at her. "Because I'm the only one in this room who'd caught fifteen years' worth of amnesia?"

Coralee pursed her lips and took a deep breath. "Well, I'm here now to help you bring up your grades, Mr. Drummond," she in-formed him, recovering quite impressively. "We can meet on your schedule, wherever you prefer."

He smiled tightly. "Yes, Miss Ceelee," he drawled, internally snickering at her responding sneer, "the schedule."

They decided on Wednesdays and Sunday at 8PM and 4PM re-spectively. The location would be an unassuming corner on the second floor in the library, a corner Coralee always used and was never bothered or noticed.

"When we meet on Wednesday, bring some of your old quizzes so we can see where the problem areas are, and bring your copy of Keats with you as well; that way we can go over themes and such," Coralee commanded, flipping her notebook closed and stacking her books. Her hold was precarious, and some books began slipping out of her arms. Benjamin didn't even hesitate in catching them before they could hit the ground.

"Guess Miss Florence taught you those lessons in manners after all," Coralee mumbled, but she flicked her eyes to him and a corner of her mouth rose.

Benjamin shrugged, mimicking her half grin. "Either that or military school, and I don't really fancy goin' to the military right now."

Coralee nodded once, sharply. "Yeah..."

Benjamin groaned, mentally cursing himself for his insensitivity. He knew about Luther Jr.'s tour in Vietnam; Patty had talked with him about it often during the summer—excited and relieved when she got a letter or sullen and anxious when she didn't. Benjamin took a cautious step toward Coralee, cocking his head to the side. "How is he?"

Coralee sucked in a deep breath and nodded, smiling too brightly for it to be authentic. "Great! Says he misses Mama's peach cobbler—"

"Oh, she makes the *best*! And she puts the powdered sugar on top just so..." His breath caught and he closed his eyes, almost tasting the sweet, buttery crust and warm, tangy peaches beneath it.

Coralee laughed a little, hugging her books closer. "Make sure to tell Mama that." He smiled slightly and took another step toward her, his look still inquisitive.

Her brows furrowed, asking a silent "what?"

"How have *you* been, Coralee?"

He was wondering why he'd spent the last fifteen years without her friendship, trying to find something in her skin tone or in her differently textured hair that made Plumville and the rest of the South deem it inappropriate for them to be friends. So far, he was coming up blank. During this last exchange alone, he'd felt more at home and in his skin than with most of the friends he'd made over their years apart. And despite what she might have thought, Benjamin had never forgotten about her. It was hard to do when her mother worked for his family, after all.

She peered at him, as if trying to discern his angle, but ultimately she shrugged and nodded. "Fine. You?"

He nodded as well, looking down and remembering he still had her books. "Suppose I should give these back."

Coralee grinned and adjusted her grip so Benjamin could stack the books atop the ones she already held. He let his hand hover as she settled her burdens, just in case they spilled again, but his fingers twitched with the bewildering urge to tuck a tendril of hair that had fallen from her bun.

The knock on the door startled him, and he masked it by shoving his hands in his pockets once more and taking a noticeable step away from her. Professor Carmichael eased his head into the room, eyes darting between them.

"Everything settled?"

Coralee glanced in Benjamin's direction before turning towards the professor. "Yes, I'll make a copy of the schedule and give it to you tomorrow."

Professor Carmichael stepped fully into his office and nodded. "All right, Miss Simmons. I'll expect it then."

Coralee said her goodbyes, leaving the two men in the office alone. Benjamin yanked his hands out of his pockets, rolling his shoulders slightly. "Professor—"

"Mr. Drummond, when I stand in front of the class, I see everything. I'm well aware of how you and your friends treat Miss Simmons during my lectures, but I also see how you look at Miss Simmons. Do you know you grin more genuinely when she answers a question correctly than when your compatriots belittle her?"

Benjamin's face flamed without his permission. "That's not tr—!"

"Or that every time you disrespect someone, I dock your grade?"

His jaw dropped. "B-but that's not fair! You can't do that!"

"I can and I have."

Benjamin could only gape at him for a moment before he felt his muscles tighten with anger and latent shame. "But I don't call her names! I haven't done anything!"

"Precisely." Professor Carmichael regarded him blandly. "Maybe this experience will force you to be the leader you are on the field off of it as well."

Benjamin snatched up his belongings and left, wondering if football was really worth all of Carmichael's bullshit.

TWO

Good ole Omega Kappa Psi, Benjamin thought dryly when his fraternity brothers bombarded him as he entered the house, beers in one hand and crumpled flyers in the other. He accepted a sip of beer from one and took a flyer from another, frowning at what he read.

"A Black Studies department? What the hell we need one of those for?" Benjamin asked on a snort. He answered his own question as he continued to read, however. Underneath the bold **"BLACK STUDIES NOW!"** that emblazoned the paper, the text explained, "Black scholarship is important and should be a part of the liberal arts education black history was American history too!"

Benjamin raised incredulous eyebrows at that.

"They're a right uppity bunch of nigras, now, ain't they?" Tommy Birch asked with a sneer, snatching the flyer from Benjamin's hand and balling it up in his fist. "Remember you used to play with one?"

Benjamin glared at him, shoving his way through the crowd to go to the living room. He plopped on the couch, throwing an arm over his eye, hoping he could avoid the conversation.

"No way," Peter, one of the younger and newer frat brothers breathed, scandalized.

"She was a *real* uppity one too. I had to set her straight one time and Benny got all bent out of shape about it—"

"Yeah, well, that doesn't matter anymore," Benjamin snapped.

Tommy shoved Benjamin's legs off the cushions and sat down, smirking at him. "Fine, I won't talk about that dark, dark time of your past. You've seen the light despite it...though I wouldn't blame you if you *played* with her now...she's a looker."

"I heard black girls do *wild* things, if you know what I mean?"

"Right animals, they are!"

Benjamin clenched his fists and forced himself to sit there and listen to the vulgarity. He was already a bit raw from the meeting and Carmichael's parting words in particularly, and the urge to flatten Tommy's jaw as he'd done when they were younger was even more pronounced. But he wasn't supposed to be bothered on Coralee's behalf. Leadership was one thing; social suicide was another.

"Anyway, me and the boys reckon we should pay the darkies a visit at this meetin' they're holdin'," Tommy suggested, tossing up the balled-up flyer repeatedly. "You up for it?"

Benjamin grunted irritably. "Why we gotta do that? Ain't like this is their first time meetin'."

"A meetin' is one thing," Tommy explained. "Havin' them spread their lies and poison around is another!"

Benjamin looked at him askance and shook his head. "Y'all, I'm not tryin' to get into trouble—"

"Your dad's a state judge *and* on the Board of Trustees for the college; we won't get in trouble! Besides, the *majority* of the school doesn't want this 'department', am I right, guys?"

There was a chorus of agreement, and Benjamin struggled for breath. He honestly didn't see the problem; it wasn't as if the classes would be *mandatory*, so why the opposition?

He looked around at his brothers and realized it was the Plumville thing to do, to fight against something that could upset the delicate, yet long-standing balance of cultural power. Being in Bakersfield while attending Solomon didn't mean Plumville doctrine didn't apply.

"Fine." Benjamin shot off the couch and hurried upstairs to his room, closing the door to his brothers' cheers and rowdiness. He dropped face-first onto his bed, his shoe-clad feet hanging off lazily.

The door creaked opened and closed, but Benjamin didn't stop staring at the nightstand, hoping whoever had just entered would get the hint he wasn't interested in being bothered.

"What's goin' on, Ben?"

It was Felix Reynolds, his roommate and one of the calmer brothers in the house. Perhaps even his boisterous brothers realized the merit of sanity every once in a while.

Benjamin flipped over to his back, resting his hands behind his head. "Rough day, man."

"At least there wasn't any practice."

Benjamin nodded. "Yep, but I still had to meet with Coach and Professor Carmichael."

"You can still play, right?"

Benjamin tilted his head towards the other man, grinning slightly. "Damn right. Even Carmichael's not that much of a wuss. Coach woulda flattened him!"

Felix chuckled, his large, broad shoulders shaking with his mirth. For such an imposing figure, Felix was one of the nicest guys on the football team, and a damn good offensive center who had saved Benjamin from many a sack and its subsequent concussions. He wasn't Plumville, either, but a military brat whose last home was in Atlanta. Sometimes they would take the hour-long joyride to the capital and go to a movie or concert that wouldn't play in small Bakersfield.

"Yeah, that's true," Felix agreed, sitting on his own bed.

Benjamin frowned a bit, sitting up as well. "Are you gonna crash the meetin' with us?"

"Yeah." For some reason, Benjamin was disappointed, but Felix's chuckle surprised him. "I want to learn more about Black Studies."

"Really?"

Felix shrugged. "Why not? My dad says if blacks and whites can fight in wars together, why not learn together? Makes sense, doesn't it?"

Benjamin gave a half-smile, impressed by the simplicity of it. True enough, Felix was among the few football players who got along with everyone, and had become the unofficial peacekeeper because of it. Perhaps if it hadn't been for Felix, the team would've combusted already, ruining their chances for postseason play.

"Makes sense, Felix," Benjamin conceded.

Felix rubbed his hands. "What about you? You don't seem too happy about crashin' it."

Benjamin shrugged. "I just don't see the point. They do their thing; we do ours. I don't see the hurt."

"It hurts folks' pride," Felix said.

Benjamin nodded, leaning back on his elbows. He thought about how irrational Coach Norman had been about Coralee and huffed. "Pride goeth before the fall."

"Aren't we philosophical this evening?"

Benjamin fell back completely onto his bed and smirked at the ceiling, but then smoothed his face into a thoughtful expression. Carmichael's words stubbornly held firm in his mind, especially now with Felix here.

"How do you do it?" Benjamin asked.

"Do what?"

"Not care? Be friends with whoever and still...I dunno...have respect?"

Felix shrugged, examining his fingernails. "I guess I treat people as people; that, and I'm as big as a truck!"

Benjamin laughed again. "That would do it!"

"Why the question?"

Benjamin sighed, rubbing his stomach idly. He wasn't ready to admit actually talking to Coralee again had been like a breath of fresh air after living in a bubble full of the same stale Southern propriety for fifteen years.

"Curious," Benjamin said finally. The two had fallen into a companionable silence when a rap on the door roused them.

"Dinner," the voice called.

Benjamin quickly sat up, suddenly very hungry. "Wonder what Babs fixed for us tonight?"

Felix smiled and stood, stretching as he did so. "She promised me some Salisbury steak one of these days. I hope it's today."

Benjamin slapped Felix's shoulder as they left the room. "You want some good food? I'll take you home where my Aunt Patty can *really* fix a good meal!"

੭

Coralee fidgeted with the scalloped collar of her cream blouse as she perused the remarks she'd meticulously typed earlier that afternoon. It wasn't as if she hadn't ever spoken to members of the Black Student Union before; but for some reason, she felt anxious.

She suspected much of that had to do with talking with Benjamin again for the first time in years.

When she'd agreed to tutor one of Professor Carmichael's students, she never thought it would be someone white, let alone *him*. Though they'd not shared a conversation since their youth, it'd been impossible for her not to follow Benjamin's progress during their separation. He or his family was always in the papers: for a controversial ruling, a well-to-do Plumville social, or an exploit on the football field. He'd obviously adjusted well during their separation; and considering he'd never spoken to her in all the years they'd been at Solomon together until now, she'd assumed he'd forgotten about her.

Coralee had chastised herself for her irrational hurt over his supposed disremembrance. He was white, after all; disavowed friendships were the norm. Yet the last moments of their meeting wouldn't leave her mind, nor did the glimpse of her former childhood friend she'd spied when he'd given her back her books. His inquisitive look hadn't changed much over the years; but the feeling his assessing gaze engendered within her was no longer as innocent as it used to be.

Now she was to tutor him in a subject with which he'd made her fall in love.

Coralee shook her head to reorient herself. Benjamin's reintroduction into her life changed nothing. He'd forget about her all over again once she helped him bring up his grades.

A firm hand squeezed her shoulder fraternally, and her eyes met kind, dark-brown ones. "You'll be fine, Coralee."

"Thanks, Jermaine," she said with a smile, bumping her shoulder against the tall man's arm. "Learned at your knee, after all!"

He laughed, and not even the thick glasses he wore could dim the brightness of his eyes. Jermaine Powell was the current president of the BSU; and his tall, lean stature and compelling gravitas made him the perfect person to fit the bill. It also didn't hurt he was quite the looker, and sometimes Coralee would still blush over the crush she'd nursed for him during her sophomore year. And though her attraction had settled on fond, yet platonic feelings for him, sometimes the sight of his inky, sable skin and warm smile would make her pause from a quick shot of lust.

Jermaine squeezed her shoulder again before drawing his hand away. "You make it sound like I'm a grandpa!"

"The way you preach and carry on, sometimes I wonder myself!"

Coralee giggled, holding up a thumb to Nick Price another senior and the BSU's treasurer. He was slightly shorter and stockier than Jermaine, but his ginger skin, short afro, and chiseled features made him very popular among the black female population. It also helped he was the star running back of the Mighty Lions too.

Jermaine glared good-naturedly at Nick, running a hand along his closely cropped hair. "Y'all, c'mon, now—"

"Passa Powell would like the congregation to say Amen!" Andre Jones teased further, nudging Nick with his elbow. Andre was the BSU's secretary and Nick's best friend. He was barely taller than Nick and a little shorter than Jermaine, but his lean, muscular frame, dark-amber skin, and wicked sense of humor lent to his boyish charm and appeal.

What made the teasing even funnier was Jermaine *was* the son of a reverend.

"Y'all ain't said nothin' but a word! All the man needs is an organ and he'll really get going!" Freda Washington added, the BSU's vice president and Coralee's best friend. Freda had been her mentor when Coralee had first joined the BSU during her freshman year, teaching Coralee the ropes and giving academic advice. That mentoring relationship had turned into a friendship, and Coralee didn't know what she would do without Freda on campus next year. She also thought she was one of the most stunningly beautiful women she'd ever met and had been among the first women on campus to wear an Afro. With her butterscotch skin, pert nose, and tall, willowy frame, Freda could easily be a *Jet* "Beauty of the Week."

"Why would I need an organ, Freda, when I have your beautiful voice to bring my message home?" Jermaine asked, grinning lightly at her.

The rest of the board whooped at that while Freda grinned in reply.

Soon, meeting attendees began to enter. They trickled in at first, all looking around the room as if they'd stumbled upon it, but Jermaine's greetings alleviated their shyness and anxiety. Thought it was a Tuesday night a month into Fall term, the meetings still were able to bring in many new, fresh faces mixed with old, seasoned ones.

Around ten minutes after the official start of the meeting people stopped coming.

The BSU board sat at the table at the head of the room. After a quick conference with Freda, Jermaine stood and address the room. "Welcome, everyone, to today's meeting. For those new here I'm—"

The door burst open, and the room rustled with anxiousness as a white guy sauntered through the door, his letterman jacket half-buttoned and his hands in his jeans' pockets. Though it'd also been years since they'd exchanged words, Coralee still recognized Tommy Birch's weasel face. He certainly hadn't changed much, wearing a smirk that meant ill will for the occupants of the room, and a gang of white boys wearing similar dress and smirk followed him. One even continuously tossed a crumpled sheet of paper, and she knew it was one of the BSU flyers.

Coralee groaned.

"This the darkie meetin'?" Tommy muttered, more to his posse than the BSU. The group chuckled.

"No, but I'm sure the cracka meetin' is just up the street!" Andre said clearly. The crashers' laughter stopped, and the one who'd been tossing the flyer threw it straight at Andre's head. In a most major affront, Andre caught it, his turn to smirk. O'Reilly gritted his teeth and balled his fists, but one of his friends put a cautionary hand on his shoulder.

Jermaine lifted his eyebrows, nonchalantly adjusting his glasses on the bridge of his nose, but Coralee noticed his jaw tightening. "Gentlemen, why are you here?'" "Gentlemen" was stressed ever so slightly, as if implying the men were anything but.

Tommy registered the slight and crept toward Jermaine. "I asked if this was the darkie meetin'."

Jermaine kept his eyes steady on the leader. "This is *not* a 'darkie' meeting. This is the Black Students' Union meeting, and you need to leave."

"Why?" asked Tommy, glancing over his shoulder to his friends. "'Cause I ain't a darkie?" Tommy's minions laughed and whistled again.

Nick now stood as well, expression flint. "No. It's 'cause you a honky peckerwood! I thought we established—!"

Tommy shoved the table. Table and chair legs scraped along the floor as board members moved back, papers and pencils flying everywhere. Fortunately, the table didn't hurt anyone on its way down, and Coralee had just managed to squelch a yelp as she jumped to her feet.

"You must be outside yo' mind talkin' to me like that!" Tommy ground out through clenched teeth, pointing at Nick with a shaky finger.

"I can talk to you however I like," Nick said as Andre and Jermaine helped him right the table. Freda and Coralee gathered the papers and pencils that were within reach.

"Nick Price...one o' the most uppity niggers at this school. Say, yo' daddy still workin' at the mill, making $2 an hour? Big man you are—"

Nick lunged for him, but Jermaine and Andre halted his progress.

The group snickered, and Tommy's eyes slid among the group until they settled on Coralee. Her lip curled as he licked his lips and grabbed his crotch, adjusting it.

"Well, well, well, boys...lookahere. 'Memba her, Benny, it's *Ceelee*—"

"You don't get to call me that," Coralee warned, not bothering to glance at Benjamin. She hadn't seen him when the group had first barged into the room. By his presence, she realized this was the Omega Kappa Psi fraternity, and she felt even sillier for the brief bout of tender nostalgia she'd felt earlier.

"I can call you whatever I damn well please!" Tommy corrected, invading her personal space by leaning towards her over the table. Coralee refused to rear back even as he leered, tilting his head from side to side as if studying every plane of her face. "You just as uppity now as you were before, thinkin' you so good 'cause yo' mama worked for the Drummonds."

"That's not—!"

"'Course it is! That's why you got this meetin' goin' on, right? Tryin' to figure out how you can be as smart as us?"

Coralee scoffed. "Why in the *world* would we sink to *your* intelligence level?"

The room went still and quiet. Tommy's nostrils flared and his eyes narrowed. Coralee honestly hadn't expected her outburst, but impatience had pushed her. He'd always been a thorn in her side, but she wasn't five years old anymore and she didn't need Benjamin defending her anymore—not that he would. And as sure as she was the other board members would've come to her aid, sometimes a woman had to handle her own business herself.

She could see Tommy's jaw working, and soon his mouth formed a derisive smile. "Yeah...you still uppity, all right. Bet you wish you was white."

Coralee said nothing, and Tommy glowered at her.

"Ain't got nothin' to say now?" Tommy asked, his voice pitching low in a way that made her skin crawl. "That's a mighty change. You used to run your mouth all the time—go cryin' to Benny." He smirked now. "You remember Benny, don't you, *Ceelee*?"

Coralee still didn't look to Benjamin and still didn't answer. She refused to give Tommy the satisfaction.

"Maybe I should clean it for you, hmm?" Suddenly Tommy's hand shot out and grabbed her neck, trying to jerk her across the table for his kiss. Coralee's stomach roiled at Tommy's fingers burrowing into the tendons in her neck and his thumb painfully bracing her jaw. She scratched at his wrists to break free, her knees digging against the table to counteract his pull. She was vaguely aware of Jermaine and Andre rushing to help her, and she flopped against them when Tommy's hold suddenly broke. Freda immediately came to Coralee's side while Jermaine and Andre created a human barrier to block Nick from attacking while. Freda ran a comforting hand along Coralee's arm, asking if she were all right, but Coralee was too busy watching Benjamin drag Tommy away from the table to answer.

"You gonna go defend that *bitch*?" Tommy spat, yanking his arm out of Benjamin's grasp.

"You ain't got a right to do that to her! She ain't done nothin' to you!" Benjamin growled, the rage in his voice so salient Coralee felt it vibrate in her blood. The reaction didn't make sense to her, especially since up until then, he'd done nothing to stop Tommy.

Tommy's brown eyes darted over Benjamin's face, then toward Coralee's, and she flinched at the lascivious grin that began to form on Tommy's face. Tommy then ran his tongue over his lips as he looked at Coralee but cocked his head toward the door. "Let's go, boys. I think the coons got our message." The goons jeered as they left, and Benjamin gave Coralee a parting glance, one so full of regret that Coralee's heart clenched, before disappearing around the door's corner.

Coralee closed her eyes and buried her face in her hands. Freda was still stroking her arm.

"You need a minute?" she asked quietly so only Coralee could hear, smoothing down Coralee's hair that'd escaped from her chignon.

Coralee did, but her knees were shaking too badly for her to stand, not to mention the rip along the right thigh of her green tartan skirt. "I'll be all right."

"Want me to read your remarks?"

Coralee glanced at the clock and licked her lips quickly, drawing her red cardigan tighter about her. They still had half an hour. As much as she wanted to crawl into bed and cry, that plan felt too much like defeat. She wasn't in a place to give any kind of speech right then, but her remarks still needed to be heard—now more than ever.

"Thank you," she affirmed, and Freda smiled her support.

The older woman stood, one hand holding Coralee's speech and the other solid on Coralee's shoulder. "If tonight's episode doesn't reinforce our need for a Black Studies department, I don't know what will. The ignorance on this campus about our people is atrocious, and it can only be rectified with Solomon setting aside a department and appropriate curriculum to go with it..."

The thirty minutes went by quickly, and by the way the others left the room, the speech garnered the enthusiasm Coralee and the rest of the BSU board wanted.

"They all seem excited now," Nick said, following the last person out with his eyes. "The real test is if they come back."

"They'll come back," Jermaine said confidently, putting his arm around Coralee's shoulders. "That was an excellent speech, Coralee."

"Yeah, well. Too bad I was too chicken to give it," Coralee mumbled, ashamed of her fear.

Freda sucked her teeth. "Girl! Don't ever confuse 'chicken' for traumatized again! Tommy Birch lucky he was able to leave under his own power!"

"Hell, Birch betta be glad Drummond had got to him first, or else he wouldn't have," Nick promised darkly.

Everyone on the board looked at each other gravely, and Coralee blew out a slow breath. If tonight's events were a preview of what might come if they pursued the Black Studies department, then the BSU needed to exhibit the fortitude they'd had and more. In a month they would hold a rally in front of the administrators' office, and they wouldn't leave until they had a Black Studies department on campus.

Not even Omega Kappa Psi could do anything about that.

And as for Benjamin, it was even clearer she should remember the Benny who'd been her friend was gone. He was every inch a son of Plumville now; small acts of kindness didn't change that fact one it.

THREE

A loud crack jerked Benjamin to reality, and muffled laughter flooded his ears. He scowled at his so-called friends as he opened his eyes before giving Professor Carmichael a contrite smile.

"You're here to learn English, Mr. Drummond, not to nap."

"Well, one usually leads to the other, Professor," Peter joked, earning snickers.

Professor Carmichael rubbed his hand along the spine of the book he'd slammed on the desk and looked at Peter over his glasses. "Then I guess you should get a pillow, Mr. Appleby, while you're writing my five-page paper on Keats due tomorrow." The class groaned and Professor Carmichael stilled the sounds with his hands. "Not the entire class, just Mr. Appleby."

"That's not fair!"

"Yet, that's how it is, Mr. Appleby. Perhaps next time you'll keep your comments to yourself—or when I'm not in earshot, hmm?"

Wisely, Peter didn't respond this time, and the rest of the class went without incident. When it ended, Professor Carmichael called down Benjamin and he told his friends he would be back shortly. Coralee was waiting at the head of the class as well, and Benjamin's insides quivered with anticipation and a bit of dread.

"Yes, Professor?" he asked upon his approach.

"Everything is set for tonight's session?"

"Yes. I thought we'd go over Coleridge tonight, unless you have other suggestions," Coralee responded, not even acknowledging Benjamin's presence.

"Coleridge is excellent, Miss Simmons," Professor Carmichael praised, and Benjamin watched her smile with praise. "You have your books, yes, Mr. Drummond?"

Benjamin nodded absently, still watching Coralee, whose expression became frustratingly neutral.

"Good. I expect a report from both of you on my desk after the second session; that way, your coach and I are kept abreast of your progress." The pair said nothing, and Professor Carmichael's eyes darted between Coralee and Benjamin. "Did something happen? You haven't even started yet and already there's tension."

"We're fine, Professor," Coralee replied quickly, still not looking at Benjamin.

Professor Carmichael's mouth flattened, obviously disbelieving her. "Would you tell me if you weren't, Coralee?"

"Because I'd automatically be the bad guy in this?" Benjamin asked with an edge.

Coralee finally shot a look his way and shrugged before turning back to Mr. Carmichael "Yes," she said, but Benjamin suspected that answer was just as much to his rhetorical query as Professor Carmichael's informative one. Benjamin frowned at her, but again, Coralee refused to meet his eyes.

Professor Carmichael regarded his two students a moment longer before nodding imperceptibly. Coralee spun on her heel and walked away, leaving Benjamin to gape indignantly after her.

"Have something else to say, Mr. Drummond?"

Benjamin shook his head and took his leave as well. Coralee hadn't gotten very far, having stopped at a corkboard and reading flyers. Immediately his mind went to the previous night when his brothers had crashed her club's meeting, when Tommy had made ugly insinuations about her. His ear twitched at the unpleasant memory, and his hands clenched.

She looked over her shoulder, eyes widening at finding him waiting there, but then she rolled them. "Are you actually comin' tonight?"

He stopped a foot away from her, sticking his hands in his jeans'
pockets. "Yeah, I'm comin'. I got football practice—"

"Don't be late," she interrupted sharply. "You're not there within
ten minutes of the assigned time, I'm leavin'."

He exhaled deeply, but couldn't blame her for her short tone.
"Look, Coralee—"

"Nothin' left to say. I'll see you tonight."

At least she'd acknowledged him this time, he thought wryly,
beginning his own walk across campus to his next class.

Things had gotten out of control last night; but until Tommy
had personally attacked Coralee, Benjamin had remained detached
from the confrontation. It was always the same thing—both groups
exchanging barbs or threats that never materialized. It was almost
sport to see which group could give the best insult, then try again
the next time. Benjamin had never really paid attention, joining in
the group jeering whenever cued, but usually used those times to
think about football plays or fantasize about Aunt Patty's home-
cooked meals.

But for Tommy attacking a girl had taken things too damn far,
especially when that girl was Coralee! He'd had to walk in the
opposite direction from his frat brothers and take the long way back
to the house when they'd left the meeting. Felix had walked with
him but remained silent, knowing any discussion would've riled
Benjamin up to the point of inflicting bodily harm.

Then again, he wasn't quite sure the urge had completely left;
and by the way Tommy and most of the other brothers had avoided
him this morning, neither was anyone else.

"Hey, Benny!"

He turned around, shielding his eyes with his hand from the
high-noon sun as Felix jogged toward him. The early October breeze
kicked up and he zipped up his letterman jacket while Felix ap-

proached. When Felix pulled even, they continued walking to Drummond Hall for their Constitution Theory class.

After four years on campus, Benjamin still felt embarrassed about his family name being on a building.

"Finish reading that John Locke essay?" Felix asked after a while, waving hello to another classmate.

Benjamin nodded. "I don't remember it."

"Lot on your mind?" Felix guessed, but Benjamin didn't respond. "Last night was pretty *eventful*—"

"I don't want to talk about it," Benjamin bit out, cutting off Felix, the roiling in his stomach returning.

"All right," Felix agreed, "whatever you say."

Benjamin nodded and trudged up the stairs to Drummond Hall's entrance. The less he spoke about it, the less he'd have to wonder if Coralee hadn't been there, would he have stopped Tommy at all.

❧

Coralee was packing her knapsack when Freda had stopped by her dorm room to chat.

Freda arched an eyebrow. "Where are you goin'? Aren't your classes done for the day?"

"Got a tutorin' session. Professor Carmichael set it up."

Freda's eyebrow rose higher. "I don't see why you can't just do it here—"

"It's a boy," Coralee interrupted. She buckled her knapsack closed and took a deep breath. "It would be inappropriate."

"Don't Trish have guys in here all the time?" Freda asked. Coralee's roommate Patricia Caldwell, who was currently at cheerleading practice, was a typically pretty blonde-haired, blue-eyed girl and very popular among the guys. Fortunately, Patricia and Coralee were friendly, and she'd let Coralee know when she had guests. Coralee usually went to Freda's room when that happened.

Coralee chuckled at Freda's insistence. "A library is the best place for a tutoring session."

"True, but I really just wanted to ask 'bout that boy—that Benny?"

Coralee paused. "What about 'im?"

"How he came to your defense like that."

She buckled her knapsack and slung it over her shoulder with more force than required. "Meant nothin'."

Freda sucked her teeth and leaned against Coralee's desk, crossing her arms at her chest. "Ain't seem like nothin'. White boys like that don't defend black girls unless..."

"Ain't nothin' like that, Freda. My mama works fo' his mama...maybe he felt some obligation because of that." Frankly, that was the only thing that made sense to her, or should anyway. Benjamin's motivations couldn't possibly extend beyond that.

"You know how many girls' mamas work for them boys' families?" Freda asked. "How many of 'em would do what Drummond did last night for you?"

Coralee shrugged, avoiding Freda's gaze.

Freda pursed her lips, clearly unconvinced. "Maybe that Tommy boy was right. Think he wants a lil' 'brown sugar'?"

"You think I'd *let* myself get suckered like that?" Coralee asked incredulously.

"As cute as he is, I'd probably let him 'sucker' me for a night."

Coralee stomped her foot. "Freda!"

"He *is*! Those blue eyes, and thick, dark-brown hair—those *lips*! Ain't never knew white boys could have full lips like that!"

"Awful!"

Freda snorted and wagged a finger at Coralee. "I'm keepin' it real, though. That's one fine white boy, Ceelee."

Coralee licked her lips, slinging her knapsack on her back. "He's a Drummond, Freda. Dad's a state judge; Mama's the self-appointed Southern belle of Plumville."

"Don't change the fact he fine."

It didn't; more was the pity.

Freda groaned at the pout Coralee sported and approached, putting hands on Coralee's shoulders.

"I'm not sayin' you gotta *date* the boy," Freda began, squeezing the shoulders lightly. "I just mean if my defender was *that* cute, I wouldn't mind."

"Or if he were *Jermaine*," Coralee specified with a smirk.

Freda sucked her teeth and pushed Coralee playfully. "You hush yo' mouth, girl!" They left her room and walked down to Freda's. Freda unlocked her door and stepped inside, leaning against the doorframe. "He *did* look cute yesterday, didn't he?"

"He was seriously scopin' you, Freda."

Freda waggled her eyebrows and winked before saying goodbye. Coralee laughed to herself as she made her way to the library. Jermaine and Freda had been dancing around each other for as long as she'd known them. Admittedly, that was one of the reasons why Coralee's crush on him had been so uncomfortable, but they were too adorable not to root for them.

However, Coralee was surprised at Freda's seeming approval of Benjamin. Granted he'd defended her, but Coralee wasn't as impressed. She was his tutor, and Benjamin wasn't dumb—she had his football season in her hands. Besides, she and Benjamin had history.

Whatever that was worth.

Not much, she thought to herself sneer, considering Benjamin had let Tommy run off at the mouth until he'd—

Coralee shuddered and shook her head, adjusting her knapsack on her shoulder. She didn't want to think about that, still irritated it'd taken her forever to fall asleep last night without Tommy's malevolent eyes greeting her the moment she'd close hers. And though she wasn't normally a coffee drinker, Coralee had drunken two cups just to get her alert that morning. The only reason she hadn't crashed yet was because of adrenaline and nerves about meeting Benjamin for their tutoring session.

"Jesus, give me strength," Coralee moaned, climbing the steps of Holtzclaw Library, named after a Georgia-born Confederate general. It was an imposing building with ionic columns and white stone exterior. The inside had cases and cases of books with ladders that rolled across them to reach the highest shelf. It was three stories not including the basement, but their corner would be on the second floor, far in the back in the foreign cultures section of the library.

Coralee found her enclave, a modest table with a small desk lamp for light, and set out her notebook and texts. She read one of them as she waited, and every few sentences would check the clock above the main entrance, even though she couldn't see the actual door. The big hand continuously crept to the twelve approaching the eight o'clock hour.

She had reached an intriguing part in her text and didn't check the clock for some time, but when she looked again, she saw Benjamin only had a few minutes before she left.

Coralee laughed shortly and began clearing the desk. She should've known he wouldn't show.

Benjamin hurried through the library's entrance, earning disconcerted looks from the librarians. He whispered an apology but kept his frantic pace, his hair still damp from the shower he took after football practice. He knew he had a minute to spare and took the stairs two at a time, his steps echoing loudly throughout the quiet building. He jogged to the corner, just in time to see Coralee sling her knapsack on her shoulder. He was about to call for her attention when she spotted him. He slowed until he stopped directly in front of her, easing one hand to his jean pocket while the other gripped his shoulder bag strap tightly. Coralee's expression was blank as she stared at him.

His lips curled into a half smile. "Sorry I'm late?"

She regarded him with a flat expression, and some of his ego deflated. He'd remained on many girls' good sides with that smile, but obviously she wouldn't fall for it.

"You took my ten minute grace-period for granted, Drummond."

He licked his lips and shrugged. "Practice ran late. Ironic, huh? I need a tutor to play, but coach makes me late for the session."

"He's protestin'. He hopes I'll drop out so you can get a more *appropriate* tutor."

"Well that's dumb, considering you're the smartest person in the class."

It was Coralee's turn to shrug, and she went back to the desk. "Frankly, I don't care what Coach Norman thinks of me, but wouldn't it kill him to show a smidge of gratitude. Without me as a tutor, your season is done."

Benjamin huffed at the reminder and settled down at the desk as well. "I brought my book," Benjamin announced, waving the text for emphasis.

She remained silent as she set up her workspace again. "Fortuitous, yet."

Benjamin frowned, peering at her. He had a feeling this was going to be difficult for all involved. In fact, something told him she was already wishing it were the end of term so she wouldn't have to deal with him anymore, and the prospect irritated him more than he'd like to admit.

"Something wrong, Ceelee?"

"Don't call me that."

Her voice was clipped and flint, irritating Benjamin more. He set his book down slowly, flipping it open to the poem they would be analyzing. She'd something similar—in the same tone—to Tommy last night, and he coughed to cover the startled sound he made.

Shame flooded him. "Coralee—"

"Turn to page 284; we're going to work on this poem first."

He sighed, but did as instructed. This would be a long session.

Gratefully, the time did not pass so slowly, and Benjamin seemed to make progress already. Coralee softened a little towards him during their session, and that relieved Benjamin to the point he could relax and actually focus.

"I think I got it," Benjamin breathed, looking at Coralee with wonder and excitement. "You made me understand!"

A tingle began in his belly when she grinned back at him. "I'm glad, Drummond. If you keep up this progress, maybe we won't have to meet beyond midterms."

His smile faltered a little, and he didn't know if it was because she called him by his last name or because their meetings could end in a few weeks' time. But he shouldn't care, regardless, right?

"I trust you, Coralee."

She glanced at him, her eyebrow quirking. "Well, good, I sup-pose. That makes this whole situation easier for both of us."

"Do *you* trust me?"

The dubious look she shot him made Benjamin want to sink into the floor, but he sat straighter and reached entreating hands toward her.

"Look, about last night—"

"This is not the time or place to discuss it."

"When *would* be the 'time or place'?"

"What does it matter?"

"Because I can't take you lookin' at me like you do Tommy Birch!"

Her eyes widened in shock, and even he had to blink at his out-burst, at the underlying terror he'd been carrying with him for years-especially when Coralee had entered Solomon. Before, it'd been so easy to be Plumville, to go with the flow and do what was expected of him. Ever since Coralee had arrived on campus, being Plumville had felt as itchy and tight like an ill-fitting wool sweater in the dead of summer. Seeing her around had reminded him of the boy he'd been, of the boy he'd liked much better than the man he was becom-ing. And though they hadn't exchanged words, her eyes would sometimes meet his across campus and say everything.

None of it good.

"Well, you know how to change how I look at you," Coralee said finally, standing and slinging her knapsack on her shoulder. "See you Sunday at four."

She left without giving him an opportunity to respond, and he figured it was just as well. He packed his own bag slowly, a small frown on his face. He knew he had a lot of ground to make up, especially considering last night's fiasco. He'd never been good at shutting off his feelings though he'd become an expert at hiding them. With Coralee now firmly back in his life, his expertise was inconveniently failing him. Maybe that feeling in his stomach had nothing to do with dread or anxiousness or even lust. Maybe that was the Benny in him trying to come back to the surface now that his childhood best friend had returned.

Perhaps Benjamin could find the courage to finally let him.

FOUR

It was Monday night, almost a full week since the disastrous BSU general meeting, and everyone had calmed down and regrouped. At the beginning of this board-only meeting in Jermaine's room, Andre and Nick spoke heatedly about Omega Kappa Psi crashing the meeting, but Jermaine eventually got them back on topic, which was determining the Black Studies Department Rally route. They knew they wanted to end at the administration building, but where to start was a harder decision.

"I think we should start in front of the chapel; you know, a symbolic gesture," Jermaine suggested first.

Andre looked skeptical. "Symbolic how?"

Jermaine shrugged. "We got God on our side...the Hebrew children—"

"I would hardly call the administrators' office the Promised Land," Nick scoffed.

Coralee grinned at Freda's eye roll. The boys were in a semicircle on the floor with sheet of notebook paper also on the floor in front of them. Freda and Coralee were sitting short ways on Jermaine's bed with their backs against the wall, watching them all bemusedly. They figured it'd be best to let them bicker each other out before presenting their own ideas.

"They don't like us in that office *anyway*; not unless it's to tell us we're on academic or financial probation," Andre muttered, making very strong strikethroughs in his notebook.

"You're gonna tear that sheet if you ain't careful," Freda warned.

Andre grunted. "Hang the damn paper."

"Yeah, well, don't be askin' fo' mine when you need some," Nick said, moving his notebook away from his friend.

"Is there no trust in the world?" Andre asked on an affected gasp, wiping an imaginary tear from his eye. The others laughed, but the question's irony struck Coralee. There *was* trust between them, and no one had had to ask.

Once, Benjamin Drummond hadn't had to ask if she'd trusted him, either, and she suddenly felt more wistful for that lost time than she cared to admit.

"You still here, Ceelee?"

She jerked at the sound of her name and realized all eyes were on her. Her cheeks grew warm as she mumbled an apology. Freda nudged her side, but Coralee shook her head, obviously not wanting to explain just then.

"What do you think about starting the protest at the library?" Jermaine asked delicately, as if repeating the question, and he eyed her with concern.

Coralee nodded. "It's fine, especially since we're trying to get a Black Studies department."

"Then we have a winner," Andre said, jotting something down. "The route will begin at Holtzclaw."

"Good; I hope the old coot is rollin' around in his grave because of it too!" Nick cracked.

The rest of the meeting went by productively, and to Coralee's relief, quickly, despite a brief tête-à-tête between Andre and Jermaine. As Coralee packed her bag, she noticed Jermaine pull Freda aside; and though usually this wouldn't catch Coralee's interest—after all, they were the president and vice president of the organization—Freda's slight blush and Jermaine's small grin told Coralee this was not BSU business.

"'Bout time, ain't it?"

Coralee jumped at the question, then sucked her teeth at Nick's dancing eyes. "Boy!"

"Aw, don't 'Boy!' me—you was watchin' 'em too! Hell, *everyone* was waitin' for it!"

Coralee smiled. "It *is* about time."

Nick smiled at her, his eyes growing a little intense. He started to say something else, then tilted his chin toward Freda as she approached them. "I guess I'll talk to you tomorrow."

Coralee was about to reply when Freda roughly linked her arm through Coralee's, whispering frantically in her ear, "We gotta talk *now!*"

Coralee barely contained a grin, but slung her bag over her shoulder and left with Freda. Neither spoke as they traversed the quad to their dorm, but Freda half-dragged Coralee during their journey.

It wasn't until Freda got them safely into her room and pushed Coralee on the bed that the older girl broke.

"Yes!"

Coralee collapsed in a fit of giggles at Freda's exclamation. Freda sucked her teeth and put her hands on her hips, but soon started laughing as well. She plopped herself on the bed next to Coralee, and the two laughed until they couldn't anymore.

"He finally did it." The statement seemed so anti-climactic now, but Coralee felt it necessary to say. "He finally asked you out."

Freda sighed. "He did, and was so cute when he did it too."

Coralee nodded. "Jermaine is a good man."

They were quiet for a bit. "We gotta find you one, Ceelee. Every good black woman deserves a good black man."

"I suppose; but, then again, every good woman deserves a good man, *period*. It's when we start gettin' particular we run into problems."

Freda chuckled. "Maybe we should call you the Sheba to the school's Solomon."

Coralee laughed, but then turned thoughtful. "She was black, you know."

"Sure was."

"Wonder how many people know that?"

Freda scoffed. "Considering how *religious* this town is, probably everyone—and in denial about it."

Silence covered them like a warm blanket. Coralee was genuinely happy for her friends; and to think, Jermaine got off his butt and asked out Freda on his own! Coralee would give him a pat on the back for his good job.

"You know, I think Nick would pee all over himself for a chance with you, Coralee."

Her grimace was immediate, reactionary, and Coralee felt instant shame for it. It wasn't as if Nick were a bad choice; after all, he was handsome, clean-shaven, tall, athletic, smart—but that was it. Coralee knew he would make someone very happy someday, she just never saw herself as that person.

"Did he tell you this?" Coralee asked eventually.

Freda shook her head. "Not in so many words, but you can't tell me you've never noticed him starin' at you."

Coralee side-eyed her friend. "So him starin' at me is supposed to be him telling me he *likes* me?"

Freda laughed then. "Fair point, but we gotta find you *someone*, Ceelee, so we can double date! I'll need someone to keep me sane while I'm out with Jermaine!"

"I really don't wanna see you moon over each other! We get enough of that durin' the meetings!" Coralee earned a pinch for her comment and she laughed. "How about I'll just be really happy for you and Jermaine and we call it even, hmm?"

Freda smiled, and they shook hands on the deal. Coralee stood, stretching languidly.

"'Bout to head out?"

"Got homework. Aside from tutoring I still have my *own* assignments to do."

"Don't *you* mess around and get behind, now. Gotta stay on top o' yo' game—"

"Be twice as good to be considered equal," Coralee finished flatly. "We're all taught that from the cradle, Freda."

"Yes. Some of us learn it better than others, you bein' one of them."

"I hear ya, Mama" Coralee teased with a wink.

Gasping Freda popped Coralee's hip maternally even as she stuck out her tongue. "Girl, get outta my room with that foolishness!"

Coralee laughed, blowing Freda a kiss before leaving and going to her room. When she reached her door, she heard multiple voices, meaning Trish had guests. Frowning, Coralee knocked on the door even as she unlocked and opened it, warning her roommate and her guests she was entering.

Coralee wished she hadn't stopped short or gasped when she saw Benjamin sitting on her bed. She wished she hadn't seen his eyes widen, then flatten as he pretended he didn't recognize her.

She wished it hadn't stung as much as it did.

"Hey, Cora," Trish said in her thick, Lamonton drawl. It was different from the Plumville drawl, less lilting and melodious. Trish always called her Cora—never Ceelee or Coralee. The nicknames didn't bother Coralee too much since she called Patricia by a shortened name as well.

Coralee almost stepped back to leave before she caught herself. "I didn't know—"

"Oh, they aren't stayin' long," Trish reassured her, glancing at her two guests. Coralee recognized the other from the Omega Kappa Psi crash; though away from the action, he'd been an enabler all the same.

Coralee's mother raised her with manners, however, and she nodded a greeting. "Hello."

The big man stood with a congenial smile and held out his hand. "Felix Reynolds, nice to meet you."

She shook his hand with a brief smile. "Coralee."

Felix's smile brightened and he dropped her hand after an appropriate interval. Coralee couldn't help but think he was a very attractive guy. "Coralee. We were just talkin' about the game on Saturday; do you like football?"

Coralee shrugged. "It's all right."

"Cora always has her head in a book," Trish said conspiratorially.

What was it with people treating her bookish nature as a peculiarity? "My family follows baseball more."

Felix nodded and smiled persuasively. "And as great as baseball is, you should come to a game and see us play. In fact, did you know Nick's the star running back and Benny's go-to guy?"

Coralee arched a brow at the heretofore silent Benjamin. "Is that right?"

He nodded once, barely sparing her a glance. "Yeah."

That was all Benjamin would give, and Coralee worked hard not to roll her eyes at him.

"I see," she ultimately replied and set her books on her desk. "Well, I don't mean to rush y'all out, but I really have to study."

Trish let out a gasp so affected it was all Coralee could do not to burst out laughing. "But *Cora!*"

Benjamin's gaze finally met hers, and this time it was she who wanted to avoid eye contact. It was that same assessing look from Professor Carmichael's office, the one that reminded her of the Benny he no longer was—no matter what his friend called him.

"No, Coralee's right," Benjamin agreed. "We should go."

Trish walked them to the door while Coralee got situated for her studying. Felix and Benjamin said goodbye to her, but didn't give into the satisfaction of meeting Benjamin's intense stare as they left.

"I'll see y'all later!" Trish called, and closed the door with a definitive click. Coralee adjusted in her seat, exhaling the tension out of her body.

"Sorry about the sudden guests," Trish said sincerely, "but they offered to carry my books and I just couldn't say no!"

Coralee frowned. "You got that many books it requires two men to help?"

"Oh, *Cora*...that's not the point!"

She didn't bother asking Trish to expand on that, too busy pretending to study and denying the relief she felt that Florence Drummond wouldn't think Patricia "Trish" Caldwell, aka the "For a Good Time Call" girl, was any more appropriate for her darling son than Coralee was.

It would be his luck Coralee was Trish's roommate.

Benjamin had no good reason to be so peeved about that, but he was. She'd looked so relaxed before realizing he and Felix were in her room; and the mistrust had been stark in her eyes. It looked out of place from the soft, pretty look of her, and he cursed himself for even noticing. But he would've been blind not to see how the beige, felt pencil skirt hugged her full hips or the pink, cotton turtleneck contoured her torso's curves.

"That Trish is somethin' else, huh?"

Benjamin didn't answer Felix, burying his hands in his letterman jacket. Trish was very pretty, but she had the depth of a puddle. Benjamin found himself growing bored quickly around her; and if it hadn't been for her obvious flirting, he would've ignored her completely.

Funny how a month ago Benjamin wouldn't have cared about the lack of scintillating discussion; but after two sessions with Coralee, the ability to hold a conversation had become a requirement for what he looked for in a girl.

"She seems interested," Felix tried again.

"Hmm."

Crickets chirped and fireflies dotted the lane as they walked across campus to their fraternity house. The soft, amber light from the lamps gave the night an ethereal glow, and Benjamin's annoyance waned a bit.

"I heard she was with Randy not too long ago."

Benjamin snorted. "The campus bicycle, she is."

Felix smacked his shoulder. "Benjamin!"

Benjamin winced, unprepared for that to have hurt as much as it did. "Not nice. I apologize."

Felix sighed, raking a hand through his hair. "If you didn't want to go to her dorm, why did you?"

"Curiosity."

Felix's nod let Benjamin know he understood. They were red-blooded males attracted to pretty females. When a girl like Trish Caldwell complained about heavy books, they couldn't turn her down—even if it only required one brawny football player to do the bidding. It'd been an opportunity Benjamin had felt compelled to take, and Trish's coy, yet abrasive laughter and light, yet practiced touches told Benjamin something *could* happen with a few more book-carrying episodes.

"Trish seems like a sweet girl, though," Felix mused.

Benjamin shrugged and stared at his feet as he walked. "Suppose so."

"Her roommate didn't look all that happy to see us."

Benjamin's nostrils flared. "Would you be, if you were tryin' to study?"

"She was very friendly considering what happened last week."

Benjamin began shaking his head. "Felix."

"Still don't want to talk about it?"

"No," Benjamin replied, now scowling at his feet.

"All right, Benjamin, then we won't."

Benjamin nodded his thanks and sighed heavily as they climbed the porch steps to the frat house's entrance. Upon opening the door, they saw the living room furniture pushed to the sides as they attempted to play tackle football.

"Hey, fellas! Babs saved some dinner and apple pie fo' y'all!" Peter called right before being downed by another guy amid whoops and hollers.

Benjamin laughed at their antics and went directly to the kitchen. Babs was there washing the dishes. She reminded him of Patty.

"Coach hold y'all late?" Babs asked, not looking up from her task, and didn't wait for an answer as she waved aimlessly behind her towards the table. "Y'all sit on down and I'll get y'all's dinner—y'all hungry?"

Benjamin's stomach grumbled in response, and the pair eagerly sat at the table. The running water ceased, and the oven door creaked open as the short, slim black woman pulled out two warm plates and set them before the boys. A chorus of "thank you, Babs" rang out right before a loud boom from the den. Babs sucked her teeth and stuck her head out of the kitchen into the den.

"Iffen y'all don't quit with that foolishness, I'mma tan me some hides! Y'all quit that roughhousin', now!" Mumbled "yes, ma'ams" and "sorrys" trickled into the kitchen right as Babs closed the door, and Benjamin and Felix tucked into their meals, making sure not to earn a dressing down too.

They had a relatively quiet meal after that, and Babs's alto humming and running water provided background music.

"How's the food, boys?" Babs asked after a while.

Felix chuckled around his glass as he took a sip of sweet tea. "Miss Barbara, every time you ask that you get the same answer—good!"

Babs laughed and winked. "Still don't mean I don't wanna hear it!"

"Excellent, Babs," Benjamin replied, clearing his empty plate and almost empty glass from the table. He set the items on the edge of the sink and kissed Babs's temple. "Thank you for savin' it for us."

"Chile, please, that's why I'm here," Babs said, not breaking her rhythm as she washed the dishes. Felix's plate joined Benjamin's. "Y'all want anything else?"

"Peter said something about pie?" Felix asked.

"Yo' slices in the oven."

"Thanks so much, Miss Barbara. I can't wait to get me some," Felix interrupted, already opening the oven to get out their slices of pie.

Benjamin made a low, pleasing sound in the back of his throat at the first bite of the dessert, relishing in the tangy sweetness of the apples and the buttery crust surrounding it. Right after peach cobbler, apple pie was his favorite dessert.

"This is so good, Babs."

"Well, thank ya, boys. I do try!"

Felix and Benjamin polished off the pie enthusiastically, also placing those dishes on the sink's edge.

"I dunno why you two boys seem to be the only ones with *manners*," Babs muttered under her breath, placing the plates in the soapy water.

"Good home trainin'," Benjamin answered.

"Military," Felix said with a slight chuckle.

Babs laughed shortly. "Sometimes they one in the same, ain't they?"

The boys laughed and wished her a good night. Once in their bedroom, Benjamin sat at his desk, pulling out his English books and doing his assignment for tomorrow's tutoring session. Coralee's tutelage had been helping him immensely; now he wasn't so lost during Professor Carmichael's lectures. Of course, it helped he paid attention in class, even going so far as to shush his friends when they were distracting him. At first they teased him about it; but once Benjamin reminded them he couldn't play unless he pulled up his grades, they stopped giving him a hard time.

He wished he could say the same for the Brontë book he was trying to read. *Wuthering Heights* wasn't particularly an easy or interesting book in Benjamin's opinion, but he had to read so he could analyze it with Coralee the next day.

He was just getting settled into the text when Peter barged into their room and sprawled on Benjamin's bed as if he belonged there.

"Get out, Pete."

The intruder sucked his teeth. "C'mon, man! Tell me about it! I *saw* y'all leavin' with Trish!"

"She needed help with her books; that's all," Felix replied. "You're sure one gossipy guy, Pete!"

"Man, skive off!"

"He has a point, Peter. You almost gossip more than my mama!" Benjamin merely laughed when he felt a pillow hit his back.

Peter glowered at them both. "C'mon, fellas! Why you holdin' out?"

"Nothin' to tell!" Benjamin insisted. "We helped her carry her books, talked once we got to her room—"

"Then her roommate came, and we left," Felix finished.

Peter groaned and fell on the bed again, the headboard bouncing against the wall. "Damn roommate! I betcha she's one of them fat girls with big glasses, the kind that can't get a date if it dropped in her lap!"

"Why you wanna know so bad?" Felix asked, nodding to Benjamin conspiratorially. "You interested in dropping in a girl's lap?"

"Aren't we all?" Peter asked shamelessly.

They all snickered at that, but Benjamin hoped they had derailed Peter's curiosity. He didn't want to discuss Trish's roommate. Further, there was just something incredibly tacky "kissing and telling" like this. For all of Trish's freewheeling, she was still a very nice girl.

"All right, no more discussing this," Benjamin determined. "Don't you have a paper to write or something?"

Peter looked at them incredulously. "Seriously? Y'all not gonna spill? Man, you two are no fun!"

"Not at a lady's expense, no," Felix agreed.

Peter sighed his dissatisfaction. "Well, I reckon I *will* go write that paper. You know the fellas will be real disappointed I'm reportin' back with nothin.'"

"I'm sure they'll survive," Benjamin predicted dryly.

Felix chuckled in disbelief once Peter exited the room. "Appleby tries too hard."

"He wants to fit in," Benjamin explained, empathizing with the young man a bit. He was young and in the most popular frat house on campus. There was a reputation to uphold, and newbies were among the most gung-ho to maintain it.

"I hope he doesn't," Felix said, opening his text to begin reading.

"Really? Why not?"

"We have enough Tommy Birches at this school without raising a crop of others," Felix replied, and looked pointedly at Benjamin.

Benjamin squirmed and shook his head. "Well? What're you lookin' at me for?"

Felix shrugged. "Dunno, just thought it might be nice if we raised a crop of Benjamin Drummonds instead."

As nice as the sentiment was, he couldn't agree with his room-mate's opinion. "If Peter should model anyone, it's you."

"Me? Why?"

Benjamin snickered. "C'mon—between your military upbringing and the fact just about *everyone* likes you, why *not* you?"

Felix nodded with humility. "Thanks, Benny."

"You're welcome," Benjamin replied, not mentioning the other, more personal litmus test he'd used.

Which was the fact Coralee had given Felix a small, yet genuine, Ceelee smile.

FIVE

Unease cloaked Benjamin upon entering the locker room, and he couldn't help shuddering. It wasn't as if the football team had never been tense, but there was something peculiar about it this time. Benjamin went back toward his locker, and a huddle of black players spoke in hushed tones in the row before his. Benjamin's confusion increased.

"What's goin' on?" he asked to no one in particular.

"Nigger huddle—"

"That's unnecessary, Randy."

Benjamin clenched his jaw and opened his locker, relieved Felix chastised Randy for his comment.

"Why you such a nigger lover, man?"

Felix didn't answer and Benjamin was glad. Felix didn't owe an answer to anyone, let alone Randy Jurgens. Randy was a good friend of Tommy's; but while Benjamin could tolerate Tommy, Randy got on his nerves.

"Look, fellas, we got an important game on Saturday, so squash whatever issues you have with your teammates. We're all in this together," Benjamin said, slamming his locker shut and going to the stalls to change. Normally he had no problem suiting up in the open spaces in the locker bank, but today he needed to be alone.

Things had been getting worse lately, and Benjamin couldn't figure out why. In the past, the players had been able, relatively, to put their problems and distrust aside for the sake of the game; but now, everything was slowly reverting to the regular social order. Perhaps their good football season made the players think they didn't have to work so hard, and the energy they spent on being civil to one another could be forfeited.

It was a recipe for disaster.

Benjamin left the stall, his commanding stride and scowl halting any conversations his teammates could've started. He was liable to snap at someone, and he couldn't afford to lose his cool. He was the captain of the team and had to set an example for the rest to follow, all the while not alienating them. It was a delicate balance that had had precarious success; now, it seemed in danger of supreme failure.

After running warm-up laps, Coach Norman called them all to the center of the field to take a knee. Benjamin only half-listened, his mind still on the huddle of Negro players. Were they planning some sort of coup or other uprising? It wasn't as if they didn't get any substantial playing time. Nick Price was his go-to wide receiver, not to mention the other Negro first-string linebackers. Then again, their behavior might not have anything to do with football, and Benjamin groaned internally. He hoped they weren't trying to do something, like cause a riot. His dad had mentioned several colleges and universities where there had been protests and civil unrest, particularly out west and up north, and had asked if Benjamin had heard any rumblings about any happening at Solomon. He'd told his father no; but now, Benjamin wondered if he'd spoken to soon.

Benjamin tried pushing the suspicion out of mind during practice, however. Coach Norman trained Benjamin hard, and his arm started burning with all the passes he had to throw. Practice also drilled the offensive line on protecting the Benjamin from rushes and sacks, and opening lanes for the running backs. Consequently, Benjamin worked on improving the passing game, testing different routes and targets. Thankfully, practice was very efficient, and it seemed outside tensions were suspended during play.

It was when the whistle blew for timeouts that things got a little more difficult.

"Honky", "cracker", "monkey", and "coon" were as common on the field as "tackle", "block", "hut, hut" and "first down." More than once, Benjamin had had to verbally chastise his teammates, feeling more like a parent than a captain.

"What the devil is wrong with the guys today?" Benjamin muttered, taking a long-needed gulp of water. He and Felix were watching the defense go through some blocking exercises.

Felix shook his head. "I don't know, but if Nick and Randy don't cool it, they may be benched for the game next week. We can't afford that, not even against Lexington."

The two guys had gotten into a shoving match at the beginning of the water break, forcing teammates to break them up and lead them to almost opposite ends of the field.

Benjamin sighed. "Yeah, well, our biggest rival is ourselves, and if we don't get our acts together, we'll—"

"Drummond!"

Benjamin winced at the tone, and Felix gave him a sympathetic glance as he jogged to the none-too-pleased coach. A string of tobacco-stained saliva shot from Coach Norman's mouth, and Benjamin had to dampen his scowl.

"Coach?"

Coach Norman grunted, scratching his head and putting his other hand on his hip, the clipboard full of plays jutting from his side like a misplaced wing. "You know what the hell's wrong with everyone? We play like this on Saturday, we'll be slaughtered!"

Though Benjamin had his theories, he wasn't ready to share them just yet. "Coach, I don't know. I've been tryin' to figure it out all practice. It seems we do fine when we go over plays, but afterwards we're ready to tear each other's heads off!"

Coach Norman looked beyond Benjamin to the defensive line going over drills and spit again. "These problems ain't start 'til we got these nigras on the damn team...they ain't nothin' but cancers—good playin' cancers, but cancers nonetheless."

"The white players ain't doin' their part to make things easy, either, Coach."

Coach Norman's eyes slid to him, and he looked at his quarterback through narrowed eyes. Benjamin worked hard not to shift under the Coach's stare. After a few seconds that dragged on like years, Coach Norman diverted his attention back to the field. "You go on, now."

"Go on?"

Coach Norman sighed again, tilting his head toward campus. "Gotta get to the library, don't you?"

Benjamin could only blink, surprised his coach was letting him leave a few minutes early to make it to his session on time. "You all right, Coach?"

"Hell no I'm not all right! But I'll be damned if I'mma have you benched all because some uppity Yank wants to follow rules! Don't he know football *is* the rule, dammit?!"

Benjamin knew better than to laugh, so he bit the inside of his lip. "I'll see you tomorrow, Coach."

"Oh, you sure will, fifteen minutes early to make up for tonight!"

Benjamin nodded and ran to the locker rooms, showering and changing quickly so he would be on time at the library.

He had just walked out of the locker rooms when someone grabbed his shoulder gently.

"Wha—?"

"Hello, Ben."

His eyes widened ever so slightly, but he quickly regained his bearings. "Trish."

Her practice uniform was dangerous on her, and he couldn't help but wonder if Trish was the single-most reason the football team had been able to beat their opponents. If he hadn't been used to practicing with the cheerleaders on the sidelines, he would be too distracted to be useful to the team, too.

"Where ya goin'? I saw you leave practice early..."

"Ah...got a prior engagement."

"A 'prior engagement', huh? Does it involve a *girl*?"

"Don't you still have cheerleading practice?"

Trish laughed, squeezing his elbow and stepping so close her chest brushed against his. Benjamin swallowed thickly, looking over and beyond her head towards the chapel, hoping to draw strength from it. "Yeah, I still have practice, but I saw you leavin' early and I just wanted to make sure everything was okay..."

"I'm fine, but thanks for the concern."

Trish stepped away from him slowly, a small grin on her face. Her eyes were hooded and full of suggestion, and had Benjamin not been a stronger man, he probably would've taken her up on it. "Maybe we could see each other later? I can ask Cora to give us the room to ourselves..."

He blinked; the chapel was still there. He had almost forgotten who Trish's roommate was, but Coralee added another reason for Benjamin not to meet Trish later, if ever. It would be awkward to date Trish, to kick Coralee out her own room just so he and Trish could fool around. Besides, Coralee was Patty's daughter; Coralee knowing would be like Patty knowing, and that was just as bad as if his *mother* knew.

"You may want to go back to practice, Trish. I know the fellas would be disappointed if your coach kept you benched from the game because of playin' hooky."

She cocked her head to the side, her grin growing wider. "And what about you?"

His grin matched hers. "Definitely."

Trish smiled full out, bracing herself on his forearms to stand on her tiptoes and kiss his cheek. "I'll see you later," she whispered, then sauntered off with a little more sway to her hips. Benjamin forced himself to turn away again. As tempting as Trish was, he couldn't, *wouldn't* allow himself to indulge—at least not until after the football season.

The walk to the library was peaceful, and it was almost as if he had the courtyard to himself. The leaves were starting to turn colors, and the red leaves of the maples and the yellow of the oaks gave the campus a woodsy character that didn't exist for most of the year. Benjamin took a deep breath, taking it all in serenely. It was good to have this alone time. Quiet was rare but cherished for him, particularly now since he had a lot on his mind.

Coralee was still standoffish; there was polite detachment during their sessions; and when he reconciled the current Coralee to the Coralee of his youth, he became wistful. Benjamin recalled his father telling him of a colored friend he'd had growing up, yet they'd had to part ways the older they'd become. Benjamin could still see the almost mournful expression his father had had during that conversation, and Benjamin wondered what Paul felt when he saw that friend nowadays. Was the nostalgia as normal for him as the sun rising in the east, or the earth being round, or did it feel like a hole in the soul that yearned to be filled?

That was what his broken friendship with Coralee felt like, and had always felt like, now that he could admit it to himself.

Benjamin nodded to the librarians at the circulation desk upon entering the building and went directly to their designated table. Coralee wasn't there yet, so he sat in his seat and pulled out his copy of *Wuthering Heights*, going over the annotations he made in the book and adding more as he re-read the assignment she had given him.

Benjamin was so focused on his task he completely missed Coralee's approach, jumping wildly at her greeting. He blushed upon her low chuckle, ducking back to his book to keep her from seeing it.

"Here early, you didn't go to practice?"

"Let me out early," he mumbled, glancing at her before going back to his text.

"Well, that was nice of him." Benjamin laughed; "nice" and "Coach Norman" didn't belong in the same sentence unless "is not" separated the two terms. "What?"

"Nothin'." Benjamin felt her eyes on him, that skeptical glance, and shifted in his seat.

"Whatever," Coralee intoned on a sigh. "Did you finish the assignment?"

Coralee's book slid into his line of vision, and all the markings, notes, and underlinings in her text intimidated him.

"How can you read through all of that?" Benjamin asked in awe.

"Helps me study and understand. Is my method working for you?"

Benjamin frowned, irrationally irritated by her professional tone. He'd yet to bridge the gap between them, to return to that place where her friendliness wasn't sterile and routine. He'd been nice, tried to open up conversations to beyond the text before them, but she remained steadfast in tutor mode.

In fact, the headway he'd made was she'd stopped calling him "Drummond."

"Benjamin?"

"I miss us."

It was the first explicit reference to their time as friends and how either had felt about it, and Coralee didn't respond immediately. She rolled her shoulders and scribbled something in her notebook. "It was a different time then—"

Benjamin shook his head. "Not so different; not really. If anything, we should be able to be friends *now* than back then. Civil rights and all—"

"Just because *the government* says we're equal in the eyes of the law doesn't mean people believe it. Your friends certainly don't."

Benjamin huffed, rubbing his palm over his face. "Coralee..."

She pulled out another book and shook her head. Benjamin knew his friendship with Tommy and the others went against everything they had been to each other.

"Coralee—"

"Why do you think Hindley was against Heathcliff's presence in the home?"

Benjamin glared at the book and gritted his teeth. He didn't care about Heathcliff or Hindley or even English III! If he didn't want to play so badly he wouldn't have even bothered *touching* the book!

"He was favored," Benjamin all but mumbled.

"Do you think his skin color had anything to do with it?"

Benjamin couldn't avoid the sensation he was walking into a trap. "Skin color?"

"Yeah...some *darkie* showing him up? Don't you think that made Hindley mad too?"

Was there something in the water? First the coloreds on his team and now *Coralee*? "What is *with* you people today?"

Coralee froze, and Benjamin immediately the trap spring. "Excuse me?"

Benjamin tapped his pen on the table, staring at the arc it made. "Nothin'."

"I'm not a simpleton, Drummond; what did you mean by that?"

He didn't want to get into it. "Bad football practice."

"And it was 'my people's' fault, huh?"

Right then, Coralee sounded so much like a female Nick Price that Benjamin became defensive. "What has that group *done* to you?"

"You wanna run that by me again?" The question was so chilly Benjamin shuddered, but he was too deep in the trap to heed the implicit warning

"Exactly what I said! You used to be so nice and polite; now you're like some...some *militant* or something!"

"*Militant*?!" Coralee laughed, but it was brittle to Benjamin's ears. "Just because I want to be treated like a full-fledged human being and not something to be tolerated, that makes me *militant*? I want my concerns and beliefs and goals considered just as important as *yours*, and whatever I do to secure that right is *militant*?"

"I think you're very human—"

"But not good enough to have the same rights and opportunities as you or people who look like you? Can't upset the social order, now, can we?"

Benjamin didn't like where this conversation was going, and he slammed his books shut, yet Coralee continued speaking

"But you and your *friends* think it's okay to barge in on a meeting that has *nothing to do with you*—"

"You're talkin' about addin' a department *most* people on campus don't want or need! Why can't y'all just shut up about it and move the hell on?!"

Coralee gasped and Benjamin's face paled. They stared at each other, Coralee's eyes pooling with tears he'd put there. The sight choked him, making his stomach bubble from self-loathing and disgrace. He wasn't the one who was supposed to make her cry; *Benny* would've never brought tears to her eyes.

He struggled for breath. "Coralee—"

Her chair slid back on the wood floor, halting whatever else he could've said, and her slamming her books closed and shoving them into her knapsack said everything else. She marched out of the library, leaving him to stare at the chair she'd vacated and wrestle with the realization he'd probably just condemned himself to a life without football.

And her.

Three weeks. It had taken Benjamin three weeks to show his true colors. They were ugly, and to see them on her former friend broke the little tiny portion of her heart that had always been reserved for him.

A narrow trail of grief slipped from her eye down her cheek, and she grew angry at it.

"I knew it."

Coralee, someone who learned just for the joy of it, was reminded once again that some lessons hurt. Some lessons, most lessons, weren't taught in the controlled, sterile environment of a classroom.

There wasn't a physical teacher who lectured out of a book and recited facts and figures long ago established and regarded as true. This teacher was Experience, that vague, indiscriminate entity who affected everyone, yet taught lessons unique to every person on the planet.

Experience taught Coralee people would hate her because of her skin color; would think her subhuman because her ancestors had been chattel; would think they had the right to think that way because their ancestors hadn't been.

Experience taught her many who looked like her would appropriate that mindset because it was safer, easier to be a "dumb darkie" than an intelligent colored person. Experience taught them that people, white people, powerful people, didn't think blacks were worth a damn, and that thinking must be true. But Experience, that mercurial teacher, taught others who looked like her they *were* worth a damn, worth the very things being denied to them despite the federal government "guaranteeing" that ownership.

Being inundated with the same message repeatedly had compelled Coralee to subscribe to it, and she'd grown to distrust all white people, including Benjamin. That hadn't stopped her from hurting every time she saw him, or feel a tiny part of her heart break every time the older Benjamin did something that was so painfully inconsistent with the younger one.

"That's just the way things are, Ceelee." That was what her mother had told her as a child as to why she couldn't see her Benny anymore. She'd accepted it because her mother had said so, and her mother never lied. These "things" were unpleasant, arbitrary, *unnecessary*. When she got older, Coralee realized "things" *didn't* have to be the way they were, but Experience had taught its lesson too well. Changing "things" was uncomfortable.

This was why the Black Studies department was so important to her, and why Benjamin's comment bothered her so much—it would teach what Experience couldn't. There hadn't been much opportunity for black progress in Plumville, and Coralee wanted to leave and learn something other than these stale lessons of inferiority and blocked ambition. She wanted to be a teacher, possibly even at Solomon College in the future Black Studies department they were trying to establish. Coralee brightened a little at the possibility.

Her dormitory crept into view as she walked down the lane and she sighed, suddenly uninspired to go to her room. She made a sharp left to the fountain and sat on the bench, staring at the churning water. The sound soothed her, and her anger and hurt lessened to disappointment. She was disappointed in Benjamin. For some reason she'd hoped *he'd* be different, that because of their brief, former friendship and her mother working for his family he'd be enlightened about black people's...humanity? Why was it on *her* to enlighten? To Coralee, white people seemed content in their ignorance—at least the Plumville, Bakersfield, and Lamonton white people. They didn't see anything wrong with the way of things, comfortable with a population of the country being systematically denied and considered second class.

"That's why we need the Black Studies department...to show them it *ain't* all right—"

"What ain't?"

Coralee started, snapping her head around and seeing Nick. She chuckled in relief before glaring at him. "You scared me!"

He smiled, sitting next to her on the bench, and nudged her with his shoulder. "Obviously. What had you all out in LaLa Land?"

"I'd rather not talk about it."

Nick shrugged, the fountain capturing his attention for the moment, and Coralee took the opportunity to look at him. He *was* very handsome; any girl would be lucky to catch Nick's eye. If Fred was right about how he felt for her, then Coralee suspected something was severely wrong with herself for not feeling the same.

"Practice was god-awful today," he said without preamble.

"Really?" The word was shock and interest rolled into one. Nick had no reason to talk about his football practice with her, and yet he was. Maybe he needed to vent, and she was there to lend an ear...yeah, she would go with that. Besides, this was the second time she heard of this "bad" football practice; maybe Nick would explain why this time.

"Randy Jurgens was being a regular honky, that's what," Nick began, standing up and pacing. "He kept botherin' me and the guys, wonderin' why we were all huddled together at the beginning of practice...ain't none of his damn business why *we're* meetin' before practice!"

"Well...why *were* y'all meetin'? You mean all the black folk on the team, right?"

Nick nodded, still pacing. "We were talkin' about the march on next Wednesday, and how we're gonna boycott the practice to go."

"Do you think that's the best idea?"

Nick's grin melted to a contemplative expression, and he sat down slowly next to her. "You don't think so?"

"I've had an...*experience* with Coach Norman, and he seems like the type who'd *jump* at the chance to kick y'all off, and y'all leavin' would only give him that opportunity. We can talk to Jermaine about startin' the march later."

Nick stared at her, and Coralee turned her attention back to the fountain. She had always wanted to throw all protocol aside and jump in it. Many students did so after big games or right before exam periods, and those students were mostly male and white. Between the gender saturation and the fact it was against campus rules *to* jump in the fountain, Coralee never had. The ones who did merely received mild punishment—if any. Coralee knew deep down if *she* did it, she could face probation or even suspension.

"As usual, Miss Coralee," Nick said finally, flashing a heart-stopping grin, "your wisdom knows no bounds."

Coralee snickered and shook her head. "You are so silly."

"*You* are so brilliant...and pretty too."

The fountain was very enthralling, even more so than before, and she almost wanted to walk toward it and let the water cool her burning cheeks, but she remained where she was, not wanting to be rude. He really was a sweet guy...

"Thank you," she said softly, glancing at him and offering a small smile. He grinned and she blushed more, turning her attention back to the fountain.

"You somethin' else, girl!" he said on a laugh. "Durin' them meetings you ain't nearly as shy as you are now! Wonder why that is?" He raised an eyebrow at her. "Ever had a boyfriend?" She shook her head. "Want one?" A shrug. "I guess that's fair..."

"Why the sudden interest?"

Coralee saw him shift out the corner of her eye, and he cleared his throat dramatically. "Jus' wonderin'..."

He scooted closer to her and she looked at him, a question on her lips. Nick shook his head, leaning closer as if about to kiss her.

"What are you—?"

"Price."

Coralee resisted the urge to drop her head on Nick's shoulder in embarrassment. The last thing she wanted was to see Benjamin again so soon after the...*conversation*.

Nick's expressive face became slate-like, and he nodded a greeting to his team captain. "Drummond."

Benjamin locked eyes with Coralee. She dropped hers quickly, but she still felt his gaze. "Miss."

Coralee only nodded. She heard Benjamin walk on and felt a hand squeeze her shoulder.

"I bet if *I* looked at one of their women like that, I'd be beat to a pulp!"

"What?"

Nick rolled his eyes. "Let me—let me just *glance* at one of them white cheerleaders on the sidelines, and they'd probably try to lynch me or some mess, but they can look *our* women up and down like they don't deserve respect!"

"I'm sure he didn't mean it like that," Coralee said half-heartedly, placing a hand on his arm to calm his ire.

He gave her an incredulous look and jerked a hand towards Benjamin. "Like I said, Ceelee, you're pretty. If *I* noticed, what makes you think these crackas ain't notice, either?"

Coralee merely bit her lip and stared at her hands. She knew that wasn't the case with *Benjamin*; he preferred lithe, busty, bubbly blondes like her roommate, not girls with black kinky hair or a little extra meat on their frames.

But it didn't matter *what* Benjamin liked...

"Well, I'm not interested—"

"*Don't matter!*"

"But they can't—they ain't allowed—"

"And I'm the pope."

She sighed and stood, slightly annoyed Benjamin had tainted the peace she'd been seeking at the fountain.

"Headin' out?" Nick asked. Coralee nodded and gathered her books. Nick plucked them from her hands and tucked them under his arm. "I'll walk you?"

"Okay." The pace was pleasant back to her dormitory, the dusky sky adding to its serenity. Nick proved an easy conversationalist, and his sense of humor helped lighten her mood. Once they reached her dormitory, he gave her back her books and Coralee smiled.

"Thank you for carryin' them; that was really sweet of you. Have a good night—"

"Coralee?"

She turned back towards him, her free hand behind her and grasping the doorknob. "Yes?"

Nick approached her and stood closely, intimidating her a little. He gave a half-smile, then bent his head and kissed her cheek lightly. Blood rushed to her face and her breath caught, her hand shooting up to graze the space his lips had touched.

"I'll see you later," Nick said, walking backwards and that same half-smile on his face. "You come to the game next Saturday? This week is an away one."

Coralee squeezed the knob and shrugged. "Maybe."

Nick laughed, and with one final wave, went down the lane towards his own dorm.

Coralee let out a long breath before entering the building, pausing briefly at Freda's room before deciding to go to her own. She wasn't ready to share what happened just yet; she wanted to keep it to herself just a little while longer.

Coralee also didn't know the first thing about football, but she would research it before the next home game. The last thing she wanted to do was annoy someone with all her questions, and she wanted to enjoy the game.

She entered her room and was glad Trish wasn't there; she didn't want her roommate's chattering to aggravate her already-overloaded senses and emotions. She changed her clothes tiredly and collapsed on her bed, falling into a dreamless, yet welcomed sleep.

SIX

"Mr. Drummond, I need to see you."

Benjamin's eyes went to Coralee, who was face down and scribbling madly in her notebook as the rest of the class gathered their belongings and left. She never came to Sunday's tutoring session, and Benjamin was angry she stood him up. The least she could've done was tell him or Professor Carmichael she didn't want to tutor him anymore!

Beside him, Peter groaned, muttering about stupid Yank professors. Benjamin chuckled, starting down to the front of the class.

"Want us to wait for you, Benny?" Peter called.

"No," he replied, his attention solely on the professor. Professor Carmichael had finished erasing the board by the time Benjamin reached his desk, the older man wiping the chalk from his hands as he turned.

"I received a message from Miss Simmons," Professor Carmichael said without preamble.

"See, Professor Carmi—"

"She says she's sorry for missing Sunday's session, and won't be able to tutor you until next week. She has a prior commitment and she's busy with preparations for it."

A prior commitment? "Oh."

"While the timing is most unfortunate, considering the big test you have on Thursday, I hope you've gleaned enough from the sessions to do well on it?"

"Yes."

"I've read the reports," Professor Carmichael continued, sitting at his desk and stacking the papers. "She says you're improving. How do you feel about that?"

"Surprised. I didn't expect—"

"She's an excellent teacher, Mr. Drummond. I thought you of all people would look beyond color to determine one's capabilities."

"I didn't mean—"

"Of course you didn't."

Benjamin clenched his jaw and counted to ten. "Anything else?"

The professor smiled. "Good luck on Saturday."

"Uh...thanks, Professor." He stood there awkwardly, even as Professor Carmichael started going through his lecture notes, then eventually left the classroom, still amazed by what the professor said. Benjamin had been sure Coralee had quit their sessions, and he felt ashamed he'd immediately thought the worst of her.

"What the *professor* have to say?"

Benjamin's head jerked up and he frowned a little bit, spying Peter. "I thought I said not to wait!"

Peter shrugged, pushing off the wall and falling into step with Benjamin. "I'm done for the day, and nobody's at the house, anyway. So, what did he say?"

"Talked to me about my grades, making sure I felt good about the exam on Thursday."

"I bet he wants you to fail."

"Except if he did, he wouldn't have even offered the tutoring sessions," Benjamin reminded Peter.

The younger boy waved the comment away. "And you trust that? He's a Yank. Bad enough they won the flippin' Civil War—!"

"Over a hundred years ago!" Benjamin exclaimed, incredulous at what he was hearing. It wasn't as if he hadn't heard the arguments before, but they sounded even more ridiculous coming from Peter. He breathed a sigh of relief when he saw Felix approaching.

"Yanks wanna control everything," Peter continued once Felix pulled level, clearly dismissing Benjamin's earlier outburst. "Wouldn't let us keep the slaves, now they wants us to give them damn niggers 'civil rights'—I bet my grandpappy's rollin' over in his grave at that!"

"They're citizens of the United States, Pete, they're due the rights," Benjamin said exasperatedly, pointing his face to the sky to let the late October sun greet it.

Peter gaped at him, then chuckled cautiously. "Oh, I get it, you practicin' that judge stuff! I was about to be worried there, Benny!"

"Worried?"

"That you meant it!" Peter scoffed, as if the very thought were ludicrous.

Benjamin's brows furrowed, and he stuffed his hands in his pockets. "What if I did?"

"Did what?"

"Mean it."

Peter reached across Benjamin to slap Felix's arm. "Are you listenin' to this guy?"

Felix laughed a little. "I got a feeling there was more to this conversation than what I've heard, but I'm gonna go out on a limb and agree with Benjamin anyway."

Peter goggled at them. "But...but—but they're no account nigras! They shouldn't even *be* here!"

Benjamin stopped walking and grabbed Peter's arm. "And why is that? What have they ever done to you?" Shock and fear crept in Peter's blue eyes and Benjamin's grip eased. "Sorry, man."

Peter yanked his arm away, his face red no doubt from embarrassment and anger. "What the hell's wrong with you? First you defendin' 'em and now you attack me! Whose side are you on?"

"This ain't a battle—"

"Oh, yes it is! They're tryin' to take over everything! First rights, then jobs, then our *women*—everything! Tommy said—"

"There goes your first problem, kid, listenin' to Tommy," Felix said dryly.

"Skive off, Felix! I ain't a kid! Just because y'all are two years older doesn't mean I'm a child, *and* I'm old enough to believe what I wanna—"

"So why believe that? What do you have to gain by bein' a bigot?"

Peter lunged for Felix, but Benjamin stopped his progress. "Cool it, kid—"

Peter shoved Benjamin's arms away. "Stop callin' me that! You see?! See what they've done?! They've turned us against each other!"

Benjamin groaned and started back up the lane, the beautiful day spoiled. He was skipping Constitution Theory; he didn't want to sit through another lecture.

No one said anything the rest of the walk to the house, Peter quickening his steps to get ahead of them. It wasn't fair for Peter to be considered "just a kid" when many older folks felt the exact same way. Besides, it wasn't as if Benjamin were all that enlightened himself, at least not compared to Felix. Benjamin's father would talk about his cases often, his tone dry and matter of fact, while his mother would nod and tsk and pity the "poor coloreds", but that was it. Neither one would *do* anything to change it—Paul would say, "it's the law," when he gave less-than-progressive rulings, and his mother rarely gave Patty days off or pay raises. Patty had never complained, though. But as Benjamin was learning, lack of verbal complaint didn't mean one was nonexistent.

When they entered the frat house, Peter bounded up the stairs to his room and Felix's eyes followed him. "I'll talk to the kid." Benjamin briefly entertained going as well, but figured Felix would be the best for the job. Though he was the most open-minded in his thinking, most of the brothers still respected him.

Benjamin envied the man's diplomacy.

"Why you standin' there lookin' like yo' dog just died?"

Benjamin chuckled, the action easing his internal tension. He looked towards the window where Babs was dusting the blinds and humming. "Well?" She still hadn't looked at him.

He sank on the couch, groaning like an old man. "Got a lot on my mind, Babs."

"Don't we all, honey."

"What's on your mind?"

"What's on my mind?" She moved to the lamp, Benjamin not understanding why, considering it seemed spotless to him.

"Yeah."

"Hmm...probably how in the devil I've been able to keep this house standin' when I got a bunch o' hooligans livin' in it!"

Benjamin laughed along with her, nodding at her point. "You're an amazin' woman, Babs, that's why."

"Guess I got some practice raisin' my own three boys, ain't that right?" Babs said with a smile, now dusting the end table on which the lamp stood.

"You have three boys?"

"Yeah, all grown now. Two of 'em joined the army and the third works in Detroit at the Ford Company. He's a floor manager now!"

"Floor manager...that's a good thing?"

Babs laughed incredulously. "You serious? Ain't no colored floor managers down at that mill! Yes, sir! My children went and done made somethin' of themselves! Sho did..."

Benjamin mulled over his next question before asking it. "What did you want to do?"

"Me?"

Benjamin shrugged, sitting up straight and resting his forearms on his thighs. "Yeah...what were your dreams? What did you want to be?"

Babs paused her movements, a small frown on her face. "What did I want to be...I ain't never really thought too long 'bout it."

"Oh."

He reclined against the back of the couch and she continued dusting. No one said anything, Benjamin trying to imagine a life without childhood ambitions.

"A queen," Babs ultimately answered.

"A queen?"

"Yeah. I wanted to be queen, but then the little girl my mama worked for said black girls couldn't be queens, so I became a house-keeper instead." She laughed as if she'd told a joke.

"Babs—"

"Want me to fix you somethin'? Sandwich? Potato salad?" She didn't wait for his answer as she went into the kitchen, and he heard pots and pans clang as she prepared lunch.

To be a queen had been Babs' dream, shot down because some-one said queens weren't black. No one had ever told him he couldn't be anything because of his color. In fact, his father always said the only person who could stop him from being whoever he wanted to be was himself. How different was it to grow up in a world where one couldn't be anything, all over something as unchangeable as race?

Had Coralee ever wanted to be a queen?

Benjamin assumed she had, given the many princess games she had forced upon him and her brother during their younger years. Benjamin was always the prince, because Luther Jr. was her brother and adored torturing the poor girl, as older brothers were wont to do. When they played, Benjamin had always vowed to protect her from big bad monsters and other things that could harm her.

Benjamin never imagined he'd become one of them.

He heard footsteps coming down the stairs, and Peter and Felix came into the living room. Peter didn't meet his eyes, nor did Benja-min try to make him. Felix sat next to Benjamin, saying nothing as well.

Peter turned on the television; some soap opera was playing. In-stead of changing the channel as Benjamin assumed he would, Peter reclined on his elbows, seemingly intrigued by the action.

"I think Jessica's gonna tell 'im!"

Babs rushed out of the kitchen, holding a dripping wet plate and a towel, her eyes glued to the set. *"Really?!* How you think George gonna react?"

Benjamin looked at Felix out of the corner of his eye, who was wearing a small grin, and became even more perplexed. "What's the smile for?"

"I think she's gonna tell him, also."

Unbelievable. *Felix* watched this too? Benjamin was truly out of sorts now!

"George's gonna be real mad, I think, real mad. I mean, hell, that was his *brother* for cryin' out loud!"

"Lawd, Peter! You all hooked on my shows, now?"

"You run this place, Miss Barbara; I just live in it."

And there it was—a small gesture of respect. She used her name only once a year when she first introduced herself to the new brothers at the beginning of the term, and never with the salutation. The fact Peter had done it was momentous. Even Babs—Miss Barbara—looked at the young man in shock, but simply nodded and went back into the kitchen, telling Peter to call her when the commercials ended. Peter's address turned Plumville protocol on its head, succinctly subverting the basic assumption of the way things were. Benjamin suddenly thought of Coralee. Perhaps the whole point of being in the BSU was to challenge those assumptions...to challenge a world that said she couldn't be queen, a world that wouldn't *allow* her to be one.

What did it say about him, being on a side that fought against her right to a crown?

❧

"He *kissed* you?! And you only tellin' me about it *now?!* Some friend you are!"

Coralee only laughed, not taking any offense at Freda's hushed comment. The board, sans Nick, who had football practice, was in Jermaine's room creating posters for tomorrow's rally. Coralee was anxious about it; it was the first major stand the BSU would take on campus and anything could happen. This was why Freda's affected affront about being out of her romantic loop was refreshing. It kept Coralee's mind off tomorrow, at least a little.

"You act like a kiss on the cheek is a marriage proposal," Coralee whispered back, carefully tracing the penciled fist with a bold, black marker.

"For you it is! I mean, you 'bout as chaste as a nun!"

"So?"

"So a fine gal like you needs some lovin'," Andre snickered, giving her a pointed look.

Coralee blushed, realizing Nick had told his friend as well. However, she didn't want this non-issue of a kiss blown out of proportion.

"I think I know what I need just fine."

The rest of the board heckled Andre, who sucked his teeth and went back to his poster art. "Ain't nice to keep a brotha down, Miss Ceelee."

"Nor is it nice for a 'brotha' to assume things, either, Mr. Andre."

Freda giggled, falling over on her back and Andre threw a balled-up piece of paper at her. Coralee laughed as well, picking up the paper and throwing it back. She was glad the group was in good spirits; she hoped it would last to the next day.

"We doin' all right?" Jermaine asked. Everyone nodded, and Coralee finished coloring in her fist.

"I wonder what they gon' do when they see us marchin'? Think they'll bring dogs out?" Andre was a little *too* excited about tomorrow's events, and Coralee told him so. "C'mon, Coralee, don't be such a party pooper!"

"Ain't no party to poop, Andre! This a dang rally! We're fightin' fo' somethin' very serious here."

"Coralee's right. We have to approach this with a sense of purpose and gravity. Ain't no half-steppin' on this, y'all!" Jermaine added.

With that, the group finished the posters in relative silence, everyone internalizing what would happen. Coralee thought she finally had the opportunity to make a difference, not just watch people on television or listen to addresses on the radio. She would be like her brother, though on a smaller, less bloody scale, fighting for freedom and a voice all the same.

They ended the meeting with a song instead of the usual prayer, and Freda sang "Oh, Freedom". Grandma Dennie said her father used to sing that song often, having been born a slave himself; and even though he'd only been seven when Emancipation came, Grandfather could remember much about it. Coralee wished she'd been born before he died, but at least she had her grandmother to voice the stories he no longer could. This rally was about more than adding a department; it was about giving her great-grandfather and countless others like him their rightful place in history instead of being ignored or only considered a footnote to something bigger.

Coralee and Freda walked arm in arm back to their dormitory, still humming the spiritual. Nothing would be the same after tomorrow, for good or ill.

"I hope it'll be a nice day," Freda said on a sigh, squeezing Coralee's arm.

"I think so."

"By the will of God...and the white people on campus."

"They ain't gonna take the rally lyin' down."

"Good. They can stand right next to me."

They wanted a peaceful demonstration, but they knew some would attempt crashing the rally. Though they'd made contingencies, the BSU realized only the ones most threatened by it, the ones with the most to lose, would try to intimidate them into silence.

"I don't know if I'll be able to sleep tonight—I'm so wired!" Coralee announced upon reaching her room. Freda entered right behind her.

"You'll put all that energy to use tomorrow when you give your speech."

"What about you?" She was relieved Trish wasn't in there.

"Sleep," Freda replied. "Gotta rest the vocal chords, 'cause I'mma sing and shout and make some noise so the people in the administrators' office can hear a sista!"

"That's right! We gotta be heard!"

"We do," Freda said, a soft smile forming on her face. "And we won't leave until we are."

"This is for our mothers," Coralee said softly.

Freda nodded. "For them."

"And for us," Coralee added.

SEVEN

"Guess what I heard?"

Benjamin was taking off his cleats, his mind on the very bizarre practice they'd just had. Most of the colored boys on the team had been far more deferential than usual, a fact not lost on Coach Norman. Coach was so baffled he ended practice early, yelling at them to get their minds straight before Saturday's game. Though practice had been productive, its mood had been eerie, ominous even, leaving Benjamin unsettled.

The queasy feeling only got worse at Randy's bright eyes and large grin.

"What?"

As soon as the question left his mouth, Benjamin wished he could snatch it back. It would open a multitude of problems he would rather keep closed, and he knew it instinctively. Tommy Birch had had a similar look when he had decided to crash that BSU meeting a month ago. Nothing good could come from such a look.

"Gonna be a nigger rally today. That's why them colored boys was all nice. Knew somethin' was off! Can't trust 'em fo' nothin'!"

He said this all with a big smile, and the juxtaposition of the action and the speech unnerved Benjamin.

"Really."

"That's all you gotta say?! I tell you the darkies tryin' to upset things 'round here, the peace and quiet, and all you gotta say is 'really'? You feelin' all right?"

"Actually, I'm not."

Randy gave him a sympathetic look, clapping Benjamin's shoulder. "I hear that. We gonna hafta stop 'em before they get outta control."

Benjamin stood, putting his cleats and padding in his locker before yanking out his towel and a cake of soap to hit the showers.

The steaming water kneaded his tight muscles, and Benjamin rested his forehead on the damp, cool tiles. A rally. It made sense: the eagerness with which most of the colored boys had left practice, the whispers and mini-conferences on the sidelines all throughout the afternoon. Benjamin even wagered this was Coralee's "prior commitment", and the thought made him sick. This was not going to be pretty, and Coralee would be in the thick of it. Benjamin wondered if Patty knew what kind of organization her daughter was involved in during the school year. Probably not. Patty wasn't the type to disturb things. Benjamin couldn't figure out where Coralee got her revolutionary streak, but it was liable to get her hurt or even killed.

That was unacceptable.

He shut off the water harshly and changed into his regular clothes, all the while hearing his teammates whoop and holler about how they were gonna "stop the darkies." He clenched his jaw, not trusting himself to say anything without incriminating himself and being made a target. He'd just been about to leave the locker room when someone grasped his arm. A snarled "what?!" died on his tongue when he saw who the other person was.

"This ain't gonna be good, Benjamin."

He rolled his eyes at the inevitability of Felix's statement and started walking again, the setting sun creating a pointed shaft of light towards the library in the distance. That unsettling feeling Benjamin had had all day now sharpened to a sense of urgency, his body priming to do *something*, yet not knowing what. Between the looming English exam he had tomorrow and the unavoidable altercation of tonight, Benjamin had never felt so helpless, overwhelmed. He decided to go to the library, determined to be in control of the one thing in which he figured he could have success. Keats and Brontë, here he came.

"The rally is starting at the library," Felix said flatly.

Benjamin exhaled a harsh breath, annoyance mixing with the slight panic he felt. That ruled out the library.

"What are you gonna do?"

"Why *I* gotta do anything?! I'm a student just like you and everyone else!"

Felix blinked, glancing at the library before looking back at him. Benjamin *wasn't* like everyone else, and not only because his father was on the Board of Trustees. He was a campus celebrity, and people looked up to him on the football field and off it. He had to choose a side.

Peter's question swam in his head: *Whose side are you on?*

Coralee complicated the question immensely, even though she shouldn't, but the last thing he wanted was for her to hate him without knowing the real Benjamin Drummond.

Who *was* he, though? Was he someone who stood for the community, or stood for himself? What was more important? Benjamin had thought Coralee selfish for trying to impose a department most people didn't want; but what about *her* people, *her* Plumville? They weren't the majority at Solomon College; and if they didn't fight for their interests, who would? What good was a democracy if the majority was apathetic about minority? When he became state judge, his state would include people like Coralee Simmons, Nick Price, Barbara Lawrence...he couldn't afford sides.

Benjamin wished he could ask his father for advice. How did he manage to decide sensitive cases and still maintain the community's respect? Benjamin was sure his father had to have made many concessions before he'd reached the point in his career where he could change Plumville slowly, probably so slowly Plumville didn't realize it was happening. This rally, however, would be fast and abrupt, requiring a split-second decision that could affect Benjamin's reputation.

What to do?

"And here they come," Felix said dryly, looking up the hill to their right. Their brothers and some white members from the football team came tearing down the hill, Confederate flags billowing in the wind and various other crude posters bearing less-than-kind words and images.

Benjamin wanted to vomit.

"Hey, fellas!" Tommy called as he passed. "We goin' coon huntin'!" Benjamin glowered at him and Tommy stopped, walking back towards him and Felix. "What's got your panties in a bunch? Think you ain't a good shot?"

"Shot?"

Tommy walked around Felix slowly, studying him. "Yeah, city boy, shot. Huntin'. That's what we do in the country, man!" The other boys laughed and Tommy shushed them. "Wanna learn?"

"I know how to shoot."

Tommy squared his shoulders and stood taller, but couldn't match Felix's height. "Know how to shoot big-ass niggers who think they as good as upstandin' white people?"

"Don't wanna know how to do that, frankly."

"Ain't you a white boy?"

"No." Tommy grinned as if he had won the lottery. "I'm a grown man."

Tommy's grin faded slowly, and his brown eyes hardened to something very ugly. "We'll see about that." He walked backwards down the hill, staring at Felix intently. "You comin', Benny?"

The way the crowd waited, almost as if on bated breath, made Benjamin realize what he had to do. Without looking at Felix, he walked by Tommy, internally wincing at the cheers that followed him.

There was no going back now.

The speakerphone felt impossibly heavy in Coralee's grasp, and it took all of her strength to hold it to her mouth.

"Ladies and gentlemen...we are here on the brink of change, of starting a new era for Solomon College, and later—the world!"

The syllables tumbled off her tongue, automatic and precise, though her stomach jumped with each word pumped from her diaphragm. This was her important speech, and she had to deliver it well.

"Too long has our history been in the hands of another, spun, molded, and shaped to fit certain perceptions, to justify the gross wrongs done to us. Tonight we take it back—but not only that, expose the *real* truth of our people. Black Studies today, Black Studies forever!"

The crowd cheered, and some of the weight on Coralee's shoulders fell away. They were responding to her, energized. Posters ranged from "Black Studies Now!" to "We Have History, Too!" Some were simply decorated with black fists or afros or black bodies holding books at their chest and a raised fist. A few people at the rally wore dashikis, other more American clothes, and Coralee thought it was a fitting tribute to their two histories. They learned about one extensively, almost oppressively, while the other was only anecdotes told by their parents or other elders.

Jermaine was right; there could be no half-stepping when it came to their cause.

The sun's rays honed in on the library like a spotlight, as if she were an actress in her biggest debut. Instead, however, Coralee felt she was a proxy for her ancestors—their ancestors—the ancestors of black Plumville, Bakersfield, Georgia, America; the many blacks who came from all classes, regions, and colors.

They were tired of being treated as second-class students at Solomon College, tired of being discounted because their skin color triggered notions of an ignorant, incapable people. They would show the school what they could do, what their people *had done*; they would show that without them, there wouldn't *be* a United States of America.

"The journey toward our goal will be long and arduous, but not as long and arduous as our forefathers and mothers, who toiled the fields and picked the tobacco, rice, and cotton that made the South what it was—the richest region in the nation. It was from *our* forefathers and mothers' blood, sweat, and tears that many of our peers' families were able to live as comfortably as they did—"

"And it was because of y'all uppity niggers forgettin' yo' place the South fell!"

A chilling breeze swooped across the gathering, strains of "Dixie" floating upon it. Coralee clenched her jaw at the Confederate flag flying high from the other group. Though it wasn't a foreign sight, it still caused an unpleasant, visceral reaction. In one piece of cloth held the hatred, humiliation, and harassment she and hers had experienced since the moment they were born. Never had Coralee reacted so strongly to something inanimate, but how could she not when most in Plumville and Bakersfield pledged allegiance to *that* flag instead of the national one.

Not that the national one was much better, but at least those under *that* flag made an effort.

Jermaine eased Coralee aside, taking the speakerphone from her. "Dixie" got louder as the group approached, and the rally members moved closer together in a show of unity...and protection as well. "This is a peaceful rally! We don't want any trouble!" Jermaine said, his static-reproduced voice echoing throughout the quad.

The second group booed, jabbing the flag and other less benign posters in the air.

"Get down," Jermaine whispered to her.

"What?"

"*Get down* from the steps, Coralee! Right now you ain't nothin' but a target!"

A whiskey bottle barreled toward them, overshooting its mark and exploding with a sickening shatter behind them. Coralee didn't run down the steps, refusing to show her fear; but as soon as she reached the bottom, Freda and Nick yanked her into the safety of the crowd.

"That Negro needs to get off those steps! What if they don't miss next time?!" Freda said, terror lacing her voice. Jermaine remained and picked up Coralee's speech where she left off, his tone strong despite heckling and vulgarity from the dissenting group. Another whiskey bottle exploded at Jermaine's feet, soaking his brand new sneakers. It was then Coralee realized they weren't missing at all, aiming just enough to show intent, to warn.

"And now we rally, my friends, rally so our voices will finally be heard...we rally for change!"

Booing and cheering fought for dominance, and Jermaine jogged down the steps to join the rest of the BSU board. They linked arms and began singing "We Shall Overcome", walking towards the office; but the other crowd moved to stand in front of them, blocking their progress and looking mighty pleased to do so.

They didn't stop singing; instead, they got louder, unleashing the power of their voices and the voices they represented. The song angered their opponents. Their jaws clenched. They gripped their sticks, branches and bats harder. They waved the Confederate flag more vigorously than earlier. Coralee felt the disgust and lust from each foe she saw, but she gasped and stumbled back when she met a particular set of eyes. Benjamin Drummond stood looking every bit as angry and severe as the rest of his group, and she tightened her arm around Nick's to draw strength. As if last week's comment wasn't enough, his presence added salt to the wound.

"Dixie" now clashed with "Didn't My Lord Deliver Daniel", the songs dueling for supremacy. However, this was not enough for some, and a scream pierced the cacophony.

A fight ensued. Nick pushed her back into the crowd, away from the oncoming opposition, and Coralee fled. Someone grabbed her around the neck, and a scream lodged in her throat. She began kicking and scratching as an arm wedged itself between her collarbone and jaw. Flashes of that fateful BSU rally strobed her mind and Coralee fought for breath.

"The only thing you nigger women are good for is a screw—and a bad one at that!"

Coralee struggled against her assailant, especially when he worked his hand down the front of her blouse to grope her breasts. Before her, a rally member stood dazed, blood seeping from a wound at his temple and small twigs from the branch used to strike him strewn at his feet.

Coralee gagged.

"I could take you right now, right here in the middle o' all this, and no one would stop me—not even yo' lil' uppity nigger boy-friends—ouch! You stupid nigger bitch!"

Coralee had stepped on his foot and jabbed him hard in the stomach with her elbow, gaining freedom. She tore through the crowd, tears of frustration, sadness, terror, and anger coursing down her cheeks. All the weeks of planning, of preparing for every possible counterattack, had fallen short because none in the BSU could fully fathom the animosity and hatred of their opposition. It seemed no amount of discussion or teaching would do anything to stop it.

Amid the chaos Coralee stumbled upon the sidewalk, not realiz-ing it was even there. Suddenly arms wrapped around her and she screamed, struggling once more. A hand clamped around her mouth, and she fought for breath—she thought he was choking her again.

"It's me, Coralee," came the familiar voice, "it's Benny."

He didn't wait for her to reply, lifting her in his arms and cra-dling her like a baby. Her eyes took in his tightened jaw and she wrapped her arms around his neck, hiding her face in his shoulder.

He ran with her, his football training coming in handy, to a far-away alcove of trees behind the chapel and library. He set her down with her back against a tree, his front pressing her against it. His arms locked her in, and he kept looking behind him, as if searching for danger. Coralee tried to relax against the tree, but she couldn't stop trembling. Blood and adrenaline surged through her and she took deep breaths as if oxygen would run out in the next five minutes. She felt her heartbeat in her wrists, temple, stomach, chest, the backs of her knees—everywhere—as the heart worked overtime.

Thunder bounced off the roofs and trees, mixing with the yelling and fighting from the melee. Lightning flashed too brightly to be unconcerned about it, and Coralee jumped, a sob escaping her. Benjamin's large, calloused hand touched her cheek, catching the silent tears she shed. Coralee jerked, glancing at his eyes that were still full of the righteous anger and severity from before. What if Benjamin *was* the attacker from earlier?

She gasped again, pushing against the tree as if forcing it to envelop her. She hadn't recognized her first attacker's voice, her adrenaline-enhanced senses distorting it; but Coralee couldn't rule Benjamin out, no matter how much she wanted to do so.

His hands moved from her face to her body and Coralee froze, feeling the backs of his fingers ghost across her stomach and the bottom of her breasts as he righted her clothes. Her bottom lip slid between her teeth and she closed her eyes tight. When he stopped touching her, she still didn't relax, but she felt that assessing gaze all the same.

Rain began falling, flourished by the thunder and lightning, and she hugged herself.

"Coralee?"

It took her a moment before she could open her eyes and watch Benjamin open his jacket in silent invitation.

It took her a moment to understand what he was offering, shelter from the downpour, but should she trust it? Him? Experience taught her not to, conditioned by her father and grandmother and everyone else who told her white people could turn on a dime. Yet here this white boy was, protecting her from molesters and now the elements, only asking for her trust in return.

Did these small acts of chivalry deserve it? Was Benjamin, for this one moment, trying to be a knight in shining armor for her?

She peered at him, hugging herself tighter. "Benny?"

The name was small, barely discernible from the pelting rain and wind surging through the tree branches. A flash of lightning illuminated behind him, casting shadows along his face. His blue eyes were totally focused on her and he stepped closer, opening his jacket wider.

"Ceelee, please."

It was the please that uprooted her feet and propelled her into his arms. She hugged his middle, and breathed in his scent mixed with the rain, whatever soap he'd used earlier, and that cinnamon scent he always had—even when he was younger. Coralee warmed up, partly from the jacket, but mostly from him. This was a familiar embrace—the embrace he'd give her when he used to protect her from Luther Jr., or Tommy Birch, or a spider.

The rain was more calming than it should've been. Her clothes were ruined, but her molester had more to do with that than the weather. Water seeped into her shoes, squishing around whenever she moved or redistributed her weight from one foot to the other.

She snuggled closer to Benjamin, taking more of his heat.

"You'd never guess this," he said after a while, one hand sweeping along her back slowly, comfortingly, "but my dad asked me to look out for you while you were here."

That should've surprised Coralee far more than it did, but it made perfect sense. Her mother still worked for his family, and Mr. Drummond was always friendly to hers. Yet if that were the case—

"You never spoke to me until this year."

"I don't have to talk to you to look after you."

"Then why did you look so surprised to see me that day in Professor Carmichael's office?"

He laughed, and his chest rumbled under her ear. "*You* were going to be my tutor!"

"Oh, yes, a black girl tutoring a white boy? Who would've thought?"

"No, Ceelee," he replied, his hand now smoothing down her hair. "The student now was the teacher."

She pulled back slightly. Water dripped off his long, narrow nose and fell to his lips. Freda had been right; they were very full...kissable.

That was certainly an inappropriate thought, and she coughed in reaction.

"Maybe we should get you inside," he whispered.

Coralee dropped her forehead against his chest again, wholly against the idea. It meant she had to leave his warmth.

"I'll walk you to your room, loan you my jacket."

Even as Benjamin shrugged out of it, Coralee remained close, staring at the ground as the rain churned up dirt and small rocks. The jacket came around her shoulders, and she slipped her hands through the arms of it. The garment was soaked and too large; and every time she pushed up the sleeves, they fell back over her hands.

Finally the rain stopped and it was quiet, the weather apparently scaring off everyone and leaving her and Benjamin alone in the quad. They didn't talk or touch as they walked on the rain-soaked path; Coralee concentrated on putting one foot in front of the other, bunching the excess cuffs in her hands. Benjamin sighed and looked around as if discovering a new place. Perhaps he was, they were; and yet, it wasn't so new.

The trust, the friendship, had been easier once—natural and automatic.

Benjamin hesitated, grasping her elbow gently to guide her in front of him, helping her avoid a large puddle she'd been one step away from walking in, and she muttered her thanks. Her attention hadn't been on her feet despite her show of otherwise. He fell into step next to her, but didn't remove his hand. In fact, he tightened his grip and eased her towards him so smoothly Coralee barely registered it.

She didn't make him let go.

They reached her dormitory and Coralee peeled out of the jacket, still staring at her feet. "Thank you," she whispered, handing it to him. Their fingers brushed against each other, and she shivered, meeting his eyes briefly before going to the door.

"Ceelee?"

She turned to him, and had the strongest urge to brush his wet-slicked hair from his forehead. Benjamin approached her, studying her. She pressed her back against the glass door.

"Ben—"

His lips were even softer than Nick's as he kissed her cheek. Coralee forgot to breathe, especially when he squeezed her shoulder a little before drawing away and going back down the lane.

Clouds cleared and the moon shone high in the sky, its man smiling down on her and the rest of campus. Tomorrow morning, after a night's sleep, she'd wake up to the same campus with the same people living on it.

But a new balance had been formed, especially between her and Benjamin.

EIGHT

The sun shone brightly on the campus as trees dripped rain from the previous night's storm. Leaves decorated the lanes, ranging from purple to gold to red, and the wind tickled the ones that remained on their branches.

A rope hung from one tree, and on the end of it was a dummy painted black with "Xs" for eyes and a bloody mouth that had a large, red tongue flopping from it. The magnolia stood in front of the chapel, and the dummy swayed with the wind's flirtations. Over the next three days a test of wills ensued, both groups seeing how long the dummy would last before someone would break and take it down. That would admit defeat, and no one was prepared to do that. Scuffles broke out so frequently school officials called in the Bakersfield police to patrol the campus. Even the football team, despite its away win, suffered from the strain.

And despite all of the turbulence surrounding Solomon College, Coralee felt as if she'd embarked on something far more daring.

Sunday's tutoring session was the first time Coralee saw Benjamin after "the event". She tried not to think about the botched rally and her assault. She tried not to think about how Benjamin's arms had felt as he'd held her, how his voice had sounded as he'd comforted her, how his lips had caressed her cheek as he'd kissed her.

Coralee *really* tried not to think about *that*!

So she'd come to the library early, pouring over her books and rereading familiar texts that had suddenly became Greek, and panicked as if she had to give a major report on what she was reading within the next fifteen minutes. As soon as she heard the floorboards creak and the soft thud of his familiar gait towards their table, Coralee snapped the book shut and hid in one of the bookcases. Juvenile, she knew, but she wasn't ready to see him yet.

After three minutes of loudly whispering her name, Benjamin found her standing on tiptoes and trying to reach for a book she didn't particularly want to read, yet needed as a shield all the same. He came behind her, pressed gentle hands on her shoulders to make her go flat-footed, and pulled the book down with little effort.

"Show off," she muttered, taking the book and going back to her seat. He laughed and followed her, then drew out the Dickens they were discussing for the week from his backpack.

Her "shield" remained untouched in the center of the table throughout their session, both very serious about the topic at hand, and both seriously avoiding the deeper one under it. The hour went by fast, yet not fast enough; and then he'd walked with her back to her dormitory. They didn't say anything during the trip, and he'd kept enough distance between them so it appeared they'd just so *happened* to be going to the same place, but he would never start for the frat house until she was safely inside the dorm building.

Coralee initially thought it'd be a one-time thing. But then he'd done it again after Wednesday's session, then the following Sunday's; and all of a sudden, it'd become an institution. And then it'd seemed with each walk, he'd draw closer and their tongues would loosen, to the point they were still discussing themes from the book or goings on in the class, shoulders brushing and strides matching. For his part, Benjamin had never gotten so close as for them to be confused as a romantic couple, but their proximity still had garnered some bewildering glances. Benjamin acted as if he were oblivious.

Perhaps he was.

Or perhaps he *wasn't*, and didn't care what they thought.

For their final tutoring session before Thanksgiving, Benjamin and Coralee searched for topics he could write for the final English paper. The library was empty, as many students had gone home already to extend their holiday, but Coralee insisted on choosing a topic now so they wouldn't be scrambling when they returned.

Benjamin sighed, probably for the thirtieth time in the last ten minutes, and closed the book hard. They still hadn't found a topic on which he could write. "I'm gonna fail."

"You're not gonna fail, Benjamin."

"So says you."

Coralee smothered a laugh behind her hand, amused as he reverted to childish retort. She began clearing their worktable, stacking the books neatly, and packing her own knapsack before leaving a sulking Benjamin at the table.

The weather was cool and the sun hung low in the western sky. Coralee held her jacket closed with her hands—she hadn't had the time to sew new buttons on it yet—and hoped her mother would have enough yarn so she could make some gloves. Despite the fact she wasn't appropriately dressed for autumn, it was her favorite time of year.

Someone tugged on her knapsack, but she kept walking, knowing it was her tutee.

Coralee twisted her lips to hide her smile. "May I help you?"

He walked backwards so he could have her and had a large grin on his face. "I figured it out."

She allowed a corner of her mouth to rise. "Did you now?"

He pivoted on his heels and walked forward again, nudging her shoulder with his. "Wanna hear?"

She nudged him back. "Sure! I know whatever it is, it'll be good. I trust you."

And at that moment, Coralee realized she did. It'd gotten to the point Coralee had stopped engaging Benjamin as solely a tutee and more like a friend. The familiarity of the shifted dynamic had felt more like a favorite blanket around her, and she'd eased to an intimacy with Benjamin that she'd thought she'd never regain.

He'd been conspicuously quiet since her admission, and his bright blue gazed at her with such gratitude that she felt humbled by it. Coralee dropped her eyes and realized how unusual this all was. She'd realized Benjamin had been trying to rekindle their friendship from the moment the tutoring sessions had begun; but ever since the rally, he'd let her control the tenor their relationship. Benjamin didn't make her feel put upon in the slightest, asking for nothing more than she could give. And admittedly, his consideration had her contemplating more than just a platonic friendship with him.

Sucking in a sharp breath, Coralee started walking again, her pace brisker than before. Benjamin matched her stride, and they passed the dummy that still hung after three weeks. She shuddered, quickening her steps even more. However, Benjamin stopped, compelling her to do the same. Then he surprised her.

He took a Swiss Army knife from his back pocket and cut down the dummy, then found a trash bin and shoved it deep inside. Coralee's throat closed with unexpected tears, and she started walking again so he couldn't see them. He fell into step next to her, still silent, and they remained that way until they reached her dormitory.

"Would you...like to come to my room?"

The red that crept into his cheeks matched her own embarrassment and shock at her boldness. Never had she been so forward with a boy, but Coralee wanted to spend time with Benjamin without worrying about Keats or Dickens. He apparently felt the same because he nodded, and Coralee was relieved most of her floor had already left for Thanksgiving, including Trish.

The room's lock threw a temper tantrum, and Coralee had a hard time fitting the key inside. Her knapsack continuously slid down her arm as she adjusted herself to get better purchase on the lock. Benjamin took mercy on her and eased the bag off her shoulder.

"Thank you," she whispered, both to him and to the key she finally got in the lock. They entered the room, Coralee shaking her head at Trish's messy side. The drawers seemed as though they had exploded from overcapacity—opened with clothes hanging out of them, as well as knocked over bottles of creams and whatever else on top of the dresser. A lipstick-imprint of a mouth was in the corner of her mirror—fire-engine red—as well as a bra slung over the mirror's post.

Benjamin coughed, quirking his eyebrows as he looked at her side of the room. "Aunt Patty taught you well, I see," Benjamin said on a chuckle. "My room can never stay this nice; then again, I have a bunch of drunk frat brothers living with me as well."

"Doesn't your housekeeper clean up after you?"

Benjamin laughed. "Miss Barbara's worse than Aunt Patty when it comes to responsibility! Some of those boys have never cleaned a room in their life, and their rooms smell it too!"

"And she lets them live like that?"

"Why not? Who's a man if not someone who can take care of himself?" She nodded and let it end there. Benjamin gingerly sat on her bed, and she arched an eyebrow at him. "It's so pretty; don't want to mess it up."

"Gonna when I go to sleep!"

"You sleepin' now?"

Coralee blushed and coughed, not needing the image of her in her bed while he sat on it.

"So," she began, clearing her throat and browsing her bookcase. "What's your brilliant paper topic?"

"Keats."

She smiled a little and chuckled. "What about Keats?"

He hopped up from the bed and began to pace. "So, I was flipping through a book of his poems because, well, I dunno—but I came across one that I think I could analyze."

"Which one?"

"'A Song about Myself'," Benjamin supplied, rifling through his backpack to find the book. He handed it to her and she scanned the poem.

"This wasn't assigned," she noted, a thrilling tingle filling her as he looked at the text over her shoulder.

"I know," Benjamin said, then he suddenly looked worried. "Is that bad?"

She shook her head. "No, I actually think Professor Carmichael would be impressed with your initiative."

"Yes!" Benjamin cheered, starting to jig about her side of the room, and Coralee laughed at his enthusiasm.

"I don't think I've ever seen someone so excited about a paper!"

He shook his head though still grinned broadly. "No, I'm more excited I actually think I can pass English III!"

She gasped with mock affront, placing her hands on her hips. "Did you forget who's been tutoring you all this time?"

His giddiness and smile mellowed, but she grew warmer at the gaze he bestowed upon her. "Of course not. Why else do you think I'm so confident?"

A soppy grin formed on her face before she could check herself, so she quickly turned her attention back to her bookcase. Suddenly Coralee gasped. "Oh!"

He was behind her immediately. "What's wrong?"

She pulled down the book from the shelf, a book she hadn't opened since her freshman year. She showed him the cover.

He smiled. "*Curious George*? You actually brought it here?" He took the book from her, turning the pages gently as if they would crumble with the slightest harsh handling. This book had sparked her love for literature and writing; it represented their past friendship and trust.

"It looks as good as it did when I gave it to you," Benjamin breathed, his voice full of awe.

"Mama always taught us to take care of our things, remember?"

And this book had been Coralee's favorite. She'd never touched it unless her hands were clean, nor could anyone else. Patty would even hide the book whenever Coralee misbehaved, which was why Coralee had been such a good child when she was younger.

"I knew it would be in good hands if I gave it to you," he murmured, tracing the illustrations with his finger. He flipped back to the beginning of the book and smiled at her sheepishly. "Mind if I read to you?"

She returned his sheepish smile. "Not at all."

They sat on her bed, side by side, and began to read. She'd always loved Benjamin's voice; even as a child it'd had the ability to make her secure. Now it was a nice tenor, and Coralee felt she could wrap herself in it and sleep in its warm drawl.

Caught up in the fond nostalgia of it all, she put her head on his shoulder, helping him turn the pages as she'd done all those years ago. His cheek rested on top of her head, his arm curling around her shoulders; and when they reached the last page, his voice had quieted so it was nothing more than a whisper.

"The end," he breathed and kissed the top of her head. Her eyes fluttered at the contact, and she stared at the book longingly. Memories had come back hard, and she wished simpler days could return too—the days when it'd been okay for them to sit as they were, for Benjamin to show affection as he'd just done.

But those days were gone now. They shouldn't be holding each other and feeling very comfortable doing so, and Coralee tensed.

"Are you okay?" Benjamin asked, squeezing her shoulder comfortingly.

Coralee nodded, not trusting herself to speak. She sat straighter, clasping her hands in her lap and stared at them. Shame flooded her. Her mother had raised her better than this. She shouldn't be in a room alone with a boy, especially a white boy, *especially* Benjamin Drummond! No good would come out of this if someone caught them. His *coach* hadn't wanted people knowing she was tutoring him; how would it appear if someone saw him leaving her room now?

"Do you want me to leave?"

To her horror, "yes" refused to sound.

"I'll leave if you ask me to."

His lips brushed against her temple as he spoke, then gently kissed her skin, and she took in a shuddering breath. She leaned into his kiss and his arms tightened around her.

Her insides matched how Trish's side of the room looked—chaos.

"You haven't asked yet," Benjamin noted against her temple, not even attempting to move.

"No," Coralee agreed. "Not yet." She didn't move, either.

The pair sat uncertainly for a few more moments, Benjamin shucked off his shoes and reclined on her bed. He opened his arms to her and Coralee looked at him skeptically, partly at his gall for making himself at home in *her* bed, but more because she wanted to lie there with him.

He wore a devil-may-care/catch-me-if-you-can expression on his face and wiggled his fingers at her.

"I'm a very comfortable pillow," he enticed, waggling his eyebrows to punctuate his point.

"This is inappropriate," she said, crossing her arms and looking away from him haughtily. Suddenly arms wrapped around her and he tugged her to him, causing them both to giggle at his antics.

"Boy! Are you outside yo' mind?"

"I'm quite cozy, actually," he replied, very unapologetic at his behavior as he settled her next to him. His hold was loose enough for her to break if she wanted, but secure enough that she didn't want to, and she rested her head on his chest.

Benjamin was right; he was a comfortable pillow.

"Remember we used to do this outside and stare at the clouds as we tried to figure out what shapes they were?" he asked, his thumb rubbing back shoulder gently.

She yawned and nodded, her eyes growing heavy. "Mama always had to wake us up because we fell asleep every time."

"Yeah," Benjamin agreed, yawning as well. "Somethin' 'bout that summer sky..."

It was autumn, and the ceiling blocked the view of the darkening heavens, but they fell asleep anyway. Coralee didn't how long the nap lasted, only knew it'd been the best sleep she'd gotten in ages. During the course of her slumber, she'd awakened periodically and taken off her shoes and cardigan. Though they were fully clothed, she'd felt his heat seep into her. Benjamin was no less active, his jacket and shirt ending up on the floor by the bed, leaving him in his tank and jeans.

He cradled her to him, his fingers never still, just as he'd done when they were children. However, his touch seemed heavy with a need to hold her, as though reassuring himself they really were reunited and not just dreaming.

If it were, she hoped she never awakened.

Benjamin's eyes blinked open to an unfamiliar ceiling, but his disorientation didn't last very long when a warm body snuggled closer to him. He smiled and looked down at his bedmate, doing his best to smooth the hair that fell from her bun. Its softness surprised him. He remembered her always wearing it in cornrows or plaits, tugging on them to tease or to get her attention. Sometimes she'd shake her head to make the barrettes clink and clank against her skull, and they'd laugh at the funny sounds.

On a whim, he took a stray tendril and wrapped it around his index finger. Never would he have imagined those plaits hiding hair as lovely as this.

Coralee sighed and snuggled closer to him, her warm breath tickling his skin. She was all soft and pliable, her features relaxed and seemingly content. Benjamin hoped it was because of him.

Rarely was he ever in bed with a girl just to sleep; but Coralee meant more to him than just a desire that needed satisfying. It bewildered him at how quickly she'd gone up the ranks. He valued her opinions above many others, especially those of his "closest" circle. Coralee had never treated him as "Paul Drummond's son" or the "star quarterback" for the college. Most of the people he met now had an angle; the only thing Coralee had ever wanted from him was to be his best, to be "Benny".

He liked being Benny.

He thought back to the rally, to her vulnerability and fear...of *him*. She'd been so terrified, and the realization had hurt far more than he thought it would. He couldn't blame her; he'd seen Randy pawing at her as a dog would a bone, had heard Randy's inappropriate exclamation and seen his frantic chase to get her in his clutches again. Randy never knew Benjamin had yanked him back so powerfully, causing him to fall and take three other people on his trip down to the ground. Coralee hadn't known that, either; in fact, the way she'd looked at him after he'd brought her to safety told him she'd thought *he'd* been the one harassing her.

He'd let her know he hadn't by righting her clothes and offering his jacket and warmth against the cold, wet insanity of the night. Benjamin hadn't forced her to take any of it, wanting the decision to be solely hers. He'd been relieved when she accepted him.

Coralee had been so small, trembled so badly, that he'd thought back to their childhood when he protected her from Tommy Birch. He'd become angry over her fright; but more than that, his role in it. Just as Professor Carmichael had said, though he hadn't been an active participant, he'd been a complacent accomplice.

Benjamin wasn't going to be complicit anymore.

At the same time, Benjamin knew he'd have to be careful. The last thing he wanted to do was put Coralee in an awkward situation or ruin her reputation. The BSU—the black student population in general—respected Coralee immensely. Benjamin would do everything in his power to make sure he and others, no matter their color, gave it to her.

Then again, their current situation would do little to stop wagging tongues if someone caught them like this, but Benjamin was too relaxed to move. He closed his eyes, trailing a gentle finger on the curve of her shoulder, a low hum rumbling from his chest.

Coralee stirred, her eyes peeking open briefly and a frown on her face. "Cold."

Benjamin kissed the top of her head, pulling up a crocheted bedspread to cover both of them as his own eyes drooped closed. It was similar in design to the one Patty had given him when he first came to college. In fact, he slept with it every night—a little bit of home with him on campus.

That feeling increased ten-fold with Coralee in his arms.

Benjamin's eyes popped open and his jaw dropped at the realization. This was *bad*! No good could come out of whatever *this* was blossoming between them! He knew Coralee wasn't the *appropriate* woman his mother was constantly nagging him to find; and yet, Coralee was the only girl with whom he'd felt completely comfortable.

He remembered declaring he was going to marry her that last day they saw each other. Aunt Patty had appeared shocked at his innocent announcement, but Coralee had only been worried about kissing and other "icky stuff"; of course, neither of them had known exactly what the icky stuff entailed then, but Benjamin now knew that stuff wasn't icky at all.

Benjamin cleared his throat, feeling the heat rise in his cheeks and other, less suitable places. Coralee only shifted again, not opening her eyes this time.

He wondered if Coralee had ever...it was none of his business, though irritation rose at the thought of someone else touching his Ceelee in such a way. Had the person been gentle with her? Treated her as the queen she was? Loved her?

"He better had," Benjamin muttered, squeezing her.

"Ow..."

Benjamin looked down to see Coralee frowning, bringing her hand to her eyes to brush the sleep out of them and sitting up slowly. She looked around her room as if she'd been dropped in a foreign country without any directions, then peered at him.

Suddenly her eyes shot wide and she popped out of bed, jerking the bedspread to her chest.

"Ceelee, it's all right," he assured her, his voice a croon as he sat up slowly. "Well fell asleep; that's it."

Coralee closed her eyes and dropped her face in her hands. Benjamin felt something heavy settle in the pit of his stomach and hoped her reaction was one of relief. He would never take advantage of any woman, regardless of color, and particularly not someone so important to him.

Nevertheless, it was best he was on his way. Benjamin found his shirt and shook it out so he could don it. "I'm sorry. I guess I shoulda left anyhow. It's too—" He'd almost slipped and said *soon*, as though a future could come of his feeling so at home with her. Benjamin shook his head at himself for wanting something he knew he couldn't have. "I mean, it's inappropriate, like you said."

Her cool hands rested on his shoulders, and Benjamin resisted the urge to lean against her. He felt the bed shift, then her knees and the front of her cloth-covered thighs against his back.

"I'm the one who should apologize, Benjamin. I know you aren't like that."

It was exactly what he needed to hear, and he relaxed a little. Her hands moved to his upper arms and she rested her chin on his shoulder, their posture typical of a couple who'd been together forever. It felt natural and fundamental to Benjamin's very existence, regardless of how new the entire dynamic actually was. It was as if they'd picked up where they left off all those years ago, even if it had taken a while to get here.

The "next time" they should've had.

Yet Benjamin had to make sure he wasn't projecting his feelings onto her. He took her hands in his, sliding them down his chest before linking their fingers together. She shifted closer to him so she wouldn't fall over, her breath tickling the shell of his ear.

"Do you trust me, Coralee?" He felt her nod, but that wasn't good enough. He needed to hear it from her. Benjamin leaned away to look in her eyes and he asked the question again, suddenly noticing flecks of gold in her brown eyes.

"Yes," she replied, her eyes never wavering from his.

He cupped Coralee's cheek and rested his forehead against hers, humbled by her simple response. He'd earned it, finally, and a large weight lifted from his shoulders.

"Perhaps you better get goin'," she whispered, squeezing his wrist.

Benjamin twisted his hand to wrap around hers, and brought the back of it to his lips. Her hand was rougher than many of the other girls' hands he kissed—a proper gentleman always greeted ladies in such a fashion, his mother used to say—but it was perfect anyway.

"Yeah..."

Benjamin put on his shirt and grabbed his jacket from the floor, shoving his arms into the sleeves. "This was the best afternoon I've had in a long while," he said quietly, staring at the vacancy in her bookcase where *Curious George* used to be.

"And productive," she added, her smile tremulous, unsure. "You have a paper topic now."

He approached her until he stood directly before her. Coralee only came up to his collarbone; and though she was a little larger than the girls he was used to, every inch of her felt right in his arms.

"Can I get a hug goodbye?" he asked, holding out his arms for good measure.

She rolled her eyes playfully yet granted his request. He was overwhelmed by the knowledge this was the first time they'd hugged since they were children and how embarrassed he'd been at the time.

Now, he didn't want to let her go.

"Remember when I proposed to you?" he asked, his lips brushing the upper curve of her ear.

She pulled back slightly, her eyes shining with recognition as she wore her Ceelee smile. Benjamin's heart swelled at the sight.

"I said I didn't wanna do any of that 'icky stuff'!" she recalled.

He waggled his eyebrows. "The icky stuff actually isn't so bad, Ceelee."

She gave him an exaggeratedly dubious look before cracking up with laughter, and Benjamin smiled, taking in her mirth. He wanted nothing more than to pull her to him to prove the "icky stuff" was anything but.

And as delicious as her mouth looked at the moment, he knew it would be *really* nice.

Unthinkingly, Benjamin leaned in closer, but she stopped him with a firm hand on his chest. He immediately dropped his arms from her and stepped back.

"I'm sorry," he immediately apologized.

"Apology accepted," she assured him, and even her gaze seemed more contemplative than accusatory. Nevertheless, Coralee went to her door and opened it. "Have a Happy Thanksgiving, Benjamin. Tell your parents I said hello, and maybe ask if they could loan my mama to me for the holiday too?"

Benjamin grinned giving her as wide a berth as he could as he stepped over the threshold. "Anything for you, Ceelee. Happy Thanksgiving."

He left with a spring in his step, realizing that this Thanksgiving he would actually have *real* contributions to the "what are you thankful for?" conversation. On the top of that list was having his Ceelee back.

NINE

Holidays were always a tricky time of year, no matter where someone lived, or how much money the person had. People were supposed to enjoy being around friends and family—or at least pretend—and some families made this easier to do than others.

Between his mother's attempt at playing cupid with the daughter of one of his father's colleagues, the mother's incessant talking, and the combined keening of "how handsome they looked together", Benjamin thought he deserved an Academy Award for playing along.

It wasn't that Laura Robinson was a plain girl. Her glossy, dark-brown hair and bright, green eyes made him appreciate her beauty; and she wasn't that horrible of a conversationalist, either. Yet, in the end, Benjamin simply wasn't interested. He understood why his mother liked Laura. She'd been groomed to be the perfect Southern lady, if a little less high-strung than Florence Drummond; but Laura's mother was almost identical to Florence, and the prospect of having her over for more holidays left an unpleasant taste in Benjamin's mouth. Benjamin's father had conspicuously made himself unavailable to support his wife's claims of "isn't she just lovely, dear?" or "she's such a lady, isn't she?" by engrossing himself in conversation with Laura's father or complimenting Aunt Patty on the delicious meal.

Benjamin thought that was funny, especially because Mrs. Robinson would always praise *Florence* for a meal she barely supervised, let alone prepared. Part of Benjamin wanted to announce he helped season the collard greens and peeled the sweet potatoes for the pie, but it was unnecessary. Patty deserved all the compliments, and the last thing he wanted to hear was his mother's chastisement about working in the kitchen.

"State judges don't do those things," Florence often said, but Paul had worked in a restaurant as a busboy during his college days. However, Benjamin continued to play the perfect son for his mother's sake. He spoke of his collegiate experiences on cue, laughed whenever appropriate, and even went so far as to ask questions, voluntarily, of all their guests—including Mrs. Robinson.

But if Benjamin had earned the Oscar for Best Actor, he thought Patty deserved it for Best Actress. He didn't think he'd have the patience to endure Mrs. Robinson with the civility Patty did. The woman was constant in her requests—more sweet tea, a little more collards, no cranberry sauce, anymore cornbread?—and all one after another. Poor Patty could barely steal a break, but she served them all with the same calm, polite demeanor she always possessed whenever Florence had guests.

When the dinner was finally finished and the sweet potato pie served, Patty gained her reprieve in the kitchen. Benjamin wished he could do the same.

"Where did you ever find that darling Patty?" Mrs. Robinson asked, taking a bite of her pie. "This is excellent, Florence."

"Thank you, Marcia! That recipe's been around for years..." Benjamin barely controlled the urge to roll his eyes. "But Patty, she's absolutely a godsend! I don't know what I would've done without her!"

"It's so hard to find decent help nowadays," Mrs. Robinson said sadly, continuing to eat her pie. "Most of the maids are either too old to be of any use or too young to have the appropriate manners. Mrs. Dowdy's maid sassed her just yesterday—"

"My Patty wouldn't sass me—"

"Because the girl thought Mrs. Dowdy gave her 'too much work'—"

"That's her job, isn't it?"

"The maid *claimed* she was missing her class, and they'd come to an understanding at six o'clock the girl would leave to go to school—"

"Why would a maid need to go to school?"

"Exactly!"

The women laughed. Laura looked positively bored and the husbands still ignored their wives.

"Patty's daughter goes to Solomon College, and I'll admit I tried to talk Patty out of sending little Ceelee there—though for purely selfish reasons. I thought I'd have an obvious replacement for Patty when she retired. She's been working here for over twenty years already, and she deserves a break."

"You may still get that daughter, yet, Florence; a colored girl with a diploma is still just a colored girl. What in the world is she going to do other than be a maid—?"

"That's not fair!"

The chatting women stopped and the men turned their attention to the rest of the table, finally finding something worth their interest. Laura continued to appear disinterested, but there was a small smile on her face.

"Benjamin, dear, what's the matter?"

"*Coralee* is one of the smartest people I've ever met; in fact, she's the best student in my English class! So 'what in the world is she going to do' once she graduates? I'll bet she'll be a teacher, or a lawyer or—or president! She will *certainly* not be a maid!"

Florence and Mrs. Robinson looked at him agape while their husbands went back to their private conversation, but Benjamin thought he saw his father grin and nod slightly. Laura smirked at the other two women.

"Things are changing, Mother," Laura said, surprising Benjamin in the process.

Benjamin blinked at her, then smiled and chuckled a little. "So, you agree?"

Laura nodded. "Completely."

Mrs. Robinson narrowed her eyes at her daughter, then turned her attention to Florence with a mocking expression. "'Got to him early', did you?"

Tension immediately settled over the table, and unease slithered into the pit of his stomach. "Mama, what's Mrs. Robinson talking about?"

Florence glowered at Mrs. Robinson, then glanced at Patty, who'd just returned holding a pitcher of sweet tea. Mrs. Robinson held up her glass for a refill, her attention darting between the hostess and her housekeeper with a knowing glance. Florence's face was red, something it rarely was without the aid of rouge, and she clearly didn't want to have this discussion now.

Benjamin, unfortunately, would have to decline her unspoken request to change the subject. "Mama, what is Mrs. Robinson talkin' about?"

"We will *not* discuss this in mixed company—"

"Mama, everyone else obviously already knows! And while I think I have an idea, I want to hear you say it!"

Patty looked sharply at him, as if willing him to be quiet.

"This is really an inappropriate time," Paul said, the husbands finally becoming a part of the bigger conversation.

Benjamin looked at Laura, and she quirked her eyebrow at him. Apparently, the look alarmed Mrs. Robinson so much she clucked her tongue in warning.

"Laura Marie Robinson, don't you dare—"

"I think there's a sense of justice in the world to know that he didn't fall for your little trick, just as I didn't."

"You mind your manners, young lady!" Mr. Robinson said, shaking his finger at Laura.

Benjamin suddenly had no appetite for the rest of the meal. What his parents had done wasn't anything others hadn't done for decades, but it didn't make the betrayal sting any less. And to hear it stated so starkly just days after spending such a wonderful afternoon with Coralee made disgust at his mother settle heavily in his gut.

"Well," Paul began, also placing his napkin on the table next to his plate. "I think it's safe to say dinner's done—why don't you go on home, Patty? You deserve to be with your family, anyway."

"Not until she cleans up, she can't!" Florence insisted.

"Florence, please," Paul appealed, then directed his attention back to Patty. "And take the rest of the weekend off as well."

Mrs. Robinson squeaked indignantly.

"Thank you," Patty said, and went into the kitchen. The silence was almost constricting, so tense it was, and Benjamin itched to get away.

"Need me to do anything before I head out?" Patty asked quietly as she stood in the threshold of the dining room from the kitchen, wrapping a kerchief on her head and buttoning up her coat.

"Yes, actually," Paul said, rising from his seat. He approached his housekeeper, murmuring softly, and whatever he said caused the woman's eyes to go wide and shake her head. "I insist," Paul said, placing an envelope in her hand. Patty's fingers closed over it slowly, and she nodded.

"Happy Thanksgiving, Patty," Benjamin heard his father murmur.

"Thank you, you too," Patty replied, glancing at Benjamin before nodding goodbye to the rest of the party. Paul sat back in his seat as if nothing happened, and Florence looked at him in consternation.

"Are you still keeping an eye on Patty's daughter?" Benjamin looked at him weirdly but nodded. "Good," Paul replied, then addressed his wife calmly. "You knew this chicken would come home to roost someday, honey." Florence sipped the swallow of tea left in her glass, refusing to say a word.

"You don't need to *explain* yourself!" Mrs. Robinson declared. "You only did what countless of other proper Southern families have done; it's not uncommon!"

Benjamin still wanted them to say it. "And what would *that* be?"

Silence. He'd never felt so angry and frustrated in his life. Benjamin excused himself and left the dining room, vaguely registering Laura's polite "excuse me" as he stalked through the front door, but didn't say anything when she followed.

Neither spoke as they stood outside, allowing the crisp, autumn air to refresh him from the stale, stuffy atmosphere of the dining room. Benjamin's neighborhood was made of handsome houses, most with porches, some with second-level verandas as well. His own wasn't the largest in the neighborhood, much to his mother's chagrin, but Benjamin thought the size was just right. Every lawn on the street was perfectly manicured with not a single leaf on the ground, and top of the line cars filled the driveways. The empty ones meant the families spent the holiday out of town.

Suddenly Laura chuckled. "Mother and I visited here all the time while you were at school. I think they were hoping we'd be announcing our engagement by the end of dinner."

Benjamin blanched and Laura laughed again, leaning against the railing and hugging herself. While the weather may have refreshed him, it still was a bit cool outside, and Benjamin offered his suit jacket to her.

"Such a perfect gentleman," Laura said with a wink. Benjamin cleared his throat and blushed. When he was younger, he'd always took that comment for granted, blindly accepting his mother's definition and following her lessons because he had to do so. But now, after three and a half years of college and especially this last semester with Coralee, he knew his mother's definition was little more than Florence's. Instead of restricting his manners and polite disposition to white people, a *true* Southern gentleman would extend it to everyone genuinely.

"You like this Cora girl, don't you?"

Benjamin narrowed his eyes at the house across the street. Who was she to ask such a personal question? They'd just met; they didn't have enough trust between them to share such confidences.

Besides, it could be possible her mother wanted to use this information for something bad.

Benjamin cleared his throat and shrugged. "We used to be friends."

"Right. So was my mother's maid and I, and her brother."

A similar situation to his childhood, and Benjamin couldn't help but be intrigued. "Really?"

Laura nodded, wrapping his jacket tighter around her. "Yes. We were all best friends when we were younger; yet her brother and I, as we grew up, became...*closer* friends."

Benjamin's eyes widened. "You don't mean—"

"Yeah, I 'mean.'"

Laura Robinson was full of surprises. This seemingly "proper" Southern belle wasn't playing by the rules given to her, either.

"Obviously your mother isn't pleased," Benjamin said dryly.

"No, especially since all she thought she had to do was break up our friendship and keep us from seeing each other anymore—you know, 'out of sight, out of mind'...according to *your* mother anyway."

It was the confirmation he needed. Everything fell into place—Coralee's abrupt absence, his mother's refusal to speak of her, Patty's forced silence—all of that was to keep their friendship from potentially becoming something more. But for all of his mother's scheming, fate, destiny, or whatever else—maybe even God—decided Coralee would be a fixture in his life, and an important one as well.

The fact Florence had decided to take that decision into her own hands made Benjamin angry.

"She had no right!"

"I had every right!"

His mother stood at the door, staring at her son with a severe expression. Laura slipped back in the house to allow them privacy, and Benjamin considered his mother carefully. Though he knew she only did what she thought was best for him, she'd been wrong. He'd grown up to be someone he didn't particularly like, but was deemed acceptable because the rest of Plumville said so.

Did his mother really think it was impossible for black and white people to have strong, genuine friendships? Things wouldn't be so tense had parents allowed their children's friendships to take their natural courses. Perhaps Benjamin and Coralee would've separated eventually, particularly when they went to school; but because of the forced interference, they would never know. Then again, he didn't think so; for despite all that had happened between them, Benjamin's affections for Coralee had deepened immensely. His mother's intervention had been for naught, and he would disappoint her just as she had disappointed him.

"I think Coralee and I are friends again." All Florence did was purse her lips at his announcement. "We're getting close—"

"Oh, don't you talk that way, Benjamin Mark Drummond! I saved you from a world of heartache, and this is how you repay me—?"

"You intentionally *broke up* a friendship, Mama! Why should I be thankful for that?!"

"She is *entirely* wrong for you! And besides, you knew it would happen sooner or later! *My* mother broke up my friendship with my little colored friend, and it was the best thing she'd ever done for me! I wouldn't have been a suitable girl for upstanding suitors if I had that colored girl around me. I never would've married your father—"

"It's a different *time*, Ma!"

"Not so different where it's okay to blatantly have colored friends—or more! They have their place in society, and we have ours. It's as simple as that, Benjamin!"

"Well, then," he said finally after a long pause. "I guess I'll have to make things a bit more complicated, won't I?"

"Now, Ben—"

"I'm a grown man, Mama. I love you, I truly do, but you will not dictate who my friends will be, particularly when the people you've surrounded me with are pretty crummy in that department."

Florence glared at him. "Those families are the most respected in Plumville, and that fraternity you're in, that's your ticket to success and status! I don't want you to suffer like I did!"

Benjamin laughed incredulously. "*Suffer*?! You've never had to work a day in your life!"

"But my father did! He was never around! I want you to be there for your family—even more than your own father was! I want people to respect you, love you."

"And I can't do that if I have a black friend?"

"Oh, Benjamin, you want that nigra girl to be *more* than just a friend! Always have!"

That comment surprised him so much that whatever else he had been prepared to say disappeared. If she were talking about that marriage proposal he made when he was *eight*, Benjamin knew his mother had been far too paranoid for too long. He tried to speak but his mother held up a hand.

"I *saw* it, Benjamin, whatever feelings of friendship you two had wouldn't have lasted for much longer. You *loved* Ceelee, and it had to be stopped before it became something dangerous—"

"How can love be dangerous, Mama? Especially love and friendship between children, how can it be dangerous?"

He was truly confused, and the weariness in his voice emphasized it. Florence's angry face melted into one of regret and sadness, and she cupped her son's cheek. "Every mother wants to save her child from heartbreak, Benjamin. Patty and I—we knew no good could come out of your burgeoning friendship."

His mother was right; things would've been precarious had the friendship been kept over the years. It would've been an uphill battle with no sign of relief, and very little chance of getting to the top. Could they have done it? Could they even do it now? He knew his friends wouldn't like it, and given the rally debacle, he was relatively sure Coralee's friend wouldn't like it, either. Should he even bother? His life up to that point had been easy...maybe too easy. He could have any girl he wanted; so why was he fixated on his colored housekeeper's daughter?

"Everything happens for a reason," Patty always said, and maybe their broken friendship happened so he and Coralee could reach their potential and gain the tools that would help them survive whatever Plumville threw at them.

Things that were broken could be repaired.

The front door squeaked open again and the Robinson family appeared, Mrs. Robinson not looking at any of them as she marched to their Cadillac. Mr. Robinson thanked Florence for a "lovely Thanksgiving" while Laura went to him and returned his jacket. He grinned and she helped him put it on, smoothing down the sleeves once he did so.

"Good luck, Benjamin," she whispered.

Benjamin smiled and hugged her. "You too."

Florence and Benjamin watched the family back out the driveway, Mr. Robinson honking the horn as they went down the road.

Benjamin leaned on the porch railing, all that he'd learned swimming in his head with no direction. He had no idea what he'd do with this new information. Did Coralee know all about the circumstances surrounding their breakup? Did it even matter to her? Benjamin hoped it did; he hoped he wasn't the only one who felt betrayed. It would make things much easier for when they...what? What *would* happen? A friendship would be difficult enough, but a *romantic relationship*? That very well might be impossible to pull off. But then he remembered how good she felt in his arms, how *happy* he was whenever he was with her...

He was jumping the gun—did she even *want* a relationship with him, romantic or otherwise? He thought back on how she'd acted around him, how she'd become much more affectionate with him since the rally. He'd gained her trust, that he knew, but had he gained anything else?

"I'm gonna go for a walk."

Benjamin said it to the railing, but knew his mother heard. Florence remained quiet for a long time, then finally told him not to be out too late and went inside the house.

He jumped from the porch to the walk and began the journey out of his neighborhood. It was cold but Benjamin didn't notice; he was a man on a mission, his stride purposeful. The large houses and manicured lawns gave way to asphalt, and downtown Plumville came into view. It was a small, handsome town, complete with a general store and the post sharing the same building. The church stood a ways back from the main road, busy this night for a Thanksgiving sermon. The Drummonds had gone to the afternoon service.

Benjamin loosened his tie and took it off, rolling it up and stuffing it in the back pocket of his slacks, but the tension around his neck remained.

He had no idea where the Simmonses lived.

He knew he was going in the right direction, however, when the houses became smaller and closer together, but no less neat and tidy. His nerves made his footing unsure, but he wouldn't let that stop him. His father always taught him if he started something, he should finish it. The relationship between him and Coralee had started from the very first moment they saw each other; and if Benjamin had his way, it was far from finished.

So Benjamin walked on, guided by a hope and a prayer, rehearsing his speech to Coralee under his breath.

There were three surprises that day for the Simmons family—one good, one bad, and one undecided.

The good: Patty's early return from the Drummonds.

The Simmonses were used to Patty's absence during the holidays, particularly Thanksgiving, so they'd started celebrating it a day early. When Coralee was ten, she began preparing the holiday meals with her grandmother Dennie, both forbidding Patty to lift even a finger. Now that Dennie was getting on in age, Coralee bore most of the responsibilities for the Thanksgiving meal. She didn't mind it, however, especially when her mother and grandmother sat in the kitchen and shared stories of past holidays, particularly the ones before her birth. They'd laugh over funny stories, rant and rave over angry ones, and shed a few tears at sad ones.

This Thanksgiving would go down as a melancholy one, all because of the bad surprise they'd received as they were preparing the early Thanksgiving meal: Luther Jr., LJ, had gotten severely injured in combat; and by the tone of the War Department's letter, his injuries were life-threatening. Luther Sr. had said little throughout the dinner, only speaking to bless the food and pray for the life of his only son, or to ask for dishes out of his reach. Coralee was no less dejected; LJ had been due to come home at Christmas; but instead, he would be returning early—possibly in a flag-draped coffin. The feeling of helplessness and loss overwhelmed her.

LJ was a typical big brother, prone to teasing and bullying as older siblings usually did; but he was also her protector, her champion, ready to fight anyone for her and support her cause. He was the one who made all the kids to stop teasing her when they were in primary school, and took the barbs he got for being in the same grade as she was with grace and dignity. LJ was not as smart as Coralee, staying behind a year because his literacy skills were lacking, but he was good at puzzles and math. He'd used those skills to their fullest potential when he'd dropped out of school in the eleventh grade to work full time at the cotton mill, making the baling process far more efficient than it had been. He'd blossomed even more in the Army, becoming a secret favorite among his commanding officers and well liked by everyone in his barracks.

When LJ had first received his assignment to go overseas, everyone had been sullen, and Coralee had fallen into a funk that lasted for almost two weeks. A few days before he'd been due to ship out, LJ had sat her down and talked to her, telling her the best thing he could do was defend this country; after all, she needed the country to become the president of it! His words had reassured her, and his subsequent letters helped even more

But now...now they might never come again.

It was only Coralee and Patty in the kitchen now; Luther Sr. and Grandma Dennie both having gone to bed early. Neither woman spoke, mugs of steaming hot chocolate settled between their hands. Patty stared at the salt and peppershakers as if willing them to move. Coralee figured her mind was still on LJ, and she reached across the table to hold her mother's hand. It was callused, yet warm, and strong like the rest of her.

"He'll make it through, Ma. Just gotta have faith."

Patty nodded and sighed, still staring at the shakers. Her eyes had a haunted look in them, her face, usually relaxed and open whenever she was at home, was pinched tightly. Her father would say Coralee looked just like her mother, but Coralee didn't see it. Patty Simmons still turned the men's heads, much to her papa's mild chagrin.

"Ma—"

"When you and Mr. Benjamin get back together?"

Coralee squeezed her mother's hand in reaction, not prepared for the question. "It's for school, Mama."

"That's it?"

Patty's voice was tired and a little fearful, and this time Coralee squeezed her mother's hand intentionally. "Yes, ma'am."

Patty twisted her hand so their palms touched, applying slight pressure to her daughter's hand. "You sure he knows that?"

Coralee averted her attention to the sink, watching the faucet drip slowly. It had been needing repair since the last time she was there in September, but money had been tight for the last few weeks. "Ma, won't you let me get a job so we can pay fo' that faucet?"

"Does he know?" Patty asked again, not to be thwarted.

"Mama, if you askin' me if I've *invited* him to do anything, then no, I haven't."

"Does he *know* that?"

"Shouldn't you have a little bit more faith in Benjamin than you givin' him? He ain't like the rest of 'em—"

"He can't love you, Coralee, not like you need!"

Love? "I know that, Mama."

Coralee wondered what brought on this conversation. Did Benjamin say or insinuate something? Aside from falling asleep together, nothing remotely...wrong had passed between them, unless the fact they were rekindling their friendship was wrong.

"I thought you liked Benjamin."

Patty nodded and squeezed Coralee's hand again. "I like him as much as I can, somethin' you should know and do!"

"Mama what're you talkin' 'bout?" Patty just sighed and shook her head, taking a sip of her now lukewarm hot chocolate. "Did he say somethin'?"

"He ain't say nothin' but praises fo' you! Takin' up fo' you in front o' his mama and her guests! You know what that sound like to them? To *me?*"

Coralee slid her hand from her mother's to wrap around her mug, unable to look Patty in the eye. She could only imagine what it sounded like, and God help the thrill that raced through her at the thought of him speaking up for her like that in front of his family and their friends. When they were younger, Benjamin would do the same; and while Patty would chastise the boy, it was often half-hearted. Even Coralee knew the difference between a real scolding and one for show, especially when she'd been on the end of a real one. But there was nothing half-hearted about Patty's worry over it now. Apparently, Benjamin wasn't supposed to do that anymore.

More to the point, she and Benjamin weren't supposed to be *anything* to each other anymore.

"We're friends," Coralee announced, still staring at her mug.

"You can't be friends with him," Patty said dully.

Coralee had heard this lecture; and she'd heard rumors about black girls getting caught up sometimes. If she were completely honest with herself, she couldn't blame them—not if they'd felt the way Benjamin was making her feel.

The doorbell rang, and her eyes darted to the clock. It was only seven minutes after 7PM, but it felt later because it was dark outside. Patty began to rise but Coralee gave her mother a sharp look and rose herself, going to the door quickly, yet cautiously. She stood on her tiptoes to look through the small window in the door, her eyes widening when she saw who it was.

She opened the door. "What are you doin' here?"

Benjamin shuffled his feet and put his hands in his slacks' pockets. "Happy Thanksgiving."

He looked very handsome standing there, the upper two buttons of his shirt were undone, and his hair unruly from running his fingers through it. Coralee could only blink, temporarily forgetting how to speak.

"Coralee?"

"Oh!" She stepped back and allowed him to enter the house. "Do you need to see Mama?"

He gazed at her intently. "I'm not here to see her, Ceelee."

Her lips stretched into a shy smile as she closed the door. When she faced him again, he was still staring at her, though this time with a shy grin as well.

"Benny?" her mother said, coming to see who their guest was.

Benjamin's face became solemn when Patty appeared, and Coralee now suspected why Benjamin had actually come.

"Ma told you, then? About LJ?"

"What about LJ?" he asked with a frown, darting his eyes to the older woman, then back to Coralee. "Aunt Patty?"

Patty shook her head, her hand going to her mouth, and Coralee saw her begin to crumple under the weight of her grief.

"Ma—"

"I'm all right," Patty said shakily, and she nodded a chin towards Benjamin. "Might as well tell him, now that he's here."

Coralee felt helpless watching her mother shuffle back into the kitchen. Her mother wasn't all right, and there was little Coralee could do to make things better.

"Coralee?" Benjamin asked, squeezing her elbow comfortingly. "What's goin' on?"

She closed her eyes and exhaled, the words brittle on her tongue. "LJ was hurt in combat. The War Department doesn't think he'll make it."

Her voice was flat, and when she saw Benjamin's eyes widen, she dropped hers, not able to take the shock on his face. His reaction had been different from hers. She'd closed off her face, packed her distress and trepidation into a tiny little box and hid it in a faraway corner in her heart.

"Ceelee...honey..." he whispered, pulling her gently in his arms. As soon he did, Coralee's throat tightened. She'd been fine just minutes earlier, so why was she on the brink of tears? Before she could answer her own question she broke down, her body wracking with her sobs. Benjamin walked them to the couch and settled her next to him, kissing her hair and rubbing her shoulders, telling her to let it all out.

Patty rushed into the room at the sound of her daughter's cries, but watching Benjamin comfort Coralee made her pause. It was as if it were fifteen years ago, with Benjamin treating her daughter as if she were the most important person on earth to him. Seeing Benjamin behave the same way now made Patty realize there was something bigger than all of them at work, and very little would be able to stop it. Patty was scared for the both of them because Plumville wouldn't appreciate or understand it. Everything happened for a reason; and God, fate, whoever, wanted these two children to be in each other's lives.

Coralee hiccupped, and Benjamin squeezed her shoulder in comfort. Patty watched her daughter shift so her head was in his lap, and Benjamin began smoothing down her hair, never lifting his eyes from

Coralee. The girl's eyes began to droop, until she finally fell asleep, tears still streaming down her cheeks. Patty knew this was hard on her, but hadn't known the extent of it until now. Everyone in their family had been in their own stages of grief, yet she didn't remember anyone asking Coralee how she was faring. Patty had been so concerned with her husband and her mother-in-law she'd forgotten that the person who'd probably take this the hardest was her baby girl.

Patty felt so ashamed of herself.

"She's a lot like you, Aunt Patty," Benjamin murmured, still caressing and staring at Coralee. "She's very strong and determined, always looking out for other people, leaving herself last." Patty grew uncomfortable by his comments, disarmed by how perceptive he was. Most would look at her behavior and think of it as typical for a proper housekeeper, never realizing Patty did that for everyone, including her own family.

"Mr. Benjamin—"

"Why is it 'Mr. Benjamin' now?" he interrupted, never looking at her. "Why didn't you tell us about LJ? Even Mama would've understood—"

"If I don't work, I don't get paid, and this family can't afford me not workin'."

"That doesn't seem fair."

"Life's not fair."

She would know better than he would; the life of a colored person in the South, the life of a colored *woman* in the South, was full of injustice and inequality. If Patty lost this job, the likelihood she could find another, especially at her age, would be small. Hard work and responsibility were important to Patty, and she tried passing those values to her children. Many times that was all they had to secure a job; reliability was a huge asset in Plumville, and personal issues had to be checked at the door. White Plumville didn't care about the problems of Negroes, so it was best to act as if there weren't any.

Unless one worked for an observant young man such as Benjamin.

Patty looked at the kids again and shook her head. As much as she didn't want to believe it, as much as she fancied herself a romantic, Patty couldn't help but think the Lord worked in mysterious ways.

Benjamin adjusted Coralee so that he cradled her, then stood. "Where is her room? I think she needs to go to bed."

Patty led him to her daughter's room, hanging in the doorway as he tucked Coralee under the covers. Patty would wake her daughter up later to change her clothes, but for right now Coralee's attire would have to do.

Her heart ached at the tenderness and care Benjamin exhibited. Too bad he was white.

"You a good man, Benjamin Drummond."

He straightened and stepped away from the bed, putting his hands in his trouser pockets. He gave Patty a half smile. "A lot of that has to do with you, Aunt Patty."

Patty nodded and led them into the living room. Truth be told, Patty often had treated Benjamin as if he were one of her children—how could she not? She'd spent more time with him than his own mother had, who was usually off making the rounds in social Plumville, being the perfect wife and hostess for all of town to praise. This wasn't to say Florence didn't love or care for Benjamin, for that would be unfair and a lie, but Florence's main objective was to groom a Southern gentleman, not raise a well-minded and fair man. The two didn't have to be mutually exclusive—in fact, if it were up to Patty, they wouldn't be—but unfortunately, Plumville thought differently.

"Would you like anything? Somethin' to eat? Drink?"

"No, ma'am," he replied, "but thank you for offering."

Patty nodded and sat in her husband's easy chair. Benjamin remained standing until she was settled, and then he sat back on the couch.

She exhaled a deep breath. "Well, I must say I'm surprised to see you here, Benjamin."

Benjamin blushed and shrugged. "I went for a walk, and my feet led me here."

Patty gave him a reproachful look. "Somethin' bad coulda happened to you."

"Nothin' did, Aunt Patty."

Reproach ceded to worry. "I don't want nothin' bad happenin' to my daughter, either."

"Neither do I," Benjamin agreed, "not if I can help it."

"You may not be able to," Patty cautioned. "This thing here is bigger than you—bigger than the both of you."

Benjamin nodded and looked Patty directly in the eyes. "Considering these feelings I have for your daughter, ma'am, I suspect you may be right."

Patty closed her eyes at Benjamin's confession, a jumble of emotions tangling inside of her. One the one hand, she was flabbergasted Benjamin Drummond had actually admitted that to her; and the fact he did so made her feel a little more confident that he was genuine. On the other hand, she couldn't sit idly by and let Benjamin pursue something that didn't have a future—not at her daughter's expense.

"Benjamin, as much as I understand where you're comin' from, you need to be very careful about who you say stuff to, and when."

He frowned. "You don't want me to see her, either?"

"Honestly? No, I don't," Patty said. "Ain't gon' be too many people who'll like this, now; particularly Coralee's daddy and yo' mama. And we won't even get into the whole of Plumville! It'll be dangerous for you but *especially* for her. Whatever you feel can't *possibly* be worth all that."

He met her eyes squarely. "The way I see it, Plumville isn't worth your daughter, ma'am."

Oh, he was good, Patty thought; but more than that, he actually believed what he said. Her heart felt a twinge of wistfulness and she sighed. No wonder her daughter was allowing herself to have tender feelings for him!

"Do you know if she feels the same?"

Benjamin shook his head and shrugged. "I dunno, but I've never been as happy as when I'm with her, and I hope I return the favor."

How could something be so bittersweet as what was happening between her daughter and her employer's son? It wasn't fair, especially when it would lead only to heartbreak?

Patty's shoulders slumped. Overwhelmed, she decided to drop the conversation for now. She couldn't appropriately deal with this on top of worrying about the fate of her eldest in Vietnam. She could only hope Benjamin would heed her concerns and leave her daughter alone.

Then again, he was a Drummond; they could sweet talk the bark off a tree if they wanted.

Patty exhaled and stood with a groan. "Let me call your father so he can get you."

Benjamin shot to his feet, he shook his head. "Aunt Patty, I can walk—"

She glared at him. "You can, but that don't mean you should. Your feet may have led you here; but in all that walkin', it never occurred to you how you'd get back in the dead o' night?"

"It was already dark by the time I got here," Benjamin mumbled.

"Boy! Ain't nothin' but the grace o' God got you to my doorstep, 'cause I know your daddy ain't tell you where we lived—so that means you had to have asked for directions. Do you know what people are gonna say? Think? You can't just be thinkin' about yourself, Benjamin Drummond. As good as your intentions are, white boys just don't come into this part of town by themselves for no reason but to create trouble! And my Coralee's a good girl. I won't have her caught up in it after whatever you feel is all said and done!"

Benjamin looked so sincerely stricken that part of Patty wanted to apologize for shattering the cotton candy dreamings he'd been having. But her daughter's safety was on the line, and Benjamin would recover just fine.

Boys like him always did.

Only five minutes passed before Paul Drummond was knocking on the door. She nodded at Benjamin's pitiful "goodnight" but kept her eyes trained on Paul standing on the steps. He glanced at his son briefly as he passed but then turned cajoling eyes to her.

He moved closer to the doorframe, but didn't cross the threshold. "Patty—"

"You need to talk to him, Paul," she said seriously, her body behind the door to ward off the late-November chill. "I'm just his housekeeper. Maybe things'll stick if they came from you."

Paul regarded her quietly for a few moments. "It's a shame, isn't it, that things haven't changed enough for our kids too..." He shook his head, unable to finish the thought.

Patty shrugged, averting her eyes. "Well, I don't make the rules."

Paul said nothing for a good while, his gaze heavy on her, then he blew out a breath and wished her a goodnight.

Later that night Patty prayed. She prayed for her son's life and health; prayed for the war and its quick end; prayed for her husband and mother-in-law and other families affected by the war, and the losses sustained by it. Patty prayed for her daughter, and for Benjamin, because what they felt for each other was as beautiful as it was dangerous. She prayed for the strength of their character, and prayed for the tolerance of a town that wasn't prone to having any. She remembered her private hope, known only to herself and to God, that change would come in Plumville, and saw potential for that it in Coralee and Benjamin.

Unfortunately, she wasn't convinced Plumville was ready enough.

TEN

The racial tension that had overwhelmed the Solomon College eased a little when students returned from Thanksgiving break. People had to worry about passing their own classes instead of the superiority of one group over the other, and everyone banded together against the common enemy of Colleton College, the school the Mighty Lions would be playing for the last game of the season.

Yet for Benjamin and Coralee, there was an additional consideration that was thrilling and terrifying. It meant their tutoring sessions were ending, and, maybe, something more was beginning.

The sessions had become longer, and at the same time, nonexistent. They'd begin talking about the lesson for the first ten minutes, but then they'd drift into more personal matters, the first usually being about LJ's condition. There hadn't been any new news since Thanksgiving, and both had decided no news was good news.

Once that topic had been exhausted, the next would be slightly more personal, more intimate, requiring hushed tones and bent heads. Benjamin would ask about Coralee and how her day had been, always taking her hand and linking their fingers together as she hemmed, hawed, and then finally steered the conversation into "safer" territories. She'd get him to talk about football, how he felt about the rest of the season and postseason, and even had him explain the game to her. He was very patient, even though she felt like a simpleton because she couldn't understand the difference between a tight end and a running back.

"Don't worry; it confused me when I first started out," he reassured her.

But he'd never let go of her hand, even if the conversation was about end zones and playbooks. Worse of all, she wouldn't pull her hand away, savoring the warmth and strength of his, of the way his thumbs would glide along her fingertips and knuckles as if to embed the shape and texture of them to his memory. Yet even despite her mother's warning lecture, Coralee couldn't bring herself to deny this show of intimacy.

"Are you okay?" he asked, squeezing said hand.

It was the first of the last two sessions they would have, and Coralee felt she was going through withdrawal already. She gave him a small smile and said, "Nothing."

That answer made no sense towards his question, and Benjamin's quirked eyebrows indicated he knew she wasn't.

"C'mon, let's go for a walk."

"But what about our session?"

"If I don't know this stuff by now, I'll never know it. Besides, there's someone else I'd like to know more."

Her hand tightened around his, but she didn't release the pressure, signaling her apprehension. "You already know what you need to know, don't you?"

Benjamin tugged at her hand, and she stood slowly. Those blue eyes were watching her, seeing her, underneath her typical cardigan and her brown skin. She'd fallen asleep thinking of those blue eyes more times than she wanted to admit, and had even wished she could wake up looking into them once or twice.

He looked down at her with a grin. "You're so small," he whispered on a little chuckle.

"Are you kiddin' me? Grandma Dennie's always tellin' me to quit eatin'—"

"You're perfect."

She ducked her head against the pleasure that filled her at his words and trembled when a gentle finger lifted her chin. His blue eyes were so clear and full of purpose, and Coralee pressed her face into his shoulder as if to hide.

But as his arms closed around her, she had to accept she couldn't hide from her feelings or from him.

Not anymore.

Benjamin exhaled slowly as he felt Coralee sink into him, and felt the knot that'd been present in his gut ever since Thanksgiving finally unravel. Between Aunt Patty's disapproval and his own father's warning lecture about ill-fated pursuits, Benjamin had been afraid all of the progress that had been made between them would be undone. However, that knot of doom would loosen each time Coralee would laugh at one of his corny jokes, or give him encouraging words, or look at him with such tenderness his insides would turn to goo. Coralee emboldened him to be a better man; he had to be if he deserved Coralee's affections. He understood the risks of entering into a relationship would be far greater for her than for him, so Benjamin was going to do this right. He wasn't ashamed of Coralee, and he wouldn't treat her as if he were. They were doing nothing wrong.

He loved her.

They heard footsteps coming their way, a rare occurrence for this section of the library, and Benjamin moved them behind one of the bookcases. He stood over her, watching her stand with her back against the shelves as she stared at him, bottom lip between her teeth. He was fascinated by her mouth, envied her teeth, for they claimed his greatest desire. Benjamin had promised to move at her pace, not to take anything Coralee didn't freely give, but that didn't mean he couldn't...*persuade* her a little.

His lips were so soft and light on her forehead that he almost convinced himself he imagined the contact. But her light gasp told him otherwise, and he was eternally grateful she allowed him to indulge in the kisses he dappled all along her hairline towards the shell of her left ear. He nipped it, and Coralee's breath caught before she whimpered a little as his tongue smoothed away the injury.

Her body trembled.

Benjamin gathered her closer while trailing kisses across her temple and hairline to pay the same homage to her other ear. Coralee dropped her forehead to the crook of his neck, her thumbs caressing the insides of his wrists so succulently it was all Benjamin could do not to crush her to him.

It was his turn to catch his breath when he felt her arms slide around his waist, bringing him closer to her. Spearheaded by her silent permission, he applied more pressure to his kisses as they danced along her cheeks, her chin, the bridge of her nose. With each contact she brought herself closer, until it appeared they were one and the same. Her eyelashes fluttered against her cheeks and suddenly he wanted to see those beautiful brown eyes, to see exactly what she felt for him.

Benjamin kissed her eyelids and spoke, his lips brushing against them. "Open your eyes, darlin'."

Coralee pressed her face further into his neck, and he cradled her nape in support.

"May I see you? Please?" he asked, keeping his tone soft and gentle as his fingers began a light caress.

He felt her exhale against him, and then he was suddenly looking into her eyes. They were wide and bewildered, but also full of a yearning he knew she would've never allowed him to see if she didn't trust him enough. His confidence soared, and a tender grin appeared on his face. He cupped her cheeks, thumbs brushing them, and rubbed her nose with his. Her sigh tickled his chin and he kissed her nose in response.

"Benjamin?"

"May I kiss you, Coralee?"

For one, anxiety-filled moment, Coralee merely stared at him, gripping his waist so tightly it almost hurt to take a proper breath.

Then her expression became determined and she licked her lips, nodding once, slowly.

"Yes."

Benjamin's hand visibly shook as he tilted up her face further. The apprehension he saw in her gaze tempered his actions and he gently settled his mouth upon hers. Her lips were soft and supple under his, and their small tremble caused his entire body to shiver.

He inhaled the tiny breath she exhaled when he pulled back.

"All right?" he asked.

She nodded, her brows furrowing. "Yeah."

Benjamin wanted to laugh wildly, but settled for a wry twist of his mouth and trailed a finger between her brows. "Then why the frown?"

She shrugged. "I dunno...I thought..."

He'd let his finger continue over the point of her nose and along her lips, and she'd drifted into silence. He watched her eyes drag shut and her body sway into him, then her lips puckered against his index finger.

"Oh, hell," he muttered.

His hand moved from her mouth to the back of her head as he bent to kiss her again, harder this time.

This was where heaven was—in Coralee Simmons. The pearly gates were her mouth, her teeth, those smooth, slightly sharp things his tongue touched because surely God spoke from within her.

"Open up, sweetheart," Benjamin begged softly, shakily. There was slight hesitation, but then, access! Ambrosia was her tongue, and Benjamin almost collapsed from pleasure. He'd kissed many girls before, but this was his first kiss, the first one that would ever really matter in the grand scheme of things. This was the first kiss of the rest of his life, and he cherished every second of it.

Coralee broke the kiss with a gasp and Benjamin tumbled back into reality. Both were panting, but Coralee's eyes were wide and glassy, as if dazed. Her brows then furrowed, as if she were trying to figure out the world's oldest and hardest puzzle; but in a way, weren't they? They were trying to negotiate a social order that had no space for them; but beyond that, they were trying to figure out why the space was missing in the first place. The answer seemed easy enough, but that superficial answer turned to ash because they were proof of its falseness. Blacks and whites *could* be friends, *could* fall in love, *could* be equal.

They *were* equal.

The library bell rang, shaking them out of their thoughts, and Coralee dropped her hand hurriedly, coughing behind it and moving away from Benjamin to gather her belongings. They'd been there all night, yet it seemed only minutes had passed. Benjamin reluctantly gathered his things as well, yet continuously glimpsed Coralee to make sure she was still there.

That she was not a dream.

When Coralee began walking away, still silent, panic strangled him and forced a small, plaintive burst of sound from his throat. She stopped her progress, but didn't turn around.

"So, that's it?"

She waited a beat. "We still have our last session on Wednesday."

That may very well be, but, "What about after Wednesday?"

What about Thursday? Friday? Saturday? What about a week from now? A month? A year? The beginning had just started, and, damn it, the ending wouldn't come for a while.

"I'll be at the game."

She would be in the stands while he was on the field. There would be thousands of people and hundreds of yards between them, but that was good enough. It had to be, until they figured out how to make it better. Besides, having her there, searching out her face among the crowd, would be his secret motivation; and, hopefully, a kiss would be his reward for winning...or his consolation prize for losing.

Benjamin approached her and took her books, tucking them under his arms before letting her lead the way. Coralee looked at him warily yet exited the library, confused and somewhat numb by what had happened between them. Her internal world had been rocked, shifted, and set in a new galaxy, spinning in a new orbit around a new sun whose light was so bright it blinded her.

Sooner than anticipated, they were at her dorm. Benjamin opened the door for her without giving her books back, and she realized he had every intention of walking her to her room, not just her dorm.

Coralee knew she should ask for her belongings and have him stay out here, but she didn't want to, afraid whatever spell cast between them would shatter once he left.

But—"Somebody might see you."

He shrugged. "It's not like I've never been to your room before."

"I don't think Trish is there."

He just smirked, which infuriated her and sent a thrill of anticipation right down her middle.

Coralee cleared her throat. "And what are you expectin' once we get there?"

He shook his head and shrugged again, his smirk softening to a serious, yet sincere expression. "Nothin' you're not willin' to give."

She licked her lips, and she didn't miss his gaze arresting on the action. Coralee spun around and headed for her room, or else his gaze wouldn't have been the only thing on her lips for all and sundry to see.

She tested the knob and her stomach dropped in relief and anticipation when it didn't turn. Unlike before, she had an easier time unlocking the door, and she quickly ushered Benjamin inside. She shut the door and leaned her back against it, watching him place their books carefully on her desk before he came back to stand in front of her.

How could eyes be so blue? she wondered. It was her favorite kind of blue too—the dark blue, almost like indigo—the blue that could turn black depending on the mood; and his mood was something...pleasant, she supposed, by the way he grinned at her. Yet the grin faded to a contemplative, almost pensive expression, as he dipped his head to hers. She met him halfway.

Benjamin pecked her lips once, twice, then began to nibble and nip. Coralee felt faint from the overwhelming sensations. If not for the door and his solid form bracing her, she knew she'd be a heap on the floor.

His mouth increased in pressure against hers and Coralee almost forgot how to breathe. Weightless, suspended in air; that was how Coralee felt when he deepened the kiss. She knew what an astronaut felt like being in Benjamin's arms, and she suddenly wanted to call NASA and tell them of her discovery. But in the meantime, she pushed herself closer to him, needing his solidness just in case she came crashing down from her high.

Right was the only word going through her mind. This kiss was right, the man giving it to her was right, the feelings burgeoning from the kiss was right. *Everything* was right despite what Plumville said. Everybody else was so quick to explain what was *wrong* that they didn't know what was *right*, and probably couldn't see it if it stared them in the face.

Coralee saw.

Right was over six feet tall with dark-brown hair and indigo eyes. *Right* was the star quarterback of the Solomon College football team and the son of the family who employed her mother. *Right* was her very first friend outside of her brother.

Right was the man she loved.

Coralee's eyes snapped open and she twisted her mouth from his with a cry. Benjamin immediately let her go and stepped back.

"Are you okay?" he apologized, sounding concerned. "Did I do too much?"

Coralee shook her head briefly, clutching a fist over her pounding heart as the realization of her feelings coursed through her, but managed to offer him a sheepish smile. "Maybe it's time for you to go, though."

He nodded once slowly and gathered his books. She opened the door and he stepped out, but spun around to regard her again. They stood there for a few moments before she offered him a tiny smile.

"Thank you, Benjamin."

His expression and voice were cotton soft. "No, thank *you*. I'll see you on Wednesday, Ceelee."

He left and she followed him with her eyes until he'd completely exited the building. She blew out a breath and closed the door, but jumped mightily when someone started banging on it.

Coralee jerked the door open. "What the devil—?"

"Was that I just saw?!"

Coralee glared at Freda, who'd all but stomped into the room, not in the mood to explain herself right now. "I'm tired—"

"Ain't that tired! I *saw* that white boy leave your room and *you* stare at him as if he had all the answers to yo' problems. I mean, yeah, he cute, but he ain't *that* cute!"

Coralee shrugged and closed the door. "We are friends."

"He ain't look at you like you were no 'friends'! And neither did you!"

Coralee glared at Freda. She'd wanted a chance to process everything that'd just happened. She'd just jumped the color line, that arbitrary barrier that had a big red "DO NOT CROSS!" sign in front of it, and it'd been one of the most exhilarating experiences of her life.

"Did you sleep wit' him?"

Coralee groaned, throwing her hands up in the air in aggravation. "C'mon now, Freda! Give me *some* credit!"

Freda sighed and placed her hands on Coralee's shoulders. "Gotta ask. One thing white men are good at doin' is connin' the hell out of people, particularly black women. All they gotta say is some pretty words, sound very sincere, and next thing you know you knocked up with a half-white baby from a man who ain't never gave a damn and never would about you and that baby you carryin'. Seen it happen too many times; too many black people here are the product of pretty words and ugly reality. I don't want to see the same thing happen to you."

"And what about the black boys who do the same?" Coralee shot back. "I don't see you standin' here and cautionin' me to avoid them!"

Freda scowled at her. "If I saw one o' them hoverin' around you, I'd be in here sayin' the same damn thing!"

Coralee grimaced, but part of her could concede that point. "I should be with a guy like Nick, huh?"

Freda shrugged, but the action might as well have been a nod.

"There's no guarantee with Nick, either," Coralee reminded her, "and I know the way of things, Freda. I know what could happen if I got caught up; and I even know the chances of this being something long term and serious are slim. But even as I know all of that, I also know I like being around him, and that's enough for now." Why should she deny herself a few weeks, months of happiness? It wasn't fair *she* had to go without because the man she loved was "the wrong color".

"Leastways you picked a cute one," Freda said finally.

Coralee snickered. "That's all you care about, ain't it?"

"I told you that Drummond boy was fine. Ain't listen to nobody..."

"I've known him forever."

"Hmm."

Either way—"I could really use your support."

"Could you?"

"Yeah."

"You sure you know what you doin'?"

There was no censure in Freda's voice that time, just concern for a friend who, by the look of it, had fallen in love with a white man— a dangerous place for any black woman to fall when the chances of being caught were slim.

"Not a clue."

Freda's hand crept along her back before drawing the girl to her. They hugged each other tightly, Coralee exhaling a long breath. She could do it; see where whatever *this* was going between her and Benjamin, all because she had her best friend in her corner.

"And if he breaks your heart, Nick'll be more than happy to break his," Freda joked as they pulled apart.

"And I'd be more than happy to let him!" Coralee agreed.

ELEVEN

It had been an exciting game with Solomon beating Colleton with a last minute Hail Mary from Benjamin to Nick. It was the first time in a long time the campus had been united, cheering a win that rested in the hands of a white man and a black man. Protests were forgotten, bygones were bygones, and the campus happily celebrated their victory with an impromptu rally on the steps of the library, a far different rally from the one that happened almost six weeks ago.

Coralee had been swept up in the excitement, glad she chose this game to be her introduction to football. She didn't know how passionate she could be about it; and for every call against the Mighty Lions, particularly against Benjamin or Nick, she screamed and ranted like everyone else. Granted, she wasn't as well versed in smack talking as Jermaine, Andre, or the others, but she picked up a few things here and there.

Coralee stayed close to Freda, Jermaine, and Andre during the post game, cheering with them during the victory rally that showcased all the major players. The coaches spoke, Nick spoke, Benjamin spoke. She cheered wildly when it was Nick's turn, yet became more subdued during Benjamin's speech, especially when his eyes searched the crowd until they locked with hers. His smile widened ever so slightly as he continued speaking. She became weak in the knees, unable to breathe, until she felt a hand creep into hers—Freda's—giving her support.

Coralee hoped Benjamin passed the class so these games *counted*!

It would be her fault if he didn't, she knew, even though she could only help Benjamin, not take the tests for him. Coach Norman would be proven "right"; she'd be accused of sabotaging the season, and racial tensions would rise yet again. The only thing that could exacerbate the scenario was if it ever came out they'd done more than study during some of those sessions; that they'd talked about hopes and dreams they weren't supposed to have; kissed lips they weren't supposed to kiss, began having feelings they weren't supposed to feel...

But she was all smiles when the group finally caught up with the Nick-half of the game-saving duo, giving him a large congratulatory hug. Nick's smile was tender to her, and Coralee's heart hurt a little.

"So you actually came down to a game, huh?"

"Last game of the season, right? And your senior year? I figured it was due time."

Nick raised his eyebrows even as he wrapped an arm around her waist. "Well, it's not the last game of the season; got a bowl game to play!"

"Yeah, man! All on account o' you!" Andre said, slapping his friend's hand excitedly.

"A team sport, now," Nick said, but his smile fully agreed with Andre.

"Sho don't take much to stroke a man's ego, now does it?" Freda said out the side of her mouth, quirking an eyebrow at Coralee.

"Not much at all," Coralee concurred, a little uncomfortable by the fact Nick had yet to remove his arm from her waist. She let him keep it there, however; he really wasn't hurting anyone.

"C'mon, ladies! Y'all *know* I was the most important half of that catch! Drummond can throw all day long but it takes a *real* receiver to catch it, ya dig?" Nick defended, earning more slaps from Jermaine and Andre.

"But it takes a damn good quarterback to throw that far!" Freda challenged, and Coralee was glad the older girl did. She was far too biased to do it herself.

"Ah, who cares? White folk got their hero; black folk got ours; everyone's happy," Andre said finally.

How convenient.

And even if Coralee was cynical about it, Andre spoke truth. The rally had been split by race, as natural as breathing, and no one batted an eyelash—not even herself. Even an interracial team effort couldn't bring social integration upon the campus, and Coralee was saddened by that.

The BSU board walked across the quad, happily listening to Nick retell the last few seconds of the game from his perspective, his arm still around Coralee, and Coralee still allowed it, praying Benjamin wouldn't notice.

"Yoo-hoo! Ceelee!"

All five of them stopped at the sound of her name, and Coralee's heart clenched when she saw who did it. Why was Miss Florence calling *her* name? More importantly, what was her mother and—

Coralee took off running, not caring if she looked like she had just lost her mind. By the time she reached her destination, her eyes were full of tears and she had choked on a sob.

"LJ!" she breathed brokenly, falling to the ground beside his wheelchair and wrapping her arms around her brother.

"Little Ceelee...how've you been?"

He had said it as if nothing had changed, as if he weren't in a wheelchair with one leg in a cast, and there were no bandages on both of his hands, or as if there weren't an eye patch over his right eye. He'd said it as if she didn't hear the exertion of every breath he made, or the fact his hug wasn't as tight as it used to be. He'd said it as if he'd returned from Vietnam just as he'd left Plumville almost a year ago.

In a way, he had—he'd returned *alive*.

Coralee felt a new hand on her shoulder, and looked up long enough to see Freda's softly smiling face.

"The rest of us are gonna go on, okay?" Coralee nodded.

"I'm Luther, Coralee's brother." LJ held out a bandaged hand for Freda to shake, and she did it gently.

"Glad to see you home. I'm Freda, and Coralee has nothin' but high praise for you."

"Is that right, little sis?"

Coralee laughed even as she wiped away her tears, kneeling fully on the ground, not caring her skirt was getting muddy. "That's right."

"Seems to me I remember a time you couldn't stand me, ain't that so, Benny?"

Coralee hadn't even realized he was there.

Benjamin chuckled. "That was a long time ago, LJ."

"Yeah..."

Freda looked at Benjamin, LJ, and Coralee again before nodding and kissing Coralee's temple. "We'll see you later okay? If not, have a beautiful Christmas break. Y'all are truly blessed."

Coralee smiled at her friend. "We definitely are."

The Simmonses went to a restaurant in downtown Bakersfield, Coralee taking a few minutes to change her skirt, but the reunion between sister and brother was full of laughs and stories. Grandma Dennie didn't come to the game because she wasn't feeling well, so Patty ordered a plate to go. Surprisingly, the Drummonds joined them, and even Florence seemed caught up in the good spirit of the victorious game and reunited family. Coralee was sandwiched between LJ and Benjamin, and they all fell back into their childhood friendship easily. Coralee didn't mind being teased by the boys, and even got in a few good licks of her own, but more importantly, she was glad she had three of her favorite men with her—her father, her brother, and her childhood best friend.

A childhood best friend whose eyes rarely left her, whose hand would sneak under the table to give hers a squeeze, whose mouth would whisper in her ear under the guise of telling her a benign secret:

"You're beautiful when you smile."

"I'm glad to see you so happy."

"I can't wait to be alone with you."

The last "secret" caused her to choke on her soda, and he, ever the gentleman, rubbed her back to make sure she was all right. She scowled at Benjamin, wondering where in the world his sudden boldness came from.

"You two still conspirators, I see," LJ commented and laughed, though his eye told a different story. It was as if he *knew* about them, knew Benjamin and Coralee were much more than they appeared to be. Panic rose in her throat, but LJ merely smiled and patted her cheek. "Good to see y'all ain't lose a friendship. Bein' in the war taught me a thing or two about that."

The mood became more somber, and Patty, on the other side of LJ, kissed her son's cheek as tears threatened to fall down hers. LJ hugged her, whispering comforting words. Luther Sr.'s eyes were a bit misty, his mouth hidden by clasped hands as if in prayer. Perhaps he was, a prayer of thanks that his son had returned to him alive, that his family would be together for Christmas, that all were safe and sound. Even Miss Florence became emotional, Mr. Drummond hugging his wife in support. Their two families had been through much together, had known each other for so long, that it was almost appropriate the Drummonds were with them now. None of the other patrons or wait staff had looked upon the group as if they were odd, perhaps sensing the profound connection all in the booth had to each other.

Benjamin's hand took hers again, linking their fingers, and didn't let go for the rest of the dinner.

Their hands were on top of the table this time.

❧

The campus was still hopping when Coralee and Benjamin returned, the Drummonds dropping them off at the gates of the quad.
Coralee's parents had gone home with LJ, but there were emotional
goodbyes and "I can't wait to see yous" in the restaurant's parking
lot. Christmas break was in four days, so the wait wouldn't be long.

"You two be careful and don't do anything crazy," Paul said as
they left the car, looking at his son pointedly. "You know how your
frat brothers get..."

Benjamin put his hand on Coralee's back and nodded. "I know,
Dad. You and Mama have a safe trip home." Florence stared at them.
He nodded again, rubbing Coralee's back a little. "I will. I promise."

His mother sighed and his father waved as they pulled away
from the curb. Benjamin watched the Cadillac's taillights disappear
around the bend. He felt Coralee shift beside him. "All right?"

Coralee began walking, effectively removing his hand from her.

Benjamin sighed but fell into step beside her. They walked into
the quad towards her dormitory, Benjamin not in the mood to deal
with his drunken, obnoxious housemates. Tommy and Randy had
cornered him about how *fine* Coralee and her mother were before
he'd left for the restaurant with his folks. They'd started making
lewd comments about what Paul Drummond probably did with
Aunt Patty when his mother was away, and wondered if Coralee
would do the same. It was all Benjamin could do not to deck them.
Weren't things supposed to be changing? Hadn't his father said the
Supreme Court had ruled on some case last year—Loving something
or other—allowing an interracial couple to be married wherever it
wanted? Of course, it was too early to talk about that as far as he
and Coralee were concerned, but if marriages were allowed, *certainly*
courtships should be!

Benjamin glanced at Coralee looking around the campus as if
waiting to be attacked at any moment. Didn't she know he wouldn't
let anything happen to her?

"Do you not want to do this?" he asked, unsuccessfully keeping
the hurt out of his voice.

"Do what? What are we doin'?"

They'd never discussed it, never put a label on their newly evolved relationship. He certainly wanted them to be, but what Benjamin *did* know was the middle of the quad in forty-degree weather was not the place to talk.

"Come with me?" he asked, holding out his hand. Coralee shied away from it, and again hurt welled inside. "Don't you trust me?"

"I do. It's everyone else I don't trust."

"A fair concern, but we have to start somewhere," he countered, and wiggled his fingers at her. "Please let me hold your hand, Coralee."

"What if someone sees us?"

"Then they see. I'm not going to hide you away in shadows and dark corners. You deserve much more than that from me."

She inched closer, eyeing his hand, but then turned worried eyes to him again. "Someone could hurt us."

"I won't let anyone hurt you. Besides, I'm a football player; I can handle eleven men gunnin' for me!"

Coralee pursed her lips, her eyes darting from his hand to his eyes before finally, hesitatingly, putting her hand in his. Benjamin squeezed it and they continued walking to her dormitory. They did pass some people, but they were too plastered and caught up in their own revelry to care about him and Coralee, so they reached her dorm without any problem. She pulled away to open the door, and walked quickly to her room. The halls were empty, probably because most were outside having their own fun, and Benjamin was thankful for their good fortune.

Her hands trembled as she put the key in the lock, and he felt a little frustration at her nerves. He resented he couldn't treat her as his girlfriend in public, that she even had to know the dangers probably much better than he did.

Benjamin covered her hand with his and kissed the back of her head. "I hate this. I hate that we have to sneak around right now; but if the dark corners and shadows are what it'll take to be with you, then so be it—at least in the beginning."

"I'm sorry," she whispered, leaning against him.

He hugged her waist from behind. "I'm sorry, too, but being without you simply isn't an option I'm willin' to take."

The door opened and she stepped inside, he following her after a moment's space. Coralee threw her cardigan on the bed and went to her dresser, rifling through it. Benjamin didn't know where to sit, so he chose her desk, not wanting to assume or suggest anything by sitting on her bed.

"I'm going to change," she said flatly, and went to the community bathroom down the hall. She wasn't gone very long, but when Coralee returned, Benjamin was deeply engrossed in *Curious George* again, jumping when he heard her clear her voice.

"You want it back?"

He grinned at her, thinking her adorable in her flannel pajamas and pigtail buns. Benjamin held out his hand, and she looked at it skeptically before taking it. He waggled his eyebrows, yanking her into his lap and banding his arms around her waist.

Coralee giggled, shifting in his lap as if to leave, but he wouldn't let go of her, putting her in a more comfortable position before he began reading aloud. She rested her head in the crook of his neck and turned the pages for him. Her fingers were gentle as they ran through his hair, bringing him to a contentment Benjamin never thought he would feel. This was the perfect way to celebrate a major game's victory—reading a children's book with Coralee in his lap.

He kissed her temple when he was finished.

"So every time you come in my room, you gonna read this book?"

He shrugged, his blue eyes bright and a small smile on his face. "I didn't read it the last time, but that's an idea."

Coralee snickered and rolled her eyes. "Why?"

"To remind me of where we've been...and the possibilities of where we could go."

Coralee grinned briefly, adjusting her head so she could look into his eyes. "I've always loved it when you read aloud. You have such a calming voice."

Benjamin grinned, kissing her temple again and hugging her closer. "*You* calm me, Ceelee, ground me."

"Mmm..."

They didn't say anything for a while, just holding each other and staring off into space. He couldn't stop touching her—whether it was rubbing her back, her shoulders, her waist; kissing her forehead, her temple, her nose—he needed contact with her, something to tell him Coralee was real and he wasn't just dreaming.

"Benjamin?"

"Yes?"

"What *are* we doing?"

He ran the backs of his fingers along her cheek, his blue eyes meeting her brown ones. "What would you like for us to do?"

Coralee dipped her head and her lips rested against his fingers. "What we're doin' right now is nice."

Nice, Benjamin conceded, but not enough. He cupped her cheek and slowly lowered his head, giving her plenty of time to move away if she desired. She didn't, her breathing becoming shallow and her eyelids growing heavy the closer he came. Benjamin grinned a little before placing his lips on hers, a soft contact that had her sighing into it.

This was the "more" they both wanted.

"Benny," she whispered against his mouth, her hand grabbing his hair with delicious pressure.

That blessed nickname—the second time she'd called him that, but Benjamin knew it wouldn't be the last. He moved his mouth from hers, pressing kisses along her jaw line to the space underneath her ear. He grabbed the lobe with his teeth and sucked while his hands dragged from her face to her waist. Coralee hugged his head to her, her breathing harsh and hitched as his kisses rained along her collarbone.

"Benny," she whispered again, the last syllable a sigh as his hand slid underneath her flannel top and up her bare back. It was then he discovered she had on no bra, and the realization caused him to kiss her harder.

Coralee shifted and he helped her, putting her in a position in which she completely straddled him. She suddenly gasped and clamped her legs tightly around his thighs.

"What's wrong, honey?" Benjamin asked, pulling his mouth reluctantly from her neck.

Coralee's bottom lip was between her teeth and she was looking off to the side, a frown on her face. Benjamin gently turned her to him, frowning himself. He kissed the crease on her forehead, then rested his against hers, his hands caressing her back underneath her shirt. "What's wrong?"

"Perhaps...we're getting too carried away..." she said monotonously, rocking against his very obvious arousal.

Benjamin blushed and Coralee grinned at him, bottom lip still between her teeth. At least she wasn't screaming for the hills and kicking him out in the process. Coralee cupped his cheeks and kissed his forehead.

"I'm sorry, Benny."

He buried his face in her neck, kissing her collarbone. "Don't apologize, sweetheart. It's a natural reaction."

She chuckled huskily, causing him to stir, and he set her further back on his lap, away from his excitement. "I never thought I could get that type of...*reaction* wearing flannel!"

"You could wear a potato sack and you'd still be desirable to me."

Coralee laughed, a happy one that made Benjamin smile in return. He lifted his head from her neck and stared at her, his smile growing as she caressed his cheeks with the backs of her hands. His were at her lower back, thumbs rubbing the small of it lazily.

"Gorgeous," he whispered, staring into her eyes. Everything about her was exquisite to him. From her wide, deep brown eyes to her dark-gold soft skin to the womanly flare of her hips and the gentle curve of her breasts. He never would have imagined she would grow up to be so lovely.

Coralee smiled, and for the first time, took initiative in beginning a kiss, just a light pressure of lips until he deepened it. Every kiss was new, different, as if he was learning how to do it all over again. Coralee wasn't the first girl he had kissed, but she would be his last, and Benjamin felt no sadness over that. He wondered if it were the same for her, but would ask about it later, because right now he liked what she was doing with her mouth.

She nipped at his upper lip, bold and saucy, and he groaned. He stood up with her still straddled around him. Abruptly she broke the kiss, eyes wide and surprised.

"Benny?"

He took calming breaths and put his forehead against hers again, even as he lowered her feet to the ground. They *certainly* weren't ready for anything other than kissing; and though with other girls heavy kissing usually went further, he wouldn't with Coralee.

"I think I should leave," Benjamin said softly, kissing her nose when he heard her sigh.

"That would be best..." she admitted as he set her down. "I reckon I'll see you over break?"

"If I have to walk to your house again to do so."

Coralee rolled her eyes, but Benjamin knew she was pleased. He was pleased as well.

"Thank you," she said, staring at the loose button she fingered. "Thank you for everything today..."

"What everything?"

She smiled, but still didn't look at him. "Winnin' the game, for one." He laughed and she joined him, glancing at him before going back to the button. "For takin' my family out to dinner...for bringin' me home, walkin' me to the dorm, for respectin' me." A tear fell and he caught it on his thumb. Coralee took in a deep breath. "Just for bein' there for me, even when I didn't know you were."

"There's no place I'd rather be, darlin'," Benjamin said softly, lifting her chin gently.

"Yeah, but—"

"*Shh*," he commanded, placing a finger to her lips. "No 'buts'."

Coralee nodded, and put some space between them. "I'll see you later then."

She walked him to the door and opened it, but Benjamin stopped her progress. "What if I said I didn't want to leave?"

Coralee licked her lips, hiding half her body behind the door. "I would say we don't always get what we want." Benjamin nodded and walked out the room. "Benny?"

He stopped but didn't turn to look at her. "Yes?"

"Maybe someday we will."

He started walking again when he heard the door click shut, but this time with a content smile on his face.

TWELVE

"Ceelee, baby, could you come here for a minute?"

Coralee wiped her hands on her apron, removing the flour from the yeast rolls she was making, before going to her mother in the living room. Patty held a box of ornaments in one arm and a small angel ornament in the other.

"Yes, ma'am?"

"Where you think it should go? LJ say it should go closer to the top."

LJ was reclining on the couch, pillows resting behind his back and his bad leg elevated on the opposite couch arm. "Angels, heaven, top...makes sense, don't it?"

Coralee smiled at her brother and nodded. "Yeah, it does. Want me to bring in a chair, Mama?"

Patty sucked her teeth and replaced the ornament in the box. "No. I'll just wait 'til yo' father gets home."

"When Grandma Dennie comin' back from the church?" Coralee asked, walking around the tree, joyous at how the decorations gave it life.

"Daddy's gonna pick her up on the way from work."

It was two days before Christmas, and the house was full of happiness and cheer. Coralee didn't need anything under the Christmas tree now that her brother was home. If she wasn't helping her mother around the house, she was keeping him company and catching him up on all the Plumville news from the past year. LJ was the most inspiring of all, always having a good disposition and maintaining the same sense of humor he had before he left. Coralee had heard some of the horrors of the war from the news, even from friends of friends who were depressed and very angry towards the government, and themselves, but LJ didn't seem to have those afflictions, at least when she was around him. Coralee knew LJ couldn't be all smiles all the time; she only hoped LJ would allow the rest of the family to help him if he hit a dark, rough patch.

"Mama, I'mma go and finish them yeast rolls."

"You do that, Ceelee, and don't forget to make that rum cake fo' the Drummonds, okay? Miss Florence always takes one to that Christmas dinner they go to at the Wilkes'."

"Yes, ma'am."

Coralee was back at her flour-dusted station, the powder-blue countertop hidden by the dough, flour, and other ingredients used during her preparation. Coralee decided—*insisted*—she would do all the work, wanting her mother to spend as much time with her son as possible. Of course, Patty argued she had every day to spend with LJ while Coralee only had two weeks, but Coralee was adamant. Patty worked very hard all the time; the very least she could have was a break in her own home!

Coralee didn't mind the work. In fact, she loved cooking and baking, her Grandma Dennie introducing it to her when she was nine years old. She didn't get much of an opportunity to do it at school since there was no kitchen in the dorms, but when she was home Coralee, Patty, and Grandma Dennie would often have much fun cooking and reaffirming their relationships.

She was alone in the kitchen now, preparing for Christmas dinner and mulling over all the changes in her life. The biggest change was the reintroduction of Benjamin and her ever-growing feelings for him. So, yes, she thought herself in love with him. What next? It wasn't as if they could waltz into the sunset and people would be fine with it! Everyone assumed she would be with Nick Price, given the way the others on the BSU board treated them. So what Freda knew? Freda had her own reservations, and Coralee greatly valued her friend's opinion. Relationships were hard enough without adding the racial dynamic to them.

And what about her *parents*? Coralee knew her father's feelings, and was pretty sure her mother deferred to whatever Luther Sr. thought, but Coralee didn't know if she could survive her parents' disappointment. Love was a gamble, everyone knew, but banking on a white man was foolishness.

Wasn't it?

Yet how could she explain Benjamin, the anomalous figure who had been the very sort of person her mother, father, grandmother, best friends, random people on the street wanted for her?

"You all right, Coralee? You just standin' there with yo' hands in that dough." Coralee jumped at her mother's soft query, and hurriedly kneaded the dough before placing it in a bowl. Patty put her hand on her daughter's shoulder and squeezed while Coralee placed a towel over the bowl so the dough could rise. "What's got you so deep in thought?"

"Just things," Coralee replied, shrugging slightly. "Ain't nothin' the same."

Patty didn't respond right away, taking one full pan of properly kneaded and risen dough pieces and putting it in the preheated oven. "If life ain't change it would be pretty borin', wouldn't it?"

Coralee looked over her shoulder, giving her mother a placating smile. "That's true."

"And if I remember correctly, you, LJ, and Benjamin always wanted to be on some sort o' adventure, no?"

Coralee laughed, wiping down the counter with a soap-soaked rag. "Yeah."

"Who knew fallin' in love would be all the adventure you needed?"

Coralee's movements slowed to a standstill, and she temporarily forgot to breathe. She desperately hoped her mother was talking about her and Daddy; but from the weight of her mother's eyes on her back, Coralee knew it wasn't so.

"Mama—"

"I didn't believe him, you know, until I saw it fo' myself with my own eyes."

"Saw what, Mama?" Patty paused, and Coralee turned to her. Patty's expression was a mix between pride, acceptance, apprehension and resignation. "Mama, what's goin' on?"

"You love him, don't you?"

Coralee gasped, but regained her bearings quickly, turning back around and placing the prepared dough on the last greased pan. "Mama, there are a lotta 'hims' to choose from."

"But there's only one white one, and that's who I mean."

Coralee bit her lip and shrugged. "I don't know—"

"A woman in love is painfully obvious, Coralee. It's all over her face, plain as day."

"Do you think he knows?" Coralee whispered, not facing her mother.

"I reckon he does, Ceelee."

Coralee gripped the counter's edge, counting to ten. No wonder Benjamin had seemed a bit more assertive the last time they were together; she'd practically given him the go-ahead! She felt embarrassed and ashamed. Now Benjamin had expectations...expectations she didn't know she could meet.

"Mama, I didn't mean for this to happen."

"I reckon none of us did, but it has. Everything happens for a reason, Coralee, and God saw it fit for y'all to be together."

"You *really* think God has somethin' to do with this?"

"Gotta have. Ain't no other reason to account fo' it."

Coralee shook her head, wringing out the rag in the sink. Admitting her feelings to herself was one thing; having someone else, particularly her mother, do it *for* her was another entirely.

Patty kissed her daughter's temple. "Take a break, sweet pea; you've earned it."

"Oh, Mama, I'm fine," she insisted even as her mother opened the oven door to check on the rolls.

"I gotta fix that," Coralee muttered absently, frowning at the rusted hinges and the grease splatters along the white side of the oven.

Patty closed the oven door again. "Can't help who you love, chile."

"I was talkin' about the oven."

"And I'm talkin' 'bout you and Benjamin."

Coralee hugged herself and shivered, feeling chilled despite the kitchen's heat. Things were moving entirely too fast between them, and maybe this holiday would bring some distance and time to cool down the intense feelings she was having. Out of sight, out of mind, right?

It didn't work the first time...

And it wasn't working now. Coralee genuinely missed Benjamin, more than she thought she would. It was as if there were a prickle inside of her that only went away when he was around.

She went into the living room, and LJ grinned at her when she entered. Coralee couldn't help but smile back and sat on the floor by the arm of the couch where his head rested, taking his hand in hers.

"How you feelin'?" she asked, rubbing the back of his hand with her thumbs.

"Just fine, Miss Ceelee, how you?"

Coralee nodded. "Fine."

"You never made a very good liar...I should know...got me in a lotta trouble that way!"

Coralee laughed, squeezing his hand gently. "What kind of baby sister would I be if I didn't get my big brother into as much trouble as possible?"

"Point taken, Little Ceelee, but what's got you so sad?"

And big brothers were perceptive, she thought dryly, but clasped her other hand over his. "I don't think it's sadness so much as...confusion."

"Hmm. About what?"

"Life."

"What's so confusing about that? You live and you die—it's that simple."

"It's the thing in between that boggles me, LJ."

LJ nodded, shifting a bit so his face was closer to hers. "Live fo' you, Ceelee. You can't live for everybody else. Just gotta live fo' you."

Wasn't that selfish? Weren't the martyrs of the world celebrated and honored for their sacrifices? Joan of Arc? Martin Luther King, Jr.? Jesus? All of them gave themselves so others could live, have a better life than the ones they had, and here was her brother telling her to live for herself? It went against everything she'd been taught.

"I can't do that, LJ. I don't *live* by myself, so how can I live *for* myself?"

Luther said nothing, clenching his jaw and the hand around hers. Coralee leaned her head against the couch's arm, near his head, and squeezed his hand back. For all the optimism LJ exuded, there was a haunted look in his eye, those times he became so still...so quiet. Some nights he would scream out, and their father would wake up to calm down his son. Just because LJ had left the war didn't mean the war had left him, and Coralee wondered if all his appearance of happiness was a show for their benefit.

"There are things people do, Ceelee," LJ began, his hand tightening around hers again, "because someone's told them to do it, or because they think it'll help someone else. In the Army, all we get are orders; we just little ants controlled by a queen thousands of miles away sitting pretty in a nice, big, White House. This queen ain't gotta see what we see; don't have to shoot innocent people workin' the rice paddies. This queen ain't gotta shoot a fellow soldier because he just so happened to have slanted eyes and in the heat o' battle ain't no one got time to check for a passport. This queen don't have to see a man get blown to bits five feet in front o' him, or see little children and babes cryin' on the streets fo' they mamas and daddies....or these same lil' children floatin' dead in the river. This queen ain't gotta see all that, but the little ant does. And the little ant's supposed to keep on, without feelin', because those are his orders. The ant becomes a killin' machine, no longer a human bein', all in the name of country."

Two tears slipped out of Coralee's eyes at LJ's speech, disbelieving what she had just heard. LJ had been one of the most kindhearted people she knew, and hearing the things he had experienced blew her away. His very *being* had been compromised in the war, and no doubt LJ was now dealing with the consequences despite the performance he put on for them—when he ate, when he brushed his teeth, when he reached for an elusive scratch hidden by a wall of plaster. Funny how it was only when the choice was taken away did LJ realize he'd had one in the first place.

Just as Coralee did right now.

She exhaled a shuddering breath and kissed the back of LJ's scarred hand. There was nothing she could say to reassure LJ it would be all better, but she wished she could.

"If you don't do anything else in yo' life, Coralee, don't be an ant. Don't just do things because you told to do 'em, because at the end o' the day, the only two people who you *really* gotta answer to is yo'self and God—not this town, and not even Mama and Pop. Remember that, girlie."

Coralee only nodded, LJ's advice swirling in her head, and the front door opened to reveal her father and his mother bearing gifts and food. Patty and Coralee helped with the load, listening and laughing to Luther sharing stories from work and Grandma Dennie interrupting to share *her* stories from the church. They released Coralee from her more somber musings as the family sat together in the living room, putting on the radio to listen to holiday songs while sharing stories and hopes for the holiday season.

&

Sitting on his bed, Benjamin held the gift in his hand as if it weighed a ton. In reality, it was a small, velvet jewelry box with quarter-carat diamond earrings inside. Perhaps the gift was too extravagant, but when he saw them in the jewelry store the other day, he knew they were perfect.

She won't accept them, his mind had told him even as he made the purchase, but Benjamin reasoned she would accept them eventually...she had the rest of their lives to do so.

His father had caught him holding the earrings earlier, only raising his eyebrows and asking, "So it's like that?" Benjamin had nodded and replied, "Yes, it is."

Paul Drummond's eyes had held two expressions at Benjamin's confession—pride and apprehension. Benjamin hoped the pride outweighed the apprehension, but he honestly didn't know.

His father then had nodded once and continued down the stairs to go to the church to pick up his wife, leaving Benjamin as he sat now, holding the earrings, wondering if it were too soon for such a gesture. They hadn't even defined their relationship aloud, both too afraid to do so. Vocalizing it made it official in a sense, closed the door on platonic and opened them to romance and hurt, possibly even danger. But he was in it for the long haul, and he intended to prove it.

The doorbell rang and he stuffed the velvet box in a drawer before going downstairs to answer it. Though it was Christmas Eve, for Benjamin, Christmas came a few hours early.

"Coralee!"

She gave him a small smile and held up the cake for him. "I brought this for your Mama...Merry Christmas."

It was cloudy outside and a little cool, and she only had a worn wool coat to protect her from the elements. "Did you walk here with just that on?"

Coralee shrugged. "It's not so bad."

Perhaps he should've bought her a coat. "Well, come inside before you catch your death!"

"I just came to drop this off—"

"Please, Coralee, I haven't seen you in days..."

Coralee frowned a little and pursed her lips, then turned to go down the steps, but Benjamin took her arm and pulled her through the front door, holding the cake with one arm while the other linked through hers. He closed the door with his foot and winked at her as they went further inside the house.

"You know the neighbors will talk—"

"Let 'em talk. If their panties are in a bunch because I let you in through the front door—"

"I'm not supposed to—"

"You're my *guest*, Ceelee; that means you come through the front door."

She said nothing after that. Benjamin told her to sit in the living room, almost pushing her on the couch, before going into the dining room and putting the cake on the table. When he returned, Benjamin found Coralee sitting on the edge, posture ramrod straight and hands clasped in her lap. Benjamin didn't blame her, though; the living room was Florence's place and it wasn't the most accommodating room in the house. White lace was everywhere—from the curtains to the doilies on the tables. The lamps were from the 1920s, a wedding present from her parents when she married his father, and was dusted and polished constantly to keep the pristine shine and glow. The furniture, all mahogany, gave the room a handsome, sturdy presence, complementing the hardwood floors that never went a day without being swept. For many of the guests, the living room and the dining rooms were the only places they would ever see, and Florence made sure they were the cleanest, most impeccable rooms in the house.

Benjamin chuckled softly and her eyes snapped to his. They were wider than necessary, and he almost thought he could see her heart hammering in her chest. He took comfort in that, realizing he wasn't the only one who was nervous.

He sat on the couch with enough space between them that a pillow could rest comfortably there, but he wanted to touch her badly. Coralee moved her eyes away from him, looking around the living room as if seeing it for the first time.

"It's been so long since I've been in here," she murmured.

"It has."

Coralee glanced at him, then looked at the lamp on the end table next to her. "Where are Miss Florence and your father?"

"Mother had a church function, some sort of food drive or something; Dad went to pick her up."

"You mean we're alone?"

"Yes."

Coralee nodded, and held her hands tighter. Benjamin took pity on her and took one of those hands, intertwining their fingers. All was right with the world now that he touched her, and Benjamin pushed the envelope further by kissing her cheek and nuzzling it with his nose.

"I've missed you..."

Her body seemed to relax at his declaration, and her eyes slid closed. Benjamin took a chance by wrapping his arm around her shoulders, and was rewarded when she put her head in the crook of his neck.

"I've missed you too."

He smiled and kissed the back of her hand. Peace was with him now; he was holding her, breathing in her scent, resting his cheek against her hair. They were just sitting there, not speaking or doing anything, and Benjamin was the least bored he'd been all break long.

"How is LJ?" Benjamin said after a while. Though the silence was nice, he didn't want to waste all the precious moments they had without hearing her voice.

"LJ is fine. Full of good spirit. I don't know where he gets his strength."

"I'd say your mother. Aunt Patty is nothing if not resilient."

"She is."

"And she passed it on to her daughter."

Benjamin saw Coralee smile, and he kissed her head again. Silence reigned. With any other girl, the lack of conversation would be awkward. With Coralee, it was comfortable, calming, like lying out in a field in the warm, spring sun and letting the breeze caress the skin.

"I think I need to be headin' home now."

And just as suddenly, thunder clapped in the sky, and the spring sun and breeze turned into a dreary rain.

It also began raining outside, and Coralee's face fell. Benjamin sent up a silent prayer of thanks, for now he had extra time with her.

"May I use your phone? I need to call home and tell 'em I'll be slow comin'," Coralee said.

Benjamin nodded and they went into the kitchen where Coralee told her mother of her predicament. Benjamin leaned against the wall, playing with the cord as he watched Coralee. She ignored his scrutiny, but he knew she felt him, saw her distribute her weight on her feet more often than necessary.

When Coralee put the phone back on the base, Benjamin's hands covered hers, pulling her to him in a hug. She sighed and returned it.

"What did Aunt Patty say?" Benjamin asked.

"She said okay. I'm to wait until the rain dies down."

"See...aren't you glad you came inside? Had you left, you would've been caught in the rain."

Coralee laughed, and he joined her. Benjamin cupped her cheek, rubbing his thumb against the swell of it. Coralee's laughter died to a simple smile, and Benjamin saw contentment in her eyes. The fear and apprehension from earlier were gone, and Benjamin's own hesitation eased.

"Have you been havin' a good break so far?" Coralee asked, eyes fluttering as he kissed her jaw.

"It's been all right," he said against her skin, going to her ear and nibbling on the lobe. "But it just got a lot better."

"Why? Your *real* girlfriend the prim and proper type?"

Benjamin removed his lips from her, bothered by the insinuation. How could Coralee think he would be seeing another girl when—?

He looked in her eyes, and the apprehension was back in them. Benjamin knew they had to talk about what they were to each other; it had to be defined, especially for her. Coralee didn't understand how much she meant to him, how much he hoped he meant to her.

Benjamin pulled away, but linked their fingers together again, and led her out of the kitchen and up the stairs to his room. He felt Coralee's resistance, but it was weaker than it could've been, her curiosity and trust in him outweighing everything else.

Coralee blinked a few times as she looked around his room. There were all sorts of football trophies on his desk as well as the cap from his high school commencement hanging on one of the desk's posts. His high school diploma was proudly displayed on the wall between the desk and his mirror, and a football lay in the chair situated in the corner. His bed was made, most of the floor was clean, but his clothes were strewn in front of the closet doors, and Coralee grinned at the sight.

"I haven't had time to do laundry," he murmured, wrapping his arms around her waist from behind.

"Too busy sleepin' and watchin' television, I see," Coralee teased, linking her fingers through his. Benjamin laughed into her neck, kissing it before pulling his head up and resting his chin on her shoulder. They looked into each other's eyes, and Coralee unlinked one hand to rub the backs of her fingers against his cheek. He closed his eyes and leaned into her caress, feeling like a cat must when it was stroked just right.

"How about we get you out of this coat?" Benjamin said as he moved his face to kiss the back of her hand.

Coralee laughed sheepishly. "I didn't even know I still had it on...I've been distracted..."

So had he, but it was more Benjamin had been *obstructed* by the coat, a barrier between him and Coralee that must be removed. He helped her shrug out of the jacket and put it on the peg behind the

room door. The extra weight on the door caused it to shut completely, but Benjamin and Coralee didn't pay any heed to it, both solely
focused on the other.

Benjamin wrapped his arms around her waist and her hands
came to his neck, thumbs grazing along the Adam's apple and
beginnings of his beard. Benjamin grinned, giving her an Eskimo kiss
that made her sigh.

"I have something for you," he whispered, kissing the skin beside
her nose. He cradled her head, pressing kisses as light as snow all
along her face.

Coralee sighed again, her arms going about his waist. "Do you
now?"

His nose caressed hers. "Yes; and if you're a good girl, maybe I'll
give it to you."

His lips were now at her forehead, and he smiled against it at her
giggle. Coralee brought him closer to her. She was so soft against
him, so pliant, as if he could mold his body into hers and never be
separated from her again. When Coralee kissed his jaw, standing on
tiptoes to reach it, Benjamin thought he would collapse from the
delicious pressure of it.

Her lips brushed his left earlobe. "When you hold me, I feel like I
could fly."

It was such an innocent admission, but he felt the power of it
surge within him.

"Coralee—"

"I love you," she whispered, hiding her face in his neck, her
mouth just above his pulse point.

He froze. It was the last thing he ever expected to come from
Coralee, but it was perhaps the most cherished. Now Benjamin
thought he could fly too.

He had to say *something*, though, anything to cover the gaping silence that now separated them, but when he opened his mouth to
speak, her fingers stilled his words.

"Don't," she whispered, biting her lip as she pulled her fingers away from his lips. "Don't say anything."

"But—"

"Please? Don't. Mama said I was doin' a poor job o' hidin' it any-way, so I came clean. I know I'm just a fascination for you—"

"*Fascination?*"

His tone made Coralee's mouth snap shut and her eyes widen. Benjamin was sharper than he intended, but he couldn't understand Coralee's logic. For someone so smart she was being very dense about the situation. And poor job of hiding it? Benjamin had thought he was in this by himself! Now that he knew he wasn't, Benjamin didn't feel so apprehensive about giving Coralee her gift.

He stepped away and went to his desk, pulling out a drawer and digging deep beneath the old papers and other knickknacks. When he looked to Coralee, he found her by the door, reaching for her coat.

"Wait!" Coralee jumped at his exclamation and he winced, im-mediately contrite. "I'm sorry; I didn't mean to startle you." Of all things she laughed, but it wasn't the full-bodied one he was used to hearing. Instead, it was mollifying, as if her laughter was in the place of crying. "Please don't go."

"I've got to..."

The rapid succession of rain pounding on the roof made her statement ludicrous. Coralee reached for her coat again and Benja-min sprang into action, his hand closing over hers as she gripped the garment. Her back was to his front, and her head was bent. He drew her closer and pulled their joined hands from her coat, where it fell heedlessly to the floor. Benjamin dragged his chin from the top of her head to her temple, his breathing harsher than normal.

"Please...?" Benjamin ignored the plaintive note in his voice and presented the small velvet box to her. He heard her sharp intake of breath and tightened his hold around her.

"*Benjamin—*"

"Open it," he whispered, closing her fingers around it and pop-ping open the lid. The diamonds glittered even in the murky gray light coming from the window behind them, and Coralee's body began to tremble upon the sight.

"I—"

"I saw these and I thought they'd look beautiful on you," he admitted, rubbing a finger along the jewels. She became heavy against him, and Benjamin lifted her in his arms and carried her to the bed. She sat across his lap, eyes transfixed on the earrings, and Benjamin leaned his forehead against her temple.

"I can't accept this," Coralee finally managed. "There's no way I could explain such a gift!"

"Say it's from your boyfriend."

Coralee looked at him sharply. "No one in Plumville could afford this."

No one in *black* Plumville was what Coralee really meant to say; and if she wore the earrings, she would have to reveal who gave them to her.

His jaw clenched in frustration and anger.

"You should give these to someone who can wear them," Coralee further explained, putting the box firmly in his hand.

"I did. I gave them to you."

Coralee sucked her teeth and shook her head, leaving his lap. She stood and began pacing in front of him. "Why do you insist on doing this, huh? Why do you keep on when the only thing that'll come out of this is my broken heart?"

Benjamin looked at her as if she had grown another head. One minute they were happy and holding each other, kissing, the next she was condemning him for loving her! Was it her monthly?

"I *know* you ain't just ask me that!"

He felt his blush burn his cheeks and he shrugged helplessly, not meaning to say that aloud. "I'm sorry, Coralee, but I don't know what else to think! I thought you liked being with me. You said you loved me!"

Coralee now appeared tired, and she sagged against the door. "I do—"

"Then don't push me away!"

She looked at him then, as if what he just said was ridiculous. "I *have* to! It'll never work for us—don't you see? When this is over you can come out virtually unscathed, but *me*? I won't have that luxury. I can't *afford* that luxury. You know how many black girls get their reputations ruined for allowing a white man to mess with them? I'm not going to let that happen to me—"

"I won't, either," Benjamin vowed. Of course he knew. He lived in a frat house full of white men who made sport of black women. Before, he had never thought anything of it because it had no real meaning to him, but now...

Coralee laughed again, hollowly. "Oh, c'mon, Benjamin! There's no way this could work," she said, pointing between them. "We're a recipe for disaster—!"

"So you *regret* loving me?"

Coralee paused, and so did his heart, growing heavy with the dread that started to fill it. Finally, she shook her head and smiled sadly. "No, I could never regret that."

He frowned, now even more confused. "Coralee—"

She walked up to him and placed her fingers at his mouth, and he kissed them. Tears welled up in her eyes, and one escaped, falling down her cheek as if in slow motion. "You're a good man, Benjamin Drummond, a really good man. You deserve someone you're free to love. I'm not that person."

"But, Cora—"

"*Shh,*" she whispered, moving those fingers from his mouth and caressing the backs of them against his cheek. "I mean what I said, Benjamin. I'm not afraid anymore; I'm not. I think I'm strong enough to love you, to watch you be happy...even if it's with someone else—"

"I don't want anyone else," Benjamin said emphatically, grasping her upper arms and shaking her a little. "*You* are who I want!"

Coralee nodded, conceding his point. "Perhaps, but I'm not who you need. You'll thank me later for this."

"No, I won't," he ground out, his hands releasing her as if she'd suddenly become too hot to touch. "How could I ever thank you for breaking my heart?"

She looked down at that, her shoulders collapsing with the force of her sob, but then her arms were around him. Coralee was kissing him, pouring all the love she claimed to have in the gesture. By the time Benjamin's despair had ebbed enough for him to reciprocate, Coralee broke the kiss. She bent down to retrieve her coat and slipped into it. The barrier was back, and each button she did seemed like a lock to which he had no key.

"Merry Christmas, Benny," she whispered, then rushed out of his room and his home.

It was still raining outside.

THIRTEEN

Solomon College won its bowl game by a landslide.

Once again, Nick Price and Benjamin Drummond were the heroes of the day.

Once again, they rallied in celebration.

Once again, the rally split along racial lines.

This time, however, Benjamin didn't search out a certain pair of brown eyes, unwilling to see Coralee standing so far away from him that she might as well be in China. It was bad enough he had to watch her run into Nick's arms at the end of the game, had to watch the other man hold her as if she were *his* girl...had to watch Coralee *let* him. It wasn't until Felix had alerted Benjamin of his staring did he tear his eyes away from the couple. He'd been primed during the game, adrenaline racing through his veins like the cars at the Indianapolis 500. All of Benjamin's frustrations carried over from the holiday break had fueled his arm to throw record-breaking passes, his legs to run yards that put running backs to shame, his body to break tackles some quarterbacks in the pros couldn't.

Perhaps he should give Coralee credit for the win.

Benjamin's parents had taken him out to a postgame dinner after the rally. He'd been polite but not nearly as excited as he should've been after winning the biggest game of the season, but his parents had acted as if all were well with their son. Florence had gushed over his performance and Paul had clapped his son on the back at appropriate intervals. When they'd dropped Benjamin off at the frat house, he hadn't known he'd feel such relief upon seeing a rowdy group of college football players; he could hide much better in a throng than with his parents.

Or so Benjamin had thought. The victory celebration was in full swing, and it appeared the *entire* campus was present. Amazingly, good will and euphoria over the win had brought upon a fragile truce between the two races, and since it was a team game, all members and their guests could come. Coralee was there, Nick's arm still attached to her shoulders. She looked decidedly uncomfortable, but her smile was warm and her demeanor cordial to all who came up to congratulate Nick. For once, she had opted out of the skirt and cardigan and was wearing a deep purple ribbed turtleneck sweater with jeans that looked as if she were poured into them. Her hair remained in its typical chignon, however, and it softened what could have been a devastatingly alluring picture of her.

She belongs with me!

"Drummond!"

Coach Norman. He was perhaps one of the reasons the party hadn't gotten as rowdy as it could've, none of the boys willing to get crazy in front of their coach. Some of them had next season to consider, after all. Benjamin glanced at Nick and Coralee one last time before going to the coach. Even with this triumph, Coach Norman still had had plenty to critique in the locker room after the game. Benjamin had tuned him out, especially since he wouldn't be playing for Coach Norman anymore. Those tips were for the new starting quarterback next year.

"Yeah, Coach?"

Coach Norman arched an eyebrow before heaving a deep sigh. "I spoke to Carmichael today about your average, wanting to make sure that colored gal helped you pull your grades up..."

Benjamin had forgotten all about that, the reason he and Coralee had been reunited in the first place. Suddenly his stomach turned to mush and his heart pounded like a jackhammer.

"Yes?" Benjamin asked, his voice even despite the desire to shout and shake the answer out of Coach Norman.

Coach Norman sighed again and grabbed Benjamin's shoulder, squeezing harder than necessary. "You're eligible, Drummond. Congratulations."

Eligible. That meant he passed English III. Benjamin didn't notice Coach Norman go to another section of the room, didn't hear the music or the people chattering about anything and everything. All he heard was "eligible."

He'd done it. With Coralee's help, he'd managed to get his grade point average high enough and keep the season legitimate for the team. He hadn't let his teammates down—he hadn't let *himself* down—and that was the most freeing feeling he'd felt in a long time.

Did Coralee know?

"Hey, Drummond, I dunno what made you play the way you did, but damn if I don't owe it a big kiss!" Randy Jurgens laughed, slapping Benjamin's back while Tommy shook his hand.

Benjamin's eyes found Coralee sitting on the couch talking to another black girl. Nick wasn't around.

The other two's gazes followed Benjamin's and Tommy licked his lips. "She's a foxy one, ain't she?"

Benjamin felt his hand twitch. "Which one?"

Randy snorted. "You know which one. I never knew purple could look so good on a nigra."

Benny stood in front of them, his eyes fierce with barely controlled rage. "Do not touch her. You hear me? You lay one hand on her and I swear to God I'll make you pay."

Their eyes widened slightly, then filled with sadistic understanding. "I got ya! You call dibs," Tommy said, jabbing Randy with his elbow lightly. "Just let me know when you're done, yeah? I'd love to sample a taste o' her brown sugar..."

Benjamin forced himself to turn and walk away. He didn't need to start a fight, not with the atmosphere being as joyous and carefree as it was. Besides, he'd gotten them to back off; he knew the other men wouldn't make a play for Coralee until they had permission.

Benjamin sent up a silent thanks for the twisted code of chivalry among the frat boys.

Nevertheless, Benjamin approached Coralee cool and collected, as if he had every right to speak to her. Both women stopped talking and looked at him, but Coralee dropped her eyes quickly. Benjamin was annoyed and emboldened by the move; it meant Coralee didn't have the courage to look at him, didn't have the courage to allow him to see the love he knew she had for him. He had to speak with her, though; Tommy and Randy's interest in her had him on edge. Not even the fact Tommy was now chatting up Trish Caldwell could dispel it.

"May I speak to you, Coralee?" The other woman started to leave and he held up a hand to stay her. "In private?"

Coralee looked at the other woman who squeezed Coralee's hand.

"Coralee—"

"It's all right, Freda," Coralee replied softly. "Tell Nick I stepped out for some air."

Freda glanced between him and Coralee before finally saying, "Okay."

Coralee went ahead of him, but Benjamin caught the other woman's eyes. They were guarded, unreadable. Benjamin gave her a small half-smile, but she didn't return it, instead standing and going off into the crowd.

The stare unsettled Benjamin. It was if she knew about him and Coralee. At least Coralee had someone to talk to about the situation. Benjamin didn't trust any of his friends with the information except Felix, but he hadn't had time to discuss it because of football practice. Now he had all the time in the world, and he had to talk to someone soon or he'd go mad with silent pining for Coralee.

He found her leaning against the side of the house, watching random drunk people enter and exit the building. Her arms were crossed at her chest as if she were trying to make herself small, to blend into the surroundings so no one would bother her. If Benjamin had anything to say about it, no one would.

He went to her, stuffing his hands in his pockets so he couldn't reach out and pull her in his arms. "Hi," he said, voice husky from too much yelling, too much emotion.

She cleared her throat and shifted a bit. "You wanted to see me?"

"Yes, uh—" The door slammed open and some guys started whooping and wailing. This was not where he wanted to talk. Things would be much calmer on the other side of the house.

"Um...can we go somewhere a little more private?" Her face darkened slightly. "I—I know a better place where we can talk." She looked at him suspiciously, and he pointed to his left, his hands still in his jacket's pockets. "Just around the house."

She nodded and fell into step with him. Her arms were still around herself, and she looked at her feet instead of directly in front of her.

This is ridiculous!

He shrugged out of his jacket and held it out to her. Coralee shook her head but Benjamin stopped walking and took her arm to make her do the same.

"Why are you treatin' me like I got some kinda disease, Coralee?"

Her eyes jerked to his, a small fire burning in them, and she yanked his coat out of his hands and slipped it around her shoulders. Benjamin didn't understand why she was so snippy. *She* was the one who broke it off, not he; and if anyone had the right to be mad, it was he!

"Enough of this!" Benjamin growled.

"Wha—?!"

He grasped her shoulders and pinned her against the side of the house before giving her a bruising kiss. He wanted her to know he couldn't live in denial, *wouldn't* live in denial like she seemed so keen on doing. Coralee struggled and he gentled the kiss, coaxing her with his mouth, tongue, and hands to respond to him. Eventually, her hands slid up his arms to grasp his shoulders.

That's more like it, he thought to himself before breaking off the kiss and resting his forehead against hers. Two weeks was far too long to go without her.

"Ben—"

"I can't stand the sight of Nick's arms around you," he breathed into her hairline. Her body trembled and he wrapped his arm around her waist underneath the jacket she wore.

Coralee sighed wearily. "*Ben*—"

"I passed English III...our season's in good standing. Coach just told me."

She gasped and pushed him away from her, her eyes wide. "Really?"

Her excitement fueled his, and a silly grin appeared on his face. "Yeah."

Coralee squealed and launched herself into his arms. "Oh! Congratulations! I'm so proud of you!"

Right. Home. *Mine*. The words bombarded Benjamin's mind as his arms closed around Coralee. She had said she wasn't who he needed, but she could not have been more wrong. Coralee was everything to him, and watching her with another man was like someone driving a rusty knife into his heart and twisting it with every touch, glance, and word that passed between them.

He closed his eyes and kissed her temple tenderly even as his arms tightened around her waist. Coralee's body tensed and her breath was warm and harsh against his cheek.

"Benjamin—"

"I love you, Coralee."

She suddenly grew heavy against him and his arms grew tighter to keep her standing upright. Her fingers clutched his hair as her forehead pressed against his temple with more than enough pressure.

"Are you drunk?" she asked breathlessly after a few moments.

He laughed, his thumb rubbing the small of her back. "I'm actually quite sober, and I've loved you for a while...in fact, I all but admitted it to your mother when I came over during Thanksgiving."

She jerked her head back to meet his eyes. "*What?!*"

He laughed again and kissed her lips softly. "I felt she needed to know. I love you. *You* know I love you. And the best part about all this? You love me too."

Her eyes darted around frantically as if searching for something she could hold. "This is *insane!* This isn't right!"

"So it was okay for you to love me, but not for me to love you."

"What does it matter? We can't be together anyway!"

Benjamin shook his head, refusing to believe it. He was a better man because of her; kept his team's record legitimate because of her; was *happy* because of her. Benjamin knew their relationship was going to be hard, but nothing came from nothing. Laziness didn't get people very far, and he wanted to go the distance with Coralee.

Benjamin framed her face so she had to look at him. A single tear trailed down her cheek and he brushed it away, ever so gently, with his thumb. "You gotta trust me, Coralee. We'll figure out something, but we need to be in this together. Quite frankly, the only people who matter to me are you and God, and as long as I make you two happy I know I've lived a good life."

She dropped her head and closed her eyes, and her shoulders began shaking with her sobs. He let her cry, saying nothing but offering his strength and warmth and love for her to hold as she navigated unfamiliar waters. He was in the same boat with her; he had never experienced life as an outcast, but he was willing to do so if it meant having Coralee. The last two weeks had been pure hell. There was nothing worse than being separated from the woman he loved all because a town would disapprove. Who the hell cared *what* Plumville thought? They didn't have to live here forever; they could move...start over in a place where relationships like theirs weren't shunned and scorned. As it was, there was a distinct possibility someone could catch them, but at that moment Benjamin didn't care. He just wanted Coralee to look him in the eye and tell him she accepted his love. He would take that for now.

"I'm so scared," Coralee whispered, her hands fisting into his shirt.

"I know, honey," Benjamin said, rubbing his hand along her back. "But we'll get through this, okay? We'll work it out."

She pulled back a little, rubbing her fingers against his cheek. "I have to go. Nick'll probably wonder where I am..."

Nick. Benjamin's jaw clenched and she gave him a small, sad smile before kissing it. "I'll see you later." She returned his jacket to him, and Benjamin snuck in one last kiss before letting her leave.

Benjamin leaned against the side of the house, the entire conversation seeping into his brain. Since Benjamin was an only child, he was used to getting what he wanted when he wanted it, but this time...he would have to wait. Of course, the waiting would be easier if there were no *Nick Price* complicating matters, but at least Benjamin knew who really had Coralee's heart. Did that matter? Fear sometimes made a person overly cautious...overly cautious meant Coralee could *try* to give her heart to Nick, just so she wouldn't have to worry about community fallout.

"No way in hell."

Tommy and Randy were right about one thing: he had dibs, and he'd be damned if anyone took Coralee away from him—white *or* black.

Benjamin walked back into the house, needing to hide from his feelings and thoughts again. Music blared, bodies writhed, Benjamin denied. He denied dancing with the bevy of women who wanted a chance to hold the hero of the day in their arms. He denied the drinks continuously passed to him by plastered teammates and housemates.

He denied the urge to forcibly separate Nick from Coralee.

They were slow dancing, if you called hugging and rocking to the beat slow dancing. Nick's hands roamed along her back as he whispered in her ear. Coralee's eyes were closed and she would nod

every now and again. When the song ended, they pulled apart, but
not before Nick ran a knuckle along her cheek and kissed the back
of her hand. More words were exchanged and then Nick went away,
leaving Coralee in the middle of the dance floor alone. Coralee's
friend gave Coralee her jacket and the two women left the party, but
not before Coralee locked eyes with him.

Benjamin couldn't decipher the glance, but he did know he
wouldn't endure another scene like that again. He would fight for
her if necessary; as he told Patty, Plumville wasn't worth *his* happiness, and the same should hold for Coralee.

&

The next few weeks proved to be full of changes for Coralee. After the post-game party, Freda, bless her, didn't prod about what
had happened between her and Benjamin, and didn't ask about what
happened between her and Nick, either. Freda had accepted her
friend wasn't dating Nick long-term; had accepted Coralee would be
mum about the white boy who couldn't take his eyes off her—Freda
had admitted she'd noticed—and had accepted her friend's lost
expression, knowing it had little to do with the new school term.
Thankfully, the BSU board meetings were not as awkward as they
could've been considering; but it seemed Nick and Coralee were still
friends, even if their attempt at something more had failed.

Coralee could not have been more relieved.

Also during these weeks, Coralee began receiving letters—love
letters of all things. They were sent through university mail, and
every letter ended the same way: *I love you.* There was never a signa-
ture, but Coralee didn't need one. She thought Benjamin was very
brave to do all this, but he was also very sweet; and if she hadn't
been in love with him before, she definitely was now.

Who would've thought?

She hadn't. She never thought childhood affection would blos-
som into adult love, and she *certainly* didn't think it would be recip-

rocated. The fact her mother had known since Thanksgiving...Coralee had had no idea. The way Patty had approached their conversation made Coralee think she'd been the only one to feel the way she did. Admittedly, even with Benjamin's admission, Coralee couldn't see them together, at least not right now. She was willing to wait until they left school, away from the eyes of Plumville. She would be content with the letters for now...

Coralee and the rest of the BSU board were currently in her room working on the second semester agenda, but Andre found one of those letters and proceeded to read it for the rest of the group. Coralee snatched the letter from him.

"*Who* gave you the right to do that?!" she snarled, folding the paper carefully and putting it in her cardigan's pocket.

Andre was taken aback by her anger. "I'm sorry, Coralee! I was only teas—"

"That wasn't funny! And it wasn't for the entire group to hear! If the writer wanted y'all to read it, he woulda sent it to the damn group!"

Everyone got quiet. Coralee rarely cursed, if ever. Freda put a gentle hand on Coralee's shoulder.

"Ceelee, honey, Andre didn't mean any offense."

Coralee put her face in her hands and took a deep breath. Thank goodness Benjamin didn't sign those letters! If the group had found out...Coralee didn't want to think about that. It was bad enough they knew there was someone else, now they would all be asking her who it was...and all would be wrong in their guesses. No way was Coralee Simmons interested in a *white* boy! No way did she dump *Nick Price* for *Benjamin Drummond*!

"Ah...I think we should wrap up this meeting anyway," Jermaine said diplomatically. "At least we decided when we wanted the first general meeting to be. That was the most imperative thing."

"'Imperative'," Nick teased, trying to relieve the tension. "Soundin' more like a white boy everyday!"

The group laughed and even Coralee cracked a smile, but she did know one white boy who wouldn't use "imperative" with the same ease as Jermaine.

Coralee stood and went with her guests to the door. Before Andre left, however, he placed a small kiss on her cheek and apologized for reading something so private. Coralee forgave him, touched by the apology. Andre's loyalty was primarily to Nick, and for Andre to show contrition showed how decent a person he was. Jermaine squeezed her shoulder and mouthed "congratulations" to her, making Coralee blush from the encouragement and the shame she felt at misleading them. They all, except for Freda, expected this new man to be something he wasn't, and Coralee didn't know if she could trust the rest with her secret. It was a very sad situation, because they'd been her bedrock while in school, had taken her under their wings and made her a part of something important and wonderful.

They were her family away from home, and being unable to share something so big with them tore Coralee up inside. Nick and Andre made her silence necessary, unfortunately. To them, white people were pigs, crackers, evil, caring nothing about their black brothers and sisters, so why care about them in return? The less interaction with them, the better; yet in many ways, that thinking was counterproductive to the BSU's aim. They wanted equality, camaraderie, within the school. However, between exams, holidays, and football practices, the BSU couldn't hold another general meeting; nevertheless, this next one would prove how many people were still down for the cause. Because of the failed rally, they'd tweaked their goal, now just pushing for one Black Studies–related class for next year. Though many of the board would have graduated by this time, it was still an important step on the road to the department. Besides, Coralee and Andre would still be there; they would be able to advocate for it aggressively after Freda, Jermaine, and Nick graduated.

But she didn't want to think about graduation, to be reminded of all the seniors who would leave at the end of the year, to remember Benjamin was among them.

"That white boy got it bad for you."

Coralee jerked at the voice. She'd forgotten Freda was there. "What?"

Freda arched an eyebrow and pointed to Coralee's cardigan pocket. "That white boy got it bad. You ain't give it up yet."

"Freda!"

The other woman shrugged. "I'm just sayin'. White men only want one thing when they pursue a black woman, and that's sex."

Coralee flinched at the crude words. "Benjamin's not like that."

"Maybe not right now, but you come talk to me after you give it to him, okay?"

Coralee pressed against her door, wishing it would envelop her and transport her away from this room, this town, this state...It wasn't fair. Most other people could be happy and in love and not worry about others thinking them crazy, but she couldn't even enjoy the very thing that was supposed to make her the happiest girl in the world.

"You don't even know Benjamin," Coralee whispered. "And I thought you were supportin' me on this!"

Freda looked at her sadly. "I still do, but do you know how hard it is for me to support this when I know he's gonna hurt you, even despite his best intentions? A guy like him can't be with a girl like you, and the worst thing about this entire situation is he thinks he can. I see the looks he gives you, and I do believe he's sincere about his feelings. But sincerity can only get you so far, Coralee. He's still white; and unless your pussy is the Holy Grail itself, he's not gonna give up his comfortable lifestyle to be with you for the long haul."

It was the exact opposite of what Benjamin had said. Was it all a line? Did he say it just because he was jealous? Maybe love didn't make Benjamin say those pretty words...maybe all he really *did* want was sex! He was always kissing her whenever he saw her, or doing that instead of talking about difficult issues. Admittedly, Coralee loved being kissed and held by him, but there had to be more to a relationship than that!

"He said he loved me," Coralee whispered more to herself than to Freda.

"Oldest trick in the book."

Well *that* was a depressing thought, but Coralee couldn't believe Freda's charge. Benjamin had seemed very genuine in his declaration; but beyond that, Benjamin didn't even have to *say* that in order to get a girl in his bed. He was the quintessential All-American boy who could attract any girl just by looking at her...even the black ones. Freda herself wasn't immune, and neither were many of the black girls she'd heard gossiping after games and such. If any black woman was to cross the color line for someone, it would be for Benjamin Drummond, and *everyone* knew it—even black men. But, of course, it was all theoretical, fancy. Benjamin Drummond wasn't supposed to be attracted to black women. He wasn't supposed to be *serious* about a black woman. He was the harmless white man black men allowed their sisters and girlfriends to fantasize about because it would never—*could* never—come true.

But it had, and the entire equation changed because of it.

"I don't care."

Freda's eyes widened, and Coralee stood straighter against the door. Coralee didn't care. She *wouldn't* care! "They were all in this together," Jermaine said often during their board meetings, and being in anything together meant one had to care. But not this time. Coralee would just flat out not care when it came to *this* aspect of her life. Something had to be for her and her alone, and this would be it. They could call her a white man's whore if they wanted, but damn it, she was going to be happy. Many people waited *lifetimes* to feel what she felt for Benjamin, and he was willing to reciprocate those feelings, even if for a brief moment. She would take it. She would sacrifice her "dignity" for Benjamin because he was worth it, despite what Freda and Patty and anyone else thought. Benjamin had told her *mother* for goodness sake! No amount of desire for sex would make someone tell the girl's *mother* he loved her. That in itself let Coralee know Benjamin was sincere. How long would the love last, she didn't know, but she knew she had the opportunity to be *happy*—and with all there was to be unhappy about, Coralee wasn't going to let this opportunity slide.

"So that's it, then?" Freda asked. Coralee nodded, waiting for the first of her friends to fall by the wayside. Freda chuckled a little bit. "A fool in love, you are."

"A happy fool."

Freda smiled and stood, coming to her friend and framing Coralee's face in her hands. "All right, little Ceelee. I warned you, you heard me, and you're still gonna pursue this. I really, *really* hope he proves me wrong."

"You should hope for that regardless of his color."

Freda nodded. "True...but old habits die hard."

Coralee knew that; she had to wrestle hers into submission, stuff them a box, and sit on the lid. Some days it was harder to contain them than others, but today, she thought it would be a little easier.

"Will you still be my friend?"

Freda laughed and hugged Coralee tightly. "Oh, chile...I promised you the first time we had this discussion I'd be there. Nothing's changed; I just felt you needed another warnin'."

The big "Do Not Cross" sign in front of that color line...Coralee was about to ignore it and go over the barrier—not a tip of her toe across the line for a night, but a full body-and-soul jump.

She hoped Benjamin came with her.

FOURTEEN

Benjamin barricaded himself behind his books, some of them open, many of them not, as he wrote in his notebook everything *but* notes from his texts.

He couldn't care less about the Populist movement in the nineteenth century.

Instead, he was trying to plan something for Coralee on Valentine's Day, and he was certainly going to do *something*. He could send her flowers, but Benjamin wanted to *see* Coralee with less than three feet separating them. As it was, the only times he did see her were across campus or in crowded halls. They hardly had a moment's privacy, and now that football season was over, there was little reason for him to be out of the frat house besides classes or girls. Since he wasn't having problems with classes this semester, that only left girls.

The frat house was little more than a women's beauty parlor, however; nothing was sacred and everything was scrutinized. If anyone discovered he was in love with Coralee, the second Civil War would probably break out soon after.

But still—it was Valentine's Day, and it had to be *perfect*.

"Hey, Drummond—"

Benjamin jumped at the sound of his name, some of his books sliding from their precarious stacks onto the desk or the floor. Felix blushed and muttered an apology for startling him.

"Yeah?" Benjamin huffed as he straightened out his mess. Felix consumed the doorframe, tapping his fingers along the plane as he watched his friend situate himself. Benjamin glanced up at him and tilted his head as if to coax him to speak. "Well?"

"Can we talk?"

Benjamin's eyes darted to his "notes" and he frowned. Maybe he needed a break. "Sure." Felix closed the door and sat on Benjamin's bed. Benjamin turned his chair to face his roommate and grew concerned with Felix's hesitancy. "What's wrong?"

"Dunno...was hopin' you'd tell me..."

"What do you mean?"

Felix sighed, clasping his hands between his legs. "You seem...out of it, dazed. You didn't get a concussion during the last game, did you?"

"No," Benjamin said on a slight laugh. "No, I'm fine."

Felix nodded, unclasping his hands to drum his fingers against each other. "Does it have to do with that colored girl from the party?"

It was Benjamin's turn to clasp his hands and he looked at his friend with a guarded expression. "What colored girl?"

"I'm not simple, Benny. I saw how you stared at her the entire party; others did too. Some were even taking bets you had scored that night. Who was she?"

Benjamin cleared his throat, his grip on his books tightening dangerously. "She was my tutor during the semester, helpin' get my grades up so the season would count."

Felix nodded. "Who else is she?"

"An old friend, you know that."

Felix nodded his head again and exhaled slowly. "You know, Benjamin...I'm not like the other guys here. It seems you've been carrying this weight on your shoulders for weeks now, and it has something to do with her. If you ever need to talk, *ever*, I'm right here."

The opening he needed, but could Benjamin take it? There was something...romantic about keeping his feelings strictly between him and Coralee, but he also knew he needed to tell someone, just in case. It never worked anyway, keeping a secret this big and significant from people; he was bound to let it slip, and probably to the wrong person. Benjamin knew Felix was trustworthy and held more tolerance in his pinky than most in the frat house held in their entire bodies.

Just when Felix was about to leave, Benjamin spoke. "I love her."

He sat back down slowly, a half-grin on his face. "Is that right?"

Benjamin laughed, already feeling thirty pounds lighter after the confession. "Yeah, leave it to me to fall in love with a colored girl!"

"Well, she seems really nice—when we're not being jerks to her, that is!"

Benjamin stared at a spot on the floor, a grin unconsciously taking over his face. "The best. She's everything to me."

"So...what're y'all gonna do?"

Benjamin looked at his hands, knowing his shrug wasn't an adequate answer. Going public was out of the question, but so was having a relationship in the lurking shadows. He wanted to take Coralee to dances, restaurants, the park, the movies...everywhere he would go if he dated a white woman. It was dangerous, though, and Benjamin wanted to keep Coralee safe.

"Got any suggestions on what I *could* do?" Benjamin asked his friend. "Because I'm certainly at a loss."

It was Felix's turn to shrug. "You could leave her alone."

Benjamin glared at his friend. "I thought *you* of *all people*—"

"I'm not saying it because it bothers me—that's not it at all!—but it *does* bother a whole lot of other people—white *and* black. And you know who they'll take out their anger on? Coralee. And as much as you wish you could, you can't fight the entire campus by yourself."

Benjamin sighed, his mind immediately going to Tommy and Randy. "I can't leave her alone, Felix. You saw me try—what an absolute failure that was!"

"You *were* pretty pathetic," Felix said on a chuckle. "But you're a guy in love. Who *would* want to let go of their woman, no matter what color she is?"

"It shouldn't *matter* what color she is."

Felix snorted. "Don't tell me you've suddenly become naïve. You forget where you are?"

Benjamin hadn't. He knew he was from Plumville, knew its history, and Coralee would talk about how black people were still scratching for rights they should've gotten long before now. He remembered Patty grieving the news of Martin Luther King, Jr. and Robert Kennedy's assassinations, and his mother's reproachful sniff while watching the race riots breaking out everywhere on television last summer. He and his father had even had many discussions about his court cases; and while at first it'd been only passing interest as a prospective judge, being with Coralee made Benjamin realize these concerns were real, valid, and very important. Too bad none of his peers did.

"I say do what you have to do, Benny," Felix advised finally. "But remember where you are...people can get hurt. This isn't just a case of lust. Love's involved, and that's a risky thing. White men just don't love black women..."

But I do, Benjamin thought as Felix left him alone in the room again. He turned back to his notebook and stared at it briefly before ripping out the page and clumping it into a tight ball. He needed to prove it, *especially* to Coralee. This was not some passing fancy of lust...he meant what he said to her the night of the party, and damn it, Coralee would believe him.

ை

Meet me at the front gate at 6:30...wear your best dress.

I love you.

Coralee pressed the note to her chest, her heart beating wildly. This Valentine's Day had been very quiet until now; in fact, she hadn't expected anything. However, she should have known Benjamin wouldn't let the day go by without doing *something*. The note had come with a large, beautiful bouquet of pink azaleas—her favorite flower. She'd been breathless when she walked into her room to see the arrangement sitting on her desk, and couldn't stop the large smile from spreading on her face.

"I can't believe you have a boyfriend, Cora!"

Coralee chuckled at Trish's remark. "I can't believe it, either, to tell you the truth."

"Is it Nick?" Trish asked, sitting down excitedly on her bed and pulling one of her legs into her lap.

Coralee bit her bottom lip and shook her head, smelling her flowers again. She couldn't tell Trish her boyfriend was Benjamin Drummond! It would be all over campus in seconds.

"Oh, *I see...*" Trish said giggling slightly. "You want to keep it a *secret*! Oh, that's so romantic!"

"Yeah...we want to keep it to ourselves for a while," Coralee affirmed with a small smile. "You know how this campus is; once everyone knows, people watch you like a hawk!"

"That's true, isn't it? White people know who coloreds are datin' and coloreds know who white people are datin'...you know what? I don't blame you. You don't have to tell me, but we should find you the perfect dress for tonight!"

Coralee grinned, then paused. "How do you know about that?" The other woman had the decency to blush, but Coralee waved away the question. "Doesn't matter."

"So can I?"

"Can you what?"

"Help! Get you out those cardigans and shapeless skirts..."

Coralee felt uneasy, but allowed her roommate to help her get ready for her date. "What about you?" Coralee asked, remembering when Benjamin and his friend had visited.

Trish's smile shrank a little. "I have a date too! It's not Drummond, but Tommy Birch has the prettiest brown eyes..."

Coralee winced internally, but didn't have time to wallow in her guilt as Trish had pulled her in front of a mirror. There was much primping, frustrated sighs, incredulous looks, and even laughs, until finally they found the perfect outfit. It was actually Trish's dress, and Coralee never thought her roommate would be so kind to as loan it to her. Considering it was sleeveless with only thin straps holding up the bodice, Coralee insisted on a cardigan, and the yellow garment softened the black dress. Trish also had convinced Coralee out of her traditional chignon, and pulled the upper half of her hair back while the bottom fell free around her shoulders.

"Knock his socks off," Trish whispered and handed her a purse. Coralee smiled at her roommate, then left for the front gate.

When she arrived, she didn't see anyone, and she checked her watch to make sure she wasn't late. Though nervous, she tried calming herself by thinking of the nice night Benjamin had somehow planned.

Luckily, her wait wasn't long, and he pulled up in his father's Cadillac. She smiled at him and went to the door, shaking her head when he tried to get out of the car. When she got inside, he immediately pressed a kiss to her cheek.

"You're beautiful," he said softly.

Coralee gave a hesitant laugh and tucked her hair behind her ear. She wasn't used to it being so free; it made her feel self-conscious. "It was Trish's idea."

"Good idea, but you're beautiful with your hair up or down."

She looked at him as he pulled the car from the curb. His movements were efficient and smooth, and when he glanced her way, she averted her gaze quickly, ashamed at being caught staring. He chuckled and reached over to grasp her hand.

"I hope you like where we're going," he said, squeezing her hand.

"Where *are* we going?"

"You'll see...you'll love it..."

Coralee settled into her seat, her hand lightly holding onto Benjamin's as the car made the drive down the dimly lit road. The scenery was becoming unfamiliar, but she trusted Benjamin. Given they couldn't just show up in a random restaurant, their options were limited, and any time with Benjamin was better than none at all.

Soon they were pulling up to a handsome boarding house with a small B&B sign out front. Benjamin pulled in the parking lot and helped her out car, telling her to wait as he went to the back seat and pulled out a basket.

Coralee chuckled. "You *cooked*?!"

Benjamin grinned and pressed a kiss to her temple. "I helped...Miss Barbara is a patient teacher, just like Aunt Patty."

They walked up the backstairs arm in arm; Coralee figured he had already paid for wherever they were going. A shiver of anticipation went up her spine, and she gasped when Benjamin opened the door to their room.

A tiny table with a white linen tablecloth draped over it stood in the center with two complete table settings and two unlit candlesticks. Azaleas were everywhere of every different color and a banner on the wall read "Happy Valentine's Day!"

She couldn't believe he'd gone through all this trouble, and she hid her face in her hands to keep him from seeing her tears.

"Oh," he whispered, removing her hands and cupping her face instead. His thumbs caught her tears and he kissed her forehead. "I hope this means you're happy."

"Very. I never expected all of this."

He smiled, his blue eyes full of love and understanding. "That's why I'm here, darlin', to make you happy. You're not a passing fancy to me, okay?"

She nodded and hugged him tightly, just needing to feel him. He obliged her willingly, his warm, large hands rubbing up and down her back as he whispered words of comfort and encouragement.

"Who helped you with this," she asked, pulling back slightly but not leaving his arms.

His arms tightened around her as he dropped a kiss to her nose. "Miss Barbara...my dad...Felix..."

Coralee tensed in his arms and her eyes widened. "They know about me?!"

"Yes, well, not Miss Barbara, but she likes me, so she automatically likes whomever I like."

Coralee rubbed his forearms and bit her lips. She didn't know this Felix character, and Benjamin's father...well, he was a smart man and generally fair. Besides, if they helped Benjamin with this, didn't that mean they approved somewhat?

"Hungry?" Benjamin asked softly. "I don't want the food getting cold."

She nodded and went to the basket. Benjamin tsked at her, grasping her arm gently and sat her down at the table. He spread out the food, her mouth watering at the roast beef, mashed potatoes, gravy, and string beans. She even got a glimpse of apple pie and her stomach rumbled in approval.

"This looks good," Coralee said, putting her napkin in her lap as he lit the candles.

"Miss Barbara is an excellent cook, Ceelee," Benjamin promised, and began putting food on her plate.

The dinner never lacked conversation, and they talked about anything and everything—their childhood, current friends, classes, family, Benjamin's plans upon graduation—and Coralee enjoyed her Valentine's meal very much.

"Finished?" Benjamin asked as she slipped the last piece of her pie between her lips. She nodded as she chewed and watched him remove the plate from the table and put it in the picnic basket. He had done everything during the dinner, not even letting her reach down to retrieve her napkin when it slipped from her lap!

"This was very sweet. Thank you, Benny."

He smiled, his blue eyes bright amid the low light. "We're not done yet, honey." He went to the 45 on the dresser and put on a record. "When a Man Loves a Woman" started playing, and Coralee couldn't help the blush creeping up her cheeks. He eased her chair from the table and grasped her hand tenderly. For some reason, Coralee couldn't look him in the eyes, so she settled for his heart instead. When he pulled her into his arms, she rested her head against his chest and closed her eyes, letting the music and his love wash over her.

They barely moved, really just hugging and swaying in time with the music. His thumb caressed the small of her back and he pressed tiny kisses atop her head. In his arms, she could forget their different races and the fact they weren't supposed to be together. He was just a man, she was just a woman, and they were in love—nothing more and nothing less—and it felt good.

The record ended but their embrace didn't. One of his hands tangled into her free hair, pulling it aside so he could drop a kiss to the side of her neck. Coralee sighed blissfully, whispering his name on a breath as his mouth moved from her neck to her ear. His tongue darted out and licked the curve of her ear right before closing his teeth around it gently.

Her breath caught in her throat and she began to smolder; so when his hands moved to the buttons of her cardigan, she didn't stop him from undoing them. He pushed the cardigan from her shoulders, his lips going to the newly bared skin as his hands slid the sleeves from her arms.

"Benny," she whispered, shivering when she felt his tongue touch her collarbone. He stopped his kisses, and she barely contained her moan of displeasure. If she had known saying his name would make him stop, she would've kept her mouth shut.

Benjamin stared at her, his eyes expressionless, and Coralee began to fidget. It was all she could do not to shrug the cardigan back on her shoulders, and she was hit with the thought he'd suddenly realized she had little experience with lovemaking and had found her completely lacking.

"What's wrong?" she asked, her voice not as strong as she wished.

"This isn't right," he whispered even as he cupped her cheek.

Coralee bit her lip and dropped her eyes so he couldn't see the tears gathering there. "I see," Coralee said finally, quietly, and started backing out of his embrace. Benjamin wouldn't let her, his grip strong and tender at the same time.

"Do you?" he asked, his tone still soft. His eyes locked with hers, and she was enchanted by the candlelight dancing in them. "Do you see how you deserve more than I can give you? More than I'm *allowed* to give you?"

Coralee blinked, not expecting that. Her jaw dropped slightly as her mind tried to process his questions, but all she could think of was, "What?"

A corner of his mouth curved, and he kissed her lightly...slowly. "You deserve kisses every time I see you, your hand held every time I touch you, my declaration of love every time I talk to you, but I can't. I'm supposed to treat you like you don't matter; and yet, you're *all* that matters to me. You don't deserve this."

Coralee didn't know what to say. She placed her palms flat against his cheeks and brought his head down so her forehead could rest against his. "Benny..."

Benjamin kissed her nose and nuzzled it with his. "I'm not good enough for you."

"Don't say that," Coralee admonished gently. "It's not your fault things are the way they are!"

"But I haven't done enough to change anything," Benjamin insisted, reaching up and lacing his fingers through hers. He brought the backs of her hands to his lips and placed a long kiss upon them. "I want to be with you, but not like this—not as if I'm ashamed of you."

Her heart hurt, and she took a few deep breaths before asking her question. "Did you plan all of this to break up with me?" It didn't matter that the rational side of her thought maybe it was for the best, she hoped this beautiful dinner wasn't done to soften the blow of a broken relationship!

He kissed her lips, more insistently this time. Her eyes remained closed when he pulled away. "No, I planned all this so you know I'm never leaving you. I'm with you forever."

"Forever is a long time."

"I know. Aren't we lucky it is?"

Coralee laughed slightly. "Don't be so hasty—you're only twenty-two years old! Besides, what if you meet someone else?"

"Of *course* I'll meet someone else; you will too. We'll meet new people all the time—especially when I'm state judge!"

Coralee rolled her eyes and he laughed. Stupid boy knew what she meant! "You're not being realistic."

"Who says that can't be our reality, Ceelee?"

Oh, how she wanted it to be, but she'd long resigned herself to the impossibility of it. She'd learned fairytales weren't for black women, and her ability to dream lessened with each year she lived. Fantasies were dangerous siren calls that could get a girl like her into trouble.

But she was flirting with trouble anyway as Benjamin pressed a delicate kiss to the inside of her wrist. Those blue eyes stared at her with love and assurance, and Coralee felt a tiny part of her start to believe in the reality he wanted for them.

"How?"

Another kiss to her wrist. "I haven't quite figured that out yet, but I'm workin' on it."

"I'm not sure I'm worth all the—"

"You are," he said seriously, kissing her palm this time. "Don't ever consider yourself not worthy, either."

"I'm just tellin' you not to try and change the world for me. You're one man, Benjamin."

"And you're my woman, Coralee," he replied. "Why shouldn't I want the world to be the best it could be?"

Coralee didn't respond. Benjamin hugged her close, inhaling deeply and kissing the crown of her head.

"We'll figure somethin' out, darlin'," he promised.

"Baby steps, Benny," Coralee warned him. "Not even the world was built in a day. Took God six."

"I hear you, Ceelee," he conceded, pulling back to look into her eyes. His bottom lip went between his teeth as his fingers combed through her free hair. Her fingers touched his cheeks and he gave her a small smile. That smile had always made her heart beat fast, but when she was five she hadn't understood why.

Though Benjamin was a man now, there was still some of the boy she first fell in love with all those years ago—particularly his idealism. He knew the way of the world but thought he could actually change it; yet wasn't he being groomed to do just that— enforce the laws or even make them fairer? Perhaps he *could* make good on his promise...even if it happened decades from now.

"What's goin' on in that pretty head o' yours?" he asked quietly, kissing her forehead for emphasis.

Coralee smiled, still caressing his cheeks with her fingertips. "How much you've changed...and how much you haven't. Even when we were younger, you looked out for me."

"You were my best friend, Ceelee; you still are."

"It's funny," she began, sliding her hands from his face to wrap around his neck. "If I were white, I think Miss Florence would be pushing us to get married by now."

"She would...and for once I wouldn't try to change the subject, either," Benny admitted with a smile.

Coralee rolled her eyes. "You crazy!"

"Maybe, but I can't lie and say I haven't imagined what our children would look like, if they would have your eyes, my hair, a combination of our skin color...I think they'd be beautiful."

Coralee kissed him then, a full one that had her flush against him. Her fingers tangled into his hair and she stood on the balls of her feet, their teeth clanking together as they tried to steal each other's breath. When his tongue touched hers, she sighed, relishing in the rough texture of it and his hands rubbing up and down her bare arms.

Suddenly he was walking backwards and falling into a chair, pulling her down with him. Not breaking the kiss, she straddled his hips, moaning when she felt his arms go around her waist. Underneath her, Coralee felt his *reaction* growing as it had before and tried to move to accommodate it, only to get a groan from him in response.

"Don't be so rough with it," he mumbled against her lips.

Coralee froze and gave a little squeak, breaking the kiss abruptly. "I'm sorry!" She hid her face in her hands and started sliding down his lap, completely mortified.

He laughed, one hand removing hers from her mouth while the other tightened around her waist and brought her back to him. He kissed her again, nipping her bottom lip gently with his teeth and said, "You're so innocent."

"Innocent?"

"You've never been intimate with someone before."

Coralee glared at him even as her cheeks reddened. "Don't look so smug about it!"

He tucked hair behind her ear and kissed her cheek. "It's hard not to, honey, to know I'm gonna be your first and only...I feel like the king of the world."

"Does that mean I should feel like any other woman? Because I know I'm not your first..."

"You're the first black girl—"

"Tryin' to see if the rumors are true, eh?"

He eyed her. "Don't be that way, Coralee. You know that's not what I meant, and just because you're not my first doesn't mean it won't be special. You're the first one I'll actually make love to...I haven't done that with anyone else." His hands moved to the small of her back, and his hardness seared her center.

Her thighs tightened about his, trying to curb the urge to rock her hips against him. "Did you...plan on this happenin' tonight?" she asked, playing with the collar of his pale yellow buttoned-down shirt. The sports jacket he'd worn had since been draped on the back of the chair he'd sat in during dinner, and his black slacks were soft—some sort of cotton. She smiled to herself; they'd matched without really trying to do so.

"I want to do whatever you want, honey," he whispered, dipping his head to lock eyes with her. "There's no pressure."

She wiggled in his lap. "Well, there's *some*..."

He chuckled as he kissed her. "Naughty."

"Your fault."

"This 'pressure' is actually *your* fault."

Her thumb caressed his bottom lip as she rubbed his nose with hers. "All I'm doing is sitting here—"

"On my *lap*, looking as sexy as you are...and you're wet."

Her face flamed. She'd never considered herself sexy, nor had anyone ever called her that. Yet his blue eyes were darker than usual; and when he licked his lips, she couldn't suppress the shiver that went through her.

His hands began rubbing her thighs, and her breathing deepened, her back arching slightly. His eyes never left hers, but his hands grew bolder, coming up her sides and underneath her arms.

Benjamin gave her an open-mouthed kiss, his eyes still locked with hers and his hands sliding back down her sides. Coralee grew restless, shifting her hips to relieve the pressure that was building inside her.

"Coralee," Benjamin breathed, his mouth going to her jaw and down her neck. Her name coming from his lips made her shiver, and when his hands slid underneath her skirt, she groaned.

"Please," she said brokenly, vaguely aware of what she was demanding. His hands were so nice and warm on her bare thigh, and the naughtiness she felt only enhanced her excitement.

"'Please' what, Little Ceelee?" he murmured into her neck. His hands slid higher up her thighs to her panties, flirting with the lace around her upper hip. "Do you want me to touch you?"

He was baiting her, Coralee realized, but he'd promised not to go any further than she allowed...and she wanted him touching her, wanted to feel his fingers at that special part of her, so she nodded.

"Look at me," he commanded gently, and she complied. When she felt his index finger press against the damp crotch of her panties, she shuddered, biting her lip and looking at him with glazed eyes.

"Benjamin," she whispered, her eyes drifting shut as another finger joined in the caress. She writhed in his lap, small little movements meant to coax his fingers where she'd been told good girls didn't allow boys to go. Yet right then, she craved the intoxicating sensations his touch created more.

"Honey, open your eyes," Benjamin cajoled. "Let me see those pretty brown eyes..."

He was touching her! His fingers had slipped under her panties and touched her *there*. Coralee gasped, her eyes widening and meeting his wildly. She began moving her hips, now unsure if she were fleeing from his fingers or inviting them.

"Relax, baby," Benjamin crooned.

"I can't," she whispered. How could she when she felt on fire? His fingers were wicked, and when one slipped inside her, she gave a very feminine squeal of surprise and arousal.

Benjamin answering groan vibrated against her chest, making her nipples harden. "I love you," he whispered, kissing her lips gently. "It's okay, Coralee...let go..."

"Let go?" Let go of what? She couldn't let go of him; she'd collapse in a disgraceful heap if she did!

"Just feel...feel the pleasure wash over you..."

Coralee couldn't, though, couldn't let him see her lose control, but she was so close. She grasped the back of his neck tightly and rested her forehead against his, her hips moving with the rhythm his fingers set.

He began kissing her again and his fingers moved faster. So did her hips, and then he found her bundle of nerves above her entrance.

"Oh, Ben—"

"Come for me, honey," Benjamin urged against her lips, his thumb running over the nubbin as his fingers thrust in and out of her.

She sighed her release into his mouth and drenched his hand, and she vaguely registered him shuddering beneath her as well.

They sat together, breathing heavily, trying to regain their composure and bearings. Benjamin pressed tiny kisses to her mouth, telling her his love, and she repeated the declarations, her fingers caressing the back of his head.

"I never thought..." Coralee trailed off, chuckling slightly.

"I didn't plan this, Ceelee," Benjamin said, "but you were so beautiful—"

"I'm not mad, Benny," she reassured him. "I'm just sorry I made a mess of your pants."

He blushed and grinned. "You're not the only one who did!"

They laughed, foreheads pressed together and arms tight around each other. This was pleasure, too, being with one another. This had been the most perfect Valentine's Day she'd ever experienced, and she wouldn't forget it anytime soon.

"Perhaps you should take off the pants so I can rinse them," Coralee suggested, rising from his lap to stand on shaky legs.

"You just want to get me naked."

She rolled her eyes and crossed her arms in front of her. "I won't even dignify that with a response, though I think it'll be embarrassing to go back to the frat house with a stain on your pants."

Pink tinged his cheeks. "Good point, but what about my boxers?"

It was her turn to blush, but she chuckled. "You plan on lettin' your brothers see your boxers, Benny? Somethin' I should know about that goes on in that house o' yours?"

He scowled at her and shimmied out of his pants, Coralee turning to give him privacy, then handed the garment to her. She stared at them with a frown.

"What's wrong?"

She gave him a shy glance. "I think I should do the same to Trish's dress...however, I cannot parade around in my underthings."

He unbuttoned his shirt and handed it to her, leaving him clad in boxers and an undershirt. "It should cover all the necessary parts."

Coralee smiled and accepted the offering, whispering, "Excuse me," as she went to the bathroom. She filled the sink with warm water and used the bar of soap to clean the stains as best she could. After scrubbing and rinsing, she hung the garments on hooks so they could dry, then slipped on Benjamin's shirt. It did cover everything, but left her legs exposed.

"Beggars can't be choosers," she whispered as she left the bathroom. When she entered the main room again, she noticed Benjamin pulling down the covers of the bed and she smiled a little. "So this turned into a sleepover, huh?"

Benjamin smirked at the sight of her. "You look better in my shirt than I do."

"Do not," Coralee insisted, but was flattered by his look and his compliment all the same. Benjamin pulled her in his arms and kissed her temple. "Hope you don't mind sharing a bed for the night."

"After all this you've done, I don't reckon you should sleep on the floor," Coralee conceded teasingly.

Benjamin chuckled, grasping her chin and kissing her lips. "Which side would you like?"

She chose the side closest to the open space, so Benjamin crawled in first. When Coralee settled next to him, he immediately enveloped her in his arms, nipping the shell of her ear and running his fingers through her hair.

"This was the best Valentine's ever, Benny," she said softly, relishing in the feel of his hand around her middle. He tangled his legs with hers.

"Mine too. I love you, Coralee," he said into her temple.

Coralee lifted the hand from her middle to kiss the back of it. "I love you, too, Benjamin. Goodnight."

Benjamin extinguished the lamp on his nightstand and the room fell into darkness. "Goodnight honey, sweet dreams."

FIFTEEN

Gentle light poured into the room at a foreign angle, and for a moment, Benjamin was disoriented. He rolled to the left, the side of the bed he usually got out from, but found a warm body instead.

A soft body...*her* body.

This certainly didn't help dampen his customary morning erection, especially since the usual phantom cause of it was materialized next to him in bed. He wiggled his fingers experimentally, feeling the buttons of his shirt she wore, then became bolder and slid them in between the closures to touch her skin. He closed his eyes and counted to ten at the feel of her, then scooted closer to look over her shoulder at her face.

She was asleep, her cheek resting on her arm and lightly snoring. *Adorable* was the only word that could adequately describe her. Her hair was free upon the pillow looking softer than cotton, and her full lips were slightly parted as breath slipped in and out of her body. He dropped a kiss on her shoulder so not to disturb her.

However she stirred anyway, her hand rubbing his that was on her stomach, and turned onto her back slowly. The smile she gave him made his breath catch; there was something surreally beautiful about waking up next to her.

"Good mornin'," she said, her voice a bit raspy and deeper than he'd anticipated.

He was robbed of speech, so he did the next best thing and kissed her. She scrunched up her nose and giggled.

"I can't believe you did that!"

"What?"

She still frowned, doing little to make her less adorable in his eyes. "I have mornin' breath! And I'm sure I look a fright—" He kissed her again, not wanting to hear the rubbish coming from her pretty mouth. When he pulled back her eyes were soft, and the backs of her fingers stroked his cheek. "But you don't care, do you?"

"Seein' as none of those things apply to you, I don't see why I should."

She rolled her eyes and chuckled, worrying her bottom lip between her teeth. "Can I tell you a secret?"

He nodded, shifting so his chin rested on her shoulder. His fingers grazed her side idly, and his erection twitched at the feel of her skin trembling underneath them. "I've wondered what this would feel like...waking up with you beside me...but actually doing it doesn't compare to what I thought."

"I hope that's a good thing," he asked, his deep voice rumbling in the quiet room.

She smiled softly at him, her hand grasping the hand at her side and intertwining their fingers. "Very good. Your eyes are so blue in the mornin', Benny..."

"Coralee..." he whispered and kissed her tenderly. Her free hand cupped his cheek, pressing him closer to her, and he could do nothing but oblige. He settled fully on top of her, her legs opening to cradle him between her thighs. Benjamin's hands trailed up her thigh, a moan coming from her, and his erection hardened further from the sound.

He had to stop before things went too far...went to the place he had wanted them to go since before last night. Benjamin broke the kiss with a small smile, once again caught breathless by the sight of hers. His eyes dragged close as she slid her hand from his cheek to his head, drawing him down for another kiss.

Again, he broke it, not sure if he were strong enough to be a gentleman now that they were in a bed and partially clothed. Her body felt so good against his...so *right*, that it was all he could do not to press himself fully against her.

"I like this," Coralee said, her grin still in place, her fingers running through his hair. "You feel so good...."

Benny groaned and buried his face in her neck, inhaling the sweet scent of her. She was trying to kill him.

"Ceelee, we gotta stop," he said, trying to insert authority in his voice, knowing it was futile because she had him under her complete control.

"Do we have to leave?"

Technically, they did, but he couldn't even if he wanted to do so, his body—*her* body—making it impossible. "I'm only a man, Ceelee."

"I know you're a man...I can feel the evidence of it against my inner thigh!"

"Oh, you think you're funny," he growled, his eyes lighting up as he began tickling her. She squealed and thrashed around, clamping her thighs tightly around him and trying to capture his arms, but instead he captured hers, throwing them above her head and kissing her soundly. Her giggles tumbled into his mouth and he gladly took them, wanting to taste her joy and feeling humbled he was the cause of it.

Soon, however, the kiss turned from playful to passionate, and he started gliding his torso along hers. He slid his hands from hers down her arms, his mouth going from her lips to her shoulder.

"Love you," he murmured against her skin, his tongue licking her neck.

Her breathing became shallow, and he made his way back to her mouth, dropping small, light kisses upon it. His fingers undid the buttons of her shirt, exposing her dark-brown skin to his lips and tongue.

"Want you," he breathed, nuzzling her collarbone with his nose.

"Benny..."

The way she said his name made Benjamin think sex was probably not even necessary to find completion. No one said it the way she did, as if she were praying, pleading, and commanding him all at the same time. He would grant all of her requests happily.

Benjamin glided his lips along the upper curve of her breast, and Coralee brought him closer. He was seeing an entirely new side to her...and it was making him lose control. He never imagined Coralee being so responsive, so willing. He thought it would take a long time for her to open up to him sexually, but there had been some heavy moments between them before this point.

She was also the first woman with whom he was totally about her. This wasn't to say he'd been selfish with other girls, but he'd expected reciprocity. With Coralee, his pleasure came only if she was having pleasure. He lived to hear her caught breaths, her sighs, those cute little sounds that came from the back of her throat. He wasn't satisfied unless she was.

"I'm right here, baby," he whispered against her sternum, his fingers undoing the last button. He locked eyes with her as he spread the shirt away from her body, her eyes widening slightly as he did.

"Benny?"

Her voice was laced with uncertainty, curiosity, and a healthy dose of arousal. He said nothing, kissing her chin first, then trailing down to the valley of her breasts. Benjamin caressed the area with his nose and inhaled, growing addicted to her scent...to *her*...he knew he would never recover.

"Who knew you'd grow into such a body," he whispered, his hands cupping her breasts. They spilled over the sides of his hands, and the nipples tightened into hard buds. His thumbs flicked over them and they grew harder, reminding him of Hershey Kisses.

He wondered if they tasted as sweet...

When his tongue touched her nipple, Coralee groaned so hard he almost came right then. Her body became supple underneath his hands. He dragged his eyes closed and sucked her nipple harder, she slid her leg up his and bucked underneath him, the damp heat of her firm against his hardness.

She was gorgeous; her movements and her sounds almost brought him to his wits' end. And her body...she was sweetness personified. His fingers couldn't stop touching her...*wouldn't* stop touching her, and they slid lower, flirting with the edge of her panties.

"Benny," she whispered, grasping his undershirt and tugging, wanting him to be just as topless as she was.

He didn't even consider denying her request, removing his mouth from her only long enough to rid his body of his shirt. Instead of going back to her breasts, he moved south, licking around her belly button. Her brown skin captivated him, skin so different from his own, so unfamiliar, but he desired to know everything about it.

"I've often dreamed of you," he revealed, his breath tickling her navel. "Dreamed of what you'd be like underneath me...how our skin would look against each other...we were beautiful then, and we're beautiful now."

"*You're* beautiful," she said, running her hands through his hair and along his face.

Benjamin closed his eyes at her caress, loving the feel of her fingers against his skin. Normally he would balk at a man being called such, but from Coralee, he embraced it.

"If I'm beautiful, it's because of you," he murmured into her tummy. His lips flirted with the edge of her panties, and Coralee snickered.

"Really? I'd think Mr. and Mrs. Drummond had something to do with that—"

"Please don't bring my parents into this right now," he said on a slight chuckle.

"Sorry."

He kissed her belly again, resting his chin on it and looked at her with a soft smile. "Don't worry about it."

They just stared at each other then, he caressing her upper thighs and she running her fingers through his hair. It almost seemed natural they were like this, sharing a bed and exploring each other as they were. Benjamin's eyes drifted closed at her ministrations, so close to purring like a cat because her fingers felt so good. He kissed his way up her body again, making sure to suckle each nipple, before burrowing his head in the crook of her neck and wrapping his arms around her. He didn't want to go any further today; he was content right where they were.

"That's it?" she asked after a few minutes.

"You want there to be more?" he asked, tilting his head to look into her eyes.

Her fingers tickled the skin behind his ears; and after a moment, her head nodded slowly.

Benjamin shivered at the contact even as he slid a hand down her body and underneath her underwear, her coarse hair tickling his palm. "It's only natural for you to feel the way you're feeling." His finger brushed against the nubbin ever so gently, and Coralee gasped, her eyes locking with his with shocked arousal.

"*Benjamin,*" she groaned, her fingernails digging into his biceps.

Her eyes rolled into the back of her head when his finger slid into her. She was so moist, making the entrance easy, yet her walls immediately clamped around it. Her hips began moving with the rhythm of his fingers, her hands clenched his shoulders.

"You're so tight, Ceelee," Benjamin whispered against her collarbone. He wanted her to know exactly how he felt inside of her...how he'd made her feel. "You're so warm and tight and wet..."

Coralee's hips moved faster. "Take them off," she whispered.

For a split second, Benjamin forgot how to breathe. Surely she didn't mean—"Take them off? Your panties?"

Her feminine muscles clenched around his finger. "*Ooh...*"

He bucked his hips into the mattress, swallowing his groan. "You want me to see you, Little Ceelee?"

It took her a second, but eventually she nodded. "Please, Benny..."

The lust in her eyes was astounding, turning her brown eyes black as he pulled the garment down her legs and over her feet. His hands grasped her ankles and played with the knot of bone at the center of them. Coralee let out a shuddering breath, lifting her hips towards his.

"Do you know how beautiful you are, Ceelee? How hot you're makin' me? How hard?" Benjamin whispered against her calf. Her eyes were glazed and she shook her head.

"Benny—"

"I wanna make you feel good, darlin'," he interrupted, his hand sliding from her ankle to her inner thigh, the backs of his fingers brushing against her center. "Am I makin' you feel good?"

"Kiss me," she pleaded, already pulling his head to hers. He complied eagerly, his tongue surging inside her mouth as he slipped two fingers inside her. His tongue mimicked those fingers, and Coralee whimpered.

The entire world was centered around his fingers. Benjamin broke the kiss and stared into her face, manipulating his digits to get her eyes to widen ever so slightly, for that sexy breathless gasp to come from her mouth. He wanted to feel that mouth on him...on his neck, his nipples, his stomach, his manhood. Benjamin figured now probably wasn't the time for all of that, but that couldn't stop him from dreaming...

"Do you feel good, Benjamin?" Coralee asked suddenly, and the concern in her eyes on his behalf made him love her even more.

"Yes, baby, I feel really good," Benjamin said, dropping a chaste kiss to her mouth.

"Really? I haven't been doin' anything—"

"Your responses have been more than enough, honey," Benjamin said sincerely. "Your whimpers and moans, the way you move, the way you bite your lips, your darkened eyes—knowin' I did all that to you makes me feel *really* good, baby."

"Do you want to do more?"

His boxers became too tight at that question, and he rubbed his erection against the bed to alleviate some of the tension. "Is that an invitation?"

His fingers moved slightly inside her and her breath caught. She glanced at the ceiling and closed her eyes, as if desperate to regain her bearings. "I mean...um, I can touch you like you're touchin' me..."

Benjamin shook his head. He wouldn't be able to last if she touched him...but he was willing to take that risk. "You sure, baby? Don't wanna startle you."

"Fair's fair, right?" she asked, even as her hand slid beneath his boxers.

The feel of her small, hot hand on his bottom made Benjamin groan into Coralee's shoulder, and he lifted his hips, allowing her hand to move to the front of him. They were no more than a breath apart, but their eyes widened when her hand closed around him.

"Ceelee—"

"It's so different from me," she whispered, her lips brushing against his. Benjamin knew he was so hard, hot, and heavy in her hand. Her thumb rubbed across the tip of him, disturbing a drop of moisture there. "You get wet too?"

"Not in the same way," he ground out as her fingers ghosted over his manhood, trailing a prominent vein from the tip to the base of him.

"I gotta tell you a secret," she said, peering at him through her eyelashes.

"What's that?"

"When I was younger...about second grade, I touched a boy underneath the table in the library...and he touched me."

"Naughty girl."

"No. Curious."

"Are you curious now?"

"A little...but I think I'm more naughty than curious." And then she squeezed him, sliding her hand back up his shaft to rub her thumb around the tip again.

Benjamin slammed his lips against hers, his fingers busier than they were before and his thumb joining in the action, worrying the nerves above her entrance. Her hand sped up in response, and soon there was nothing but frenzied fingers and hands and breathless moans.

When Coralee broke the kiss and looked at him wildly, he knew she was close. He doubled his efforts and stroked her nub even harder.

"Benjamin," she breathed and he groaned. Something about hearing his full name from her at that moment got him so aroused.

"Say it again," he demanded, biting her upper lip. "Say my name again."

She dragged her eyes closed, moving her hips so his fingers could go deeper. "Benjamin..."

He moved his mouth from her lips to her breasts, suckling her as he worked his hand even more. She was no less busy, pumping him with faster, surer strokes that had his body begging for release.

"I'm almost there," he announced, letting her nipple slide from his mouth and resting his forehead on her shoulder. She squeezed him, and he delved deeper, feeling her body begin to shake.

"Benny—Benjami—Ben—"

"I love you," he whispered in her ear.

Apparently, that was all Coralee needed; and with a small gasp, she exploded. Her hand gripped him hard and tugged, and he climaxed as well, closing his eyes and falling against the pillow next to her head.

They took deep breaths before removing their hands from each other, and Benjamin used the bed sheet to wipe their hands before linking their fingers and bringing them to his chest. Coralee looked numbly from the ceiling to his eyes, and graced him with a small half-smile.

"Thank you," she said, chuckling a little when he nuzzled his nose against hers.

"No, baby," he said, kissing her lips lightly. "Thank *you*."

ᔕ

Benjamin whistled, a bounce in his step, as he entered the frat house. He'd just returned from his Valentine's Day festivities after dropping off Coralee first—a process that took almost an hour because he couldn't stop kissing her—before driving the car home to change his clothes. Aunt Patty had been there, and she didn't ask him any embarrassing questions, merely looking at him with a pointed, parental curiosity and asking if he wanted breakfast. Benjamin had mumbled a no and avoided her eyes. Though he and Coralee hadn't had made love, he wouldn't tell his girlfriend's mother how close they *had been.*

"And just *where have you been?*" came the mock-feminized voice from the living room.

He deflated, falling flat-footed onto his feet, as he saw just about all of his frat brothers convened before him.

Benjamin cut his eyes to the ceiling. "Stopped by to see my old man...is that a problem?" This was the last thing he expected or wanted, the guys waiting and ready to hear juicy details he would never tell.

"You didn't come home last night," Peter said. The other brothers heckled Benjamin and he rolled his eyes.

"So what? I'm not the first and I certainly won't be the last—"

"You weren't with Trish, though," Tommy said with a smirk. "I know that because she was with me..." The boys hollered and hooted at that, and Benjamin took that opportunity to go upstairs.

"Nosy," Benjamin muttered to himself when he made it to his room. He sat on the bed as if lost and bewildered, wondering how he'd made it through the minefield virtually unscathed and how he'd even managed to leave Coralee at her dorm when all he wanted to do was hold her through the night again. She'd spoiled him. He wouldn't have a good night's sleep until the next time Coralee was by his side.

The door opened and the protest died in his throat when Felix entered. The blond man didn't say anything, his face expressionless, but his eyes were focused upon him. Benjamin looked to the door and Felix closed it before sitting on his bed and waiting for Benjamin to start talking.

Benjamin rubbed his fingertips against his jean-clad thighs, trying to find a more masculine way to express his feelings. "It was the best night of my life."

Felix grinned and Benjamin rolled his eyes. Gah, he sounded like a simpering debutante gushing to her girlfriends! Part of him expected Felix to squeal and bounce in his seat with joy, but was secretly glad *one* of them remembered they were men!

"I know; otherwise you would've been back much earlier."

"I didn't intend to stay the night—"

"I'm not judging you, Benny." Felix leaned forward, pinning Benjamin with his gaze. "But please tell me she returned the same way she left."

Benjamin glared. "She didn't *lose* anything, if that's what you want to know. I've already had this discussion with Dad, thanks."

Paul had given Benjamin a ride back to campus, and he couldn't forget the profound sense of relief the older man had expressed when he'd also told him he and Coralee hadn't gone too far. Paul Drummond had managed to keep his lecture to a minimum, however, and promised should he ever hurt Coralee, he would come after Benjamin himself.

Felix nodded, unapologetic for his insinuation. "Her losing it from you will create all sorts of issues—"

"On top of the ones we already have? Yeah, I know; but you know what? For a brief moment—a *tiny moment*—I had a glimpse of what my life would be like if we were married. Waking up next to her this morning was...indescribable."

Felix smiled, reaching over the space between the beds to clap his friend's shoulder. "Never thought you'd be the kind to want to marry right out of school."

Benjamin raised his eyebrows. "Part of me doesn't even want to wait that long."

Felix blinked in surprise, clearly not expecting that admission. To be honest, neither had Benjamin. The words had slipped out without his permission, desires so buried in his heart he'd barely known they existed. They were out in the universe now, for fate or God or whomever to do as they wished.

Benjamin feared he'd been too forward when he'd told Coralee about thinking of their children. He wouldn't dare impregnate her and then leave her to fend for herself and the little one—he wasn't so heartless and careless to do that to any woman—but perhaps that was why he didn't go as far with Coralee as he would've with another girl. Both definitely had been ripe for it—nude, willing, and ready to make love—but the timing was off. If they gave in too soon, it would be a disaster. By waiting, Coralee or anyone else didn't have that card to play against him.

"You want to *marry* her now?" Felix asked, incredulity coloring his voice. "One night together and now you're talking *marriage?*"

Benjamin chuckled, standing up and going to his desk, just to have something to do. "Actually, I've been talking marriage since I was eight—"

"*Eight?*"

"Yeah...mama separated us after that. She said she saw it then."

Benjamin turned to see Felix shaking his head and chuckling. Between Felix and his father, Benjamin was in danger of thinking the entire campus would understand once he *explained* he loved Coralee, but Felix was right. This was no time to be naïve, not when there were real, mutual feelings involved. Things *had* changed, but not about relationships like his and Coralee's, which threatened that very tenuous foundation of Plumville social life.

"Then we move," Benjamin said aloud. It wasn't the first time he'd thought about it, but now he was more convinced.

"Move?"

"Yeah. Move. Move to a place where it doesn't matter so much...where she and I can be married and raise a family and be left alone."

"No where can you go and be left alone. Bigots are everywhere."

"But not as many."

Felix snorted. "They just hide it better."

"You're not making this any easier, Felix."

"Why should I, Drummond?" Felix asked, standing and stretching his arms over his head. "It's better you see reality and take off those rose-colored glasses you seem so fond of wearing. Now I agree moving's the best thing for you to do, but don't think moving will solve your problems; it'll just lessen them."

Benjamin's eyes furrowed and he regarded his roommate carefully. There was too much passion, too much *knowing* in his tone to be a simple matter of a friend giving sound advice.

"Are you speaking from personal experience, Felix?"

Felix lowered his arms slowly and returned Benjamin's gaze unblinkingly. "Unfortunately, I've never had the pleasure."

"You would've liked it, though?" Benjamin pressed.

Felix shook his head once. "Ain't the same with me, Ben, and we'll just leave it at that."

Benjamin pursed his lips against the onslaught of questions that had suddenly filled his mouth. There was obviously a story here; but if Felix didn't or couldn't discuss it, then he'd respect his friend's request.

"We could move out of the country," Benjamin mused, reverting back to their original topic.

Felix pulled a dubious face. "Now you're bein' ridiculous. You really think she'll let you move her out of the country, away from her family and friends, just to be with you?"

Benjamin plopped in his chair, rubbing his hand across his face. *He* couldn't leave the country, not unless Felix came with him to act as his common sense.

"We could still get married," Benjamin murmured.

"You mean elope. In a courthouse. I dunno, she seems the traditional type—"

"She fell in love with a white man."

Felix shrugged. "You got me there." He ran a quick hand through his hair and went to the door, grasping the knob but not opening it. "At the very least, if you elope, she'll be under your legal protection...and nobody can undo the fact you're married except for you two."

"Exactly."

Felix still didn't look too keen on the idea. "At least *present* it to her first before you just blurt out 'we're getting married.' Best way to get on her bad side, Ben, is to tell her what she's gonna do."

Benjamin laughed. "You're right about that!"

Felix chuckled. "I'll leave you be. Got some studyin' to do, anyway. I'll call you when Miss Barbara sets out dinner."

Benjamin nodded his goodbye and Felix left. It was strange to think about marriage; there was finality to it. Never mind that Benjamin wouldn't be able to provide for a wife upon graduation and he knew Coralee wouldn't drop out of school to follow him to wherever he wanted them to be. School was very important to her, and though he was only *now* concentrating on law schools—thank goodness for rolling admissions!—she still had a year left of school.

And she's so young, Benjamin reminded himself as he opened his textbooks. Granted she was only three years his junior, but that was still young to be thinking about marriage. Then again, his mother had been married for a year when she was Coralee's age, but that was at least a quarter century ago. Girls weren't getting married so young anymore, and even Coralee had seemed hesitant when he brought up marriage and children.

He smiled as he stared at the page, not really reading it at all. They *would* have beautiful children—he just knew it. He wanted a little girl first, one who looked just like Coralee...hell, he wouldn't mind if they *all* resembled Coralee in some way. Benjamin knew she would make a wonderful mother, and he would have the best time spoiling her as she carried every one of his children inside of her.

"Slow down, Benny...slow down..."

Children meant conception, and conception meant...his body knew, and was reacting accordingly. This was bad. He hadn't even made love to her and already he was addicted. Coralee in the throes of passion was the most erotic thing he had ever seen, and knowing he was the cause made his chest swell with pride.

And something else below the belt as well.

Benjamin cleared his throat and shifted in his seat and began to read, hoping to cool his ardor. "The antitrust laws of the late nineteenth century were to prevent monopolies from occurring, most notably, the Sherman Act of 1890..."

One night didn't necessarily portend a lifetime—his father had told him that during the mini-lecture—and he knew better than to indulge such fantasies. Yet it was hard not to want paradise once one had been there, and that was what last night had been. He had to be patient—he couldn't always have what he wanted when he wanted. "Good things come to those who wait," Benjamin reassured himself, turning the barely read page and scribbling notes into his notebook. Last night had been a dream—a blessing—and he knew it would have to sustain him for the upcoming weeks.

SIXTEEN

It was one of those rare times that Paul Drummond had the house to himself...or at least, without his wife around. Florence was off at a tea party one of the neighbors was hosting—wives only— and it was the weekend.

He went to the kitchen but didn't enter, standing near the threshold and watching Patty wipe down the countertops. She was always so efficient and thorough, never complaining about her workload. She'd played the cards life had given her with dignity and grace, and Paul thought the world could do better with more people like her. He cleared his throat, gaining her attention. She looked at him with an expressionless face, never ceasing her work. Paul pulled the corner of his bottom lip between his teeth and tapped against the doorframe, looking around the room before settling back to her.

"Need any help?"

Patty blinked then frowned, turning her attention back to the countertop. "Sir?"

Paul walked further into the kitchen, stopping a good ways from Patty but close enough that she tensed ever so slightly. "I asked if you need any help."

"No, sir," Patty said breathlessly, her motions a bit more energetic than before. "I'm just fine."

He watched her jaw clench and her fingers tighten around the rag, and he sighed. He had no idea what he was doing right now other than making her uncomfortable, and that was the last thing he'd wanted to do, but he needed to talk to her.

He decided to get her used to his presence first, reaching above him into the cabinet and pulling out a glass. He filled it with water and downed the contents, peeping her in his peripheral vision as she moved to the kitchen table. She was good at making herself invisible; she barely made a sound. But his staring at her, ruining her illusion, had her jumpy, so he turned and faced the sink as he filled his glass again.

"How are things at home?" Paul asked, taking a sip of water this time.

"Fine."

"And LJ?"

"Doin' fine, sir. Gettin' stronger every day."

Paul nodded, pressing the glass to his cheek. He cocked his head to the side as Patty shook out the rag in the trash before coming over to the sink. She stood as far away from him as humanly possible and still be able to reach the running water, and Paul took another step back. Her rigidity didn't lessen, but she did move closer to the sink, her breath hissing softly through her teeth.

"How's Luther?"

Patty glanced at him then, her lips pressed into a thin line before nodding. "He's good too. He just got a pay raise—makin' five dollars an hour now."

"Good for him," Paul nodded, wondering how a family of five lived off a combined income of ten dollars an hour. This was why Patty insisted on working weekends, because with that extra income, they could at least breathe a little.

Paul would increase her pay...it was the least he could do...given what his family was putting hers through.

Patty wrung out the rag and draped it on the side of the sink before going to a corner and pulling out a broom. Paul felt conspicuous and unnecessary; why would she need his help, after all? She'd been cleaning his house for almost twenty-five years and no one had helped her in all that time.

He cleared his throat again, drinking the last bit of water and refilling the glass.

"He loves her, you know." Patty didn't stop sweeping, didn't make any indication she'd heard him, so he said it again. "He loves her a lot."

"That's what he says all right," Patty replied flatly.

"You don't believe him?"

"I believe him more than when you said it to me, yeah."

She turned her back to him then, her body shaking with the force of her strokes. In all the time she'd worked there, never had she made such an explicit remark about their time together. Patty didn't know it, but he always looked back at that time fondly, still holding a special place in his heart for her. She'd been his first love, and he hers; people didn't forget firsts—no matter how good or bad they were.

"I meant it, Patty," Paul said, staring into his glass and hearing the broom slow down its frantic pace. "If things were different—"

"Like they are now, you mean?" Patty asked. He looked at her, but she was staring out the back door window. "Things ain't that different, Mr. Paul."

"He loves her."

"She loves him too," Patty admitted. "But so what? She's a colored girl; he's a white man. Things ain't change that much to make that love all right."

"We could help them," Paul said, setting down the glass and walking slowly to her. "We can give them the chance we never had—"

"He can't be a state judge with a colored gal on his arm," Patty said, whirling around to face him. Her eyes were wide and her brows were in her forehead. "Ain't that what you told me?"

Paul slipped his hands into his pockets and nodded sadly. He couldn't be a state judge with Patty, and Benjamin couldn't be one with Coralee. He'd become a state judge because *his* father had been a state judge. Patty's grandmother had been the housekeeper in his father's house and had apprenticed Patty to be one in his. They'd known each other mostly all of their lives...had fallen in love just like Benjamin and Coralee had, but neither could do anything about it.

Yet Benjamin and Coralee...maybe their story would have a happier ending. Paul remembered how full of optimism, skepticism, Benjamin had been the morning after Valentine's Day. Benjamin knew, intellectually, things wouldn't be easy if he decided to make a go of it with Coralee, yet part of Paul knew Benjamin was passed that; the night at the bed and breakfast had proven it. In fact, the first thing Paul had asked his son was had he taken advantage of her; and from the horror on Benjamin's face and the emphatic shaking "no" of the head, Paul had breathed the sigh of the relief he hadn't know he'd been holding for that last twenty-four hours.

"Your son's settin' up my baby for a world o' hurt, and there ain't a thing I can do about it," Patty said, her grip on the broom's handle tightening.

Paul reached out his hand as if to cup her cheek before dropping it heavily to his side. "Benjamin's stronger than I am."

Patty took a small step back but kept her eyes to his. "Is he strong enough to walk away like you did?"

"Don't confuse his strength with my cowardice, Patty," Paul insisted.

Patty shrugged. "Ain't no strength in tilting at windmills. That's insanity."

"Love is insanity," Paul quipped.

"And judges can't be insane, can they?" Patty argued, smirking a little.

"Then again, Solomon threatened to cut a baby in half, and he's considered the wisest man in the Bible," Paul returned, grinning even as Patty glowered at him, folding her arms at her chest, broom handle tucked between her chest and biceps. Right then she reminded him so much of herself when she was younger that his nostalgia couldn't be contained.

"I still think about that first kiss...the one by the big tree in my backyard."

"You stole it from me," Patty mumbled, but with a fondness in her voice that made Paul smile.

"You tasted like sweet lemons...you were dipping in the mix for the lemon meringue pie."

"And you tasted like the peppermint I distinctly remember yo' mama tellin' you not to have, so don't talk about me!"

They were both smiling at each other now, reminiscing of a time that was so much simpler than it currently was. Patty had been a skinny little thing of eleven, ashy-kneed and rambunctious, making messes instead of cleaning them—with him helping. They'd hidden behind a tree, Patty giggling and resting against it with him trapping her with his arms. On impulse he'd bent and kissed her, a quick contact of lips that had left her blinking, confused, as if she'd had no idea what had just happened.

His thirteen-year-old mind hadn't fully understood the implications of the kiss, so when he did it the next time, it was longer and deeper, and all he'd known was that he'd thoroughly enjoyed her taste and wanted to do it again. He'd leaned in for a third but Patty's grandmother had called for her, mad about the mess she'd made from the flour war they'd had earlier. He'd wiped a smidge of flour from the corner of her lip with his thumb then put the pad of it in his mouth, watching her pigtails tap against her head as she'd hurried off into the kitchen.

"I think I fell in love with you then," Paul revealed, this time following his impulse and cupping her cheek. Patty leaned into his touch and closed her eyes, nodding imperceptibly.

"Yeah."

"It wouldn't be right for me to say I still love you, would it?"

"No." Patty exhaled. "I love Luther."

Paul inhaled. "And I love Florence."

His thumb caressed the swell of her cheek briefly before dropping away. "Benjamin loves Coralee."

"You think he'd give up state judge?"

"In a heartbeat."

Patty turned from Paul and finished sweeping. She put the broom back in the corner and rested her back against the wall, staring at him with a pained expression.

"I don't want my baby hurt, Paul," Patty implored softly, and Paul was secretly glad she became familiar with him. "Seems all a black woman's good for is being hurt."

"He won't hurt her," Paul promised.

"And what about other people then? Miss Florence ain't gonna like this. She ain't like it when Benny was eight; she sho' ain't gonna like it now!"

"She wants Benjamin to be happy, Patty."

"Yeah...happy like you are."

Happy enough... just enough that the world could go on like it had been. Paul wanted more than that for his son.

"I'm a state judge...I can marry them," Paul said.

Patty rolled her eyes and pushed off the wall, washing her hands in the sink before pulling out pots and pans. "Again with the crazy talk. Love don't necessarily lead to marriage."

"Benjamin wants to marry her."

"He say that?"

"No, but—"

"Benjamin can't always get what he wants."

"You don't want Coralee to marry him?"

"I don't want my baby hurt!"

It was the third time she'd said it, and it was then Paul realized how deeply his actions had affected Patty. Love wasn't always the wonderful thing poets and the movies made it out to be. Love caused pain and tears and yearning that would never be fulfilled. Love was sometimes not strong enough against pride and loyalty to one's race.

It was something that could be compromised, and Patty didn't want that to happen to Coralee.

"Do you want me to tell him to stop seeing her?" Paul asked. "I'll do it if it means that much to you."

She pulled out chicken wings from the refrigerator and began sprinkling pepper on them. "And have that gal hate me? No, sir! She caused me enough problems the first time they separated."

"Then how—?"

"I don't know how!" Patty snapped, slamming the bowl she'd taken down from the cabinet onto the countertop. "I don't know how to protect my baby's heart without breakin' it...I don't know how to tell her she should find a decent man instead of bein' with someone she can't have. I don't know how to tell her to stop lovin' someone—I shouldn't have to do that!"

She looked as torn as she had the night he'd broken things off with her—just as beautiful and haunted and worn from almost twenty-five years ago.

"Then don't," Paul said, placing a tentative hand on her shoulder. The tension immediately relaxed and she leaned against Paul, borrowing some of his strength. "Benjamin won't make the same mistake I did."

"Coralee's heart's gonna get broken," Patty whispered, her hands still preparing the chicken though her focus was in a faraway place.

"Benny will be there to pick up the pieces," Paul guaranteed, pressing a fleeting kiss to the top of Patty's head. "I know he will."

Even if he were the one who broke it in the first place.

It was a very gray day and just cold enough to make snow a definite possibility. Coralee wore many layers and lined the pockets of her coat with newspaper so her hands wouldn't be so cold. In a rare move, she wore her hair out to give her ears some protection, and constantly muttered under her breath that it should never get this cold in Plumville.

Because she kept her face to the ground, she never noticed the presence slightly ahead of her...watching her. There weren't many students outside braving the weather as she was doing, but she had to study—there was a major test in her philosophy class that week, and she didn't know Kant as she should.

She'd just passed by the large tree in front of the library's steps when suddenly she heard a shout of her name. She jumped, startled, then narrowed her eyes when she saw a laughing Benjamin sagging against the tree. She marched up to him, glaring, but then he spun her around so that her back hit the tree's bark, and a pair of familiar lips covered hers.

She'd missed him so much.

"You was so wrong fo' scarin' me like that," Coralee murmured when Benjamin broke their kiss. He merely grinned, rubbing his nose against hers and playing with her hair.

"You should wear it out more," he said softly, pressing a kiss to the bridge of her nose. "It's like a mass of black fire."

"An uncontrollable mass of black fire," Coralee mumbled. "Can't go out my room with my hair every which way!"

"Doesn't look that way to me."

"You're a bit biased, Benny."

"You're a bit beautiful, Coralee."

"Just a bit?"

Benjamin pretended to think long and hard about it. Finally, he grinned, leaning his head towards hers to kiss her lips lightly. "A really big bit..."

Coralee rolled her eyes and bunched her hands near his waist. He was so *warm*, and she snuggled into him. "I'm glad you're here."

"I'm glad I'm here too," he whispered, caressing her temple with his nose. "You know, I've been having trouble fallin' asleep lately..."

Coralee blushed and sniffled a bit, her nose runny. "Warm milk should help that."

Benjamin chuckled, pulling back to rub his thumb against her cheek. "Only you can, honey. You felt really good in my arms that night."

That was almost two weeks ago, and she had to admit it'd been harder for her to fall asleep since then as well. Coralee nodded and buried her head into his chest.

"Someone could see us," she whispered, a bit belatedly, but she'd been too high on Benjamin to realize this was the most public she'd even been while showing him affection.

"Let them see."

"Ben—"

"I know," Benjamin sighed, bringing a gloved thumb to her lips. "It's not fair."

"I know," Coralee echoed before stepping away from him. She looked at the gray sky and took a deep breath. "Think it's gonna snow?"

"Dunno...you want it to?"

"Dunno..." Coralee giggled, adjusting her bag on her shoulder. "I don't think I'm adequately prepared for it!"

Benjamin gave her an assessing look, frowning as he fingered the newspaper sticking out of her pockets. "What's this?"

Coralee knocked his hand away and stuck her hands in the pockets. "They keep my hands warm...and provide light readin' too!" Benjamin scowled at her even as he began pulling off his gloves. "No, Benny—"

"Don't tell me 'no', Coralee," he replied, pulling her hands out of her pockets and putting the gloves on them. He rubbed his thumbs along the backs of her newly gloved hands. "Don't tell me not to take care of you."

His voice was low, deep, and cozy, and she shivered at the affection cloaked in it. Unable to stop herself, she pulled him to her even as she stood on tiptoe and pressed a light, chaste kiss on his mouth. He smiled underneath her lips and nuzzled her as they separated.

"So what you doin' out here, anyway?" Coralee asked, making an indignant sound when he pulled her bag off her shoulder and placed it on his, though was secretly pleased by his consideration.

"I was goin' to the library to study, but it's closed." Coralee huffed and Benjamin grinned at her, squeezing her hand. "But imagine my luck when I see my girlfriend comin' towards me...I knew it wasn't a wasted trip!"

"It *is* a wasted trip," Coralee muttered, though couldn't help the flutter in her heart when he called her his girlfriend. She had walked in the cold for nothing! Hopefully, it wouldn't be bad weather tomorrow; she really needed to study.

Benjamin kissed her temple and shook her hand a little. "I'm sorry, honey. I know how serious you are about your work. Trish givin' you problems?"

"I haven't seen Trish since Friday afternoon," Coralee mumbled, glaring at the library as it seemingly mocked her. "It's Kant! I was going to go to the library to get more books but clearly I can't do that anymore..."

Benjamin brushed his lips against her forehead, linking their fingers together. "If you want, I can help you with that; I *am* a political science major after all."

"Where?"

"Dining hall?"

Coralee knew Benjamin rarely went there because he took his meals in the fraternity house, but she, like he, reasoned the dining hall would be open, considering the rest of the campus had to eat.

It would be their first "public" outing...though they were just studying together...

"Are you sure?"

He smiled against her skin and Coralee shivered deliciously. "Are you askin' if I'll be able to keep my hands off you while I help you with Kant...I won't make any promise other than I'll *try*."

Benjamin allowed her to lead them to the dining hall. There weren't many people when they entered, a fact that brought Coralee much relief. She chose a corner of the dining hall far from where the main traffic would be, and told Benjamin to sit opposite of her. Benjamin set her books out before her in the same manner she would set them—text to the left and slightly ahead her notebook, and placed her marking pen inside the book and her pencils next to the notebook.

Coralee blushed at the care he put into the setup as she slipped off the gloves. "I can't believe you remembered that."

Benjamin grinned sheepishly, his cheeks red from either the cold or embarrassment. "I remember almost everything about you, Ceelee."

It was Coralee's turn to become shy, pushing her hair behind her ear and sitting down primly. "That's sweet..."

Benjamin sat as well, turning her text so he could get a look at it. "So what, exactly, is givin' you problems?"

"Everything," Coralee said with exasperation, crinkling her forehead and rubbing her thumb against it. "His categorical imperative concept should be straightforward but it's not; I guess I'm having a hard time understanding why someone doing a good deed for not-so-good motivations would be immoral to him...why the end won't justify the means."

Benjamin picked up her marking pen. "May I?" Coralee nodded and watched him underline key parts in the text or circle ones she'd already marked. He explained them patiently, not even bothered by her questions when she still didn't understand. She scribbled notes furiously, taking in his explanations as if they were water and she were dying of thirst, and she did a little dance when she felt she was beginning to understand.

"So basically...people can't apply one set of standards for themselves, then turn around and apply another set to someone else—no matter the reason?"

"More or less," Benjamin said, reaching across the table and squeezing her hand.

"And *if* the categorical imperative isn't applied when or as it should, then actions become...null? Like, if I asked to borrow something of yours and promised to give it back, but never do, then I've basically set two different standards; and if *everyone* did that, then there would be...moral chaos?"

Benjamin squeezed her hand again. "And you were worried..."

The tension in Coralee's shoulders left and she settled spinelessly in her seat. "I thought I'd *never* get that! Thanks so much!" Benjamin nodded, sliding his hand from hers and settling in his own chair. His expression turned flat and Coralee frowned. "What's wrong?"

"Just how that's easier said than done."

Coralee snorted, pulling her book in her lap and annotating the text. "Morality usually is."

Benjamin licked his lips, glancing at her, then around the dining hall. "According to Kant, I should be able to pull you in my arms and give you the biggest kiss...but I can't."

Coralee gave him a sad smile, then winked at him. "It's a categorical imperative now?"

Benjamin leaned across the table, his fingers playing with the leaves in her notebook. "It's *always* an imperative when I'm around you, baby."

Coralee giggled, slapping her hands over her mouth and shaking her head. Benjamin could be something else when he wanted to be!

Without looking her way, he turned her notebook around and flipped to a clean sheet of paper, then took the pen and began writing. Coralee felt heat rise in her cheeks, just knowing he was writing something *entirely* inappropriate on her sacred paper. She pretended to be disinterested in *whatever* he was writing, but the circles she drew in the margins of her book did little to satisfy her curiosity.

The notebook appeared in her line of vision and she slid her book down just enough so she could peek at what he wrote.

BMD + CRS = *Categorical Imperative*

"You are so silly," Coralee murmured, tearing the page out of her notebook and folding it carefully before slipping it into her bag.

"And right," Benjamin said, tapping the pen against the table. "You know it."

The racket from the kitchen suddenly became audible, and Coralee knew dinner would start soon. She looked at him sadly. "I guess you gotta go, now?"

"Why?"

She looked at him, then around the dining hall, before settling back to the book in her lap. There really wasn't any reason for him to leave other than the fact he *never* ate in the dining hall and she usually ate with the BSU board members. Besides, most of the white people didn't eat until towards the end of each meal, and Benjamin being there at the beginning would be unusual.

"I'm sure they serve better food in your frat house," Coralee said, beginning to pack her bag. Some students began trickling in, two of them Freda and Jermaine. They were holding hands, Jermaine looking at Freda as if she held his world in her hands...it was a similar expression she noticed on Benjamin whenever he looked at her.

The realization made Coralee blush.

"I can deal with subpar food as long as you're with me," Benjamin teased. "But if you cook anything like Aunt Patty, I know I won't have to worry about that!"

"Cook! Who said anything about cookin'?" Coralee asked, tearing her eyes away from Jermaine and Freda. Benjamin's face suddenly became very red, and he laughed hesitantly.

"Doesn't matter," he said, waving away the comment with his hand though looking at her intently.

Coralee decided to let it slide, her own mind going towards a dangerous fantasy. He was about to graduate; she still had a year left of school...and she wouldn't even mention the *obvious*...

"I guess," Benjamin continued as he stood, "I'd better be going." Coralee forgot herself just then and pouted, and Benjamin's face looked pained. "Don't do that, baby...makes me wanna kiss you when you do."

Coralee stopped pouting and fought back a grin. He said the sweetest things sometimes.

"Coralee?"

She jumped and panicked slightly when Freda and Jermaine appeared at their table. Coralee glimpsed Benjamin and saw his face turn slightly pink. Coralee prayed to *God* they hadn't heard Benjamin's confession.

"Drummond," Jermaine said with a curt, though polite nod.

"Hi," Benjamin said, acknowledging them both. He turned his attention back to Coralee and nodded again. "I hope that helped," he said, glancing at her books before looking in her eyes.

Coralee saw Benjamin's hands clench at his sides, then watched his face as he licked his lips unconsciously. Coralee bit hers in response, knowing exactly what he wanted to do but knowing they couldn't...not now, and definitely not in front of Jermaine and Freda. Instead, Coralee nodded and patted her Kant text. "Yes it did, Benjamin; I appreciate it."

Benjamin gave a small smile, nodding once more before leaving the table and exiting the dining hall. Coralee's eyes followed his progress, and she didn't tear her eyes away until a throat cleared next to her ear. Coralee blushed again and glared at Freda as the other girl slid into the seat next to her. "Ma'am?"

"You starin'! Jermaine's lookin' at you like you grew another head!"

Coralee looked briefly at him; and sure enough, his eyebrow was raised curiously. Coralee tilted her chin, trying act innocent. "How you, Jermaine?"

Jermaine shook his head, then smiled a little. "Nothin', Ceelee...just, y'know, chillin'."

Coralee laughed and rolled her eyes, putting up her books to keep them free of food debris. "That's literal, I take it. Your glasses are startin' to fog!"

Jermaine made a face at her, then at Freda who had started to giggle, and muttered something under his breath. Still giggling, Coralee stood, telling them she would get her own tray of dinner. She said hello to the cafeteria workers as she gathered her meal, but felt a sensation on the back of her neck, as if someone was watching her.

She looked around, but saw no one paying attention to her. Coralee shrugged; maybe she was still nervous about Jermaine and Freda seeing her with Benjamin. At least the books were still out, so it didn't look so bad, but Coralee knew it would only be a matter of time before someone found out about them.

SEVENTEEN

The following week passed by uneventfully; the excitement of Valentine's Day and the fact it had snowed—though it'd melted in less than twenty-four hours after falling—was gone, leaving in its place a listlessness that not even professors could combat. Lectures were more like monotonous drones, and no one was surprised, or necessarily bothered, when students punctuated lessons with hearty snores.

Coralee was a hapless victim of the academic lull, but at least the downtime had provided the BSU with inspiration. Jermaine thought of a proposal to present to the Board of Trustees about implementing a Black Literature course next year on a trial basis. He'd asked her to help establish a syllabus, and explained the specifics he and Freda thought were important for the course.

Coralee immediately took to the idea, and she worked endlessly on the subject for the rest of the week. There was also a general meeting of the BSU, because there hadn't been one in a while, where they would just listen to concerns of the blacks on campus and possibly garner support for their new proposed course.

Much of the group were anxious about the escalating war in Vietnam and worried about being drafted—especially the seniors. Her mind immediately went to LJ, whose life had been turned upside down by a war he'd never wanted to fight, but had because it was his duty as an American citizen. Not only that, there was bitterness that black men were usually on the front lines in the war, and they'd glare at the body bags they saw on TV.

Another big topic was the growing Black Panther party out of California. Andre was particularly vocal about his support for the group, and while Coralee didn't blame Andre or the Black Panther leaders for their position, she couldn't jump so readily on the bandwagon. Self-defense was one thing; blatantly antagonizing the establishment was another.

"We gotta stop rollin' over like we been doin'," Andre said to the group, earning a chorus of encouragement and agreement. "We gotta stand up for ourselves—"

"That doesn't mean we gotta go startin' mess, now! Look at what happened in DC and Baltimore—" one attendee called.

"Yeah! Don't start none won't be none, right?" said another.

"But there comes a point when enough's enough!" piped up someone from the back.

"Yeah, except *they* started it almost four hundred years ago, so I say it's time we shove back!" Nick said, standing with his friend.

Coralee shot a worried glance to Freda, who gave her a sympathetic smile. Just because the campus was bored didn't mean the solution was to start a fight, another riot like last time. All that would do was entrench sides and solve nothing, reinforcing the gross misunderstandings each group had for the other.

"We cannot improve through fighting; we cannot improve alone," Jermaine said quietly, his subdued authority cooling the ardor somewhat. "A house divided will not stand."

"What good is the house if it's built on shoddy foundation in the first place, Jermaine?" Andre returned. "This country was built on a lie, and you want to keep a house built on that together? Let it fall! It needs to be rebuilt, anyway."

"And yet we're only a small fraction of the population, Andre," Freda joined in. "Like Jermaine said, we can't do this by ourselves!"

"And who on this campus gonna help us?" Nick said sarcastically. "Ain't a white person here who gives a damn about black people, and if they say they do they're lyin'!"

"That's not fair," Coralee countered. "You doin' the same thing you accuse them of doin' to us—stereotyping. You can't just lump the lot of 'em together—"

"I can, I did, and I will," Nick said, unapologetic. "They don't give a damn about us so why should we give a damn about them?"

"Because *they* control everything," Coralee said, glancing at Nick before going back to the notepad in front of her. She'd been writing notes for what to put in the proposal, and this conversation was perfect material to consider. "And you're right, a lot of them couldn't care less about what's goin' on in our community, but not caring about them won't solve anything. *We* have to care. We have to care enough to make *them* care. As long as they think what happens to us doesn't affect them, and as long as we keep givin' them that impression, ain't nothin' gonna happen."

"I don't trust 'em," Andre said. "It's been four hundred years of nothin' but pain. Why should I turn the other cheek?"

"It's in the Bible," Jermaine said on a small chuckle.

"Yeah? And so is eye for an eye. I like that method better."

"Our 'eye' ain't as big as theirs, so we'll just end up blind," Freda muttered, earning a chuckle from Coralee and some other people.

"Ah, but *they're* already blind, aren't they? Blind to us, blind to things different from them—"

"Just like we are," Coralee insisted, staring at Andre and Nick. "You should hear yourselves. Just as closed-minded and blockheaded—"

"Damn, girl!" Andre asked on a laugh, but his eyes were completely serious. "Just whose side are you on?"

Immediately Coralee shut her mouth, not liking the accusation laced in the question. She was losing ground with the very people she needed. Maybe she was being a bit harsh, but Nick and Andre sounded just like Tommy Birch, if a little more civil.

"Whose side you *think* she on?" Freda asked, standing up and leaning forward. "You know Coralee just as committed as everyone else in here in improving our situation! Just because she has a more inclusive method doesn't make her what you're accusin' her of being!"

"Sorry, Ceelee," Andre muttered.

Coralee nodded, unwilling to look Andre in the eye. She was afraid he'd see all of her secrets, all of her ulterior reasons for working with instead of against white people. That he'd realize she was very much in love with one and was selfish in her desire to make the world a better place. She'd been renewed in her quest for equality all because she wanted to be free to love a white man, to affirm she had the *right* to love a white man...to affirm there was no shame in him loving *her*.

She laughed sardonically.

"Have something to share, Ceelee?" Nick asked tightly.

She shifted in her seat and focused back on her notes. "Not if I'm gonna get hostile reactions to it, no. I'll just sit here quietly like a good girl," Coralee said, her tone saccharin.

"You ain't gotta be that way, Coralee—"

"Be what way? Deferential? Seems that's how I should be...like I'm not supposed to have an independent thought; that I'm supposed to think how every other black person's 'supposed' to think, and if I don't I'm a traitor?" Coralee had surprised herself with the outburst, but the relief she felt was overwhelming. It was practice, she realized, for when her relationship with Benjamin came out in the open...practice for how to protect herself against the accusations and rejections. Practice for how she'd navigate the divided world alone.

It was completely silent in the room, and Coralee felt the air press against her until she couldn't breathe. She gripped her notebook tightly. Someone cleared her throat.

"Ah, I guess now would be a good a time as any to schedule the next meeting. How about two weeks from now, same place, same time?" Jermaine asked cautiously.

The other participants in the room murmured approval and began leaving, but Coralee kept her head bowed. She sorely disliked getting in arguments, and it was even worse when in public. It should not have happened; what kind of message were they sending to the others if the board members couldn't even agree on a plan of attack?

She felt a hand on her shoulder and gave a wan smile to Freda. The other girl smiled in return, sitting in the seat and kissing Coralee's temple.

"You right, y'know," Freda whispered in her ear. "Nick and Andre may not wanna hear it, but you right."

"Even if I wasn't...you know...I'd feel the same way," Coralee said wearily, closing her notebook and drumming her pen against the cover.

"I know, Ceelee," Freda said, squeezing Coralee's shoulder again. "You don't gotta explain it to me."

But she would have to explain...eventually.

❧

Books were spread open every which way, pages crumpled or dog-eared, some inching ever so slowly off the bed, some already on the floor with the pages smooshed from the weight of their spines. Their owner, however, seemed oblivious; and if he'd noticed, he didn't care, a pencil clamped between his teeth as his hands tore through the pages of yet another hapless book.

"I *just* saw that damn passage!" Benjamin muttered around the pencil. It was awful putting off a major paper until the last minute. It was due tomorrow; and though it was only four in the afternoon, he had the horrible habit of writing his paper first in pencil, correcting mistakes with a red pen, then typing it. Just the actual transfer could take hours, so the fact he was just starting put him in an awful pickle.

And it didn't help he'd been daydreaming about Coralee in the interim.

They'd not been able to meet since the day it snowed, only catching glimpses of each other as the spring semester went into full gear. As it was, he wished she were here with him, if not so he could just gaze upon her, but for her help in writing this paper. She was always so organized; so thorough in whatever she did, that though she didn't study political science, she'd be able to find all the quotes and information he needed, sort it just so, and make this process go far faster and much more smoothly.

But it was not to be, and he grew more frustrated because of it.

"Oh, forget this!" Benjamin yelled, throwing the book on his desk and pushing back, only for the legs of his chair to catch on one of his haphazardly strewn books. The chair tipped back and he crashed to the ground, the back of his head smacking against another one of his abandoned books.

A book's revenge had never been so sweet.

"Kill me now..." Benjamin winced and rubbed the tender spot on his head.

"Hey, Ben—"

Benjamin glared at Peter, daring him to say anything about his current predicament. Peter, though not always quick on the uptake, wisely kept his mouth shut about it and shrugged.

"You should see *my* room..."

"What is it?"

Peter shook himself as if to reorient his mind. "Oh! You have a visitor."

"A visitor?"

Peter shrugged again. "Some colored man in a wheelchair, says his mama works in your house?"

"Yeah, yeah."

Benjamin eased himself off the ground, now more confused than anything. What was LJ doing here? What did he want? Benjamin couldn't help but be a little intimidated—even in a wheelchair, Luther was not to be taken lightly, and it seemed even Peter had grasped that fact.

He hurried down the steps, annoyed no one had invited LJ in from the cold, but at least they hadn't turned him away outright.

"LJ," Benjamin said as he got to the porch. LJ smiled and held out his hand, which Benjamin took.

"How you doin', man?"

Benjamin nodded, pointing back inside. "Wanna come in? It's pretty nippy out here."

"There's no ramp, so I can't," LJ said with a little smile. "But Miss Barbara was kind enough to give me some hot tea and a blanket."

"How did you get here?"

"Oh...Mama came and got Coralee for the day—she don't have classes Fridays. I said I wanted to come see you, so here I am."

Benjamin cracked a smile; but as he looked over the campus, he thought that was an awfully long way to go by oneself in the cold. "I can push you back."

LJ's face immediately closed off and he shook his head. "It's okay—"

"Why not? Besides, I want to see Aunt Patty," Benjamin said. He knew LJ wouldn't deny him that.

LJ rolled his eyes and nodded. "All right, then." He finished his tea and shrugged out of the blanket. "Here."

Benjamin took the teacup and saucer but ignored the blanket. "Put it back around. It may be March but it's still pretty cool. I'll be back in a jiff."

Benjamin set the teacup and saucer on the countertop in the kitchen before going to his room and packing his bag full of his books and slung it over his shoulders. What better excuse to see and spend time with Coralee than for help on his paper? That wouldn't be suspicious...besides, her mother and brother would be with them!

Benjamin didn't bother telling the rest of his housemates where he was going, or who was with him; it wasn't any of their business, anyway. Instead, he grabbed the handles of LJ's wheelchair and began the trek across campus to Coralee's dorm.

They talked about Benjamin's classes, where he wanted to go to law school, or if he wanted to pursue professional football instead.

"There haven't been any scouts," Benjamin muttered, wincing as he rolled LJ over an uprooted branch. "Sorry."

"Couldn't be helped...the dang thing was all along the path." LJ shrugged. "And how you know there weren't any scouts?"

"No one came up."

LJ scoffed. "Don't let that stop you. I'm sure the coach knows people or knows where you can get a tryout."

Benjamin didn't respond. In truth, he didn't want to play football for a living; it wasn't in his blood like the law. Besides, playing for a team meant away games or moving out of the state entirely, and he didn't want to do that, especially not while Coralee was here.

"But I reckon as long as you keep throwin' 'em like you do, you always liable to change yo' mind, no?"

"Yeah..."

"Yeah..."

There was silence again, the cool, cloudy day feeling massive. The trees were beginning to bud shoots of brilliant flowers that would soon turn pink and white or just green of long-missed leaves. Benjamin knew that by Easter break, which was not far off, spring would fully set in on the campus and renew everyone's spirits from the harsh winter months.

"So how's Ceelee been doin'?" LJ asked, surprising Benjamin so much he stumbled slightly.

"Um...fine?"

"Fine? That's all you gotta say to me?"

"LJ..."

"I may be a lot of things, Benny, but dumb ain't one o' 'em. Even with my one good eye I see how you look at her...how she look at you. So does everyone else with half a brain. Y'all bein' careful, I hope?"

"No one's seen us."

"Doubt that. Can't go far with a relationship like that without someone knowin' *somethin'*."

People knew—Felix, his father, Aunt Patty—but the less people knew, the better.

"I hope y'all've been careful," LJ repeated when Benjamin didn't speak. "Things may've changed, but not so much that people would be okay with you takin' out my sister."

"It's not any of their business," Benjamin muttered. "What does it matter—?"

"It matters because you two are basically tellin' everyone in this town to go to hell, and who would take kindly to that? Would you? I doubt it."

"Still none of their business," Benjamin insisted lamely, gripping the handles of the wheelchair more tightly.

"Look, white folk in this town still mad Negroes even procrea- tin', so you think they gonna like *you* of *all* people choosin' a Negro girl...boy, man...you need to wise up!"

"Free country, ain't it?"

"C'mon on, now, you can't possibly believe that! Ain't been free fo' us since the moment we stepped foot on this continent! And what's free fo' you ain't free fo' me...or my sister."

"You tellin' me I can't see her?"

"I'm tellin' you to be *careful*. If somethin' happens to her, I'll kill you myself, and if somethin' happens to *you*...I don't even wanna know..."

That had, admittedly, brought Benjamin up short. He'd never considered the possibility that someone would attack him—he'd always been focused on Coralee. Why? Because she was a girl...or because she was colored? He thought he was safer because he was white, but he was also...what did Tommy call it?

A nigger lover. A traitor.

Americans never did cotton to traitors.

"Well, I haven't really seen Coralee in weeks," Benjamin muttered.

"Can't say I ain't glad. Maybe you should think about school up North. They more forgivin' of couples like y'all."

Benjamin was never gladder to see Coralee's dorm, and was more than a little surprised to see Patty standing outside. Apparently so was LJ, because he began chastising his mother.

"I was about to come get you," Patty said by way of explanation, glancing at Benjamin. "Thank you."

"It's no problem. How are you?" Benjamin asked. He stepped around the wheelchair and kissed Patty's cheek. "Well, I hope?"

"Well, yes," Patty agreed, smiling a little. "Told you it was cold! You should've let me stay—"

"I told you Benny would walk me back...he's a good friend."

It heartened Benjamin to hear LJ consider him such, and he blushed a little. "Just returnin' the favor, LJ."

LJ grabbed the wheels and maneuvered himself towards his mother. Patty tightened the blanket around him, earning LJ's protests and comments about how he wasn't five years old anymore.

"You can be eighty-five but you still my baby," Patty said, even going so far as to lick her thumb and wipe away imaginary smudge from LJ's cheek.

"Ma..."

Benjamin laughed. "You know you like it, LJ!"

LJ rolled his eyes but winked, and Benjamin glanced at the entrance to Coralee's dorm again, wondering if it were appropriate to go inside with her mother and brother knowing his intentions.

"Got work, Benny?"

Benjamin started and adjusted the bag on his shoulder to cover it. Patty snorted, however and shook her head. "You almost as transparent as your father."

"My father?"

"*Mmm hmm*....whenever he gets caught dippin' in somethin' he ain't supposed to be dippin' in, he pretends he's adjusting somethin' instead. You Drummonds are all the same..."

Patty looked at him pointedly as she said that, and Benjamin got the feeling there was an underlying meaning to her comment. However, he fiddled with his bag again. "Um..."

"She in there studyin'." Patty sighed. "She's always studyin'."

"I know," Benjamin said. "I keep trying to get her to go out more but she won't listen."

"She's determined to graduate on time...she'll be the first in the family," Patty said, pride tinting her voice.

"She will," Benjamin said, just as proud. "She's too smart not to."

"She is," Patty agreed, squeezing her son's shoulders. "I reckon I should get you home now, hmm?"

"Do you need me to help you?" Benjamin asked.

"No, dear. You should get out of the cold, can't have you gettin' sick."

"But you make the best soup, Aunt Patty!"

"You can have that soup, sick or not!" She gave him a mild glare and sucked her teeth. "Promise to make you some durin' Easter break, how about that?"

Benjamin smiled and kissed Patty's cheek again. "Love you."

"Right. You Drummonds..."

Benjamin laughed and shook LJ's hand. "Take it easy, man."

LJ gave Benjamin the blanket. "You too. Don't *study* too hard..."

Benjamin clapped his shoulder and went into the dorm, walking down the hall to Coralee's room. He knocked on the door, but instead of Coralee answering, it was Trish.

"Haven't seen you in a while," Trish said, leaning in the frame. She gave him a smile that made him antsy, and he clutched his bag's strap for support. "How you doin'?"

"I'm good, Trish. You?"

"I'm just fine," Trish said, batting her eyelashes. "Come to see lil' ole me?"

"Um...well...I—"

"Excuse me."

Benjamin nearly choked when Coralee tapped him on the shoulder, barely sparing him a glance as she passed him and went to her side of the room. Coralee made a point to keep her back to them and Benjamin clenched his jaw. He wanted her to look at him...at least to acknowledge his presence! After all they'd gone through, they could at least do that, couldn't they?

Trish chuckled and shook her head.

Benjamin noticed this and frowned. "What?"

"Well...I know you didn't come to see me, at least."

Coralee's head snapped up, and she looked at them in horror. "Trish—"

"Never would've thought it'd be you..." Trish said, the smile still on her face as she looked at Benjamin.

"I'm just here to study..." Benjamin muttered.

"Maybe...but nothin' that's in them books," Trish said, moving away from the door and further into the room. When Benjamin didn't follow she looked over her shoulder at him. "Coralee's over there, sugar, or do you want her to follow you?"

Benjamin swallowed, still hanging by the door. He had no idea what her intentions were, and there was no way he would do anything to confirm Trish's suspicions.

Trish looked between the two of them and rolled her eyes. "Honestly...if you're gonna study, study! Ain't no law against that!"

Trish had a point, and Benjamin shuffled inside. "Coralee."

"Benjamin."

"I'll just leave you two alone, then...wouldn't want to *disturb* you..."

Trish grabbed a coat and some books of her own and left the room with a little wave. The pair didn't move or look at each other for a good amount of time after she left. Trish didn't give any indication whether she was okay with what she saw or if she'd tell anyone, but Benjamin knew they'd have to be more vigilant.

"I really did come here to study," he said quietly, breaking the silence between them.

"I know you did."

Coralee still wasn't looking at him, instead staring at her bedspread as she held a pillow to her chest.

Benjamin set his book bag on the ground and went to the bed, sitting across from her and cupping her cheek. "Ceelee..."

"My heart's racing as if I'd just gotten caught doing something wrong."

"Oh, Ceelee—" He had been moving forward to kiss her forehead, but Coralee moved back and shook her head. "Coralee?"

"We can't do this here. Not in my room, not with Trish knowin' you're here..."

"But—"

"Perhaps you should leave."

"Leave?"

Coralee nodded and held the pillow to her tighter. Benjamin didn't want to leave...he didn't think he *should* leave. So what if he wanted to kiss her?—she was his *girlfriend*! That was what couples did! He passed his thumb over the swell of her cheek and shook his head.

"I'm not leavin', Coralee," he said quietly. "Especially when I'm not doin' anything wrong."

"But Trish—"

"Trish ain't here and Trish won't tell anyone."

"How do you know that? You know who she's seein', don't you?"

Benjamin did know, but it wasn't as if Tommy didn't know he'd "called dibs" on Coralee. Then again, Benjamin didn't think that would make her feel much better. "Even if she tells Tommy, who cares? He knows I know you, after all. I can just explain it away—"

"But you came to *my* room—"

"To study, darlin'," Benjamin said, his lip quirking a bit.

"Your book bag is all the way over there, Benjamin," Coralee reminded him with a raised eyebrow and a chin jut toward the door.

"But like Trish said—who said anything about books?"

Coralee rolled her eyes, but a ghost of a smile flitted upon her face. Benjamin grinned and kissed her forehead, glad that she didn't move away this time. "I could stare at you for hours and learn everything I needed to know."

"Could you?" Coralee asked. "Like what?"

"Well..." he began, moving his hand from her cheek to her jaw. "I can learn what beauty is by looking at your smile...about grace by watching you walk and move...humility from how you interact with others..." He dropped his hand from her face and grabbed hers, kissing the back of it. "Love by just being with you and thinking about you."

Coralee squeezed his hand, chuckling even as a tear fell down her cheek. "Lord, Benny, you make it seem so easy! Like people won't be angry if they find out about us!"

"I'll protect you from them." He squeezed her hand and kissed her cheek. "I'll protect you from everyone..."

"You can't do that, Benny," Coralee said sadly. "No matter how much you'd like to."

Benjamin squeezed her hand again, worried about the crease between her brows and the tension in her shoulders. Something had spooked her, and he needed to find out what.

"Coralee, what happened?"

"Nothin'."

He cupped her chin to force her to look him in the eyes. "Don't lie to me, Coralee. First, because you're very awful at it; and second, and most importantly, because you're supposed to trust me. You said you did, remember?"

"I do—"

"Then what's wrong?" Benjamin asked. "Do you think I'll make fun of you? That I won't understand? I can't understand anything if you won't tell me—!"

"And then there are things I'll tell you and you *still* won't understand," Coralee replied on a sigh.

Dread overcame Benjamin and he shook his head. "No...don't do this, Coralee—not now. Not after all we've been through..."

"What have we really been through, Benjamin? Huh? What— what *test* have we had to endure?" Coralee stood and went to her desk, staring at the books on it, fingering *Curious George* in particular. "No one but a select few knows about us, but are we really, *truly*, ready to make that big step and go public? Will we ever? You can still back out of this—"

"Whoa, whoa—wait a minute!" Benjamin interrupted, leaving the bed and approaching her, grasping her upper arms and shaking her a little. "Where's this comin' from? You still doubt me?" She didn't look at him, and Benjamin bent so she had to. There was anxiety in her eyes, and he cupped her face. "I'm not goin' anywhere, Coralee."

"You say that—"

"I *mean* it!"

She shook her head. "The fallout from our relationship—"

"Forget about that—"

"That's a luxury I can't afford, Benjamin," Coralee snapped, jerking her head out of his grasp and going back to her bed. She picked at a loose yarn on her afghan. "Without my community, I have nothing! All we have is each other and *this*...could cost me that! I'm afraid to be alone."

Clenching his jaw, Benjamin shook his head and picked up his backpack. "I keep tellin' you, Coralee, that I'm in this for the long haul, that you *won't* be alone, but it seems nothin' I say can convince you of that."

"Benny..." She sighed and blinked rapidly, though Benjamin noticed her watery eyes.

"I'm runnin' out of ideas, Ceelee," he said, a mixture of sadness and frustration. "I told you that you're worth anything and everything. The least you could do is extend to me the same courtesy."

Benjamin ignored her gasp and the call of his name, walking out of her room with a bag full of undeciphered notes, an unfinished report, and a cracked heart.

EIGHTEEN

"They're *what*?"

"*When*?"

"Today...in about thirty minutes."

Brother and sister looked at each other agape, then their mother, then each other again, trying to wrap their minds around the fact their mother's employer and his family would have Easter dinner with them.

"Why?"

Patty shrugged, flitting around the kitchen to make sure everything was in order. "I invited them."

"*Why*?"

"Coralee, I thought you of all people would be happy about this," Patty said quietly, looking around the room as if it were tapped or Luther would come jumping out the walls at any second.

Coralee could only blink at her mother. Why should she be happy about this—because Benjamin was coming? The last time they were together had ended poorly, and she hadn't seen Benjamin since. Now she had to be "happy" their families were together *and* try to act like they were "just friends"? It had been hard enough the first time they'd done it during the mutual dinner after the last regular season football game, and then they *had been* only friends...who kissed.

"Mama..."

"Don't 'Mama' me, Coralee," Patty said, pulling rolls out of the oven and putting them in a towel-lined bowl. "I thought it was the least I could do since I couldn't prepare *their* Easter dinner."

"Maybe they should learn how to cook for themselves," LJ said as he helped Coralee set the big table in the living room. "You do everything for them people, Ma—"

"I thought you liked the Drummonds," Patty said.

"I do, but I *love* you, and you need a break," LJ insisted. "You work too damn hard—"

"Language."

"He's right, Mama," Coralee said, coming into the kitchen for more utensils. She hugged her mother from behind. "You need to take a break...relax. I wish I could help you—"

"You'll do me a world o' help if you just stay in school and gradu-ate," Patty said, turning around and framing her daughter's face. "Yo' daddy and I ain't work all this time so you couldn't make somethin' o' yo'self. You smart, Coralee, too smart to be a housekeeper fo' somebody—smart enough to hire yo' *own* housekeeper someday—"

"A white one!" LJ called.

"White, black, blue, green, purple—I expect greatness from you," Patty said. She kissed her daughter's forehead. "Now hurry up and finish."

"Grandma Dennie comin' out?"

"No; said she ain't hungry and she tired," Patty murmured. "I think she needs to go to the doctor. She ain't had an appetite in a while."

"Really?" Coralee asked. She looked to LJ for confirmation and he nodded. "Why didn't y'all tell me when you last visited?"

"What can you do about it, Ceelee?" Patty sighed. "Besides, yo' daddy's workin' overtime at the mill so we can afford sendin' her to the doctor."

"He's gonna eat with us, right? I set up a place fo' him," LJ said, rolling his wheelchair into the kitchen.

"Yeah. I'll wake him up in about ten minutes. The Drummonds should be ten minutes away by then."

The three of them worked efficiently until that time, making sure everything was in order and that there would be enough food for everyone. Patty was nervous, Coralee could tell, because she went over details multiple times, something she rarely did when it was just family. Coralee wasn't that much calmer, but she hid it better, hopefully.

"Mama, the dinner's gonna be fine," Coralee promised.

"Ain't the food I'm worried about, Ceelee."

Coralee put a hand on her mother's shoulder and squeezed. "Why are you worried then?"

"Your father doesn't know about you and Benny."

"So? Not like we're gonna do anything—I won't even sit next to him."

Patty chuckled and shook her head. "That ain't gonna be enough. That boy won't be able to keep his eyes off you."

Coralee blushed at that prediction. "Mama..."

"If he was black, I'd be as happy as a clam about this," Patty muttered. "Now I'm just filled with fear and dread."

Coralee hugged her mother's waist and rested a cheek to her shoulder. "If I could've chosen..." *If she could have chosen...honestly...she* didn't want to finish that thought, knowing, instinctively it would have been Benjamin anyway.

"But you can't," Patty said, resting her forehead to Coralee's temple. "I know that better than anyone."

Coralee couldn't ask her mother to explain further, for it was time to wake up Luther. Coralee went to her room, straightening out the wrinkles in her dress and smoothing out her hair. She shouldn't be nervous. It wasn't as if he hadn't been in her house before, and it wasn't as if their parents didn't know each other, but this dinner felt different, like there was more at stake.

There was a knock on her door and she told the person to enter. LJ rolled in and closed the door behind him. She glanced at her brother. "Yeah?"

"I can't come in here and just be with my baby sister?"

She laughed. "You never had the inclination to do it before!"

He smiled and shrugged. "Things change..."

"Sometimes not fast enough."

"Sometimes *too* fast."

Coralee went to him and kissed his forehead. "I love you."

"I love you, too, Ceelee," LJ said, squeezing her hand. "It'll be all right."

She took a deep breath and laughed a little. "How you so optimistic? Given everything that's happened to you, no one would blame you if you was a little bitter...or even a lot bitter."

Luther's expression shuttered for just a moment, and then his responding smile was brittle. "Bitterness is a wasted emotion, Ceelee," LJ said, squeezing her hand again. "It's a poison that worsens a problem instead of solve it."

Coralee squeezed his hand back, her mood more solemn than before. "Do you think you'll ever walk again?"

"I hope so," LJ said. "You think there's a chance for you and Benny?"

Coralee didn't answer him, treating the question as rhetorical. Now was not the time to talk of a phantom relationship anyway. Outside the campus's bubble, she was just the daughter of Benjamin's housekeeper—no more and no less.

"Coralee! I need you, baby."

LJ kissed the back of Coralee's hand and turned his wheelchair around. Coralee opened the door and turned off the light in her room before following her brother to the living room. The Drummonds were already there, Mr. Drummond making himself at home on the couch while Mrs. Drummond looked around as if she were a caged animal. Benjamin was in the kitchen, his mouth practically watering in anticipation of the meal, and Coralee bit her lip to hide her smirk.

"Coralee, baby, can you go on down to the store for me? I ran out of tea and I just don't feel right servin' our guests water—"

"Now, Patty, I told you it was fine. You don't have to—"

"Mr. Paul, if it's all the same to you, I'd feel better about it. Ain't but a mile and a half up the road and if she hurry, she can get to it befo' it closes. Besides, Mama Dennie needs some talcum powder so she may as well go up there anyway. Abner has opened it for a few hours today after church."

"She this bossy with you, too, Mr. Paul?" Luther asked on a chuckle.

"Your wife is very assertive when she wants to be, Mr. Simmons."

Luther's laugh was still husky from his nap and he waved off Paul's comment. "Man, how many times I told you to call me Luther?"

"And how many times have I told you to call me Paul?"

Luther laughed again and nodded. "Plenty times, Mr. Paul, plenty times..."

"Coralee!"

"Ma'am, sorry," she said sheepishly, walking around LJ's wheelchair to the door. It was getting chilly, and by the time she came back from the store it would be dark out.

"Benny, go with Coralee."

"Mr. Paul, I'll be fine—"

"No, I agree with Mr. Paul," Luther said. "If it wasn't so close to sundown, I'd let you go out by yo'self; and if LJ was able he'd go, but I don't feel comfortable with you by yo'self, Ceelee—"

"Daddy, ain't like I never—"

"Abide by me, Ceelee," Luther said sternly. Benjamin was at her side now, but Coralee refused to look at him.

"And just who is going to protect my son out there?" Florence asked.

The hustle and bustle of the room stilled at that question, but Luther began laughing quite heartily. "Miss Florence, yo' son is huge, and not to mention the son of a state judge. Ain't nobody over here that stupid to do anything to him!"

"And if you're that concerned, he can just take the car," Mr. Paul said, though Coralee heard a slight edge to his voice.

"That was uncalled for, Mother," Benjamin said. He placed his hand on the small of Coralee's back, giving her a slight push. "Let's go, Ceelee."

Coralee hurried down the steps, slipping her hands into her pockets and began walking, not even waiting for Benjamin. He caught up with her in two strides. "Where are you going?"

"To the store."

"But we're taking the car..."

"The car offers more *protection*," Coralee said sarcastically.

"It does," Benjamin said. "For you."

"Yo' mama wasn't a whit concerned about me, Benjamin," she said, going over to the passenger's side of his car.

"But I was—am—more than a whit, actually. If my father hadn't suggested it, I would have; this isn't campus, Coralee. You can't just go wherever you please without someone walkin' with you. It's not safe!"

"Me bein' with you ain't safe, either, and yet I am!"

Coralee winced the second she'd said it; and when Benjamin got in the car, not looking at her or saying anything, she knew she'd hurt his feelings. He pulled out the driveway and the only time he spoke was to ask directions. Lately it seemed no matter what she did or said, it was the wrong thing. Her relationship with the BSU board was strained; now she was lashing out at Benjamin. Coralee was tired. She wanted to apologize to Benjamin about her outburst, but knew it wouldn't be as sincere as she wanted it to be because, in a way, she'd meant it.

When they reached the store, he remained in the car despite her assurances he didn't have to do so.

"I wouldn't want to be dangerous to you, Coralee."

She could've spit and cried at that.

Coralee wasn't long in the store, and Abner had said she made it just in time because he was about to close. He asked all the usual questions about her parents, LJ, and Grandma Dennie, and how she was doing in school. All of her answers were positive and upbeat, though she was anxious to leave.

"You need a ride, Ceelee? It's dark out."

"No, sir, I have one, thank you...Happy Easter."

"You too. Tell Mama Dennie Maebelle and I should be comin' up there soon, maybe a week or so?"

"Yes, sir. Bye!"

When she returned to the car, Benjamin still didn't speak to her, but she wouldn't press him. If he wanted to sulk, she would let him.

The ride back to her house was even quieter than the drive to the store, for this time he didn't need directions. She didn't like him silent like this, but they wouldn't have an opportunity to talk since they had to have dinner, and was sure that afterward, he and his family would leave.

Maybe it was better this way.

She would spend the better part of the dinner trying to convince herself of that.

Benjamin hadn't realized how hard it was not to talk to Coralee until he'd actually done it. Though he had been frustrated, he didn't like not talking to her at all, and when his parents had told him about their dinner with the Simmonses, he thought this would be a perfect opportunity to patch up things. So far, that attempt had gone horrifically. Of course now he was smarting from her previous comment—he, dangerous!—but the fact she hadn't even tried to talk to him at all made him feel even worse. He seemed to hit one brick wall after the other, and it made him feel frustrated and helpless because he didn't know how to reach her.

"What's wrong with you, Benny? Only time you've opened yo' mouth was to stuff food in it!"

Benjamin gave LJ a little smile but shrugged, shoving a piece of cornbread into his mouth. It was a lovely dinner, as expected since Patty prepared it, but he hadn't tasted anything. Coralee was sitting on the opposite side and end of the table next to her father, and Benjamin was sitting next to his and across from his mother. The two fathers sat at the heads of the table, appropriately, and the families were segregated because of it. Florence was as far away from Coralee as she could get, as if Coralee were contagious with an incurable disease.

Yeah...the Negro "disease"...

"Patty, I swear you should open a restaurant."

"A restaurant? Mr. Paul, you know I ain't got no time or money to do such a thing—"

"I'd back you. I've said it before and I'll say it again—you're the best cook in Plumville, hands down!"

"Why else you think I married her, Mr. Paul?" Luther laughed.

"Humph. And here I thought it was because of love," Patty muttered, but there was humor in her voice.

"That too," Luther said, leaning over to kiss his wife's cheek. Benjamin watched Coralee smile faintly at her parents and sip her sweet tea.

"A good cook and the love of a good woman is all you need," Luther said, pulling away. "Ain't that right, Mr. Paul?"

"Yes it is," Paul said, eating more of his food. He didn't even look at Florence when he said it, instead focusing on his plate.

"One out of two isn't bad, is it, dear?" Florence chuckled, trying to make a joke.

Paul smiled, eating another bite of food.

Benjamin winced. His parents weren't nearly as loving as Coralee's were, and that exchange highlighted that fact. He didn't want what his parents had; he wanted what Coralee's parents had...and he wanted it with Coralee.

"How did you and Aunt Patty meet, Mr. Simmons?" Benjamin asked.

"Oh, no, Benny, why you ask him that?" Patty frowned, but he could tell it was a fond story just by her tone.

"Curious."

"Curious, ha!" Luther laughed. "He wants the secret of gettin' a good woman, don't you, Mr. Benjamin."

"Oh, sir, call me Benny..."

"You sure?" Luther asked, though looking at Paul.

"Of course," Benjamin replied, and Paul nodded.

"Then call me Luther."

"It's not right—"

"Uncle Luther, then?" Luther said, glancing at his wife. "If she Aunt Patty, make sense I'm Uncle Luther, don't it?"

Benjamin laughed at the flawless logic. "Yes, sir—I mean, Uncle Luther..."

"Good heavens," Florence muttered. Paul and Benjamin ignored her. She'd had the snippy attitude since his father had announced they were coming; and though Benjamin didn't understand his mother's behavior, it was embarrassing and a little irritating.

"Well...I met Patty at church. Or rather, I ran right into her. Bein' chased by someone—"

"Floyd Wright."

"You ain't had to say *who*, Patty-Cake—"

"Just wanna make sure you get the story straight, that's all," Patty said, winking at Benjamin.

"*Anyway*," Luther started again, giving a mild glare to his wife. "*Floyd Wright* was chasin' me 'cause I'd beat him in a game of marbles and he had to give me his toffee—"

"Gamblin' at the Lord's house, the lot o' 'em. Heard they both got whipped real good fo' it—"

"Patience, *please!*" Coralee and LJ started snickering, and Luther tickled his daughter as she was the one within reach. "What I told yo' kids 'bout laughin' at yo' daddy?!"

"It's funny, Dad," LJ said, quite unapologetic.

"I'm sorry," Coralee insisted, kissing her father's cheek.

"Baby girl's forgiven. *You*," Luther said, pointing at his son. "Got work to do."

LJ rolled his eyes and Benjamin bit his lip to keep from laughing.

"So I gotsta runnin', 'cause Floyd Wright's 'bout as big as the church's steeple and as mean as a cock in a fight, and if Miss *Patience Reese* wasn't standin' in my way, my name's Jesse Jackson!"

"Now, Luther—"

"I was yellin' at people to move, but she was too busy talkin' to one o' her friends and she plum stood in my way!"

"Shouldna been gamblin'," Patty muttered. "You ruined my dress too! Brand new and my mama just sewed it!"

"And *you* ruined my escape!" Luther exclaimed. Suddenly he smiled, leaning across and kissing his wife's lips. "I ain't tried to get free, since..."

"Wasn't that lovely?" Florence said faintly. "Paul and I met at my coming out. A cleaner method, yes, but...same result!"

"Not quite," LJ muttered into his tea. Benjamin smothered a snicker.

"But fo' you, I'd recommend yo' Mama's method," Luther nodded. "Future state judge shouldn't get dirty fo' no woman."

"Yet if that's what it takes, I will," Benjamin said. He felt stares on him, his father's the strongest, but Benjamin kept his attention on Luther.

"There isn't any cause to get dirty," Florence insisted. "In fact, the May Day Ball is coming up soon, and you, of course will be there—"

"Mother, I don't want to go—"

"We've been putting it off long enough anyway," Florence continued. "Since you didn't like that Robinson girl, and thank heavens for that—what a dreadful choice *that* was!—this is the only place for you to find eligible, appropriate girls."

"But, Mother—"

"No 'buts', Benjamin," Florence said. "You are almost twenty-three years old, and it is time for you to start thinking about your future and settling down. I'm not getting any younger!"

The entire table was focused on him and his mother, even Coralee. Benjamin looked at her, and she dropped her eyes, her fork held limply in her hand. Appropriate and eligible girls...didn't Coralee realize she was both for him?

"Perhaps we should talk about this later, hmm?" Paul said, looking at his wife pointedly.

"You were his age when we got married, Paul," Florence said in a stage whisper. "I think we've indulged him too long."

"Excuse me," Coralee said softly, taking the pitcher with her to the kitchen as it was low on tea. Benjamin wished he could have followed her, but the kitchen was open with no door, so it wasn't as if they'd be able to have a private conversation.

"Would anyone like some tea before I sit?" Coralee asked upon her return.

"I would, dear, thank you."

She went to Florence's side and poured the drink. "Have you been training her, Patty?"

"Training her?"

"Yes, she pours so well."

"I'd like some tea, too, please," Benjamin said quickly, noticing the way Coralee's hand tightened on the handle and hearing LJ's groan. Coralee came around and began filling his glass, but Benjamin took her wrist, forcing her to set down the pitcher so she wouldn't spill its contents.

"Yes?" she asked, eyes slightly wide as she tried to figure out if he had completely lost his mind.

"Thank you," he whispered, looking right into her eyes as he kissed the back of her hand. It had been an impulsive move, but it felt natural...necessary. Coralee needed proof that he was serious about her, and what better way than to show their families he was.

It was very quiet again, and Benjamin took a deep breath before he began speaking. "I met Coralee when I was six years old and she was three. Aunt Patty used to bring her and LJ to work with her and we'd use to play games. Her favorite, if I remember correctly, was Princess; and I would be the prince and LJ would be the dragon, and of course, the noble Coralee was the princess." Benjamin squeezed her hand. "That was my favorite game too," he whispered to her.

"Are you crazy?" she asked.

"In love with you, yes," Benjamin said. Suddenly he stood, and Coralee moved back, but he didn't let go of her hand. He pulled her into his arms and looked at her father. "I love your daughter, Mr. Simmons." It felt good to let go of the secret that should've never been.

Luther couldn't say anything, his eyes wide as he stared at him holding his daughter. Benjamin looked at his mother who glared at Coralee with an ugly look he had only seen in Tommy Birch's eyes.

"Is she pregnant, Benjamin?"

"Florence Drummond!" Paul exclaimed.

"That's the only reason I can think of for my son to make such a *stupid* announcement!"

"You touch my baby girl?" Luther asked, his tone not as genial as it had been earlier. In fact, it made Benjamin hold Coralee tighter to him in fear.

"No, sir," Benjamin said. "She still has her honor, sir." He didn't think Mr. Simmons would want to be called Uncle Luther anymore.

"You're fired, Patty!"

"No, you aren't," Paul reneged.

Florence shot to her feet and pointed a shaky finger to Coralee. "You *will not* have my son! The Drummond name won't be sullied for the likes of you!"

Coralee shoved out of Benjamin's arms. The look on her face shattered his heart; but before he could say anything, she ran into her room. He started to go after her, however his father's cleared throat stopped him.

No one spoke, and Benjamin sat down under the weight of the strain in the room. Florence glared at Patty; Patty stared at her plate; Mr. Simmons looked like he wanted to break something—Benjamin guessed his neck; LJ continued eating his meal; and Paul looked around the table.

This dinner hadn't gone as any of them had planned, Benjamin was certain.

"Perhaps it's best we go," Paul said finally, setting his napkin down gently in his plate.

No one said anything still, but Benjamin stood and Paul pulled out his wife's chair. Florence was blotchy with fury, and Mr. Simmons' face was granite. Benjamin kept his head bowed like a puppy that had been kicked.

"I, uh, think it would be best for you to take the next week off, Patty," Paul said softly.

"Yes, sir."

He nodded to the remaining Simmonses. "Thank you for the meal. It was wonderful." He glanced back at Benjamin. "Come on, son."

Benjamin tried to meet their eyes, but the only one who would look at him was LJ. He'd ruined it. Coralee had tried to warn him but he wouldn't listen, and now he'd ruined not only her, but probably the entire family. Florence wouldn't take this atrocity of Southern etiquette, and the Simmonses might be blacklisted.

Me bein' with you ain't safe, either.

She was right.

Coralee was always right.

NINETEEN

"We're almost done with the proposal, people," Jermaine announced, looking around the room at BSU members with a slight smile. "By the time we're finished, the Board of Trustees will have their meeting next week; and, God willing, we'll be on the agenda to present our case."

Coralee felt his eyes on her, but kept hers on the tablet before her. That was her job, after all, to talk with Mr. Drummond to see if he could get the BSU a spot on the agenda to propose the Black Literature class. Trouble was, she hadn't spoken to anyone named Drummond since that fateful dinner two weeks ago. In fact, she'd been deliberately avoiding Benjamin because she couldn't face him.

Idiot boy! she thought, a frown marring her features as she half-listened to Jermaine continue his speech. She'd *told* him to play it cool, not to say anything, but he'd been pig-headed and opened his mouth anyway. Luckily, her mother hadn't lost her job, but her father had been given a mysterious pay cut at the mill.

He also wasn't talking to her.

Coralee felt robbed, jilted out of the bliss of a man declaring his love for the world to hear. She couldn't bask in it as other girls could; instead, she shied away from Benjamin and his love. She couldn't hold hands with him as Freda and Jermaine could. She couldn't go up to Benjamin and kiss his cheek as Trish could with her boyfriends. She had to treat Benjamin as if he were a stranger. His one flaw, the one snag, was the color of his skin, something so immutable and simple that caused such complex issues. Coralee knew Benjamin had grown sick of hearing about race and color and everybody else, and Coralee had as well; but when those two things were the very *foundations* of their lives, such a plain, and theoretically insignificant, human characteristic became the root from which everything else branched.

She had to publicly rebuff a love she'd waited her entire life to have.

"You feelin' all right, Ceelee?"

Coralee looked up to see the room starting to empty out, and felt Andre squeeze her shoulder. The other board members were all giving her concerned looks, and Coralee felt tears sting her eyes. She'd been crying far too much for her pride and peace of mind, but she'd always saved the tears for the privacy of her bed, muffling her sobs in her pillow right before falling into dreamless slumber.

"Yeah, girl, you've been avoidin' us," Freda said, and Coralee could hear the hurt in her friend's voice.

Coralee covered her eyes and took a series of deep breaths, warding off the impending flood. She'd been staying away for this very reason. She didn't have her emotions in check; and once she started crying, people would ask her what was wrong. Since she was already an emotional wreck, she wouldn't be able to evade the true answer. Then not only would she have lost Benjamin and her family, but her friends as well.

She would truly be alone.

"Stress of the proposal?" Jermaine supplied kindly. Coralee shook her head, and another, larger hand began sweeping up her back in a calming motion.

"What is it, girl?" Nick asked.

Coralee blew out a breath. The Lord had a sense of humor, making her fall in love with someone so wrong, when someone so right was perfectly willing to give her whatever she needed. Nick Price, the man she should have chosen, the man with whom she should be in love, comforting her like the good friend he was.

She started crying.

"Ceelee, honey..." Freda said, sitting down beside Coralee and smoothing her hair down. "What's wrong? Is it LJ?"

Coralee shook her head, unable to talk for the lump in her throat. Jermaine took her free hand and squeezed, and they just sat there, allowing Coralee her catharsis. When she finished crying, Freda wiped her face with a tissue and kissed her forehead.

"I'm sorry," Coralee croaked, taking another deep breath.

"Don't apologize," Jermaine said, squeezing her hand again. "Lately you've been walking around here like you were a zombie— only a matter of time before you snapped."

"Have I really been that bad?"

"You hadn't chewed me out for somethin' or other, so yeah, I'd say so!" Andre teased, earning a small smile for his efforts.

"You shouldn't sound so happy about that," Coralee muttered, and the group laughed.

"That's my girl," Nick murmured, kissing the top of her head.

"You wanna talk about it?" Freda asked gently.

"Want us to leave?" Jermaine asked, looking at the other two men briefly.

Coralee shook her head and took another deep breath, sitting up straighter and drying her cheeks with her hands. "No...what I got to say kinda affects everybody."

"All right, then," Jermaine said. "Let me close the door and then you can talk, okay?"

Coralee nodded, immediately missing the warmth of Jermaine's hand when he left, only to have Nick replace it with his own. Coralee tapped the eraser of her pencil on the tablet and bit her bottom lip, anxious and scared about what she was going to do. Should she tell them everything? Could she trust them? Her father giving her the silent treatment was bad enough, but bearable, since she didn't live at home; if her friends did the same...

She couldn't continue her silence, however. Despite her father's and Miss Florence's reactions, Coralee was relieved she didn't have to lie to them anymore; and she knew when she told her friends, another burden would be lifted from her shoulders.

The truth shall *set you free and all that, right?*

"Back," Jermaine said, taking a chair from one of the other desks and sitting in it opposite Coralee on the small dais. "Whenever you're ready."

Coralee started off slow first, going off on tangents, or staying too long on unnecessary points; but soon, she got to the meat of her predicament, and then she couldn't stop talking. She spoke of tutoring Benjamin, then the reforming of their friendship and how it'd bloomed into something more. She didn't look at anyone as she spoke, and she didn't tell them everything about her relationship with Benjamin, but she did mention Benjamin's declaration to their families and the subsequent fallout. By the time she was finished, Coralee felt refreshed and exhausted.

No one said anything at first, but Nick slid his hand from hers and left the dais. Coralee's heart clenched because she knew Nick was, inadvertently, a casualty of her relationship with Benjamin.

"He really said that in front of y'all's parents?" Freda whispered.

Coralee nodded.

"I wonder what his angle was for that." Andre said, more subdued than normal. "You ain't pregnant, are you?"

Coralee sucked her teeth and glared at the ceiling. "Why is that the automatic question from people's mouths? I'm *not* pregnant—in fact, we've never even done that!"

"For real?" Andre asked.

"Andre," Jermaine chastened.

"Come on, now," Andre said, "everyone was thinkin' it!"

"Because God forbid a white man loves a black woman, right?" Coralee muttered.

"Though I will admit," Jermaine said, giving Coralee a small smile, "Benjamin isn't as bad as the others—"

"Birds of a feather, man," Nick scoffed.

"Well," Andre said, cutting off his friend hastily, "Never figured you to—"

"Colorstruck—"

"Don't go there, Nick," Freda warned. "You know Coralee ain't like that—"

"She goin' out with Benjamin Drummond, ain't she? Tell me that ain't colorstruck—he's one of the most popular white boys here! Figures if you so naïve to fall for him in the first place, you'd fall for anything he tells you—!"

"Naïve?" Coralee asked quietly, staring at Nick with a challenging expression. "You know me better than that—!"

"I thought I did, 'til I hear now you runnin' behind some white boy!" Nick exclaimed, slamming his hands on the table in front of her. He invaded her personal space by bringing his face into hers, his eyes murderous. "That why you couldn't be with me—'cause you was with *him*?"

"*Be with you*?" Coralee repeated, internally wincing at her behaving like a parrot, but too flabbergasted by Nick to behave otherwise. "You never asked—"

"I took you on a date! To the after party after the bowl game!"

"A date," Coralee said flatly. "A date does not a relationship make!"

"And neither does a few tumbles in the hay, either, Coralee!"

Coralee stared at him, then looked around the room to the others. Jermaine had a sympathetic expression on his face, but Andre looked just as upset as Nick, just as accusatory. Oh, how they just *knew* the nature of her relationship with Benjamin! How they *assumed*! She'd just said she and Benjamin had never had sex, but they'd ignored her. Since it didn't mesh with their preconceived notions, it was disregarded.

"You're not listenin' to me," Coralee said, not backing down from Nick's challenge.

"Why should I listen to you? You nothin' but a liar and a traitor—!"

Her eyes almost popped out of her head. "What did you just call me?!"

Nick scowled and sucked his teeth. "Here we are trying to carve out a place for ourselves here, and you're sleepin' with the enemy!"

Coralee shook her head, and a small smile formed on her face, not even bothering to defend herself against his baseless accusation again. "No, Nick, he's only the enemy because you want him to be. It's convenient. Just as it's convenient for all the white people to think we're coons, it's easy for us to think of them all as enemies or out to get us. We're all in our nice, neat little boxes—everything's predictable...safe. White hatred is safe, isn't it, Nick? Mutual love and understanding...that's dangerous, and yet that's exactly what Dr. King wanted, right? 'Not by the color of their skin, but by the content of their character'? That applies both ways, and I thought that was the purpose of the BSU—to foster that mutual love and understanding!"

"Yeah, but we didn't mean literally!" Andre said, and Nick's nod corroborated the insistence.

"And yet, you didn't have any problems trying to get me to talk to his father," Coralee accused. "You have no problem usin' me to get what you want—to 'take one for the team', right?"

"Yo' mama works for 'im...then again, does she? Doubt they'd keep her around when her *daughter's* turnin' the son's head! Or *maybe* like mother like daughter—"

Everything suddenly became still, but the smack was as loud as a firecracker.

"Shit," Andre said, his mouth agape.

Coralee brought up her shaky, red-palmed hand to cover her own opened mouth. Never—*never*—did she think she could lose control like that; and as angry as Nick was making her, the last thing she'd ever intended was to hit him!

Nick didn't say anything, merely nodded and worked his jaw to relieve the stinging. He held up his hands in a surrender position and backed away from the table, his expression completely blank.

"Sellout," Nick whispered, then dropped his arms heavily and left. Andre left as well, but not before sending a very nasty glare Coralee's way as he rushed after Nick.

A fresh round of tears began, and Freda rubbed her back and cooed in her ear. It really wasn't fair.

"Let's get you home, huh?" Freda whispered after a time. "You and I can talk more later." Coralee nodded, and assisted Freda in wiping away her tears. "We'll get through this, Ceelee. We'll get through."

Jermaine nodded and offered her a small smile. "I'm gonna go...make sure they don't do somethin' stupid." Jermaine squeezed Coralee's shoulders and went out ahead of them.

Freda kept her distracted on the walk home, talking about her spring break and plans for the future. Coralee was glad she had good news to share, even as she felt her world collapsing.

"They're gonna tell other people, aren't they?" Coralee whispered when they approached her dorm.

Freda looked at her before she sighed and nodded. "More than likely, but you know I got your back, and I'm sure Jermaine does too!"

As president of the BSU, Jermaine was among the most influential black students on campus; so if Jermaine supported her, he would be a major ally.

Freda invited Coralee to spend the night in her room. She accepted the invitation, glad she had a late-morning class the next day. Trish was not in the room, so Coralee left a note for her roommate before changing into her nightclothes and stripping her bed of her pillow and blankets. Freda had a tin of cookies out for them and smiled.

"Movin' in?" Freda teased.

"It's cold in your room," Coralee returned, getting comfortable on the floor and taking out a cookie.

"Don't seem all that cold when Jermaine's in here," Freda said slyly.

The women shared a giggle and Coralee relaxed. Freda was do-ing a very good job of taking her mind off her problems, and Coralee was thankful for it. It was in times of crisis one found out who her real friends were, and she knew they didn't get any better than Freda Washington.

ॐ

Though it was mid-April, and the weather was starting to get warm, Benjamin couldn't help but feel chilly as he walked around campus. More than once, he caught himself on the receiving end of unpleasant and ugly stares, and multiple conversations stopped whenever he encountered a group of people.

But it wasn't until lunch back at the frat house did he figure out why, when Peter walked in, red-faced and harried, almost panicked.

"Tell me it ain't true, Ben; tell me it ain't true!"

His ham sandwich hovered at his mouth as he looked at Peter as if he were crazy. "What's not true?"

"You and some ni—"

"I know you ain't 'bout to go there, Peter," Barbara said from the sink as she washed a head of cabbage, not even bothering to turn around to address the boy.

Peter swallowed and lowered his voice and himself into a chair. "You and some Negro girl! Tell me it ain't true!"

"'Me and some Negro girl' what?" Benjamin said, taking a bite out of his sandwich. How did Peter know—how did *anyone* know? Did his mother tell someone? Did Coralee? Was she upset about it? Benjamin was, but mostly because he wished Coralee had told him she was going to tell someone. However, he hadn't seen her since "the announcement".

Peter glared at him, yanking the sandwich from his hands and dropping it on Benjamin's plate. "You went out with her? You're *in love* with her? Tell me it ain't true!"

Benjamin was suddenly very glad he no longer had his sandwich in his hands, or else he would've taken another bite and choked on it. He gaped at Peter instead. "What?"

"It's all around campus! Says you and that Simmons gal were to-gether—that you love her!"

Benjamin recoiled, looking over his shoulder at Barbara. She was still washing the same head of cabbage, and even he knew it didn't take that long to wash it. "Peter, I—"

"Tell me she's lyin'," Peter pleaded. "Now, I don't necessarily blame you—she's fine as far as Negro girls go—but tell me you ain't mean it...tell me that..."

"Why does it matter?"

"Why does it *matter*?" Peter repeated, aghast at Benjamin's au-dacity. "Don't you remember who you are? *Where* you are?!"

"Kinda hard not to!" Benjamin said bitterly. "Who told you all of this?"

Peter took a series of deep breaths and exhaled the last one slow-ly. "I overheard Nick Price talkin' to some of his friends...and he wasn't happy."

Benjamin winced, recalling the brief time when Nick had tried to start something with Coralee. "Do the other brothers know about this? Have they said anything to you?"

"As soon as I overheard Nick I came straight here," Peter admit-ted. "And you know they're gonna blow a gasket once they do—Tommy and Randy in particular! You need to squash this rumor and fast!"

"It's not a rumor," Benjamin said softly, staring at his ham sand-wich and realizing he no longer had an appetite.

"Lawdhavmercy," Barbara said, and Peter shot up as if his seat suddenly became very hot.

"No..."

"Peter—"

"Don't talk to me," Peter said, shaking his head and waving his hands in denial. "Just...don't..."

He rushed from the room then, and Benjamin dropped his head in his hands. Everything was unraveling right before his eyes, and he could do nothing to stop it. He hated feeling so out of control, so helpless; and worst of all, Coralee had warned him about this.

"You put yo'self in a mighty fine pickle, Mr. Drummond," Barbara said after a few moments.

"Yeah..."

She sat next to him at the table and held his hand. "And that girl...she ain't in trouble, is she?"

Benjamin sighed. Why was that always the automatic assumption? "No, ma'am. We never did anything like that."

"Really?" Barbara sounded skeptical. "I been in this house fo' a long time, and believe you me, you ain't the first one to jump the fence, and I doubt you'll be the last; but you *are* the first one to...not deny...*kinder* feelin's, if you catch my drift."

"How could I deny the best thing to ever happen to me?" Benjamin asked honestly. "Miss Barbara, she's...amazin'. This beautiful, intelligent, amazin' woman said she loved me, and I love her; and now people lookin' at me and treatin' me like I'm some sort of traitor!"

"You are!" Barbara chuckled. "You committed the cardinal sin and loved one o' us, and she...well, she let you, I guess. Y'all wasn't supposed to do that, y'know."

"I know," Benjamin said. "She told me, and I didn't listen."

Barbara scoffed. "Men never do."

Benjamin had to quirk a lip at that. "I told her it would be okay; that things had changed...but given my mama's reaction to this whole thing, they haven't changed all that much."

"It's all right 'til it's *their* child." Barbara sighed. "So, she ain't in trouble—that's good. Maybe it's best fo' you to end it? This'll blow over soon and you'll be able to get yo' life back in order—people mighty forgivin' if you repent."

"I didn't commit a sin, Miss Barbara," Benjamin insisted. "Loving Coralee could never be a sin."

"Coralee..." Barbara's eyes widened. "Miss Patty's girl? Lawd, Benny! You know how to pick 'em, don't you!"

Benjamin laughed a little and nodded. "Head over heels and it snuck up on me before I could even blink. But we've known each other all our lives...it was easy...seamless."

"Foolhardy!" Barbara said. "Like father, like son—"

"What?"

Barbara sucked in a breath. "Lawd, me and my mouth..."

Benjamin stood. "My father—?"

"It ain't my place," Barbara interrupted. "But given the circumstances, you should probably talk to yo' daddy."

Benjamin was getting a headache. Too much was happening and he couldn't process it all. "I need to see her."

"That gal's goin' through enough right now," Barbara surmised. "And as for that Nick boy—it sound like nothin' but sour grapes. The only reason a man would ever spread a woman's business around is because o' jealousy—"

"I'll fix him," Benjamin said seriously.

"Boy, sit down and finish that sandwich!" Barbara ordered, finally pulling the leaves off the cabbage and putting them in a pot. "You'll do no such thing, 'cause all that'll do is make things worse. Don't do that to that girl."

"I'm not hungry," Benjamin muttered, and instead pushed his chair under the table and went to his room.

He skived off the rest of his classes, knowing he wouldn't be able to keep it cool if he did, and tossed a football in the air as he lay on his bed. What possessed Coralee to tell Nick?

He snorted to himself. "You're the one who caught the confession virus first, man."

He'd been swept up in the moment, wanting to share after listening to Mr. Simmons talk about Aunt Patty that way. Benjamin felt as much for Coralee as Mr. Simmons obviously did for Aunt Patty, and in his joy had forgotten something very significant: Coralee wasn't the same race as he was.

"That pesky little matter—"

The door opened, and Benjamin physically relaxed when it was Felix. "Hey."

"It's all over campus," Felix said without preamble, closing the door and locking it for good measure before sitting on the edge of his bed. "How are you doin'?"

"How am I doin'?" Benjamin said under his breath. "What about Ceelee? How is she doin'?"

"I don't know, Ben; I haven't seen her all day," Felix said apologetically. "But what I hear…it's not good."

"She's hurt?"

"I would be if someone said the things about me they're saying about her," Felix admitted.

Benjamin caught the ball and sat up. "Like what? From who?"

Felix shook his head and looked at his hands that were hanging between his legs. "I don't wanna repeat, but suffice to say, it ain't nice."

"Who?"

"It doesn't matter who," Felix said, "you just keep your cool. I've never known you as a hothead before, so don't go tryin' to be one now!"

"That's my girl they're talkin' about," Benjamin muttered, sitting on the edge of his bed.

"Yeah, well, the best thing to do is not fan the fire," Felix advised. "You have more important things to worry about—like the other brothers here."

Benjamin groaned and stamped down the sudden urge to hurl the football through the window. "Why couldn't I keep my big mouth shut?"

"Dunno, but it was only a matter of time."

"A matter of time…" This was not how he wanted things to be, and he'd been a fool to think his parents would understand. And then the comment Miss Barbara made about his father—

"I gotta talk to her," Benjamin mumbled. Felix was right behind him as they went down the stairs, only to see the majority of the brothers circled around Tommy.

This was not good.

"Well lookey here, gentlemen—the nigger lover and his nigger lovin' friend!" Tommy said.

Benjamin ignored Tommy and the stares that were pinned on him as he and Felix reached the bottom of the steps. He didn't have time for Tommy Birch just then, and wondered why he'd ever made time for him in the past.

"So..." Tommy said, seemingly unaffected by Benjamin's lack of response. "How was she?" The others snickered and again Benjamin ignored him, poking his head in the kitchen to find Barbara not there.

"Who you lookin' for?" Tommy asked. "*Ceelee?*" Benjamin tensed, and Felix touched his shoulder. He didn't like her name coming from Tommy's mouth, and Tommy knew it too.

"*Hmm,*" Tommy continued, and the way he said it finally garnered Benjamin's attention. "Figure she'd let me have a go at her? Think she'd put out if I told her I *loved her* too?"

"You touch her and I'll kill you," Benjamin said quietly.

Tommy's smile turned into a scowl. "You were always so quick to defend that girl, even when we were younger."

"She's my friend—"

"*I'm* your friend!" Tommy snapped, walking up to Benjamin until they were nose to nose. "They're just no account niggers, and you chose them over me and everybody else—?"

"Never had to be a choice, Tommy," Benjamin said, his body locked and primed should Tommy start something. "Wasn't a law sayin' I couldn't be friends with all of y'all—"

"The hell there ain't!" Tommy exclaimed, standing straighter and looking down at Benjamin. Tommy was slightly taller than Benjamin, but lankier and not as strong. If it came to blows, Benjamin would be ready.

"You just leave her alone," Benjamin said, and began to walk around Tommy. He grabbed Benjamin's arm and dug his fingers into the muscle.

"Why I gotta leave her alone?" Tommy asked. "You had her, why can't I? You know what they say—sharin' is carin'—"

"Do you go around sharing *your* girlfriend with other men?" Benjamin asked. "Do you even *have* one?"

The men in the room whistled lowly and Tommy smirked. "Ain't like you do—you bein' in love with a *coon*—"

Benjamin yanked his arm out of Tommy's grasp and shoved the other boy hard. "You watch your mouth around me—"

Tommy tackled Benjamin to the ground, and the two men began wrestling, neither getting the upper hand over the other. Tommy caught him good in the cheek and the eye, while Benjamin got Tommy's jaw and stomach. No one tried stopping them, which was fine, because only God could stop Benjamin from tearing into Tommy—

"Y'all *bet' not* be gettin' blood on this carpet! I just cleaned it yesterday!"

And Miss Barbara.

People finally stepped in to break up the fight, Felix holding onto Benjamin while Randy held Tommy. They looked at him with such hate that Benjamin knew he would've been heartbroken if he cared. In fact, the majority of his brothers shared the same looks the other two men had, if to a lesser degree—mostly disbelief and confusion—and Benjamin knew he should feel as though his world had ended.

But he didn't.

"You go to hell!" Tommy hissed.

"I'll meet you there," Benjamin returned, and Felix shoved him out of the frat house. Benjamin kept walking, however, not even looking back to see if Felix was following.

He was, however, coming up shoulder-to-shoulder with Benjamin and looking straight ahead. "Your stuff may be broken and in the front yard when you get back."

"Miss Barbara's not gonna let them do that," Benjamin said confidently.

Felix chuckled. "That's true...but still, things might get a little frosty for you in the house, and it's too late to move out."

"If I have to move out, I'll go back home. Term's basically over anyway; and the less of Tommy I see, the longer he lives," Benjamin groused.

"That's good; homicide doesn't look too well on a state judge's résumé," Felix said. "Even with your last name."

"A blessing and a curse."

"A blessing," Felix said, "because if your name wasn't Drummond, I'm sure more of those guys would've gotten their licks in just now."

Benjamin winced, more at the throbbing in his eye than the truth Felix spoke. No one would risk irreparable harm on a state judge's son—not over a colored girl. Besides, Benjamin wasn't the first white man to sow his oats with one, and he wouldn't be the last.

"But I meant what I said," Benjamin began after a few moments, "if Birch or any of 'em touches her, I'll fix him good."

"I think he's jealous you got her," Felix said.

"Jealous? He hates her and every other colored person on the planet."

"No man hates anything more than somethin' he can't have."

"And he can't have her," Benjamin growled, his hands balled into fists. "She's mine."

"And always has been, from the sound of things," Felix said with a slight smile. "It would be romantic if it wasn't so tragic."

Benjamin gave Felix an odd look. "I didn't know you.... talked like that."

"I love *Romeo and Juliet*," Felix said, shoving Benjamin a little when he started to laugh. "I have a soft side, what can I say?"

"So what are you—the Friar?" Benjamin asked sarcastically. Felix stopped walking, and Benjamin did the same. "What?"

"I can't believe you knew that!"

It was Benjamin's turn to shove Felix. "You can thank Coralee for that."

"Next time I see her, I'll make sure I do so!"

Benjamin sighed. "At this rate, you'll see her before I ever..."

She was at the fountain with her friend, crying, and Benjamin's heart hurt. He went to her cautiously, not knowing how she would receive him, but unable to ignore her.

"Coralee?"

Her head snapped up, her eyes red and puffy. "What happened to you?"

"What?"

She came up and touched his face gently. "Have you been fightin'?"

He nodded, hissing when she touched his swollen cheek. "For you...us..."

"Benny..."

"Benny," he repeated, taking her hands in his and kissing the backs of them. "I'm glad I'm still Benny." That meant she wasn't angry with him anymore.

"I'm sorry."

"I'm not," Benjamin said. "Now we don't have to hide—"

"Maybe not," Freda piped up, standing from the fountain and approaching them, "but you two should back off a bit. A lot of people aren't happy with the two of you right now—"

"I don't care," Benjamin said, staring into Coralee's eyes as he wiped away her tears with gentle thumbs. "I shouldn't have to sacrifice my happiness for everyone else—"

"Well, how about happiness for safety," Freda said. "And what's gonna happen when you leave campus and she's still here? Who's gonna protect Coralee then?"

Freda had a point, and Benjamin pulled Coralee into his arms, heartened that she returned his embrace. He would stay for her—he could wait to go to law school.

"I'll figure something out—"

"Freda's right," Coralee said, pulling back, but Benny refused to let her leave him completely. "Our parents are at odds...friends...the campus—everything—"

"You're gonna let them win, Coralee?" Benjamin asked, cupping her face again. "Baby, no..."

"Benny." Coralee sighed, covering his hands with hers. "Benny...I don't do well with isolation. I don't like people talkin' about me behind my back...or in front of it. I don't like bein' called all these names by people I thought were my friends—"

"They're not really your friends, and you can do without them—"

"It's not that simple!"

"But is it worth it?" Benjamin asked, shaking her head a little. "Are *we* worth it?"

Coralee stood on her tiptoes and kissed his lips lightly...sadly. "We are...but not right now."

"Coralee—"

"Not right now," Coralee said, starting to cry once more. "I'm sorry..."

Benjamin disregarded that, pulling Coralee in his arms again. He kissed her hard, framing her face and pouring every bit of emotion he could into it. "I love you."

"I love you too," Coralee whispered against his lips, kissing them again almost chastely. "I do—even if I shouldn't—but we have to wait, Benjamin, just for a little while. Now's not the time..."

Freda eased Coralee out of Benjamin's arms and looked at him sadly. "You should put some ice on your face."

Coralee walking away from him hurt more than any punch or kick ever could, and it wasn't until Felix physically turned him around and guided him back toward the frat house did he finally feel his world crashing around him.

TWENTY

Each stare felt like a dagger stabbing into her body to the hilt, kept there to maximize the pain but to keep Coralee alive...serving as a reminder of how much her betrayal hurt, of how they wanted her to feel that hurt she'd inflicted upon them a thousand times over. The gossip, looks, and hostility had been going on for a week. Conversations stopped when she passed, letters were tacked to her door or thrown her way, revealing the writer's disgust at her and her relationship with Benjamin. No one made eye contact with her, no one wanted to come close to her, as if she were diseased and unclean. To them, however, she was. She'd loved a white man...crossed over to the other side...and now she had to pay the price.

Trish didn't speak to her anymore, not that they'd ever been very talkative; but her roommate's condescending looks made Coralee glad it was the end of the year and not the beginning. In fact, she spent most of her nights with Freda, anyway, so at least that tension was livable.

Coralee supposed Trish had been okay with her and Benjamin until she'd discovered real feelings had been involved.

The BSU had decided Freda and Jermaine would present the proposal at the Board of Trustees meeting a few days ago, hoping to avoid biasing the members any more than necessary. After all, if the campus knew about Coralee and Benjamin, it was safe to assume the Board did too. The Board had said it would think about it, but no one expected much from the decision.

"Floozy!"

Coralee didn't even bother to see who called her that, holding her books tighter to her and keeping on the path to the dining hall. Freda still had class, so she had to make this walk alone. A week earlier, she would've been waving and smiling to her fellow class-mates; but not now, not anymore. She'd been preparing herself for this, had been preparing *Benjamin* for this, but he was off on his own side of campus because she'd foolishly thought putting things on hold would appease people somehow.

But the damage had long been done. She'd chosen the quarter-back over the running back, the Drummond over the Price, the white man over the black man, and that was unforgivable. How could black folks have a united front if one of them was involved with someone from the other side? Benedict Arnold had more tact.

She entered the dining hall, relieved to see it relatively empty as it was the beginning of dinnertime. She glanced at the table where Benjamin had helped her with her Kant essay. She remembered his note saying they were a categorical imperative, and she smiled a little. Things had been so simple when it was just the two of them.

Coralee grabbed a tray and plates before going into the food line. The usually cheery cafeteria workers now had dour faces, their eyes flat and their postures unwelcoming. One worker sucked his teeth and looked her up and down as if she weren't worth their time. Another drummed her fingers on the counter.

Coralee licked her lips. "May I have mashed potatoes with gravy, a slice of roast beef, green beans, and a roll, please?"

The workers looked at each other, then the mashed potato server rolled her eyes before plopping a scoopful on her plate and dribbling the gravy haphazardly on it. Most of it ran in a river off the side of the plate, and maybe a teaspoon of the gravy actually made it to the mashed potatoes. She shoved the plate to the roast beef server who chose the absolute thinnest slice he could get and threw it on the plate, shaking his head to pass it on to the next person. The man didn't even bother to drain the juice from the scoopful of green beans, dropping it all onto the plate where the greenish liquid mixed with the gravy, opaque roast beef slice, and potatoes. The bread lady flipped the roll right into the potatoes and didn't give her a packet of butter.

"Enjoy," she said, her lip curled and eyebrow raised, shoving the plate onto the serving shelf where juice, gravy, and some mashed potatoes flew off and hit Coralee in the face and collar. The servers snickered at her predicament.

"Maybe y'all should start adding *respect* to the menu," Coralee said tightly, wiping her jaw and collar with a napkin. She would write yet another note to the cafeteria manager about their behavior, and it would probably remain just as ignored as the previous eighteen.

"Oh, no, Miss Thang—don't get uppity with *us*," Bread Lady said, "treatin' po' Nick like that—"

"We always liked you, always thought you and him would be good together, but Nick betta off without ya!" Roast Beef Man said.

"Tramp!" Mashed Potato Lady condemned.

"I'mma pray fo' you, girl," Green Beans Man said. "You sho'ly need Jesus, now!"

Coralee looked at them all as if they had lost their minds, surprised and hurt by their comments. Just a few days ago, before everything came out, she'd had a very nice conversation with them about being a teacher, and they'd said how proud of her they all were and what a great teacher she would be. They'd even given her extra corn, two rolls, a nice portion of meatloaf, and two helpings of rice completely covered in gravy. Now it was as if it physically pained them to serve her.

"I'll pray for y'all too," Coralee said, looking each of them in the eye, dampening a smirk at their shocked faces. "Have a good day."

She chose the "Kant" table and began eating, pulling out one of her texts so she could study. As she ate and read, the dining hall grew louder, and the stabbing feeling returned.

"Missed you this mornin', *Ceelee*...was wit' Whitey today?"

Others chuckled but Coralee didn't respond. They weren't her parents; she didn't have to answer to them. She knew better than to mistake their curiosity for concern of her dietary intake, or the lack thereof, since she'd skipped breakfast completely.

"You always been a lil' uppity thang," someone else said, "Suckin' up to the white professors, bein' their teacher's pet...always thought it strange you joined the BSU—"

"She was a *spy*! She probably tipped off those white boys at that rally—"

"Always talkin' 'bout unity and workin' together...now we know why!"

Tears stung Coralee's eyes but she refused to let one fall. If they thought she could've sold out the BSU at the rally, then they really didn't know her at all. She was one of the staunchest fighters against the racism and prejudice on campus, and for them even to *conjecture* she could've done such a thing was a punch in the face.

"Coralee."

She looked up to see Nick, Andre, and other black athletes standing at the table. Her heart clenched, and she had half a mind not to reply, but she wouldn't be petty.

"Evening."

The rest of the dining hall went quiet. Everyone looked at them in anticipation.

"Wanted to know if we could borrow the salt," Andre said while Nick rolled his eyes and pursed his lips.

"She may not give it to you," one of the guys said.

"Yeah, seems to me you've always been partial to the salt," one of the boys said, and they snickered.

"I guess pepper ain't good enough fo' ya?" someone else asked.

The neighboring table also chuckled and Coralee clenched her jaw. "This comin' from a man who has 'salt with fries' instead of the other way around." She glared at the first boy who spoke—a basketball player—amid cough-covered laughs. "I didn't know what I eat or how I eat it was of great concern to you, Chris."

"When it affects my man here," Chris said, slapping Nick on the back, "it does."

"I'm not the first girl not to date Nick," Coralee said.

"You are for a white boy!" someone else said, and the men pinned him with silencing looks.

"Yeah! Here we are, tryin' to fight for our just due and gettin' ours, and you sittin' there *givin'* yours away! Y'know, when he dumps yo' black behind, don't come runnin' 'round after us—we don't like *used goods*."

"*Oooh...*"

Coralee rolled her eyes, annoyed by Chris, by the dining hall getting into her business, by everything. This campus, this town, was entirely too small, and Coralee felt suffocated. Every single move was scrutinized, analyzed, scandalized, to the point where Coralee wanted to scream. Hadn't this been why she'd been fighting for the better part of the year? It hadn't just been for the Black Studies department or even for civil rights. It'd been about her having the same freedom as everyone else and not having to apologize for it. Benjamin had assured her he was in it for the long haul, and she couldn't even grant him the same courtesy—too busy preparing herself for the community fallout instead of fortifying herself in Benjamin's love. Now that she had neither Benjamin *nor* community support, Coralee realized she was the biggest fool of all.

"Truth hurts, don't it?"

"Oh, is that what we're calling this bullshit now?"

He blinked at her and others gasped, clearly taken aback by her cursing, but Chris recovered with a cough and a grin. "Girl, that white boy don't love you! You just a fad! You know how they love dippin' in chocolate—!"

"And so do you! You see how many hearts you break in a given *semester*?"

"Tell *that*!" someone exclaimed.

"But I stick wit' my kind, *Coralee*," Chris said, scowling at Coralee and the exclamation. "I don't think I'm too high and mighty—"

"He goes with women who can *handle* a black man," Nick said, speaking to her for the first time.

Some people actually clapped for that, but Coralee could only laugh. That was the funniest, most asinine thing she'd ever heard in her life. "Negro, please!"

"No she *didn't* go there!" a nosy, high-pitched voice said.

"Negro! Yes, I am one," Nick said, leaning down to her and crowding her personal space again. "And you can't handle it! You're *ashamed* of it! I'm more man than you could ever hope to handle, that's why you gotta go with them white boys...you've been so brainwashed by the system that you was simple enough to fall for their lies and lines! Forget you, then! You deserve 'em! Hell, I even feel *sorry* for 'em—gotta deal with a weak-ass *girl* like you!"

Coralee stood and got in Nick's face in return. "You be very careful with how you speak to me, Price."

Nick started to lean closer, but Andre tugged him back. "Watch yourself, Nick."

"And *I'm* the weak one?" she asked, then laughed derisively. "Is that why you had to use Chris as your mouthpiece just now?" Coralee smirked, knowing those thoughts were as much Nick's as they were Chris's...as much as everyone's thoughts were in that dining hall. "Seems to me, *you're* the one who can't *handle* that I love Benjamin and he loves me back! You so busy clingin' to stereotypes that you don't even *check your boy* when he goes around using black women like toilet tissue! So how about this—make sure your house ain't made o' glass before you go throwin' rocks elsewhere!"

It was utterly silent now save for her voice ringing through the hall. It was liberating to say that out loud to all of them, though, to take ownership of her feelings instead of being scared of them. It was one thing to do it in private, or even with the BSU, but it was a completely other thing to do it in this forum. They weren't going to make her ashamed of how she felt—not anymore.

Nick started forward again but Coralee held her ground.

"Back up off me."

She trembled with anger, adrenaline, and apprehension. She didn't want to slap him again, but he was really working her nerves; and she knew, instinctively, that he wouldn't let a second slap go unpunished. He wouldn't take the public affront to his manhood lying down.

"Yeah, Nick, c'mon," Andre said, grasping Nick's arm to ease him away. Nick yanked his arm out Andre's hold and stuck a finger in her face. Coralee swatted it down.

"I let you get away with puttin' yo' hands on me once, I ain't gonna let you do it again—"

"Then you respect my personal space—"

"*Respect*? I know you ain't throwin' that word around at me! *Respect*! How much respect you showin' me and all the other black men on campus by flauntin' yo' whitey in our face! *Bitch, please*! You ain't nothin' but a house slave!"

Gasps echoed throughout the hall and Coralee shook her head, willing herself not to hit him...not to cry. Nick was being too cruel, and for this to come from someone she'd considered a good friend broke Coralee's heart. "Don't call me outside my name like that, Nick. You're behavin' no better than *whitey* does right now!"

He grabbed her shoulders and shook her, and this time Andre forcefully removed his hands from her body. "Don't you *ever* compare me wit' them, you hear me?!"

"Well you are!" Coralee yelled, her voice echoing. "You keep talkin' about respectin' our 'sisters' and here you are grabbin' and yellin' at me like I'm no better than a dog! Bein' a jerk isn't reserved for one race, Nicholas!"

"Damn, she brought out his full name!" Andre said, struggling to keep Nick calm.

"A jerk, huh?" Nick repeated, eyes widening. "Neither is bein' two-faced! And as far as I'm concerned, you ain't no 'sista' o' mine!"

"Come on, man! Let's go sit down!" Andre said, his voice belying the anxiousness he felt. "I know you angry, but you're takin' this a little too far!"

Nick shoved Andre away from him and left the dining hall. The others also went to their table but Andre remained, concern stark on his face.

"What?" Coralee asked, eyeing him askance. "Your turn to have a go at me?"

Andre looked horrified and shook his head. "No! He's just hurtin'," he explained, shrugging his shoulders. "You chose Drummond over him—"

"I didn't *choose* Benjamin *over* anybody! I fell in love with him! This has *nothin'* to do with Nick! I loved Benjamin before I even *met* Nick!"

"But you're turnin' yo' back on your race, Coralee," Andre said.

"How does that follow?" Coralee asked, looking at her cooled, coagulated food with distaste. "All I did was fall in love, and y'all treatin' me worse than any white people ever could!"

"So now you hate us—"

"This isn't about *hate*, Andre! It's about *love*! I love Benjamin and I love black people and I love myself! I was unaware that lovin' one meant hatin' another! I don't want to be *white*! I'm proud of myself and my heritage, but that don't mean I'm not allowed to love other heritages or someone *from* another heritage!"

"Other people don't see it that way."

"Yeah, well, they should," Coralee snapped. She wasn't hungry anymore, and she was sick of people staring at her as if she were an alien. "And that's why nothin' will ever get done—we're too busy hatin' each other to make any real progress! Hate ain't just fo' white people...black people can do a pretty good job of it too!"

Andre groaned and shook his head again. "Coralee—"

"Naw, I'm mad now!" She stood and gathered her things. "I'm goin' to my room."

She left Andre sitting there, and tried to balance her books and her tray as she walked towards the trash. She didn't make it, but at least her books fell instead of the food, and she was too upset to be embarrassed.

"I got this," Andre said quietly, having stooped next to her to mop up the food with a wad of napkins. "I'm real sorry about everything, Coralee."

She took a deep breath, blinking rapidly to stave off the tears. "Thanks, Andre, and I'm sorry too."

With as much dignity as she could salvage, Coralee picked up her books and left the dining hall, making a detour to the fountain instead of going to her room as she'd originally planned. The sun was beginning to set and a cool breeze fell upon the campus. Fresh air and light—two things she had gone without for the past week— rejuvenated her body and spirit. Everyone was either eating or studying, so the fountain was all hers. Sitting there with nothing but her thoughts, the wind, and crickets to keep her company did she finally feel some peace.

The only thing missing was Benjamin.

She hadn't seen him since their last meeting, and this separation was worse than the first time they "broke up". That hadn't lasted very long, either, and Coralee should've realized then that keeping Benjamin out of her life wouldn't work. He wouldn't allow it; and if she were being honest, neither could she. Every time she tried to do the right thing, it felt terribly wrong.

Coralee now realized it was because it hadn't been the right thing for *her*.

A shiver went through her, and it had nothing to do with the breeze. Her muscles tensed and bunched, and she looked around her, surveying her surroundings and finding nothing out of the ordinary. Her heart beat just a little faster, however, and she didn't relax.

Perhaps it *was* time to leave; the sun was gone now.

She stood and stared at the fountain before reaching into her cardigan's pocket and pulling out a shiny penny. She whispered a little wish on it, kissed it, and threw the penny into the fountain. She watched it sink to the bottom, clutching her books to her chest. It was silly to put a wish on a piece of copper.

It was even sillier to give up love to make everyone else comfortable.

A whim suddenly came upon her, and instead of going to her dorm, she walked up the gradual hill towards the frat house. *What are you doing?!* she asked herself, feeling more nervous the closer she was. It probably wasn't the best thing for her to do or even the safest, but what she had to say couldn't wait. Benjamin had asked her a question the last time they saw each other and she'd answered it wrong.

They *were* worth it right now. They'd been worth it all along.

All Benjamin had seen was the hopeful side of things, the optimism, and Coralee had been looking for doom for so long she'd finally found it. She only prayed Benjamin still held his beautiful hope for them...she was ready to accept it now.

"Where do you think you're goin', nigger bitch?"

Coralee stopped and whirled around, her heart beating even faster, still not seeing anyone. That voice sounded eerily familiar, and the feeling she'd gotten at the fountain returned. She began walking faster towards the house, wondering how something so close could seem miles away.

"I said—" The man grabbed her, one arm over her chest and the other around her waist, "where do you think you're goin'?"

Her books' corners cut into her body and she winced, then recoiled when she felt his nose drift along her jaw. "Who are you—what do you want?"

He squeezed her again, making Coralee bite the inside of her lip so she wouldn't yelp in pain and fear. "What does it matter who I am? Huh? As for what I want.... I want a go..."

"What?"

"I want a go at you. You must give pretty sweet lovin' if you made Drummond so soft—"

"Let go of me," Coralee said in a low, threatening tone. She began struggling, and some of the books fell out of her arms and onto their feet. The pain from that didn't compare to the creepy feeling of his hands and breath on her body. This was nothing like Benjamin's touch...nothing like the warm, loving embrace of his arms around her. This was what hate and power felt like, and Coralee wanted no part of it.

"Did you struggle like this with him?" he asked, sniffing her hair. "I'll bet it turned him on just like it's turnin' me on—"

Coralee knocked her head against his, causing him to relax his hold on her. She stomped her heel on his foot and gained freedom, now running for the house and screaming. She didn't get far before he tackled her to the ground, twisting her arm behind her back and pulling her head back by her hair.

"You did that the last time, you fuckin' nigger! But this time you won't get away—" He cut off his speech and began hiking up her skirt, twisting the arm behind her back even harder as she began kicking and thrashing to buck him off her. He was too strong, however, and her body was fatiguing quickly, but she continued yelling for help.

"You think anybody gonna come?" he asked, far too confident for her liking. Her skirt was now around her waist and he was working at her underwear. "They all hate you! In fact, if they come out, they'd probably have a crack at you once I was done—"

"Benny—!"

"Benny?" he asked, incredulous, then cackled. "Benny's not there! I don't know where the hell he is and I don't give a shit—he's moved out!"

"No..."

"Yeah!" He whooped. "We ran him out—can't have a nigger lover in the frat house, no matter what his name is—"

He managed to get her underwear down her hips, and Coralee's panic threatened to choke her. "No!" she cried, her throat burning as badly as her eyes did. This would *not* happen to her. "No!"

"Yes!" The man crowed, his nails digging into her wrist. "Maybe when we're done, Benny and I can compare notes...talk about what it was about you we liked the best!"

The street lamps clicked on, and Coralee realized they were underneath one, right on the pathway towards the frat house. He wasn't even trying to hide what he was doing, so sure no one would care, no one would help. The scary thing was, Coralee started believing that too.

Her elbows and knees stung from thrashing and scratching against the asphalt, and her hair tumbled into her eyes, long fallen from her chignon. Suddenly he straddled her waist but released her arm, and the sickening clink of metal let her know he was unbuckling his belt.

"Help," she whispered, unable to scream anymore, panic clogging her throat. She continued to buck as much as she could, but his thighs were too strong. She swallowed and took a deep breath. "HELP!"

He struck her across the face. "Shut up, bitch!"

Her vision blurred and her eyes watered, but she fought for consciousness. She couldn't pass out. She had to fight!

She weakly punched his shoulder and bucked again. "No!"

"Yes," he said, moving from her waist and between her legs. "Ye—!"

Suddenly all pressure went away from her body, but Coralee dared not move. It was as if she were in a tunnel, and she heard the wet, bloody sounds of a fist meeting flesh. Her body trembled so she could barely grasp the underwear around her knees, but she did, and scrambled them back to their proper place.

"Coralee?"

She jerked towards the voice, not able to recognize the person who spoke. Her eyesight was hazy and unfocused, but a rough, callused hand cupped her cheek. She shied away from it instinctively.

"I told you they were no good," the voice murmured, lips drifting over her forehead. The stench of alcohol was so strong that she gagged. "No good...shoulda been wit' me..."

She shrank back again, but he didn't allow her to go too far. The brief relief she'd felt when he'd pulled her attacker off left again, and she trembled. "Please..."

"I'd never hurt you," he whispered, words slurred, mouth moving down her cheek. "They don't know how to treat a woman...all they do is hurt...they can't love you like I can..."

"Nick," Coralee croaked, crying, angry at herself for hurting him, for him hurting her, for everything. All she'd ever wanted to do was love Benjamin—that was it. "I'm sorry..."

"Please, Ceelee...I won't hurt you..." His hand slid down her neck and collarbone...breastbone. He was pushing her back onto the asphalt, and Coralee began struggling again.

"Nick? Nick! Nick, let me up!"

"I'm not gonna hurt you, Coralee," he whispered, kissing her cheek, her jaw. He tried going for her mouth, but she moved her face away. He grabbed it tighter and moved her mouth back towards him, inserting his knee between her legs. "I'm *not* gonna hurt you—"

"But you *are*," Coralee insisted, wriggling to relieve the pressure of him, to remove the icky feelings he was creating in her.

Suddenly his eyes grew dark, his expression menacing. His nails dug into her skin and he pressed his knee painfully against her. "Even now, after everything, after that white boy just now, you *still* don't want me? You *still* don't get it!"

This was spiraling out of control, and Coralee nodded her head emphatically. "I *do*! I do! I appreciate you helpin' me, but Nick, you gotta get off me—*please*!"

"I ain't good enough fo' you," he said flatly.

She shook her head rapidly. "It's not that—!"

"It is! You think I ain't fit to touch ya! Well I am, Coralee! I am!"

He set his mouth to her neck and sucked so that it brought pain, not pleasure. Terror, more of it than before, raced through Coralee and she shook her head and bucked her hips frantically. "Nick! Please! *Please* get off me!"

"I'm not gonna hurt you; I'm gonna love you like you deserve...no white boy can love you like I can—"

"Get off her!"

Nick was yanked away, and Coralee curled into a tight fetal position. A coat fell upon her body, and a hand rubbed her back. "It's all right now...everything's all right now..."

She couldn't stop shaking.

"Coralee, it's Freda, okay? You're all right...everything's gonna be fine..."

Freda cradled Coralee in her arms, and she sagged against Freda's chest, spent. It was as if it were all a bad dream, Coralee seeing Felix trying to pull back a red-faced, straining Benjamin as he pummeled her first would-be rapist while Jermaine and Andre held down Nick. Coralee didn't recognize the person Benjamin kicked, but that didn't matter...she was safe now.

"I'm sorry," she whispered.

"Coralee?"

"I'm sorry..."

"Oh, no," Freda said softly, "none of this is your fault..."

"It is..."

"No," Freda said more firmly, "and don't you let me hear you say that again." Freda tightened her hold on Coralee. "Benjamin!"

Benjamin all but fell to his knees in front of them, holding out his arms so Freda could place Coralee in them. She snuggled immediately into Benjamin, breathing in his scent as he pressed kiss after hard kiss along her temples and face.

"Baby—"

"I'm sorry—"

"*I'm* sorry..."

No one spoke after that. Freda went with Felix to the nearby frat house while Andre monitored the still-unconscious attacker. Nick was babbling and Jermaine was looking between him and Coralee with sympathy and distress. Benjamin and Coralee held each other tight, neither saying a word. Benjamin's heartbeat beneath her ear reassured her. His fingers combing her hair relaxed her. His arms around her body comforted her.

This was much different from five minutes ago.

"Freda was right," Benjamin muttered, resting his forehead against hers. "She was right."

"Right about what?"

"Leavin' you alone. If I'm not here, you're vulnerable...I can't leave you here..."

"Benny—"

"No," he whispered. "I'm not leavin' you alone on campus. What if I'd come just a minute later? What if no one had *heard* you? What if—?!"

"Just hold me, Benny," Coralee interrupted, pressing her fingertips to his lips. "Don't speak...just hold me..."

"Forever," he vowed, pressing a long kiss on her forehead and holding her tighter.

Coralee was sleeping now, thank heavens; and despite the scratches and bruises on her forehead and cheeks and the lacerations on her arms, she was flawless. Benjamin hadn't left her side since arriving to the hospital; and though the nurses had looked at their ragtag group oddly, they'd left them alone. Coralee's doctor didn't even try to pry Benjamin from her side, his smile knowing and reassuring.

He was a transfer from a hospital in Chicago.

Benjamin looked across the bed at his father who gazed at her with concern. Benjamin then brushed an errant lock of hair from Coralee's forehead before re-clasping the sleeping girl's hand.

"You look tired," he said softly.

His father chuckled, though his mouth didn't smile. "Not too tired..." *Not compared to Coralee*...Benjamin heard the unspoken part just as clearly as if it had been.

A nurse walked in, staring at the both of them, her expression shocked and judgmental. She glanced at Coralee and harrumphed as she checked the hospital chart.

"A man can't be concerned for his girlfriend?" Benjamin snapped.

The nurse gasped, then threw her head back and left.

"Benjamin," Paul chastised half-heartedly.

"She's not important," Benjamin said flatly, his thumb running across Coralee's knuckles. "None of them are."

"Coralee's parents should be arriving soon," Paul began, almost feebly. Benjamin nodded. "Son—"

"This should've never happened," Benjamin murmured, looking at Coralee's sleeping form. He should've been there...he should've put his foot down and not allowed her to walk away from him. This would've never happened had he been there with her.

Paul shook his head, leaning across the bed to cover his hand over Benjamin's and Coralee's. "Don't do this to yourself. It's not gonna change anything—"

Benjamin laughed sardonically. "*Randy Jurgens* tried to *rape* her, *Nick Price* tried to finish the job, and the police aren't going to do anything about it!"

"Coralee decided not to press charges against Price," Paul reminded him quietly. "And you know they weren't going to charge Jurgens with anything...the Simmonses are a private people, Benjamin, and something like this won't let them get any peace! Bad enough she's seeing you—"

"So this *is* my fault!"

"Damn it, Benjamin, no, but you knew better! You can't always have what you want!"

"What about what I need, Dad?" Benjamin asked, now squeezing Coralee's hand with both of his. "What about that?"

"Need?"

"I need her, Dad," Benjamin said without shame.

Paul again chuckled without humor. "I'd thought the same thing when I was your age."

"Right," Benjamin said in disbelief. "Forgive me for saying, but you and Mom don't act like you need each other."

"I wasn't talking about your mother," Paul said softly, staring at his fingers as if he was seeing them for the first time.

Now Benjamin was confused, if not his mother, then, "Who?"

Paul clasped his hands together, the bottom fingers tapping against the bed. "Let's just say.... like father, like son."

Despite the cliché, Benjamin thought the phrasing familiar, and suddenly remembered Miss Barbara saying the same thing earlier. He gasped, staring at his father through incredulous eyes. "You and...Aunt Pa...?!" Benjamin rested his forehead on the bed as if it were too much to comprehend. They were the last two people he ever thought would be in a relationship together, and yet, strangely, it made sense. "Not that I can say I blame you..."

"Nor I you." Paul laughed more genuinely this time, then took a deep breath, smoothing his palms on his slacks. "In many ways, I envy you."

"Envy me?"

"Yes. You did what I couldn't—take a chance."

Benjamin didn't need to ask why. It was moot anyway. "Coralee had given me plenty of chances to change my mind—sometimes even trying to change it for me."

"You've always been a stubborn goat," Paul said with a hint of pride. "I'd like to think I had something to do with that."

"You taught me to stand up for myself."

"Did I?"

"Yes, and for those who couldn't," Benjamin said. He'd idolized his father during his youth, and in many ways still did. Paul's fairness and honor was something Benjamin strove to have and maintain.

"I am proud of you, Benjamin," Paul said after some silence. "You're doing what I couldn't."

"What's that?"

"Stand alone."

Benjamin shook his head, kissing the back of Coralee's hand. "I'm not alone, Dad," he insisted, "I have Coralee."

A knock sounded on the door, and it opened revealing Coralee's parents. Their worry was palpable; Mr. Simmons's face was stern and Aunt Patty looked as if she'd just stopped crying.

"She's resting now," Benjamin said, smoothing out imaginary creases in the bedspread. "The doctor cleaned up as much of the cuts as he could and prescribed her some medicine for the pain."

Patty nodded, hand at her mouth to cover her sob. "My baby..."

Mr. Simmons glared at Benjamin. "If it hadn't been fo' you—"

"A whole lot worse would've happened to her!" Mr. Drummond said, interrupting the accusation forcefully and not backing down from the distrustful look Mr. Simmons now gave him.

"Benjamin," Patty said, effectively defusing the tension and turning everyone's attention to her. "Will she be okay? Will my baby be okay?"

Benjamin stood and embraced Patty, and she returned the hug hard. This woman was like a second mother to him, someone his father had apparently loved just as he loved her daughter. "I'm sorry—"

"You saved my baby," Patty said, dismissing his apology. "Ain't no need for you to say you sorry. You saved her..."

Benjamin helped Patty into the chair he had vacated, and Paul and Benjamin left mother and father alone with their daughter. Freda, Jermaine, and Felix stood when they entered the waiting area, all with concerned expressions.

"I'm going to call your mother to let her know what happened," Paul said. Benjamin nodded.

"How is she?" Freda asked. Jermaine hugged her shoulders and kissed her temple, wanting to calm her.

"She's resting now...sleeping. They're gonna keep her overnight for observation—she has a nasty bump on the head, but they think she'll be fine."

"Y'all had to pull some strings to get her admitted here," Jermaine noted. Though the hospital legally had been integrated for a few years, few black patients ever came there.

"Coralee would get the best care here," Benjamin said. Unfortunate, but true.

"You really care for her," Jermaine noted.

"I love her."

"You do, don't you," Freda said with a watery smile, and Benjamin returned it. They all sat down again, though Benjamin couldn't sit very still. Felix clasped his shoulder in support.

"You can't hog up all her time, Benny; her parents need to see her too."

"I know..."

"I know you know. She'll be there when you go back."

It felt like days had passed before the Simmonses left the room. Mr. Simmons said nothing and looked at no one, going directly to the car. Patty said they'd be back in the morning to check her out of the hospital, and thanked them all for their support before following her husband.

Benjamin stood. "I'm goin' back in there." No one was surprised, and no one stopped him.

He went inside the room, shutting the door softly behind him, and sat next to the bed again. He trailed a finger along her hairline and kissed her softly. Her eyes fluttered open at the contact, and they stared at each other for a long time.

Coralee licked her lips. "I was comin' to you."

Benjamin nodded, exhaling a wobbly breath, and slid onto the bed, wrapping his arms around her waist and bringing her flush against him, needing her warmth, the reminder that she was okay and safe and with him.

They both fell asleep, remaining that way all through interruptions from his father and her doctor.

They slept until morning.

EPILOGUE

1975

Benjamin stroked his wife's belly softly as she slept. She was big, round, and beautiful, and he couldn't wait to greet his little one—a girl he predicted, while she insisted the baby was a boy.

Even after two years of marriage and a lifetime of love, his wife left him in perpetual awe. Coralee Ruth Drummond, née Simmons, a childhood best friend who grew to be the love of his life. It didn't matter they'd met when both were too young to know what "soul mate" meant or that "race" mattered, all Benjamin had known was the little dark girl with her braids, curiosity, and love for *Curious George* was important to him.

And now, this glorious woman was giving him a child.

Benjamin couldn't stop touching Coralee, gazing at her, loving her. She was his air, and he always breathed easier when she was near. It was so difficult going to work, being separated from her, while she was like this. During the first few weeks of her pregnancy, he'd called her on the job every half hour, and it wasn't until Coralee had threatened to exile him on the couch did he ease up. She was a kindergarten teacher, so the many disruptions by her husband were incredibly unappreciated. He hadn't realized his wife could get so surly and snippy; but if it meant his wife and child would be perfect, then so be it.

Then again, one would think he could handle the separation considering they'd gone long stretches not even being in the same state before, and the time apart had been good for them. For years they'd rarely seen each other, their contact limited to phone calls and letters. Their love hadn't waned, however; and even though Coralee had told him he wasn't beholden to her relationship-wise, he could never punch in the pass she'd given him.

He *loved* her, and it was a forever type of thing. He'd never done well with settling, and he wasn't going to start just because he was in Athens, Georgia going to law school while she was in Massachusetts to finish her undergrad at Thoreau College before beginning the two-year teaching program. Open, long-distance relationships might work for some of his peers, but it didn't and couldn't work for Benjamin. Besides, Coralee was worth the wait and more. Attending Thoreau was the best decision not just for her education, but for her safety as well. In fact, he still hadn't returned to Solomon since graduation and he didn't foresee that changing any time soon.

Conveniently, Benjamin had taken a job in Boston upon graduating law school after his father had recommended he'd reach out to an old classmate who practiced Civil Rights law. Benjamin wasn't the biggest fan of the cold, but Boston was too big to be overly concerned with the dating habits of its citizens, and the opportunity to live in peace was much more attractive than mild winters.

Benjamin had asked Coralee to marry him on a random day in May, a week after she'd ended her first year of teaching school. They'd been snuggled on his futon, listening to records, and she'd laughed, thinking he was teasing her. Then he'd showed her the small diamond that adorned a white gold band, and she'd cried and accepted.

They were married in Boston in a courthouse during her Christmas break, a gray, snowy day with both sets of parents and her grandmother present, Felix and LJ as his best men, and Freda as the matron of honor.

They'd consummated their marriage and love that night, both trembling from the rush of emotions they'd felt. Coralee had been shy, but totally trusting of him. Benjamin had been breathless at the sight of her in a silken nightgown and her hair in the French braid she'd worn for their wedding.

The first lovemaking didn't last long, the culmination of a twenty-year relationship too much for the both of them. Coralee had cradled his face in the crook of her neck and his body between her thighs, and he'd remained inside her until both were ready to try again. The only words between them the second time were, "Baby", "Ceelee", "Benny", "I love you." The last had become a mutual mantra the closer they'd reached climax; and when both had exploded simultaneously, "I love you" had been a harmony of the sweetest sounds he'd ever heard.

Benjamin had cried at the exquisiteness of it.

There would be more "sweetest sounds" during this first year of marriage, he'd come to realize. The next had happened in the midst of the fireworks presentation during the Fourth of July. Benjamin and Coralee had been sitting the banks of the Charles River watching the colorful explosions in the night sky. Benjamin's attention would continuously drift from the heaven above to the heaven he held in his arms. Coralee was no less distracted, but instead she'd kept staring at a dancing toddler nearby with a tiny smile on her face. Benjamin had commented on how adorable he was, then Coralee had placed his hand on her middle and asked if he'd thought their little one would be as adorable when it came in February. He'd wept joyfully into his wife's hair, too overcome to respond properly.

It was February now, days away from their child's arrival. Benjamin paused caressing Coralee's belly and rolled away briefly, his hand still on her swell where he could feel the press of what he assumed was a foot. Through the sheer drapes that were slightly separated, he could see gray skies and fluffy snowflakes falling. It was the second snow in as many weeks; and though he'd been in Boston for three years now, he wasn't sure if he'd ever get used to it.

"You need to get ready for work."

Benjamin smiled and kissed Coralee's nose. "I'm already working."

Her lips spread into a small grin and she burrowed her face in the crook of his neck, eyes still closed. "Are you now?"

"Loving and protecting you and my baby."

She snuggled into his side, the gravid weight of her so very precious to him.

"And how you gonna feed me and your baby if there's no income because you didn't go into the office?" Coralee was on maternity leave, which meant they were living on one paycheck at the moment. Luckily, however, Coralee had always been a robust saver, so they had a little nest egg to help them along.

Nevertheless, his wife was right; but he was warm and cozy cuddled with his family underneath the thick blankets.

"Benny."

It was that no nonsense tone that got him moving, though he was a little heartened she'd used his diminutive name—it meant she wasn't that irritated with him.

He tilted her face to his and pressed a gentle kiss to her lips. "I love you."

"*Mmm...*"

He grinned, knowing that was her way of returning the sentiment when she was still mostly asleep.

Benjamin showered, dressed, ate a bowl of cereal, and gave Coralee's tummy one last kiss before going off to work.

"You'll call me if—?"

"Yes, my love, yes," Coralee promised with a drowsy grin and tugged on the hairs at his nape. He kissed her forehead and didn't remove his lips until she pushed him towards the door.

The day crept by and the snow fell steadily. The endless, dull paperwork made him resent being a responsible adult when all he could think about was his toasty bed and the darling wife he'd left in it.

He nearly cheered when his secretary buzzed his phone, desperate for the break in his ennui, but that cheer quickly turned to panic when he heard the message.

"I've gotta go," he said monotonously, the receiver limp in his hand and his eyes staring unseeingly into space.

Mrs. Perkins, his secretary, burst into his office with wide eyes and beaming smile. "You've got to *go!*"

The excited affirmation propelled Benjamin into action, and he hightailed it to Boston Women's Hospital. When he reached reception, he gave Coralee's name on a breathless pant, but Freda rescued the bewildered receptionist from his panic and took him to Coralee's room.

"How—?"

"Fine," Freda said with a little chuckle. "You haven't missed anything."

Freda and Jermaine Powell, two people who'd become as important to him as they had been to Coralee, had married a few years before he and Coralee and had a two-year-old son, Geoff. Jermaine had recently entered Boston University's divinity school, and the Powells had eventually settled only a few blocks away from the Drummonds. In fact, Benjamin and Coralee were Geoff's godparents; and it seemed they would be returning the favor before the day ended.

Coralee was walking around the room when they entered, her belly button poking against the cloth of the gown as it was stretched tightly across her abdomen. She blinked and held out a hand to Benjamin.

"Ceelee," Benjamin murmured, approaching his wife and framing her face in his hands.

"Calm down, honey," Coralee said, kissing his lips chastely and cupping his elbow. "We have hours."

Benjamin fell to his knees and kissed her belly. "Hours..." He didn't know if he could bear the wait.

The snow started to fall heavier, and Benjamin was glad he'd decided to take public transportation instead of drive. Coralee breathed as her mother and grandmother had told her to, and squeezed the very life out of Benjamin's hand whenever she had a contraction. It was hard to watch his wife exert so much effort to bring his baby into the world, and would if he could switch places with her. He dabbed a towel about her brow to blot up the sweat and kissed her whenever she got through a particularly hard contraction.

"I love you so much," he'd whispered into her ear, feeling helpless and hating it; but knowing if he could do nothing else, he could at least remind her of that.

She would nod and say, "*Mmm...*" then have another contraction.

"Hours" turned out to be a number more than two.

"This baby is coming now," Dr. Michael Reeves said, a very distinguished physician and known as one of the first black obstetricians to be hired by a major Boston hospital.

"I'll go wait outside for Jermaine; he say he's on his way with Geoff," Freda informed Coralee with a kiss to her temple. "You'll have a beautiful baby in your arms soon, sweetheart!"

Coralee nodded, her face a mixture of joy and pain as she kissed Freda's temple goodbye.

Benjamin had never heard such screams of agony; and if Coralee hadn't been giving birth, Benjamin would've killed the doctor for making his wife hurt so much...and then he remembered this wasn't the doctor's doing at all.

"I'm sorry," he murmured against Coralee's temple. He'd promised never to hurt her, and here she was, damn near splitting herself in two.

"Sorry? What?" Coralee gasped between pushes, her breath scarce from her screaming and efforts.

"I'm hurting you!"

A growl erupted from his wife's throat, and Benjamin jerked back in alarm.

"I see the head!" Dr. Reeves exclaimed.

Benjamin felt faint. A head! That meant a baby was on the way. His baby. Her baby. *Their* baby. He knew the child would be beautiful because it was borne of love, and nothing ugly could come from what he and Coralee shared.

"Two more pushes, Mrs. Drummond. You can do it!"

Benjamin used the towel to dry perspiration from her face. "I love you. I'm right here, baby."

"I love you," Coralee mouthed, and Benjamin nodded.

These last two pushes were excruciating to watch and hear. He thought of all the injuries he and others had sustained during football, and he felt ashamed for making such a big deal about them. Coralee's was pain in the most extreme sense, and no amount of broken legs, torn ligaments, or pulled muscles could ever compare to what a woman giving birth went through. His mother had said it was the closest a woman got to dying without actually doing so if one survived it, and now Benjamin understood why.

Suddenly, Coralee plopped down in the bed, her chest working overtime as her lungs drew in large gulps of air. Her eyes drifted closed and her head lulled to the side in exhaustion. Benjamin's panic reached its pinnacle when suddenly—

"WHAAA!"

Benjamin collapsed to his knees next to the bed. It was the sweetest sound he'd ever heard. His baby. *Their* baby. He looked to Coralee who had a smile on her face, her eyes closed. Her body was the most relaxed he'd seen it in months, as if God had squeezed her shoulder and had told her she'd done good.

"It's a little girl," Dr. Reeves said reverently. He held up the bundle for the parents to see, and Benjamin let out a sob. She was brown, large, and squalling. She had a healthy set of lungs too.

"You were right."

Benjamin tore his eyes away from his daughter to look at his wife. He brushed back strands of her hair from her sweat-slicked temple and nuzzled her nose.

"I was?"

"You said the baby would be a girl. You were right."

"I wouldn't have cared," Benjamin said honestly. "But I am glad...a little girl who looks like you."

She let out a breathless cackle. "I think you're going to regret she's a girl."

He gasped in shock. "Why would you say that?!"

"When she starts dating—"

"She's never gonna date," Benjamin said with finality. Their daughter wasn't even five minutes old and his wife had her fifty years into the future!

Coralee's laugh was husky and she cupped Benjamin's cheek. "You sound eerily like *my* father right now."

Benjamin bristled, remembering the less than pleasant times between him and Mr. Simmons; but now that he was a father to a daughter, Benjamin understood completely.

"I'll send him an 'I'm sorry' card. Had I known then what I know now—"

"You still would've married me."

Benjamin grinned and kissed Coralee tenderly. "You bet your life I would've."

A few moments later, a nurse approached them holding their daughter. She put the baby in Coralee's arms, and mother and father let out a sigh of pure love. The baby's eyes were closed, and she had a head full of curly brown hair with a face that would become almost identical to Coralee's when she became older.

"She's never leaving the house," Benjamin said, mostly serious.

Coralee shook her head, giving her daughter a finger to hold. A tiny brown hand curled around a darker finger, and Coralee kissed those precious fingers around it.

"Look at what we created," Coralee whispered. Benjamin noticed tears falling down her cheeks and he kissed them away.

"Thank you," he whispered against her skin.

Benjamin kissed his daughter forehead. She opened up her eyes, and he was taken aback by how large and green they were.

Oh, yes. She was definitely *never leaving the house!*

Freda, Jermaine, and Geoff came in to see the baby, and Benjamin stepped out to call down to Plumville. Patty had answered the phone when he rang his house, and Benjamin had started to weep at the sound of her voice. This woman had given him Coralee, and Coralee had given him a daughter. He was a father because of Patty.

"She's so beautiful..."

It didn't take long for Patty to realize who he meant, and Patty had started crying too. Patty asked how her grandbaby was, who she looked like, how much she weighed—eventually, his father came on the line, and Patty gave them privacy so they could talk and she could get Benjamin's mother.

"I have a granddaughter," Paul said with awe.

"She's gorgeous."

"These Simmons women..."

"Drummonds, now."

"I reckon you're glad Coralee's your wife instead of your sister, huh?"

"Dad."

Paul chuckled, but Benjamin could hear the tint of sadness. "Everything is as it should be." There were muffles on the other end. "Your mother would like to speak to you."

"Okay."

He still felt a little sad on his father's behalf, to know he could never be with the woman who truly held his heart. Perhaps Paul could be happy he and Patty shared a grandchild anyway, even if it wasn't from a mutual child of their own.

Florence was cordial. Though she still wasn't pleased Benjamin had married Coralee, she wasn't as virulent in her dissent as she had been. Besides, her son was happy, happier than he had ever been, so Florence couldn't begrudge the woman who was the cause of it.

"We'll come up soon, dear," Florence said.

"Yes, Mother. I love you."

She returned the sentiment and the phone went back to Patty. "Do you have the number to the room? How is she doing, Benny? Oh, my baby had a baby!"

Benjamin gave her the information, and Patty said the family would try to come up soon. Benjamin, though glad to hear Patty and was happy she was so happy, was anxious to get back to his two favorite girls.

"All right, Benny. Tell her I love her? And my grandbaby..."

"I will, Patty. Love you."

"Love you, too, Benny. Thank you so much."

He was returning to the room just as Jermaine was leaving. Geoff was asleep in his arms.

"Hey, Papa," Jermaine said, squeezing Benjamin's shoulder.

"I get it, now," Benjamin said, looking at the sleeping toddler.

"Yeah..." Jermaine agreed, kissing the top of his son's head. "Nothing like it."

Benjamin clapped Jermaine on the shoulder before he went inside. The doctor and nurses were all gone. Coralee was breastfeeding their daughter and Freda approached him, pulling him into a large hug.

"Congratulations, Benny."

"Thank you. Aren't they beautiful?"

"You're never letting her leave the house, are you?"

"Not even to the front yard!"

"Benjamin..."

Freda laughed and kissed Benjamin's cheek. "Seems like your wife has a different say in the matter, huh?"

Benjamin felt his cheeks heat, but the sight of Coralee nourishing their child made him breathless. Every time he thought he'd seen her at her most beautiful, she would go and prove him wrong.

"We'll be back tomorrow, okay?" Freda said, squeezing Benjamin's hand. He nodded, but didn't respond, too transfixed on the sight of his wife and child.

"Bye, Freda," Coralee said. Y'all be safe out in all that snow!"

The sound of the door closing sparked Benjamin to move. He sat where Freda had just vacated, his large, trembling pale hand brushing against the downy soft, dark hair of his daughter. The suckling action seemed vigorous, and he winced on his wife's behalf.

"Does it hurt?"

"Almost as much as the actual birth!" They laughed. "Freda says I'll get used to it."

Their daughter had finished her meal, and Coralee's nipple fell out her mouth. Benjamin righted Coralee's gown for her, earning a loving smile and thanks.

"We need to name her," his wife whispered after a few minutes. The baby had gone back to sleep, her hand now wrapped around her father's finger. "And you need to hold her too."

Benjamin nodded, unable to speak at the prospect of holding this treasure in his arms. The transfer had a few bumbles, but none enough to rouse his princess. His daughter seemed to weigh no more than a football would.

"Any thoughts, honey? You did say she would be a girl...makes sense for you to have the honor of naming her."

He stared at his daughter for a moment, thinking of all she represented. Suddenly, he smiled.

"Simone."

"Simone?"

"After her mother and grandmother," Benjamin said, looking at Coralee. "Simmons women...so very loved by us Drummond men."

Coralee nodded in understanding and approval. They'd never spoken about their parents' young love, but both knew it hadn't completely died. "Harmony."

"Harmony?"

"For her middle name," Coralee explained, reaching out to hold the hand he'd offered. "What do you think?"

"Perfect," Benjamin said, smiling down at the baby he held adoringly. She would always know love. He guaranteed it. "Simone Harmony Drummond. Welcome to the world, dear heart."

ABOUT THE AUTHOR

Originally from Blythewood, SC, Savannah J. Frierson has been writing since she was twelve years old, debuting with the novel *Being Plumville* in March 2007. She has released more publications since then, and they are available all online book retailers or by request at brick and mortar bookstores. For more information about other titles, please visit Savannah's Web site at http://www.sjfbooks.com or contact Savannah by e-mail at sfrierson@sjfbooks.com.